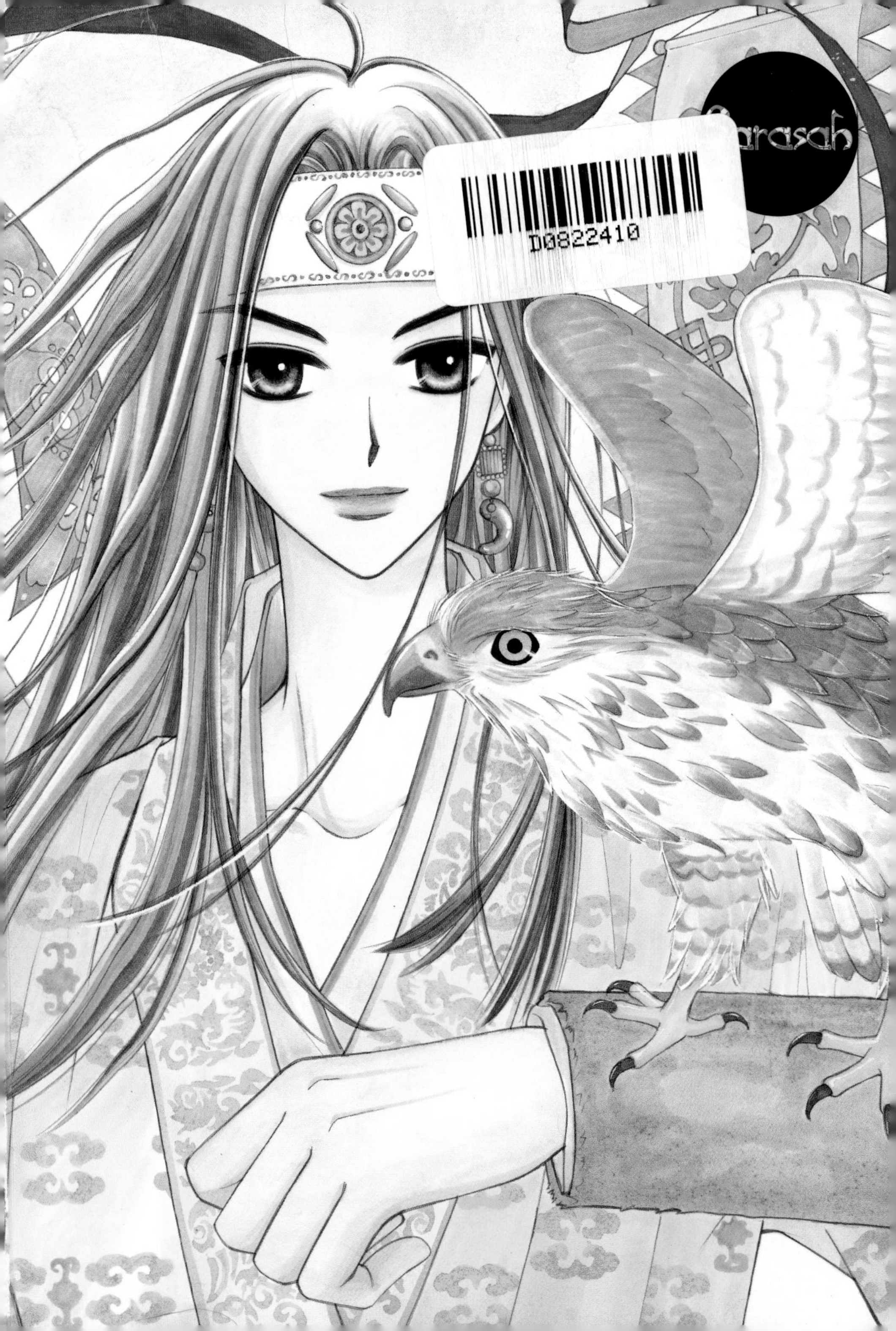

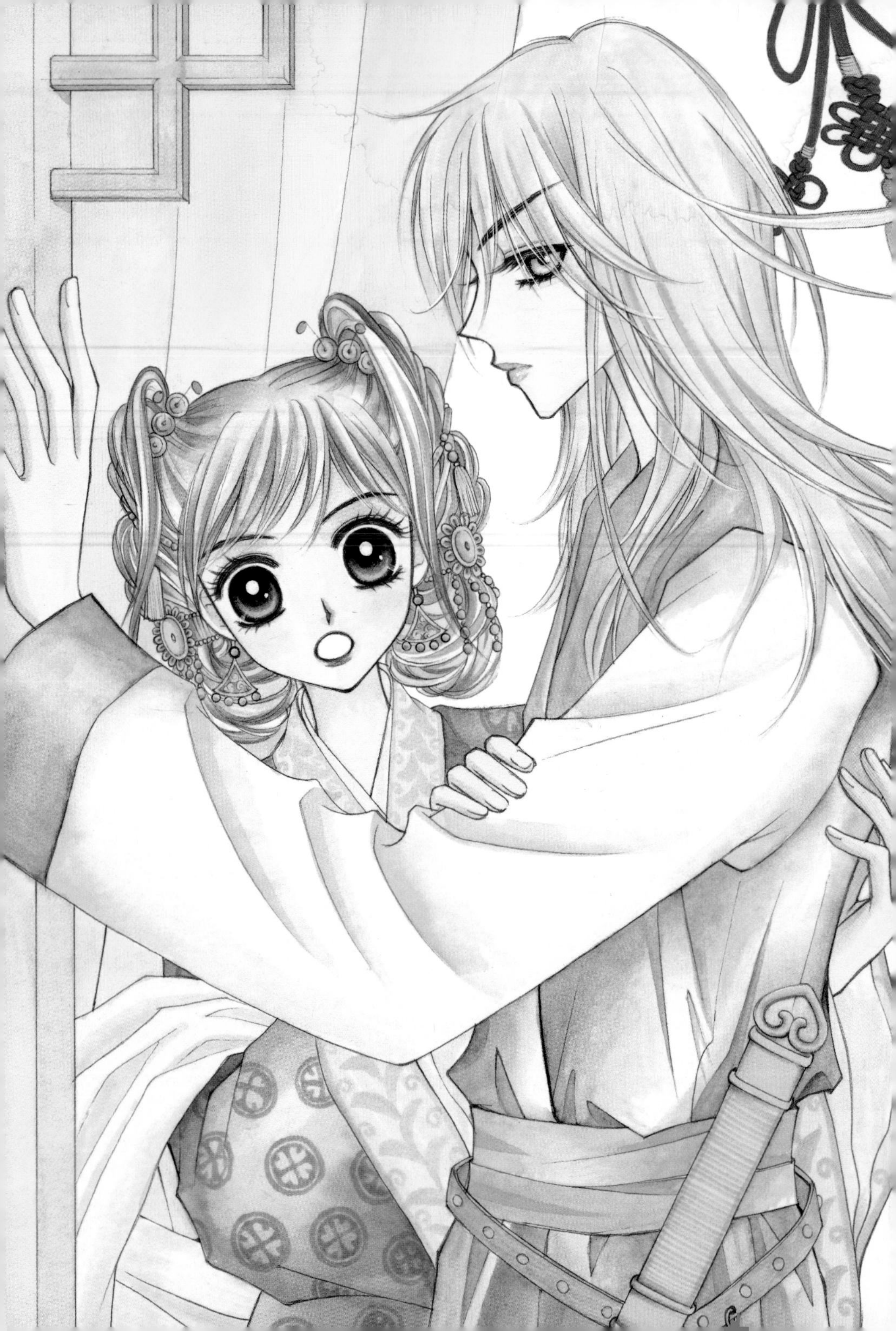

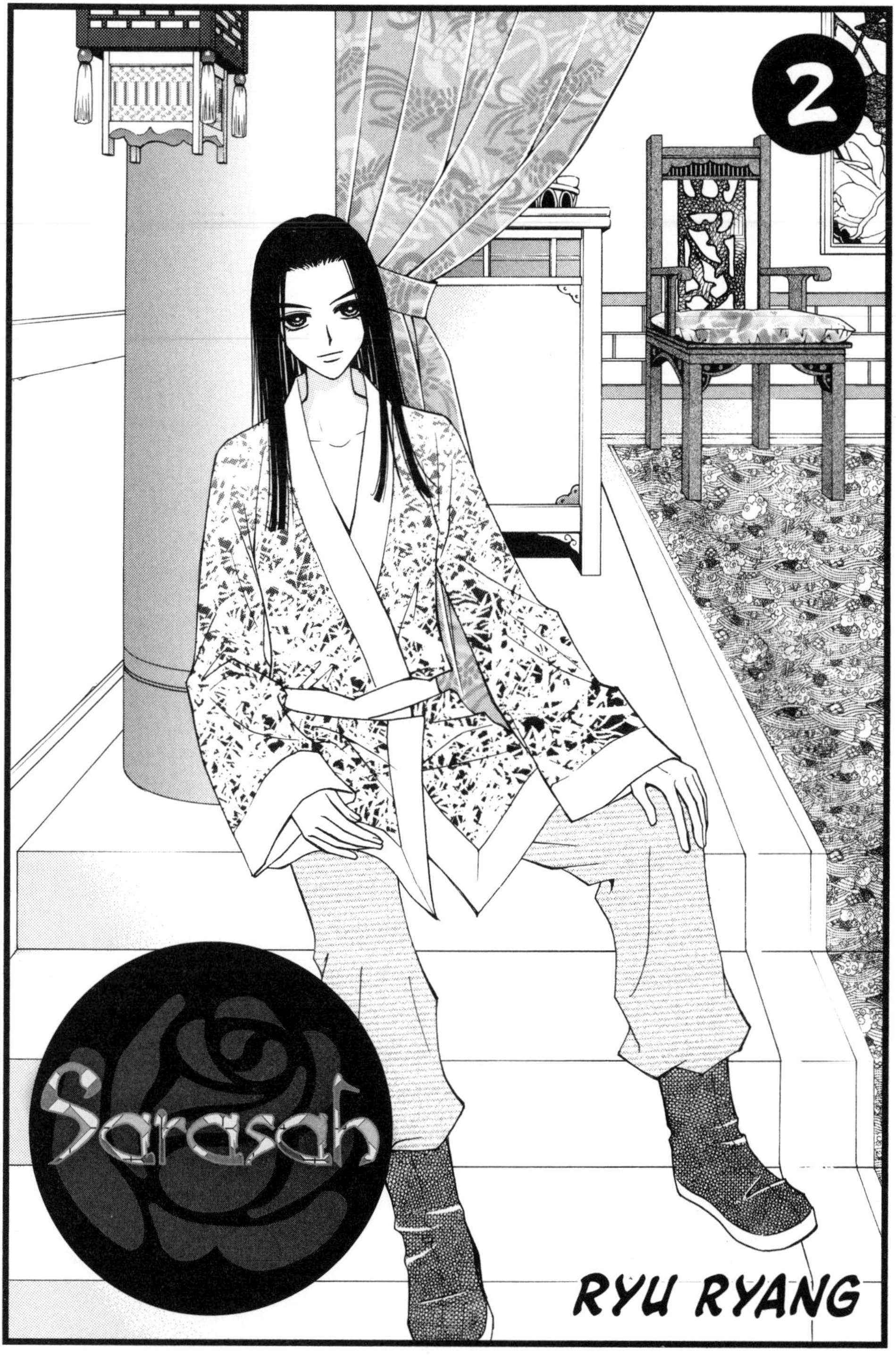
2
Sarasah
RYU RYANG

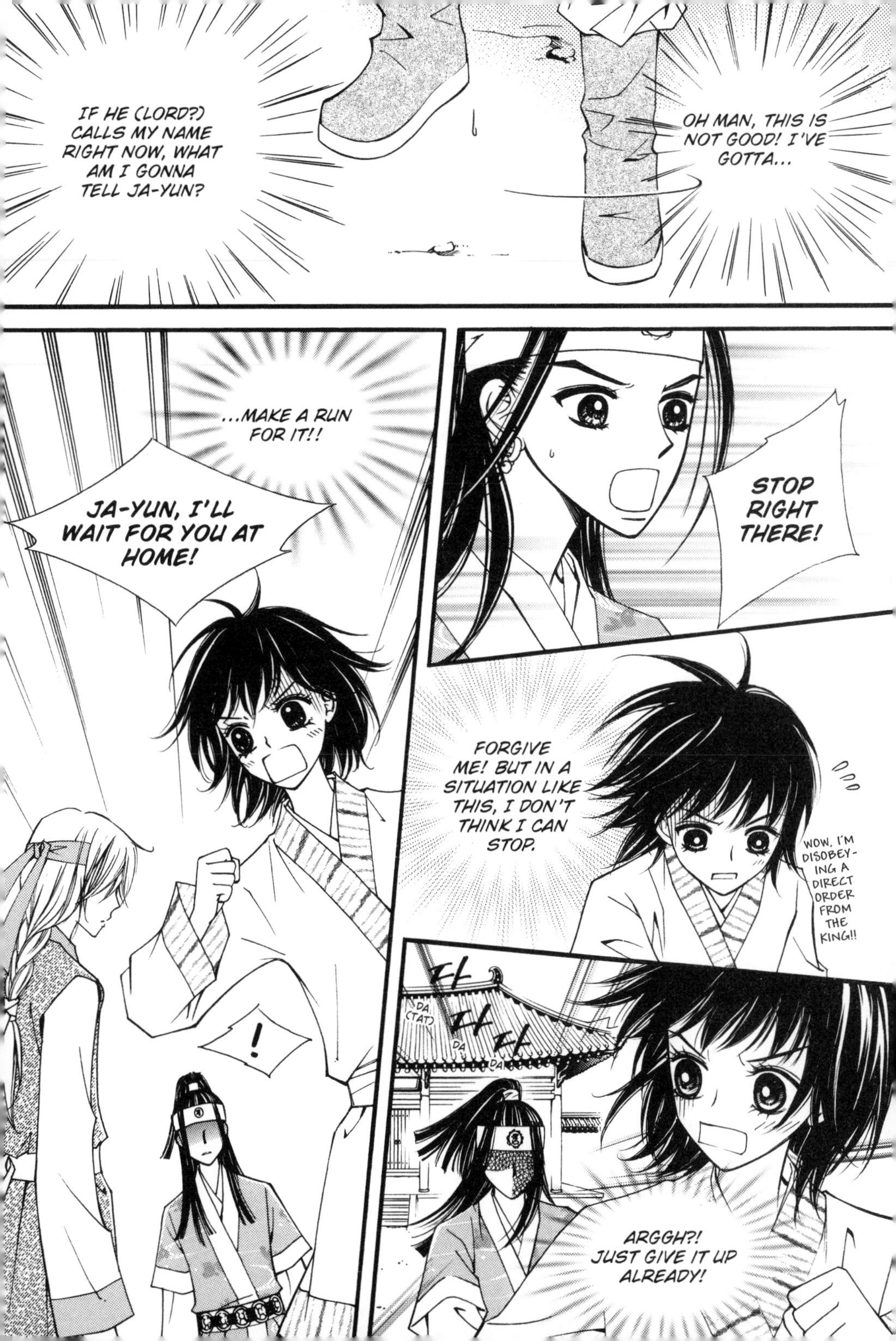
IF HE (LORD?) CALLS MY NAME RIGHT NOW, WHAT AM I GONNA TELL JA-YUN?
OH MAN, THIS IS NOT GOOD! I'VE GOTTA...
...MAKE A RUN FOR IT!!
JA-YUN, I'LL WAIT FOR YOU AT HOME!
!
STOP RIGHT THERE!
FORGIVE ME! BUT IN A SITUATION LIKE THIS, I DON'T THINK I CAN STOP.
WOW, I'M DISOBEY-ING A DIRECT ORDER FROM THE KING!!
DA (TAT)
DA
DA
ARGGH?! JUST GIVE IT UP ALREADY!

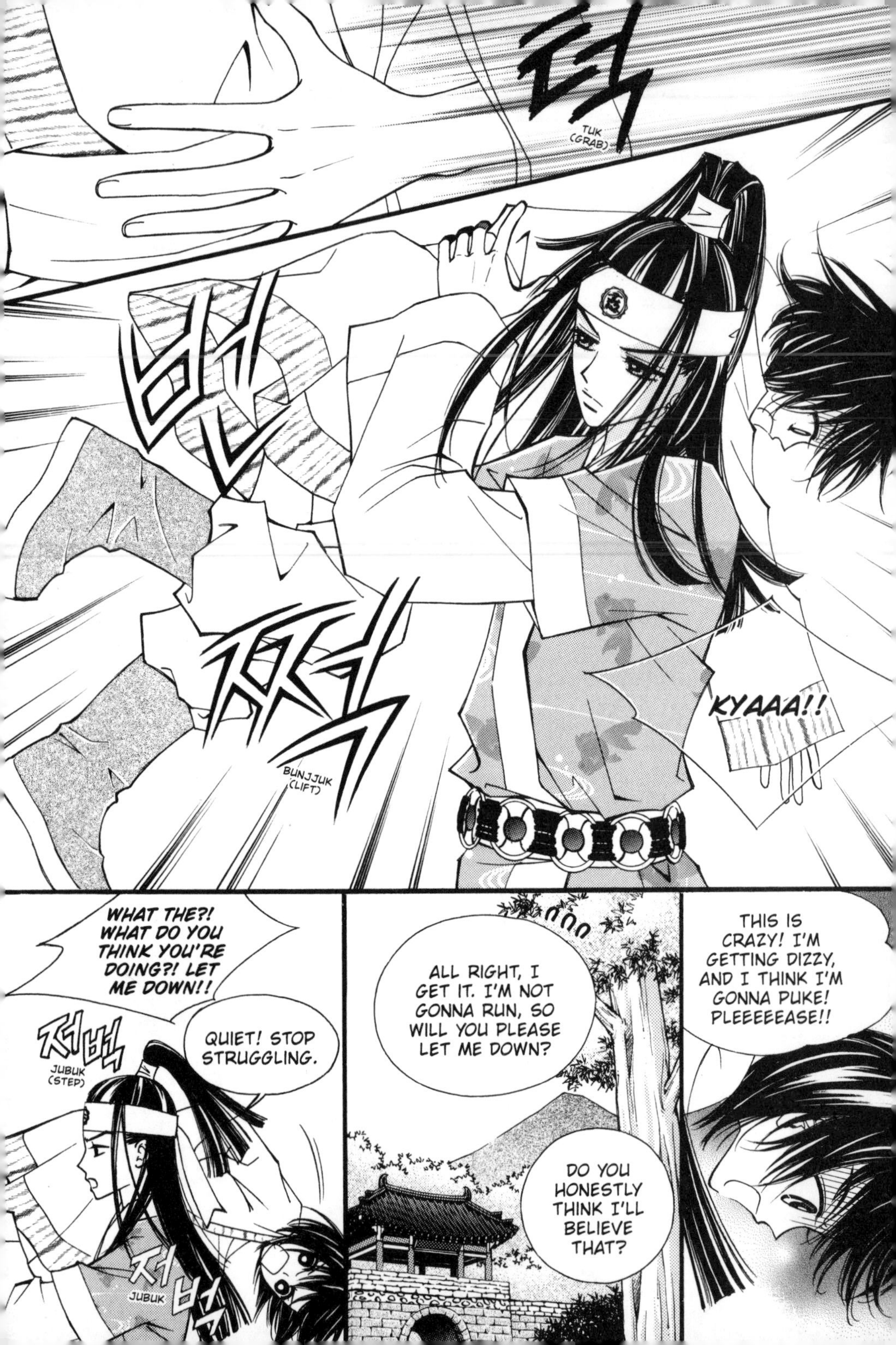
턱
TUK (GRAB)
번쩍
BUNJJUK (LIFT)
KYAAA!!
WHAT THE?! WHAT DO YOU THINK YOU'RE DOING?! LET ME DOWN!!
저벅
JUBUK (STEP)
QUIET! STOP STRUGGLING.
저벅
JUBUK
ALL RIGHT, I GET IT. I'M NOT GONNA RUN, SO WILL YOU PLEASE LET ME DOWN?
DO YOU HONESTLY THINK I'LL BELIEVE THAT?
THIS IS CRAZY! I'M GETTING DIZZY, AND I THINK I'M GONNA PUKE! PLEEEEEASE!!

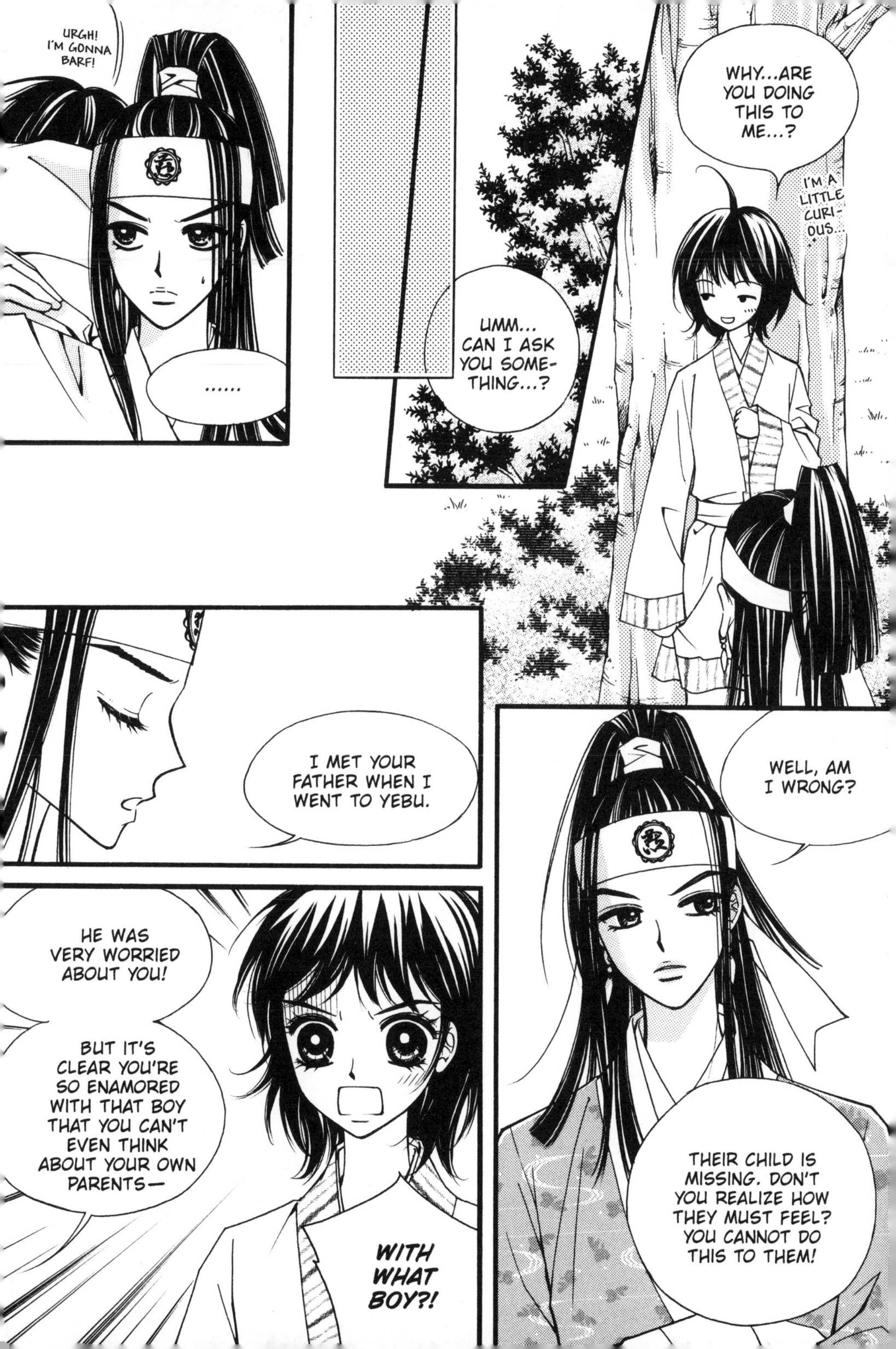
URGH! I'M GONNA BARF!
......
UMM... CAN I ASK YOU SOME-THING...?
WHY...ARE YOU DOING THIS TO ME...?
I'M A LITTLE CURI-OUS...
I MET YOUR FATHER WHEN I WENT TO YEBU.
HE WAS VERY WORRIED ABOUT YOU!
BUT IT'S CLEAR YOU'RE SO ENAMORED WITH THAT BOY THAT YOU CAN'T EVEN THINK ABOUT YOUR OWN PARENTS—
WITH WHAT BOY?!
WELL, AM I WRONG?
THEIR CHILD IS MISSING. DON'T YOU REALIZE HOW THEY MUST FEEL? YOU CANNOT DO THIS TO THEM!

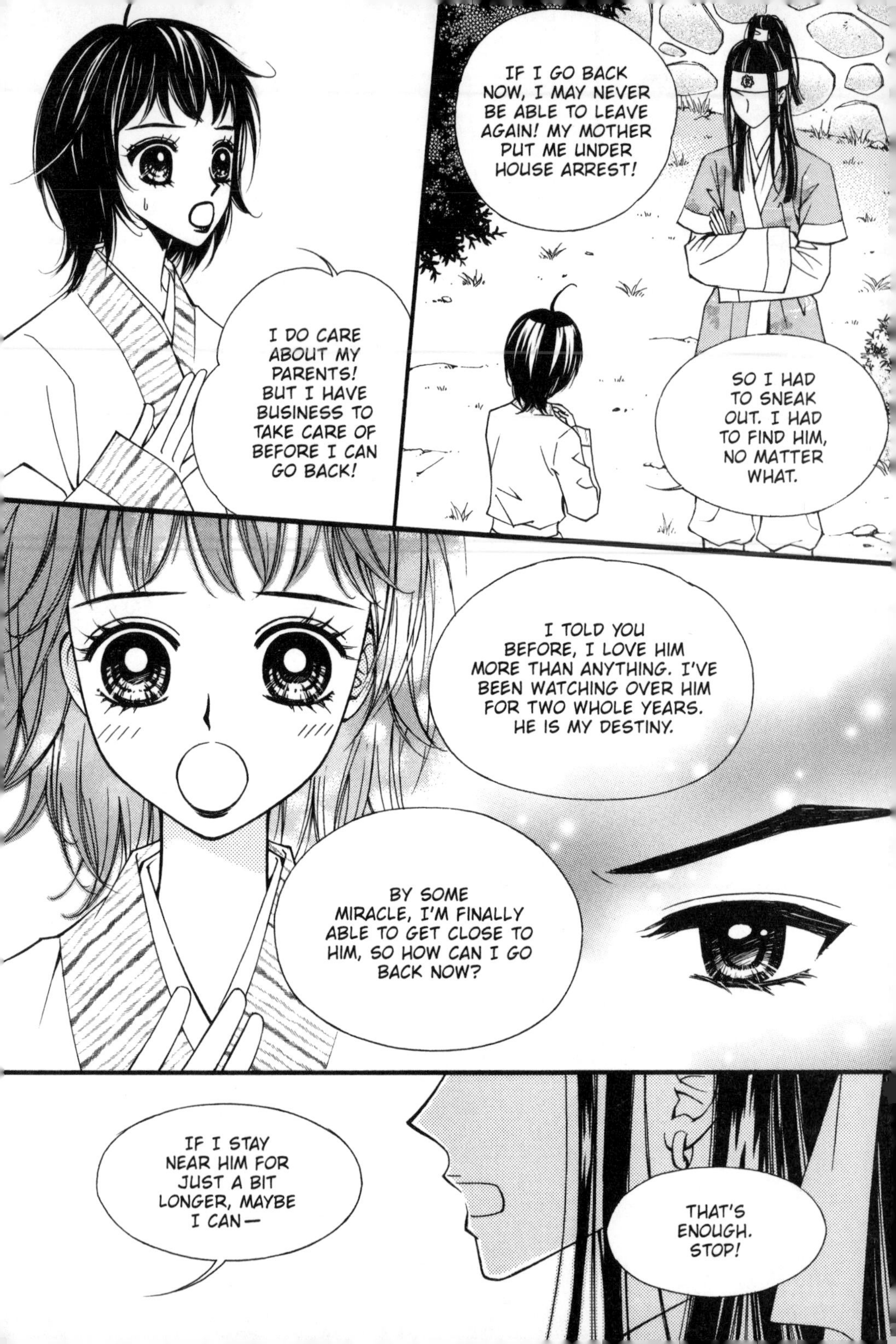
I DO CARE ABOUT MY PARENTS! BUT I HAVE BUSINESS TO TAKE CARE OF BEFORE I CAN GO BACK!
IF I GO BACK NOW, I MAY NEVER BE ABLE TO LEAVE AGAIN! MY MOTHER PUT ME UNDER HOUSE ARREST!
SO I HAD TO SNEAK OUT. I HAD TO FIND HIM, NO MATTER WHAT.
I TOLD YOU BEFORE, I LOVE HIM MORE THAN ANYTHING. I'VE BEEN WATCHING OVER HIM FOR TWO WHOLE YEARS. HE IS MY DESTINY.
BY SOME MIRACLE, I'M FINALLY ABLE TO GET CLOSE TO HIM, SO HOW CAN I GO BACK NOW?
IF I STAY NEAR HIM FOR JUST A BIT LONGER, MAYBE I CAN—
THAT'S ENOUGH. STOP!

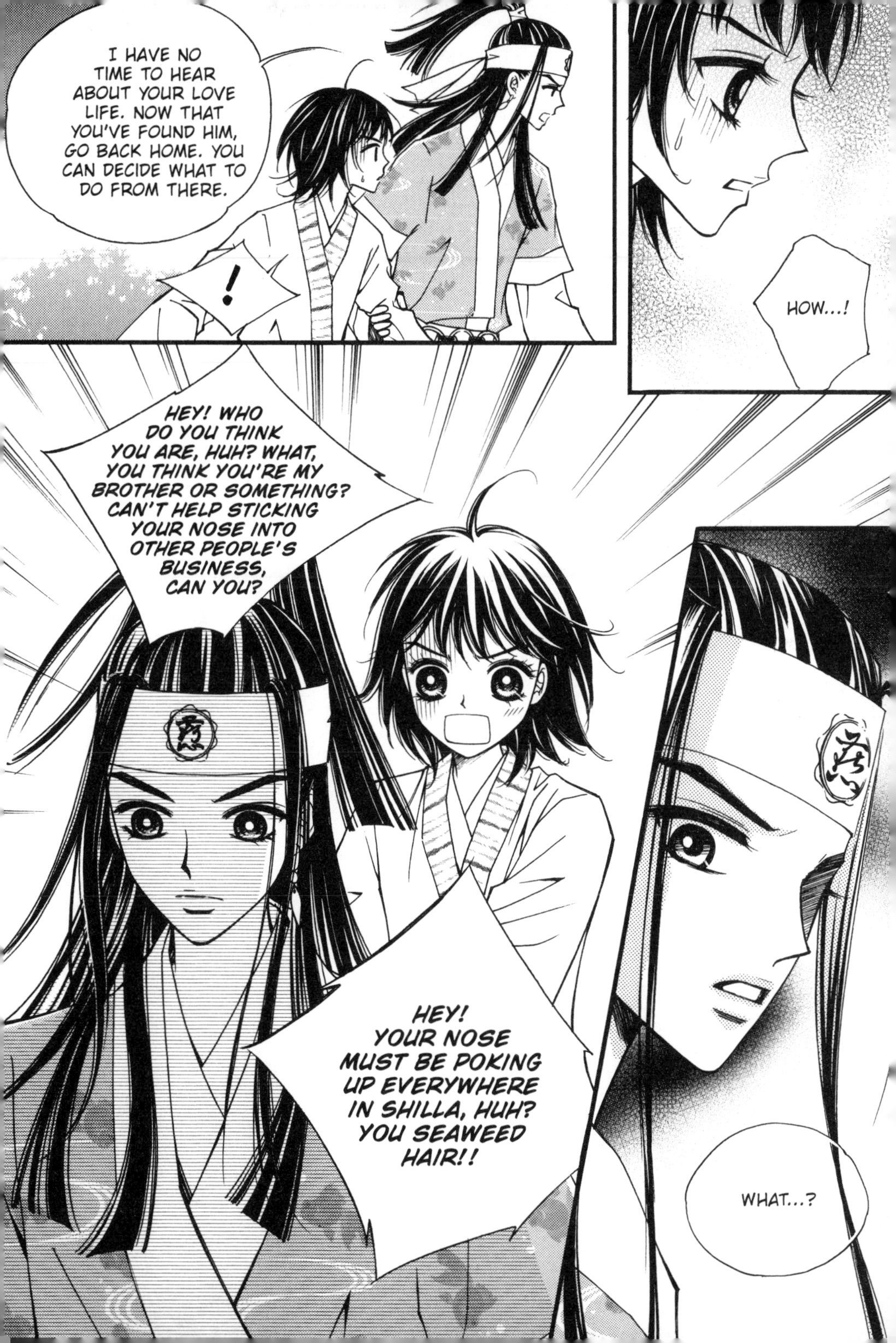
I HAVE NO TIME TO HEAR ABOUT YOUR LOVE LIFE. NOW THAT YOU'VE FOUND HIM, GO BACK HOME. YOU CAN DECIDE WHAT TO DO FROM THERE.
!
HOW...!
HEY! WHO DO YOU THINK YOU ARE, HUH? WHAT, YOU THINK YOU'RE MY BROTHER OR SOMETHING? CAN'T HELP STICKING YOUR NOSE INTO OTHER PEOPLE'S BUSINESS, CAN YOU?
HEY! YOUR NOSE MUST BE POKING UP EVERYWHERE IN SHILLA, HUH? YOU SEAWEED HAIR!!
WHAT...?

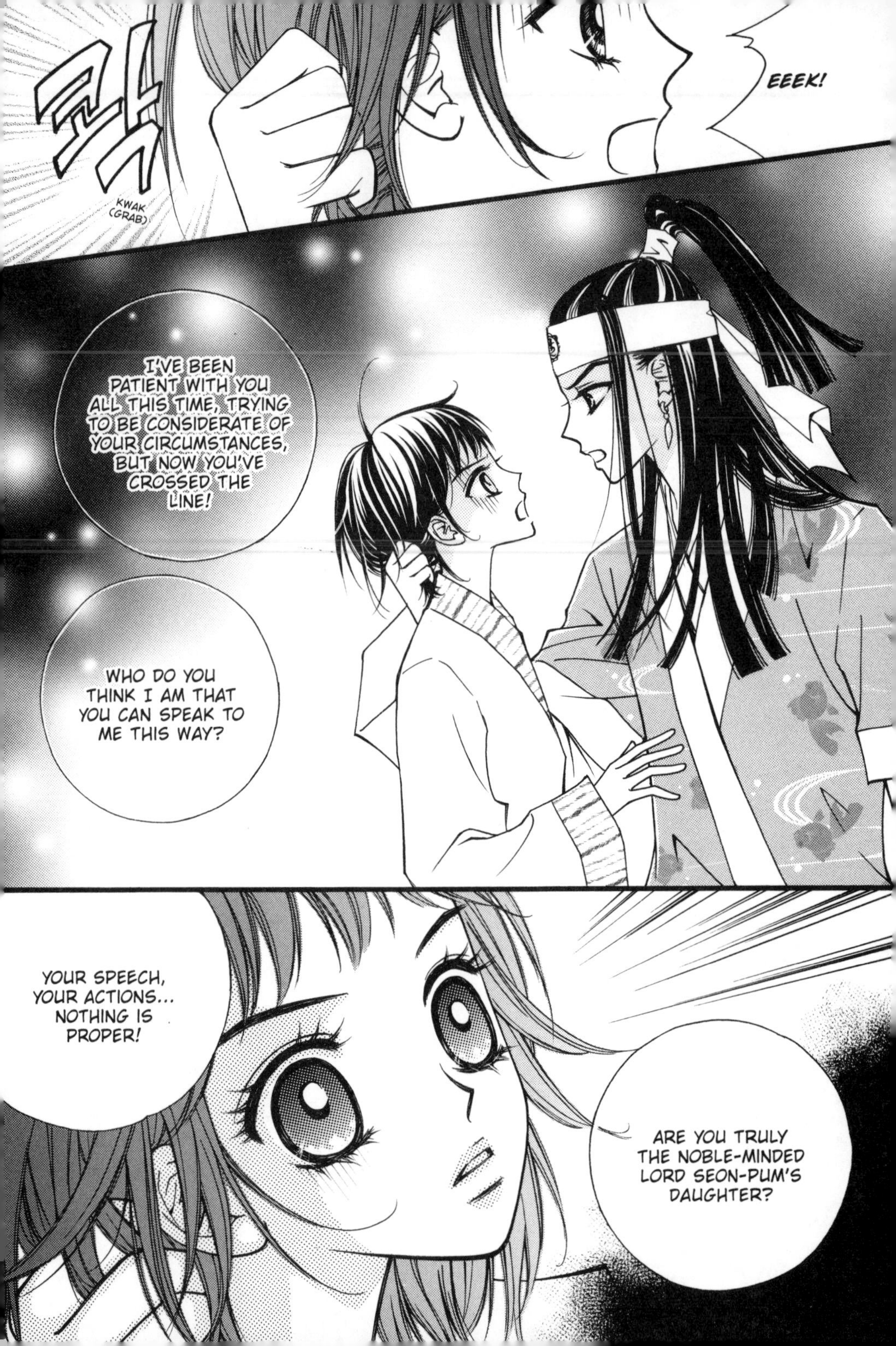

콱
KWAK (GRAB)
EEEK!
I'VE BEEN PATIENT WITH YOU ALL THIS TIME, TRYING TO BE CONSIDERATE OF YOUR CIRCUMSTANCES, BUT NOW YOU'VE CROSSED THE LINE!
WHO DO YOU THINK I AM THAT YOU CAN SPEAK TO ME THIS WAY?
YOUR SPEECH, YOUR ACTIONS... NOTHING IS PROPER!
ARE YOU TRULY THE NOBLE-MINDED LORD SEON-PUM'S DAUGHTER?

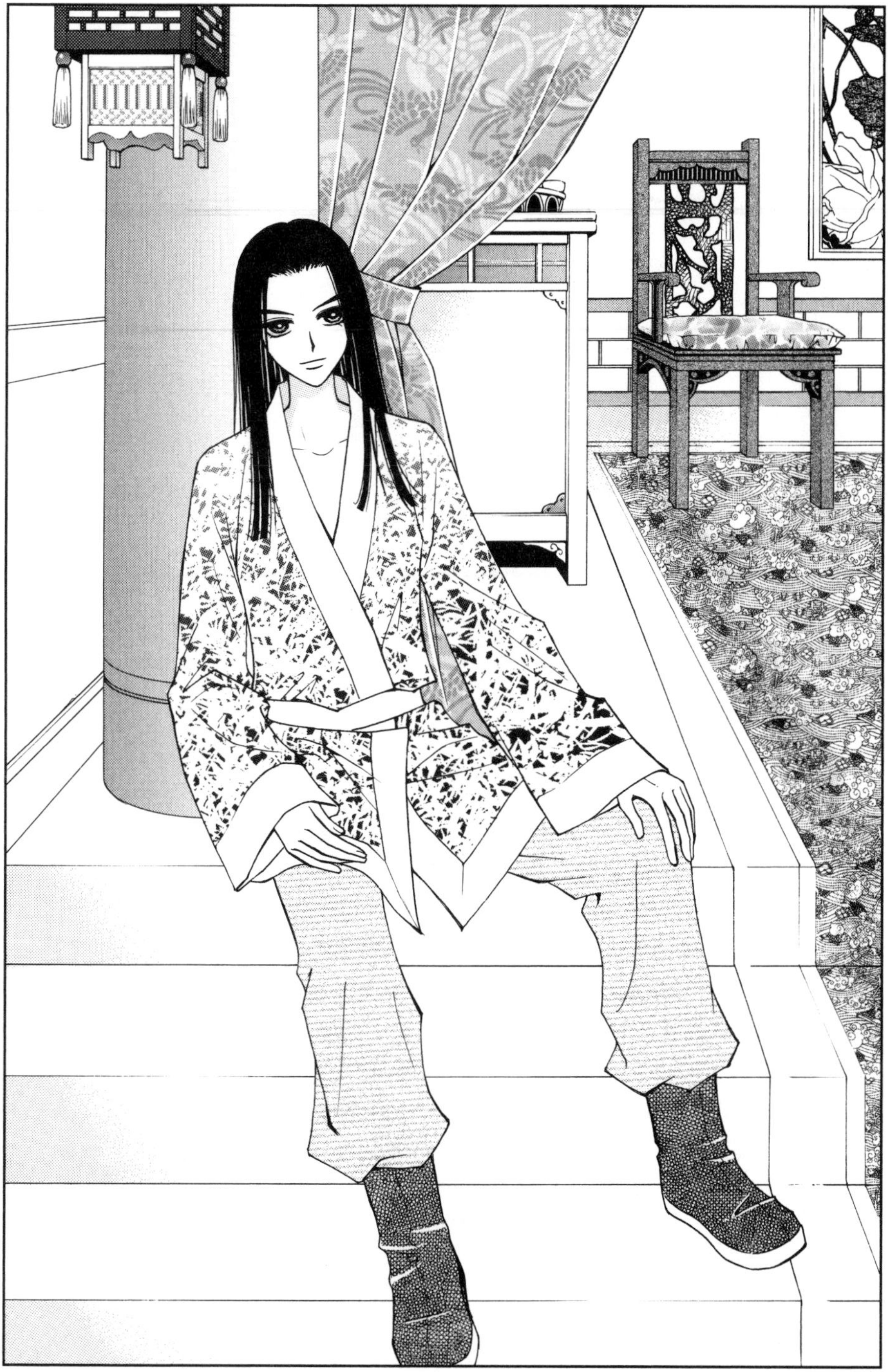

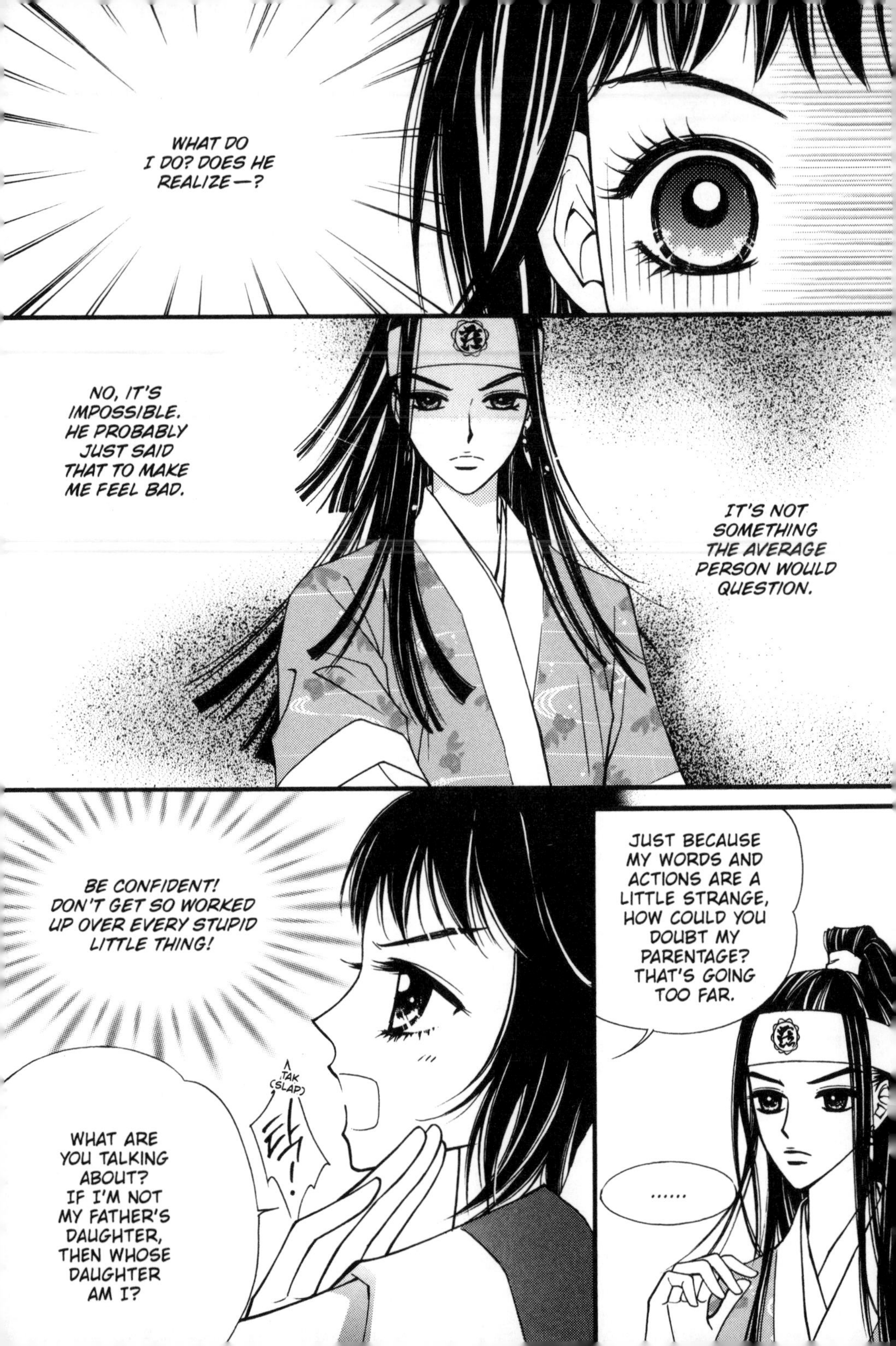

WHAT DO I DO? DOES HE REALIZE—?
NO, IT'S IMPOSSIBLE. HE PROBABLY JUST SAID THAT TO MAKE ME FEEL BAD.
IT'S NOT SOMETHING THE AVERAGE PERSON WOULD QUESTION.
BE CONFIDENT! DON'T GET SO WORKED UP OVER EVERY STUPID LITTLE THING!
TAK (SLAP)
WHAT ARE YOU TALKING ABOUT? IF I'M NOT MY FATHER'S DAUGHTER, THEN WHOSE DAUGHTER AM I?
JUST BECAUSE MY WORDS AND ACTIONS ARE A LITTLE STRANGE, HOW COULD YOU DOUBT MY PARENTAGE? THAT'S GOING TOO FAR.
......

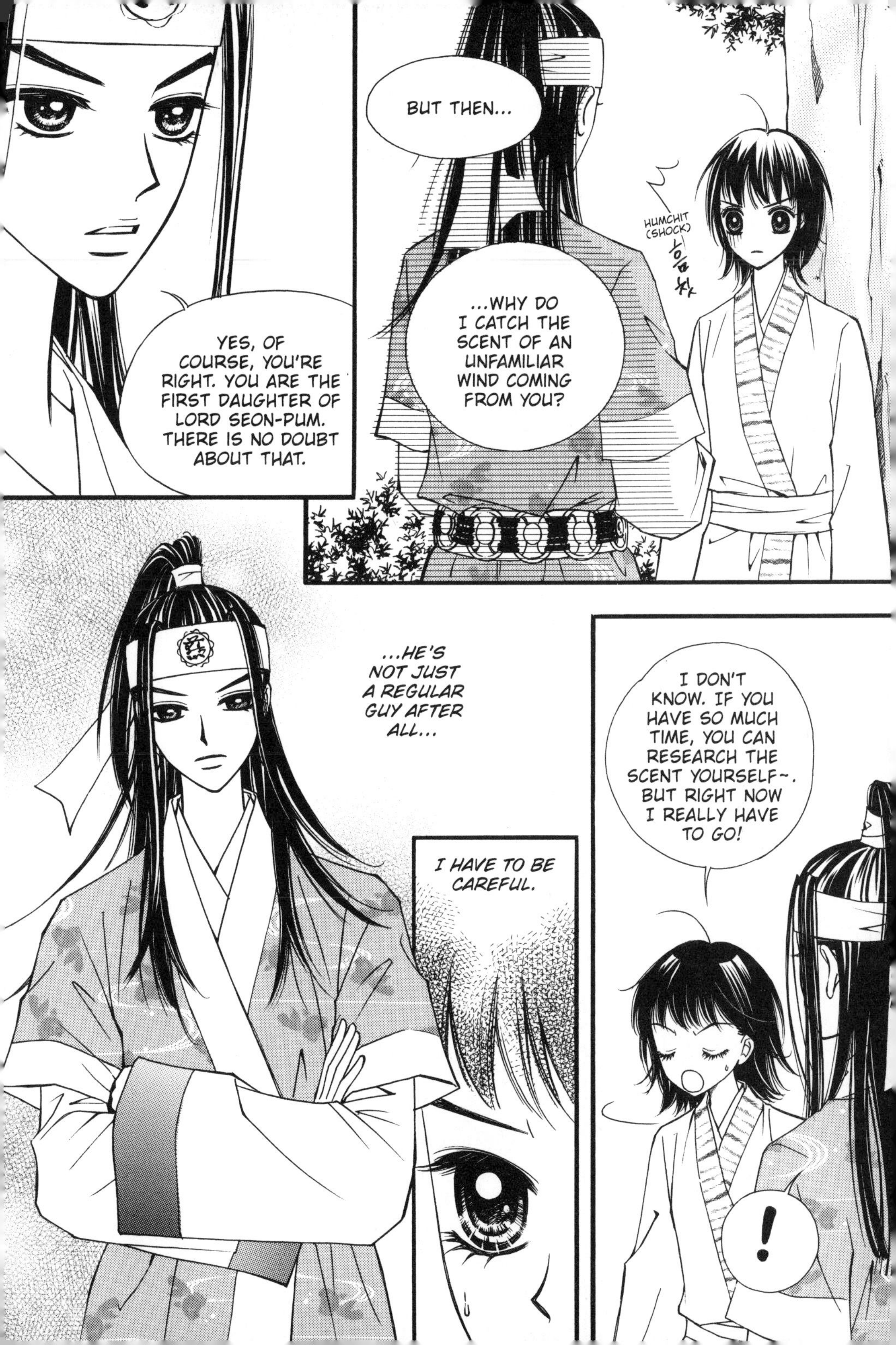
YES, OF COURSE, YOU'RE RIGHT. YOU ARE THE FIRST DAUGHTER OF LORD SEON-PUM. THERE IS NO DOUBT ABOUT THAT.
BUT THEN...
...WHY DO I CATCH THE SCENT OF AN UNFAMILIAR WIND COMING FROM YOU?
HUMCHIT (SHOCK)
...HE'S NOT JUST A REGULAR GUY AFTER ALL...
I HAVE TO BE CAREFUL.
I DON'T KNOW. IF YOU HAVE SO MUCH TIME, YOU CAN RESEARCH THE SCENT YOURSELF~. BUT RIGHT NOW I REALLY HAVE TO GO!
!

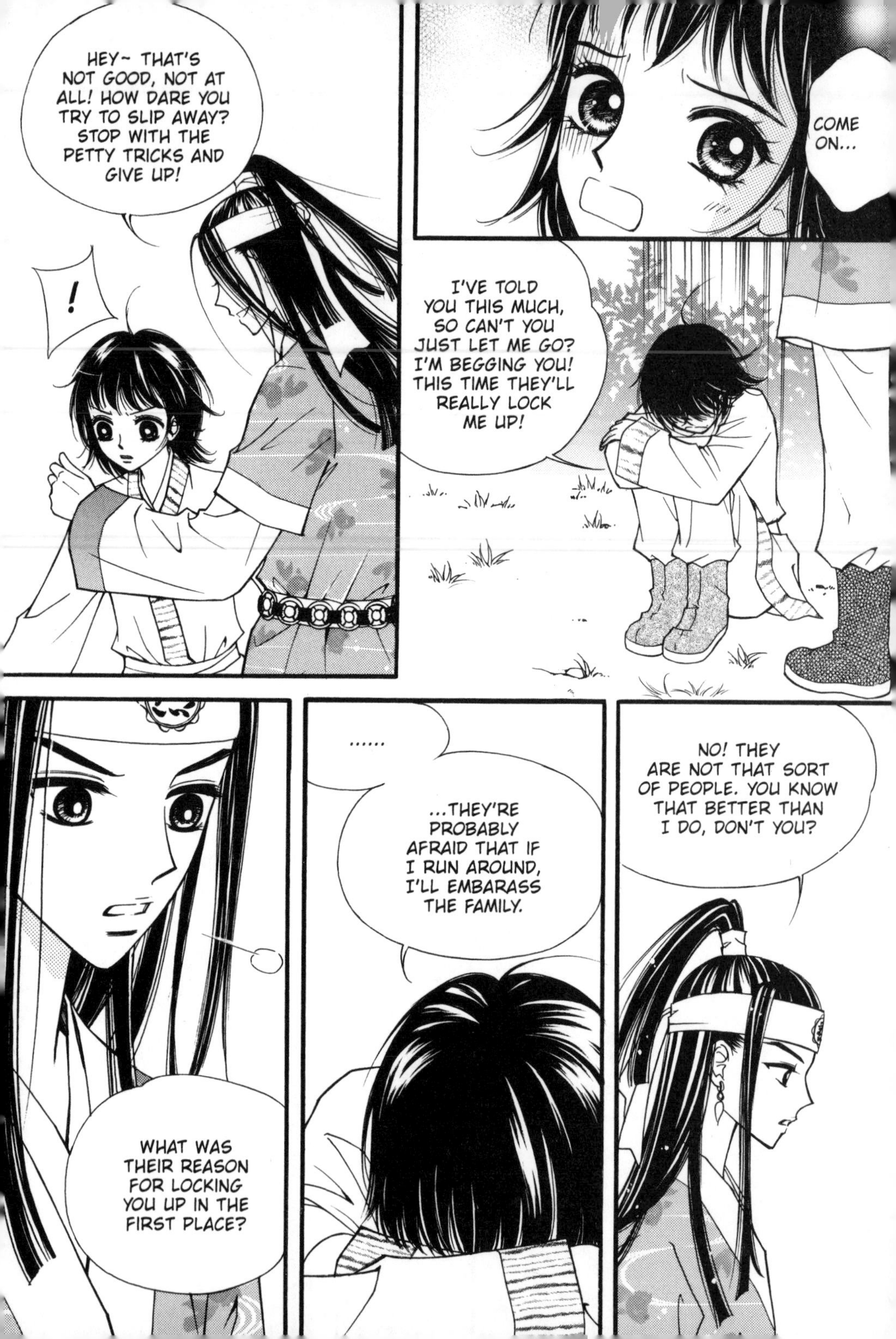
HEY~ THAT'S NOT GOOD, NOT AT ALL! HOW DARE YOU TRY TO SLIP AWAY? STOP WITH THE PETTY TRICKS AND GIVE UP!
!
COME ON...
I'VE TOLD YOU THIS MUCH, SO CAN'T YOU JUST LET ME GO? I'M BEGGING YOU! THIS TIME THEY'LL REALLY LOCK ME UP!
WHAT WAS THEIR REASON FOR LOCKING YOU UP IN THE FIRST PLACE?
......
...THEY'RE PROBABLY AFRAID THAT IF I RUN AROUND, I'LL EMBARASS THE FAMILY.
NO! THEY ARE NOT THAT SORT OF PEOPLE. YOU KNOW THAT BETTER THAN I DO, DON'T YOU?

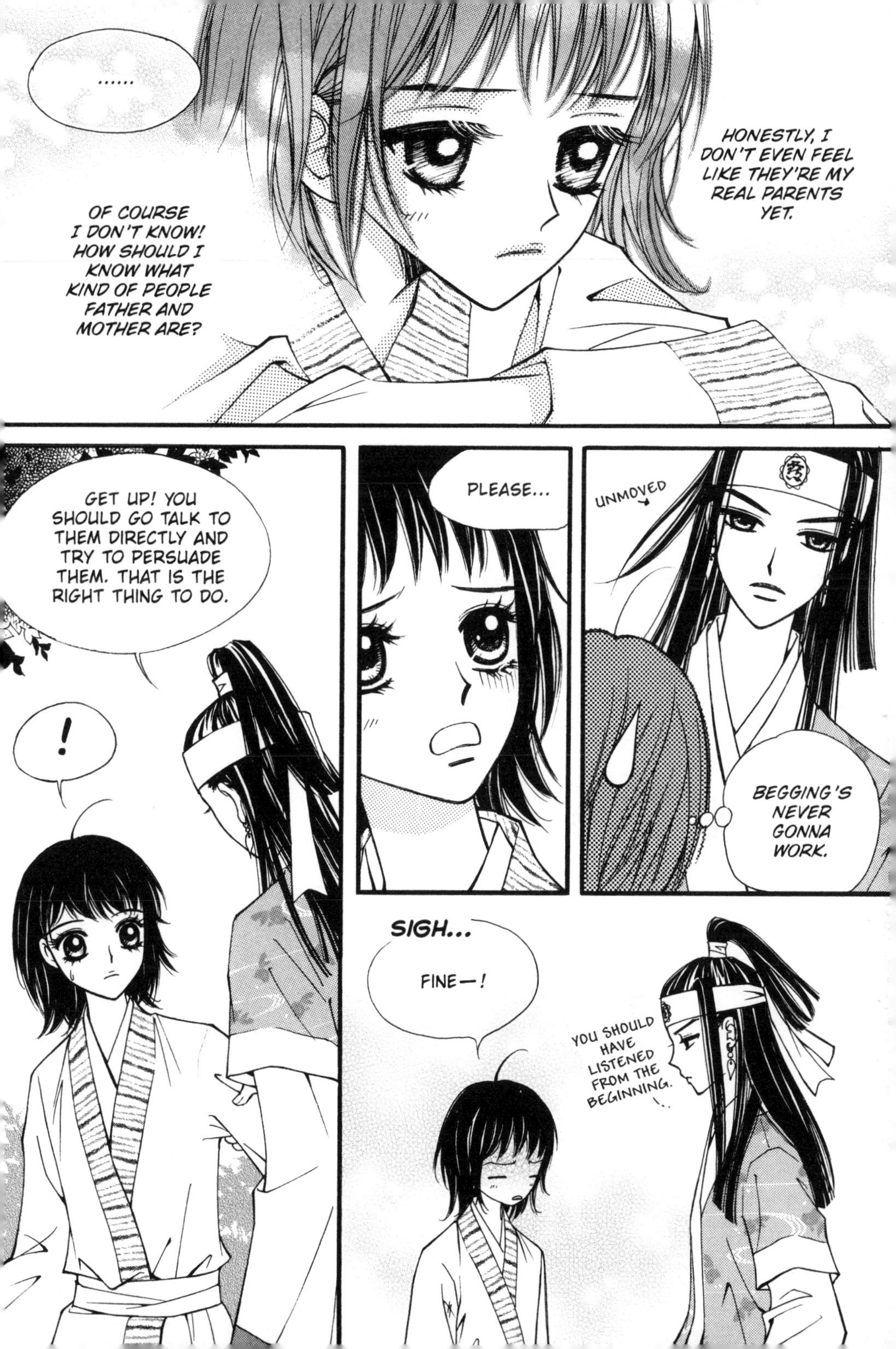
......
OF COURSE I DON'T KNOW! HOW SHOULD I KNOW WHAT KIND OF PEOPLE FATHER AND MOTHER ARE?
HONESTLY, I DON'T EVEN FEEL LIKE THEY'RE MY REAL PARENTS YET.
GET UP! YOU SHOULD GO TALK TO THEM DIRECTLY AND TRY TO PERSUADE THEM. THAT IS THE RIGHT THING TO DO.
!
PLEASE...
UNMOVED
BEGGING'S NEVER GONNA WORK.
SIGH...
FINE—!
YOU SHOULD HAVE LISTENED FROM THE BEGINNING.

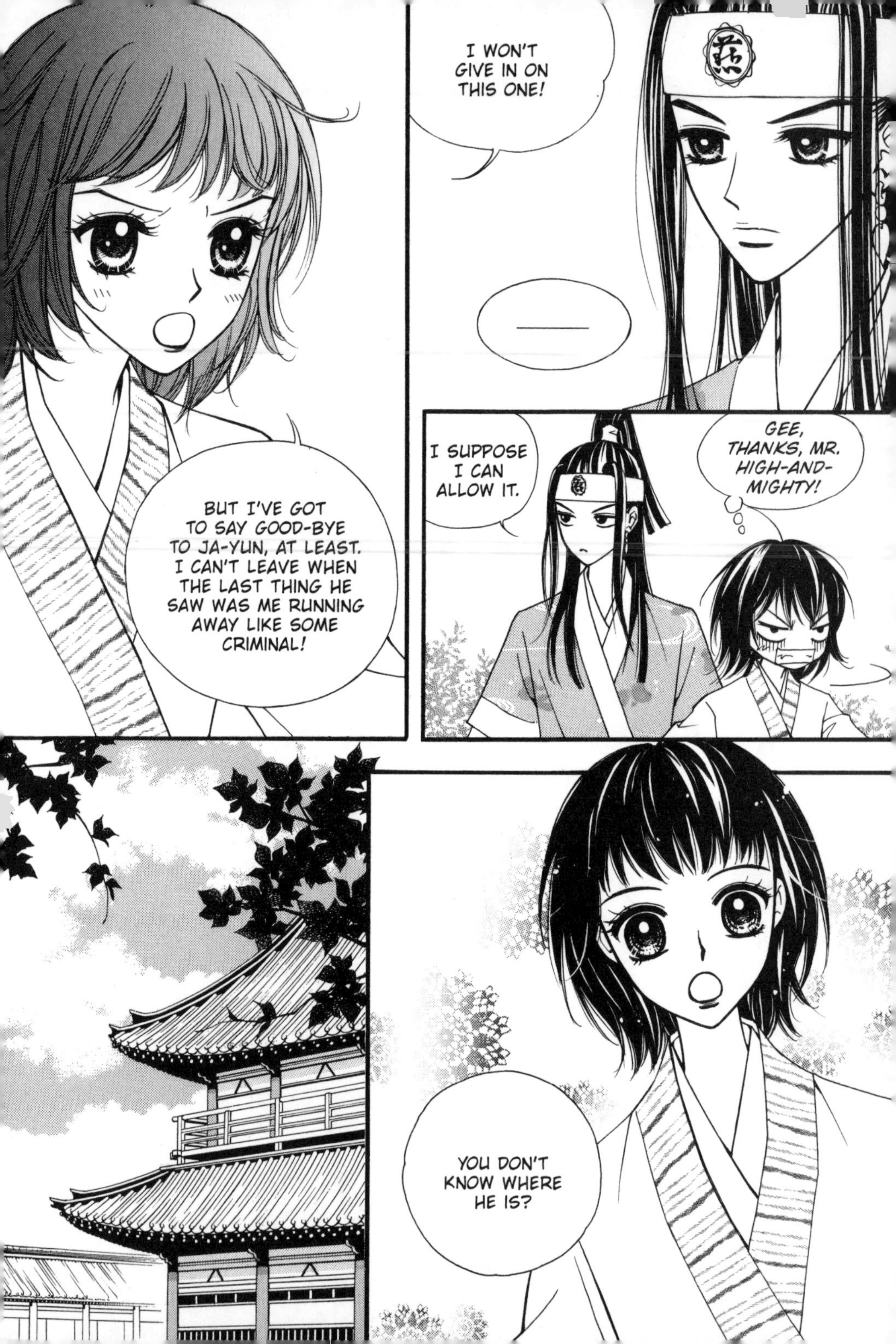

BUT I'VE GOT TO SAY GOOD-BYE TO JA-YUN, AT LEAST. I CAN'T LEAVE WHEN THE LAST THING HE SAW WAS ME RUNNING AWAY LIKE SOME CRIMINAL!
I WON'T GIVE IN ON THIS ONE!
——
I SUPPOSE I CAN ALLOW IT.
GEE, THANKS, MR. HIGH-AND-MIGHTY!
YOU DON'T KNOW WHERE HE IS?

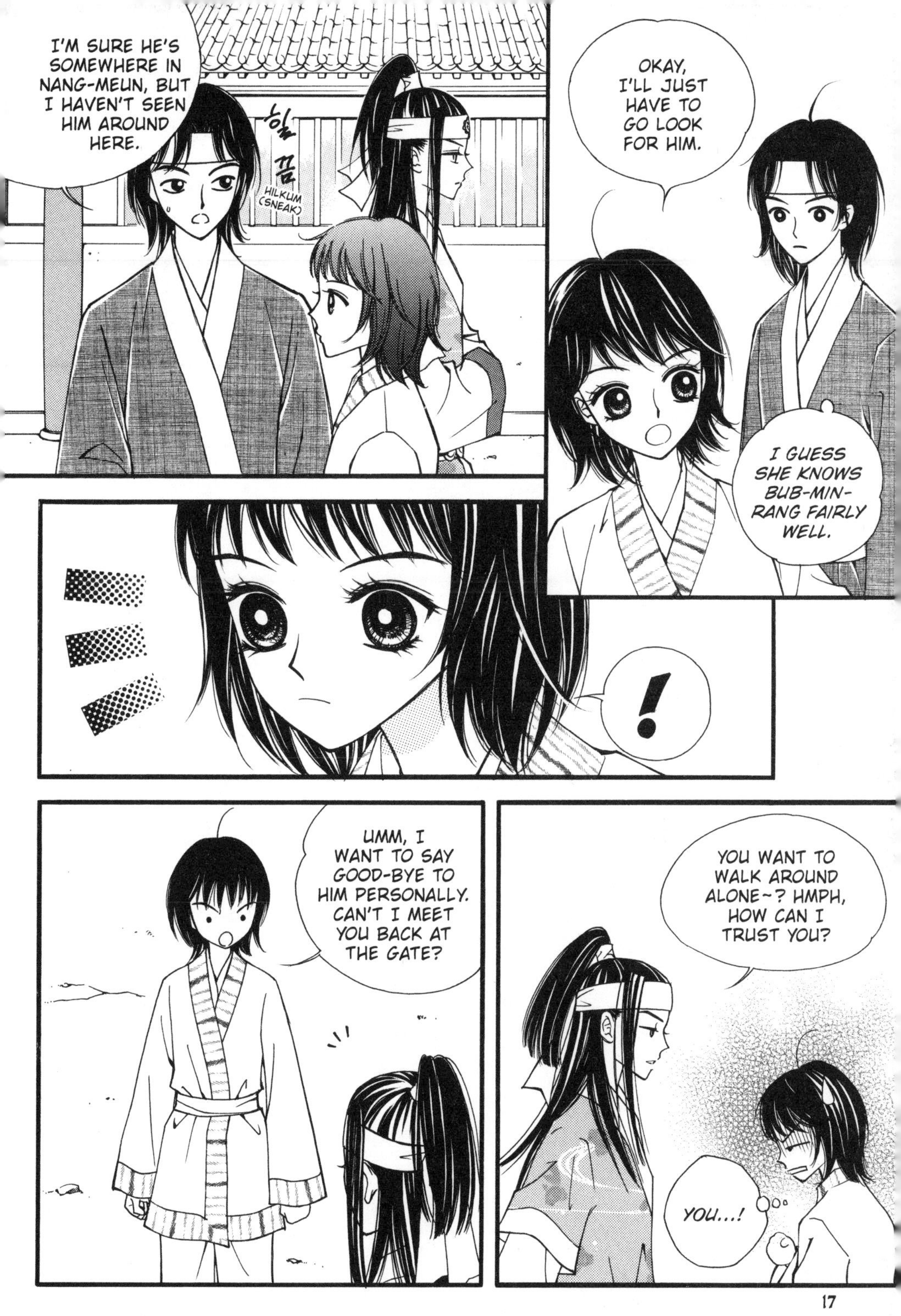
I'M SURE HE'S SOMEWHERE IN NANG-MEUN, BUT I HAVEN'T SEEN HIM AROUND HERE.
힐끔
HILKUM (SNEAK)
OKAY, I'LL JUST HAVE TO GO LOOK FOR HIM.
I GUESS SHE KNOWS BUB-MIN-RANG FAIRLY WELL.
!
UMM, I WANT TO SAY GOOD-BYE TO HIM PERSONALLY. CAN'T I MEET YOU BACK AT THE GATE?
YOU WANT TO WALK AROUND ALONE~? HMPH, HOW CAN I TRUST YOU?
YOU...!

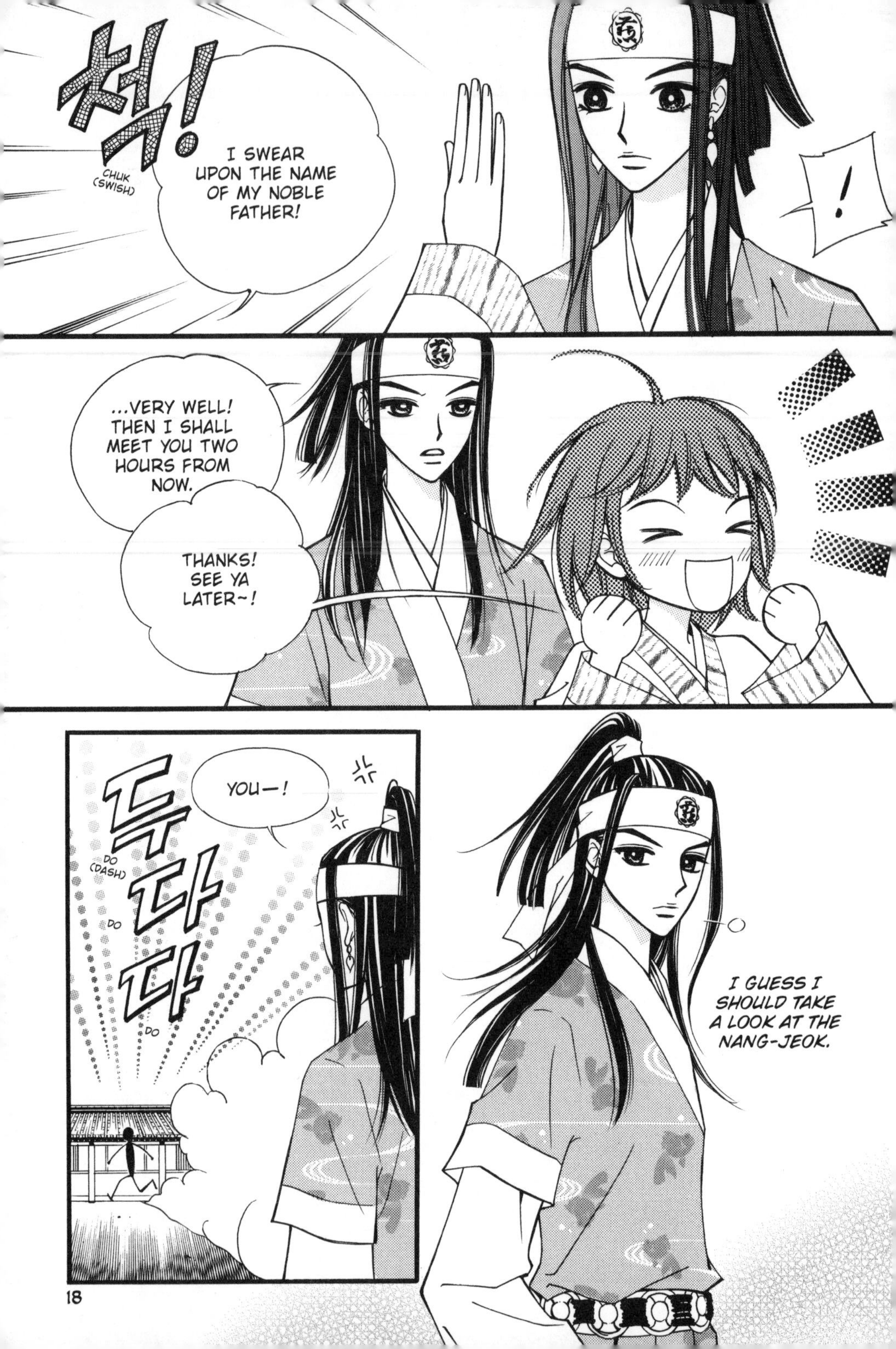

척!
CHUK (SWISH)
I SWEAR UPON THE NAME OF MY NOBLE FATHER!
!
...VERY WELL! THEN I SHALL MEET YOU TWO HOURS FROM NOW.
THANKS! SEE YA LATER~!
DO (DASH)
DO
DO
YOU—!
I GUESS I SHOULD TAKE A LOOK AT THE NANG-JEOK.

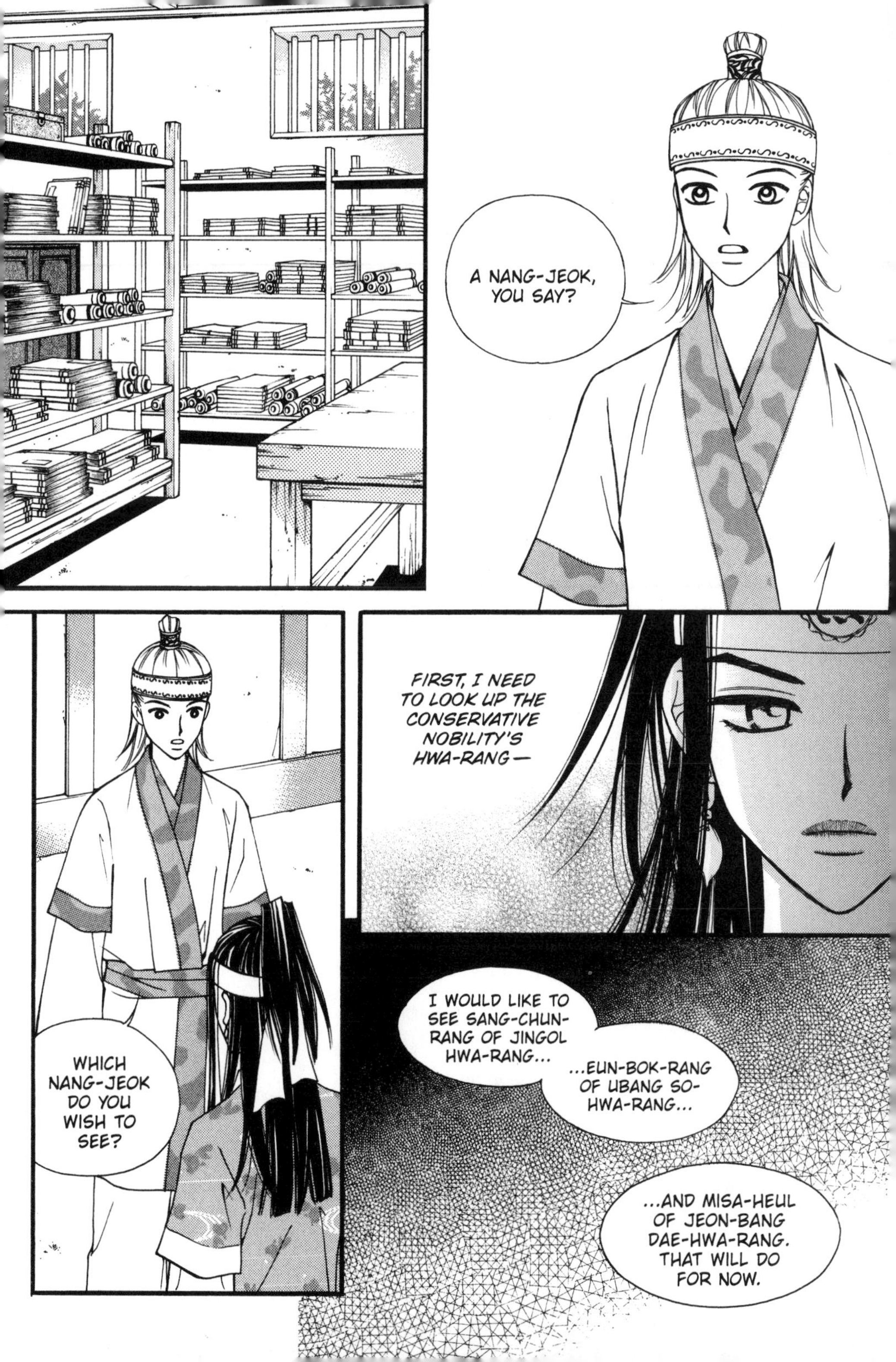
A NANG-JEOK, YOU SAY?
WHICH NANG-JEOK DO YOU WISH TO SEE?
FIRST, I NEED TO LOOK UP THE CONSERVATIVE NOBILITY'S HWA-RANG—
I WOULD LIKE TO SEE SANG-CHUN-RANG OF JINGOL HWA-RANG...
...EUN-BOK-RANG OF UBANG SO-HWA-RANG...
...AND MISA-HEUL OF JEON-BANG DAE-HWA-RANG. THAT WILL DO FOR NOW.

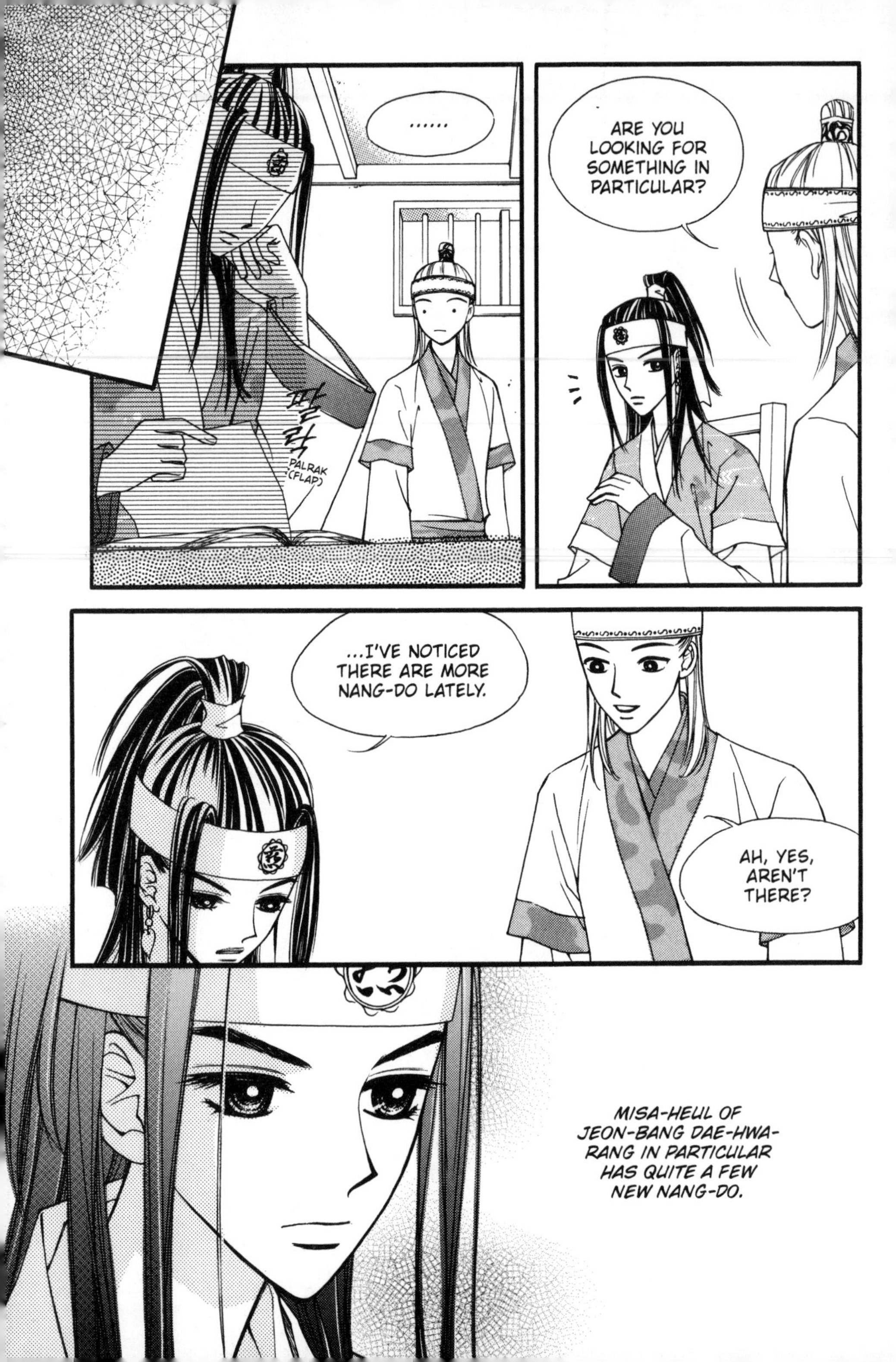
......
팔락
PALRAK (FLAP)
ARE YOU LOOKING FOR SOMETHING IN PARTICULAR?
...I'VE NOTICED THERE ARE MORE NANG-DO LATELY.
AH, YES, AREN'T THERE?
MISA-HEUL OF JEON-BANG DAE-HWA-RANG IN PARTICULAR HAS QUITE A FEW NEW NANG-DO.

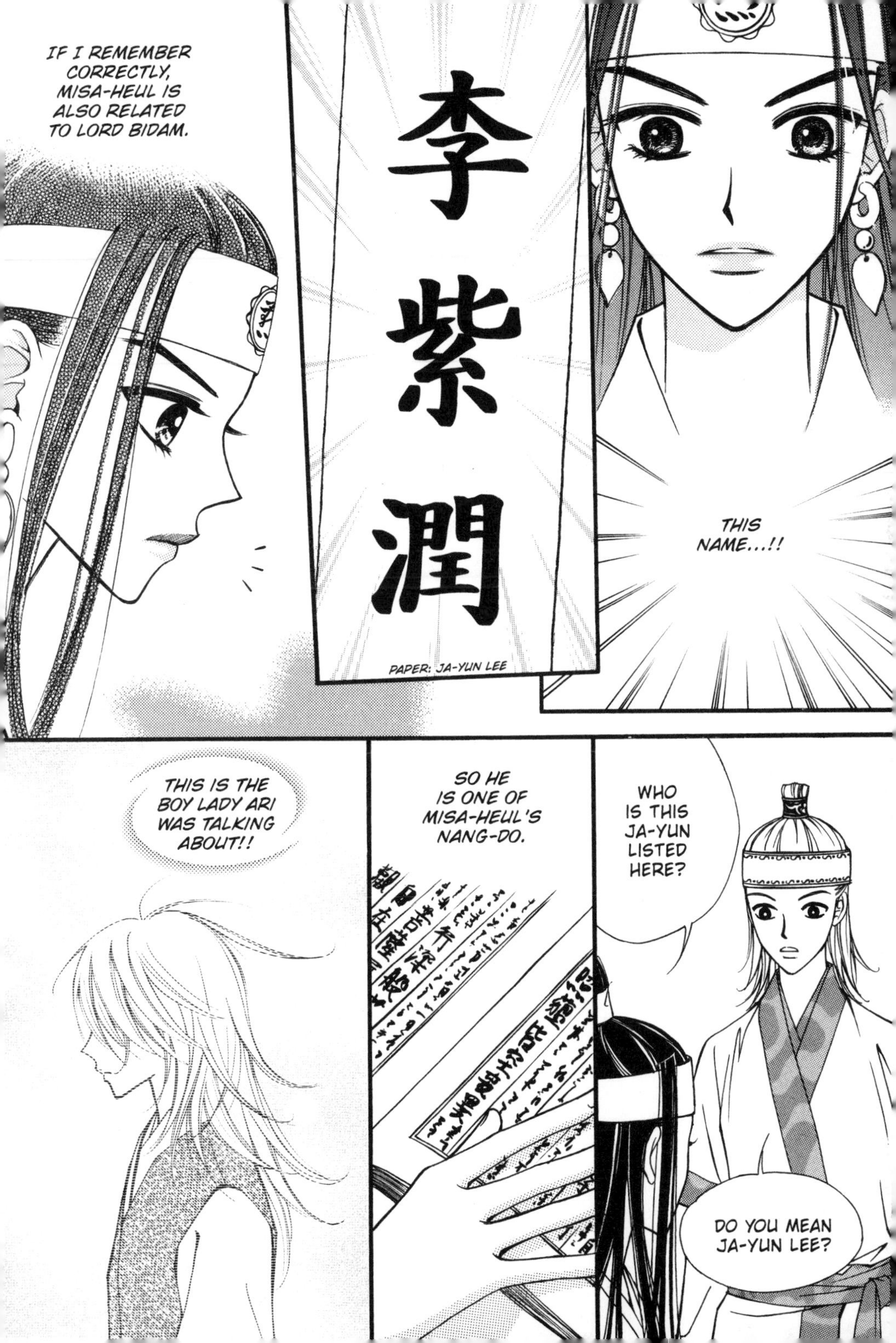
IF I REMEMBER CORRECTLY, MISA-HEUL IS ALSO RELATED TO LORD BIDAM.
李紫潤
PAPER: JA-YUN LEE
THIS NAME...!!
THIS IS THE BOY LADY ARI WAS TALKING ABOUT!!
SO HE IS ONE OF MISA-HEUL'S NANG-DO.
WHO IS THIS JA-YUN LISTED HERE?
DO YOU MEAN JA-YUN LEE?

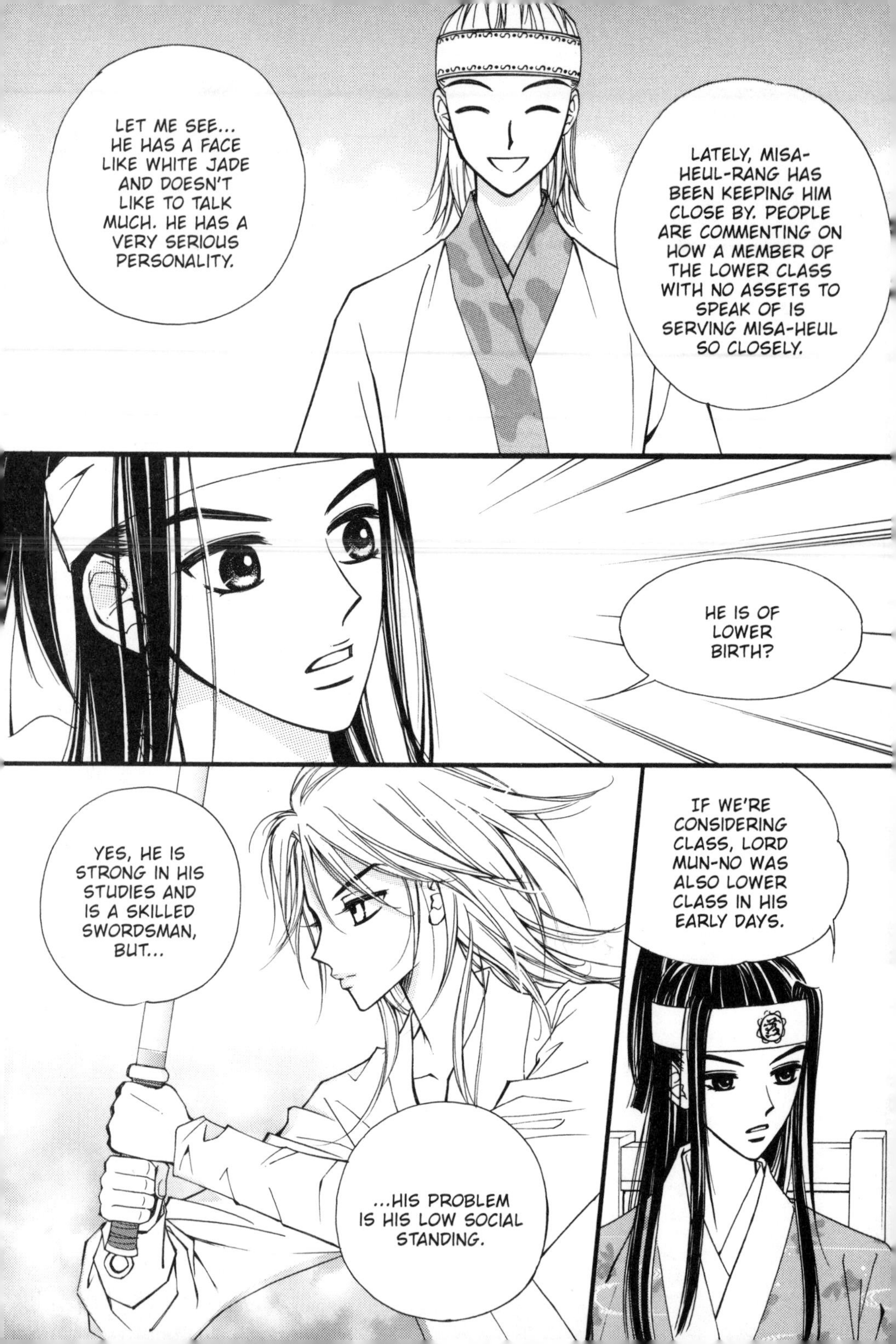
LET ME SEE... HE HAS A FACE LIKE WHITE JADE AND DOESN'T LIKE TO TALK MUCH. HE HAS A VERY SERIOUS PERSONALITY.
LATELY, MISA-HEUL-RANG HAS BEEN KEEPING HIM CLOSE BY. PEOPLE ARE COMMENTING ON HOW A MEMBER OF THE LOWER CLASS WITH NO ASSETS TO SPEAK OF IS SERVING MISA-HEUL SO CLOSELY.
HE IS OF LOWER BIRTH?
YES, HE IS STRONG IN HIS STUDIES AND IS A SKILLED SWORDSMAN, BUT...
...HIS PROBLEM IS HIS LOW SOCIAL STANDING.
IF WE'RE CONSIDERING CLASS, LORD MUN-NO WAS ALSO LOWER CLASS IN HIS EARLY DAYS.

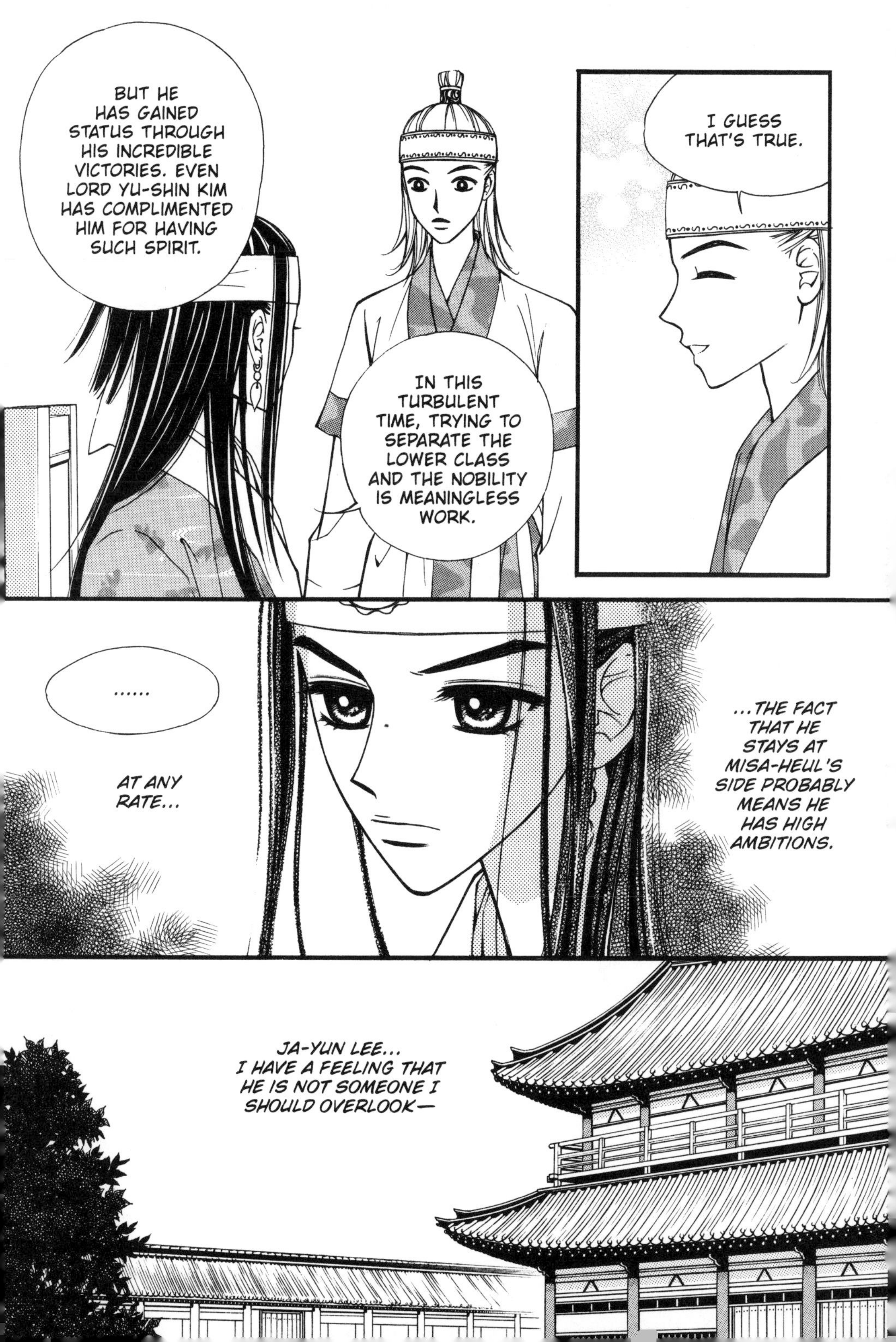
BUT HE HAS GAINED STATUS THROUGH HIS INCREDIBLE VICTORIES. EVEN LORD YU-SHIN KIM HAS COMPLIMENTED HIM FOR HAVING SUCH SPIRIT.
IN THIS TURBULENT TIME, TRYING TO SEPARATE THE LOWER CLASS AND THE NOBILITY IS MEANINGLESS WORK.
I GUESS THAT'S TRUE.
......
AT ANY RATE...
...THE FACT THAT HE STAYS AT MISA-HEUL'S SIDE PROBABLY MEANS HE HAS HIGH AMBITIONS.
JA-YUN LEE... I HAVE A FEELING THAT HE IS NOT SOMEONE I SHOULD OVERLOOK—

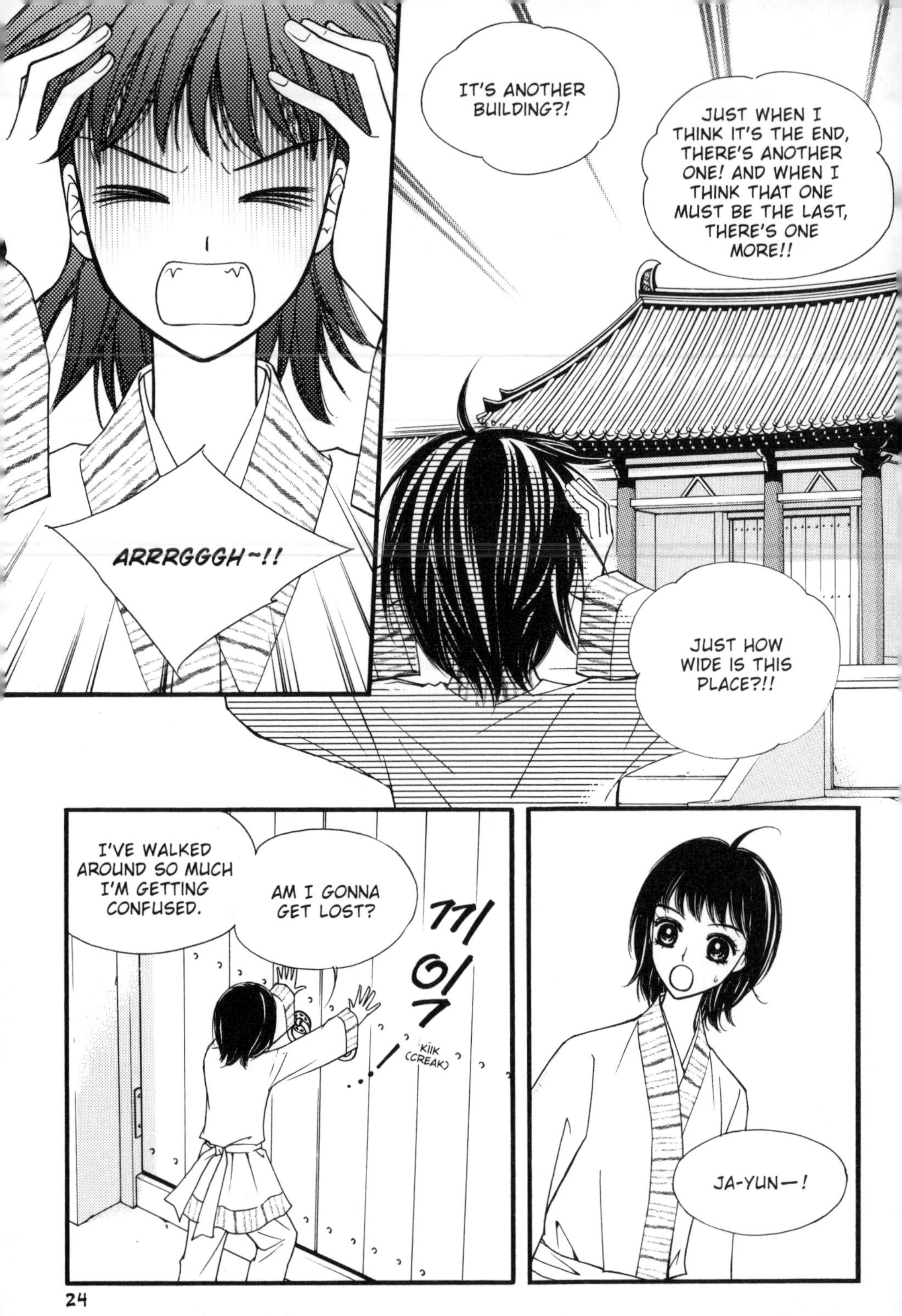
ARRRGGGH~!!
IT'S ANOTHER BUILDING?!
JUST WHEN I THINK IT'S THE END, THERE'S ANOTHER ONE! AND WHEN I THINK THAT ONE MUST BE THE LAST, THERE'S ONE MORE!!
JUST HOW WIDE IS THIS PLACE?!!
I'VE WALKED AROUND SO MUCH I'M GETTING CONFUSED.
AM I GONNA GET LOST?
끼익
KIIK (CREAK)
...!
JA-YUN—!

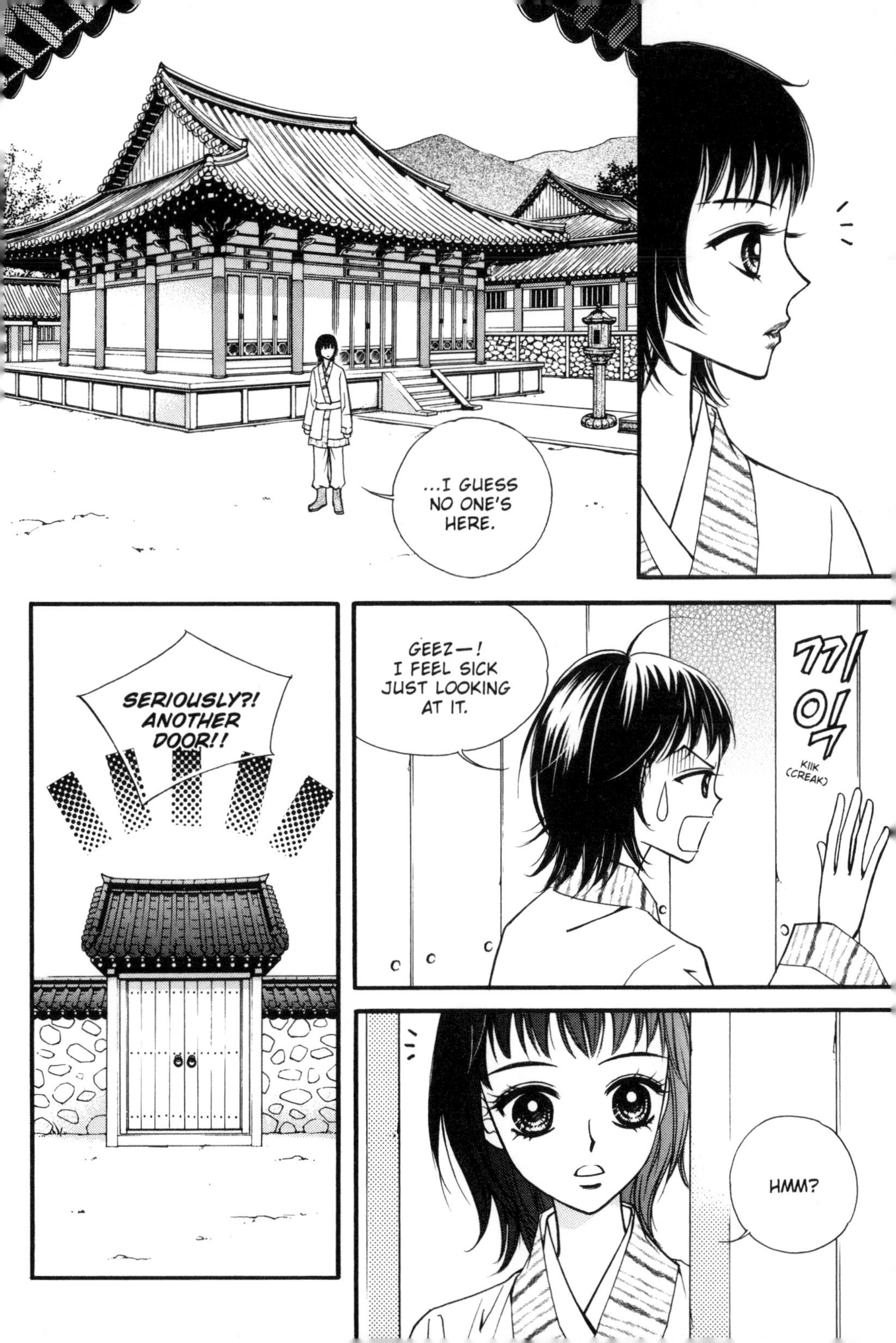
...I GUESS NO ONE'S HERE.
SERIOUSLY?! ANOTHER DOOR!!
GEEZ—! I FEEL SICK JUST LOOKING AT IT.
끼익
KIIK (CREAK)
HMM?

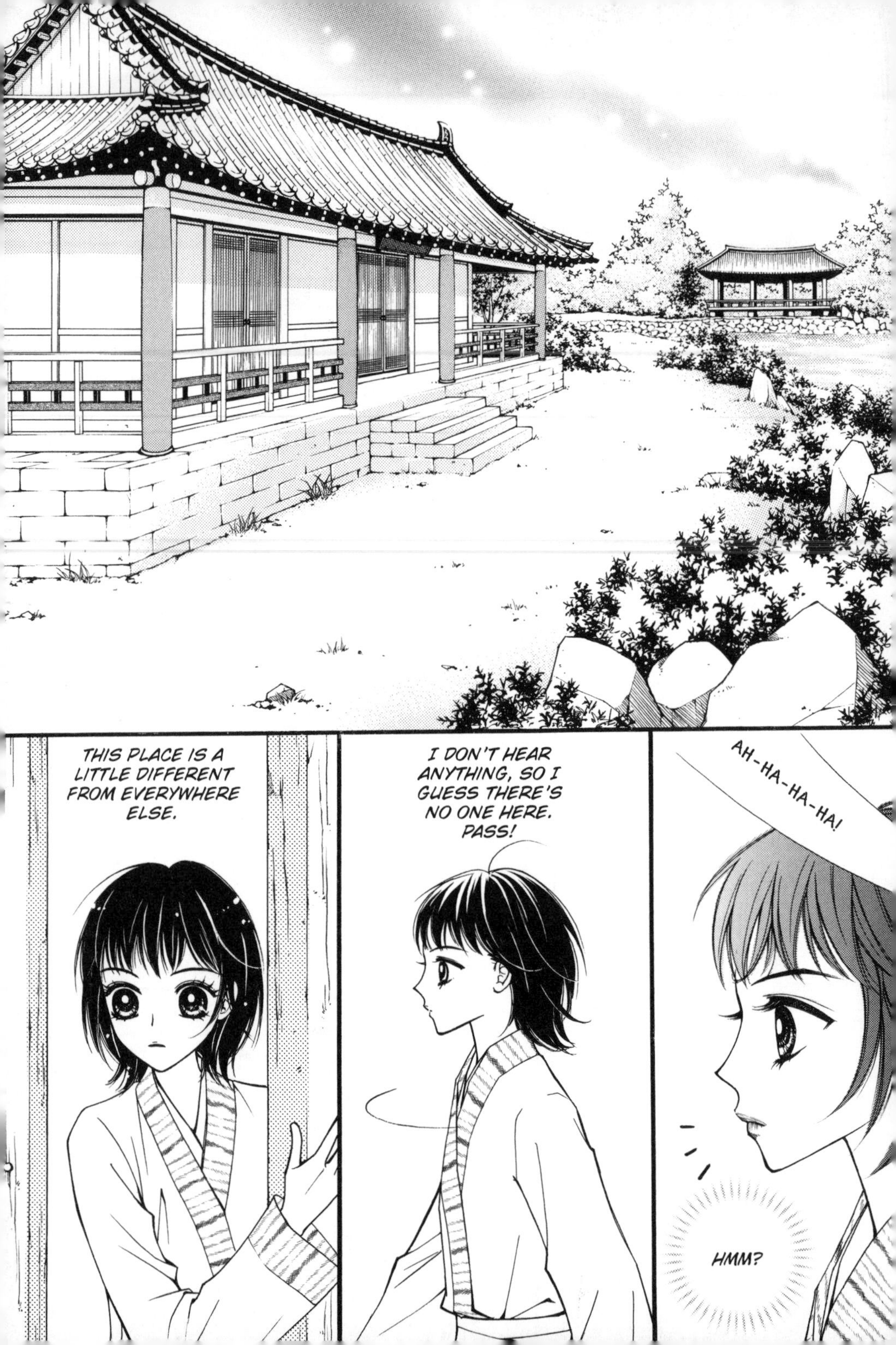
THIS PLACE IS A LITTLE DIFFERENT FROM EVERYWHERE ELSE.
I DON'T HEAR ANYTHING, SO I GUESS THERE'S NO ONE HERE. PASS!
AH-HA-HA-HA!
HMM?

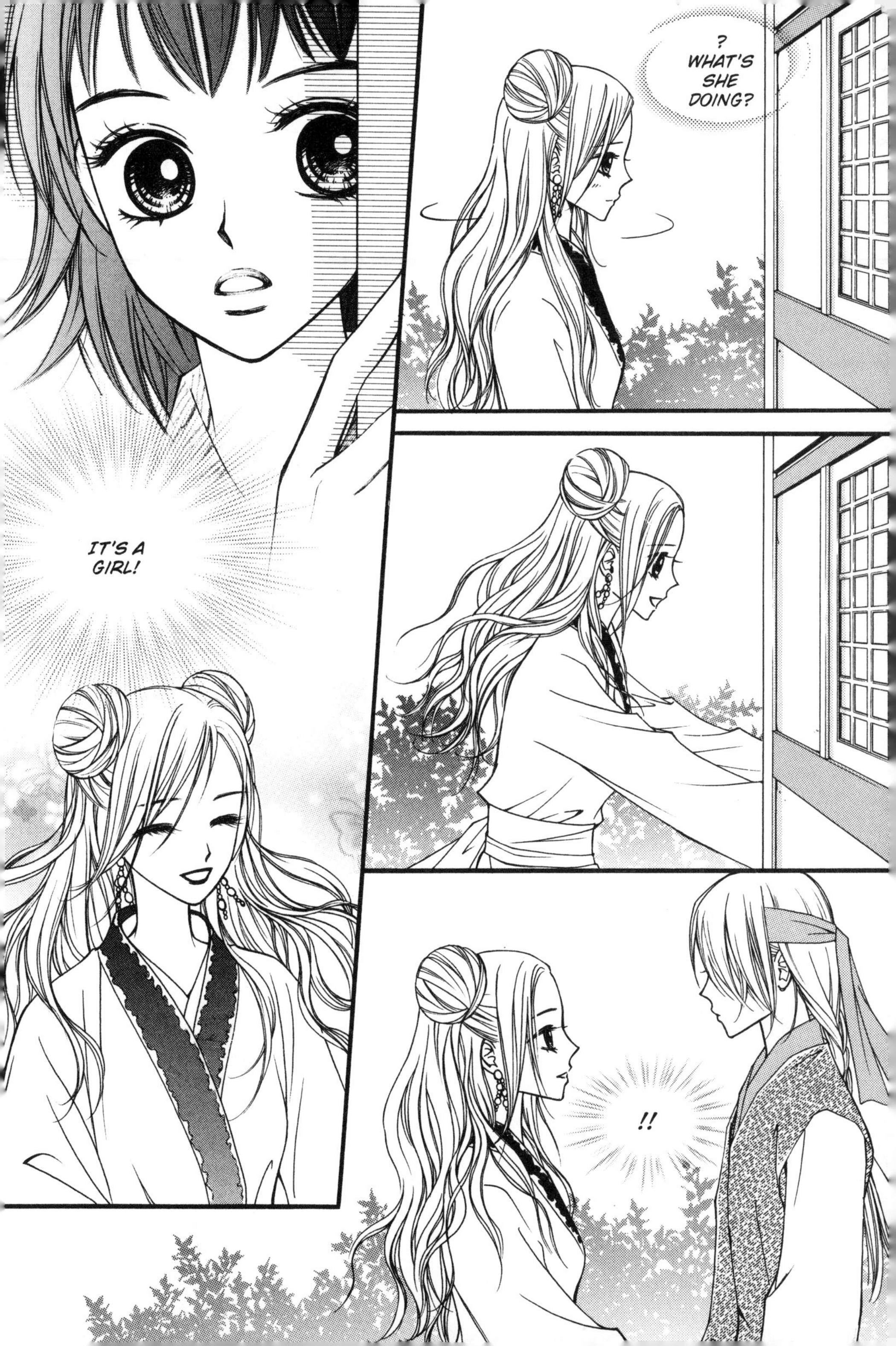
IT'S A GIRL!
? WHAT'S SHE DOING?
!!

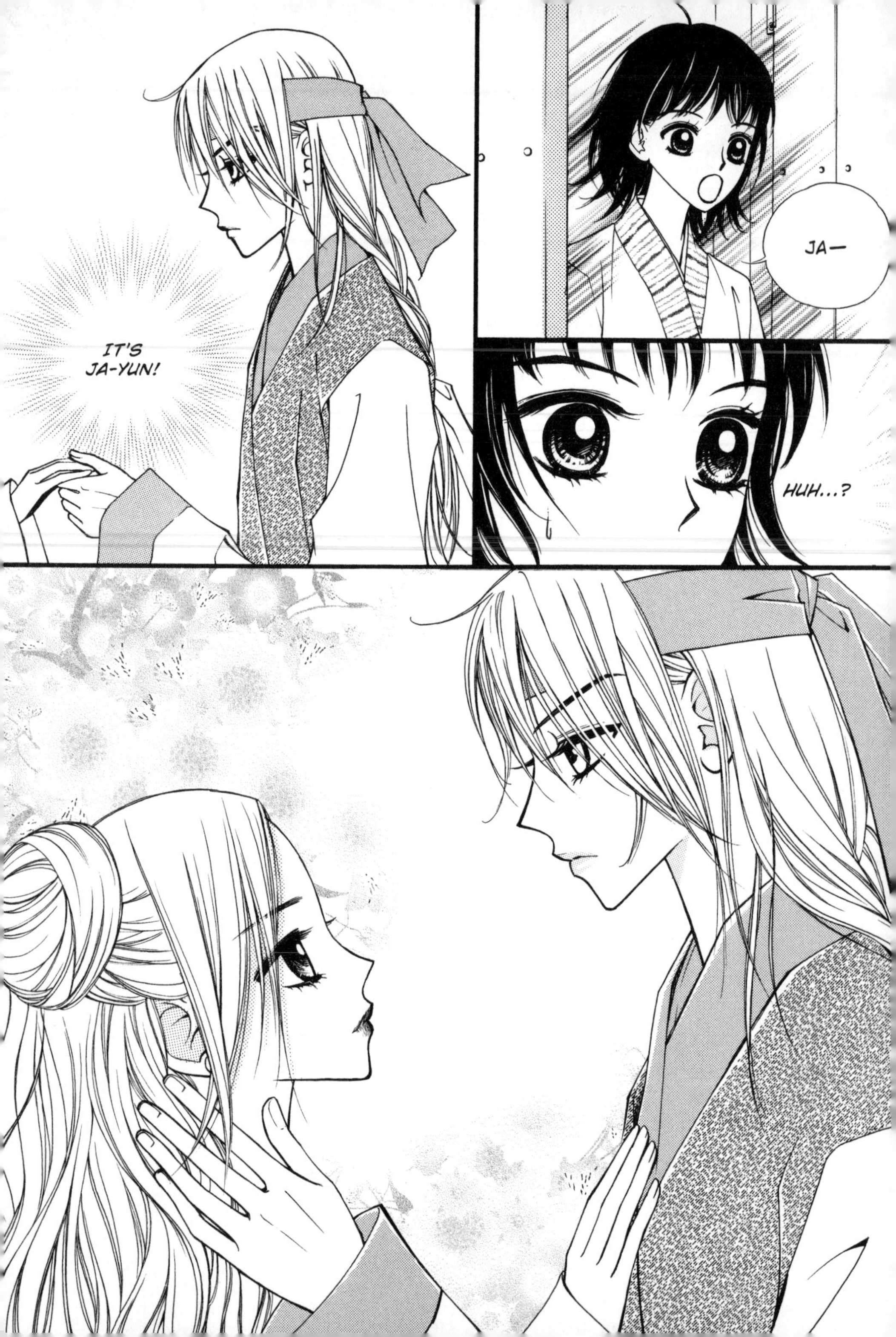
IT'S JA-YUN!
JA—
HUH...?

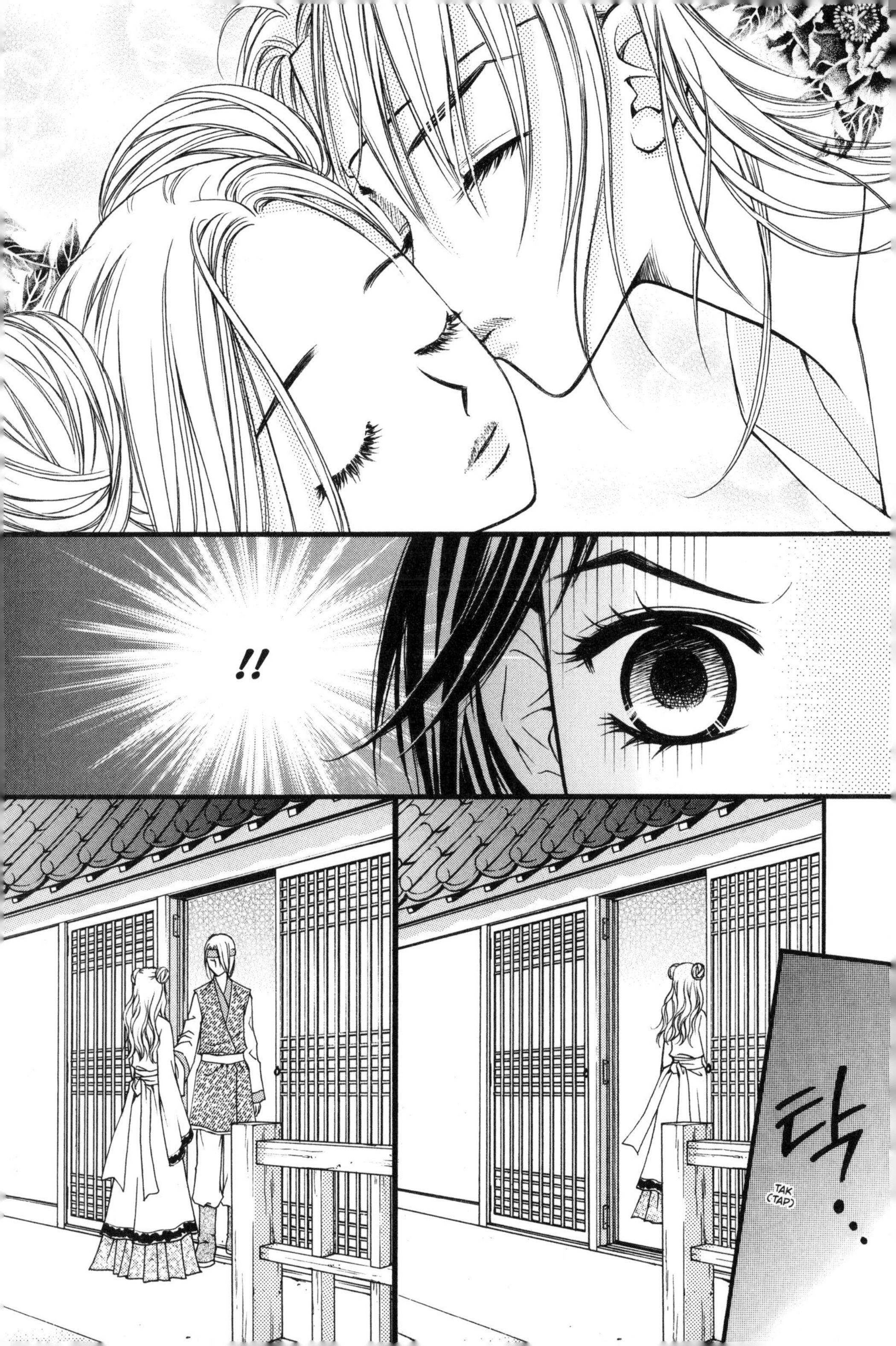
!!
탁
TAK (TAP)

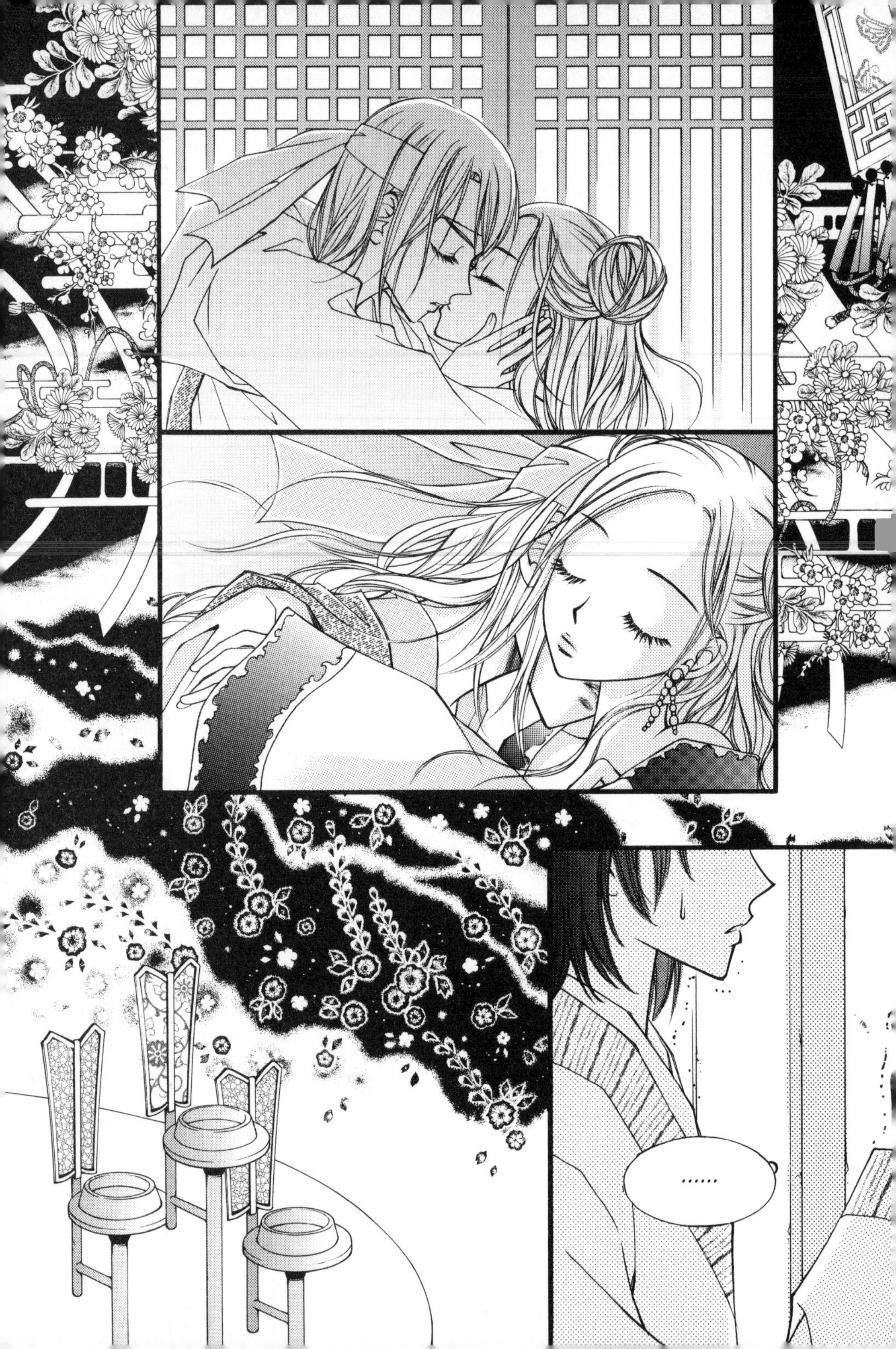
……

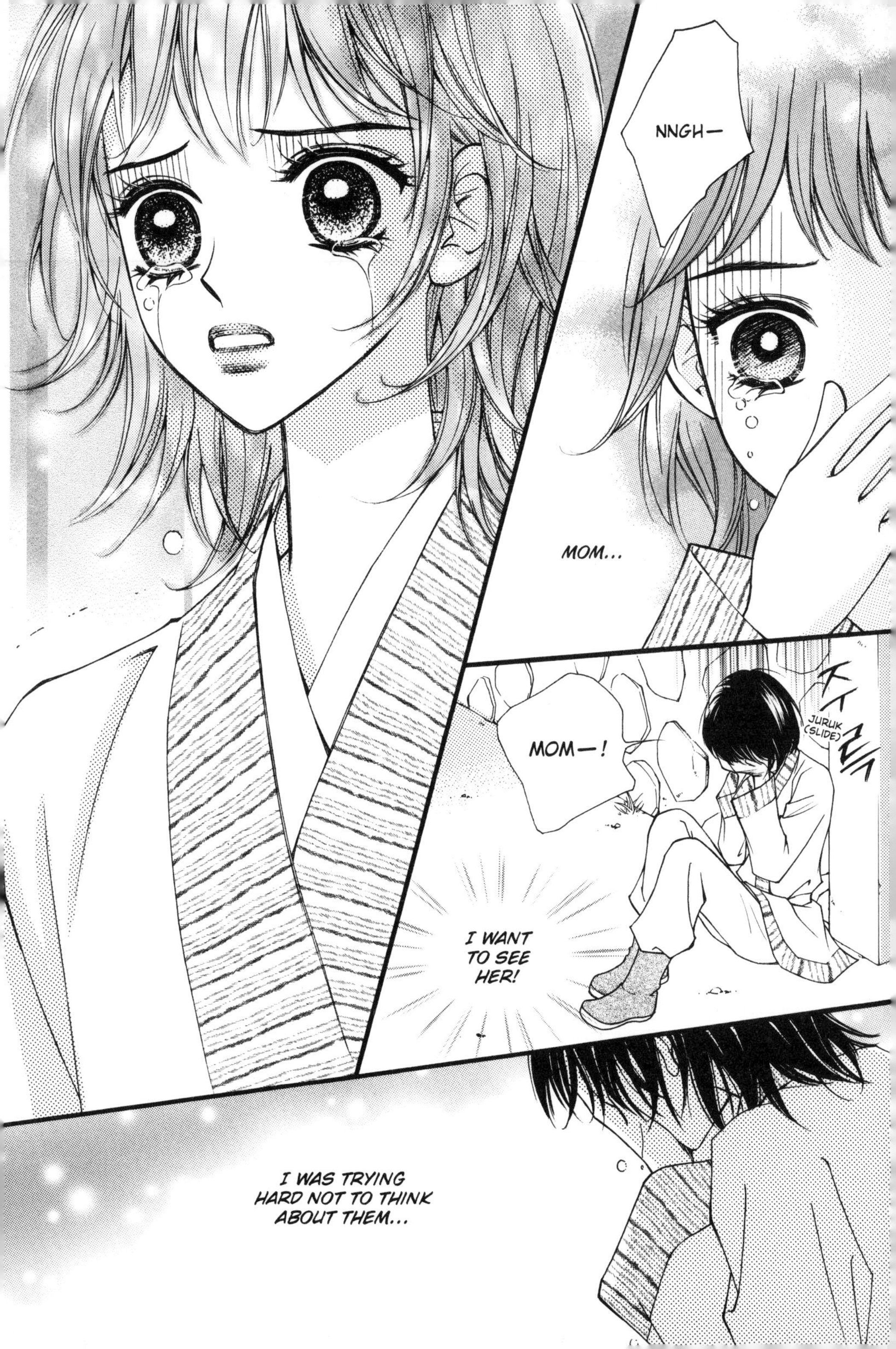
NNGH—
MOM...
MOM—!
JURUK (SLIDE)
I WANT TO SEE HER!
I WAS TRYING HARD NOT TO THINK ABOUT THEM...

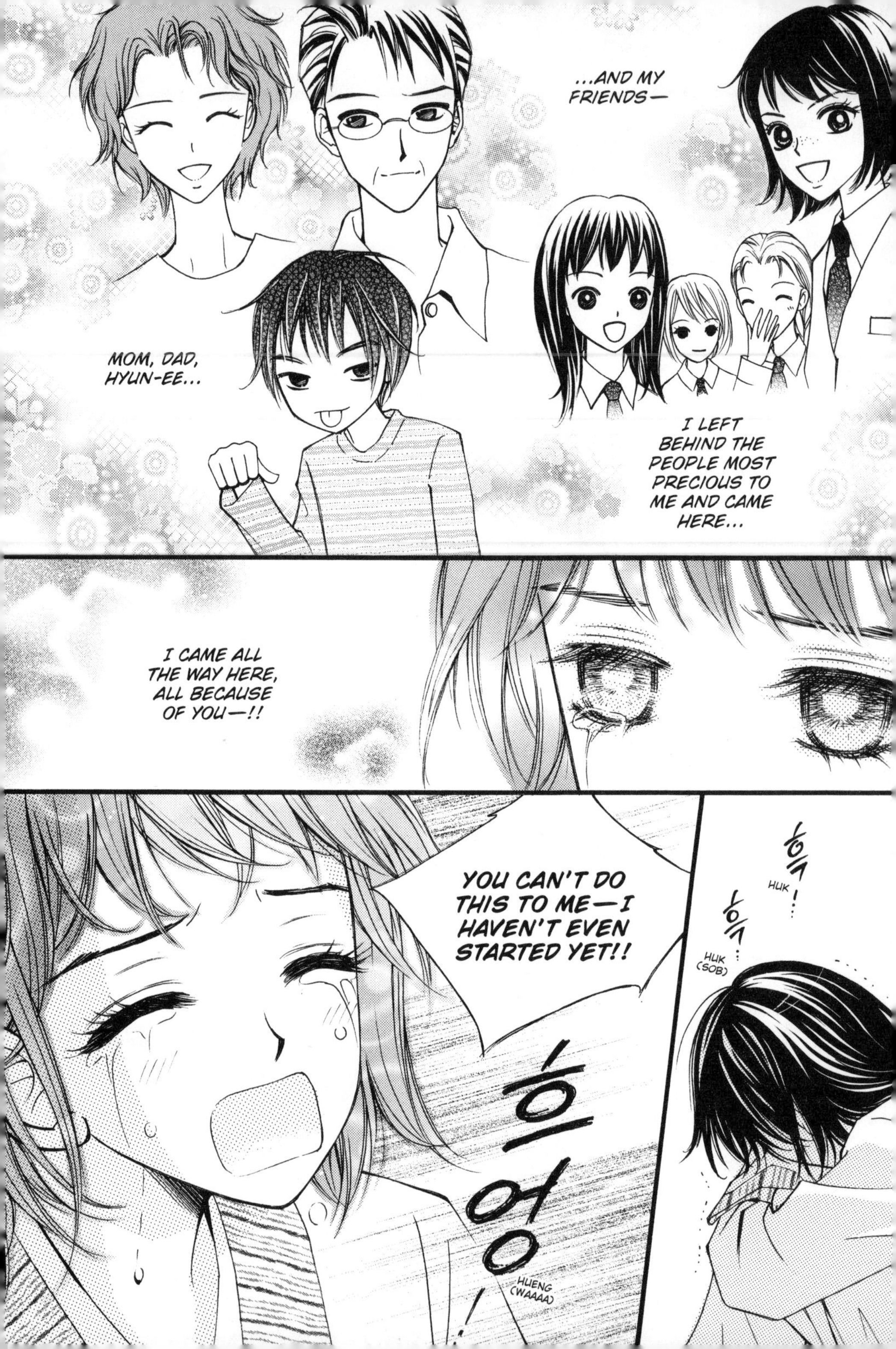
MOM, DAD, HYUN-EE...
...AND MY FRIENDS—
I LEFT BEHIND THE PEOPLE MOST PRECIOUS TO ME AND CAME HERE...
I CAME ALL THE WAY HERE, ALL BECAUSE OF YOU—!!
YOU CAN'T DO THIS TO ME—I HAVEN'T EVEN STARTED YET!!
흐어엉!
HUENG (WAAAA)
흑
HUK!...
흑
HUK (SOB)

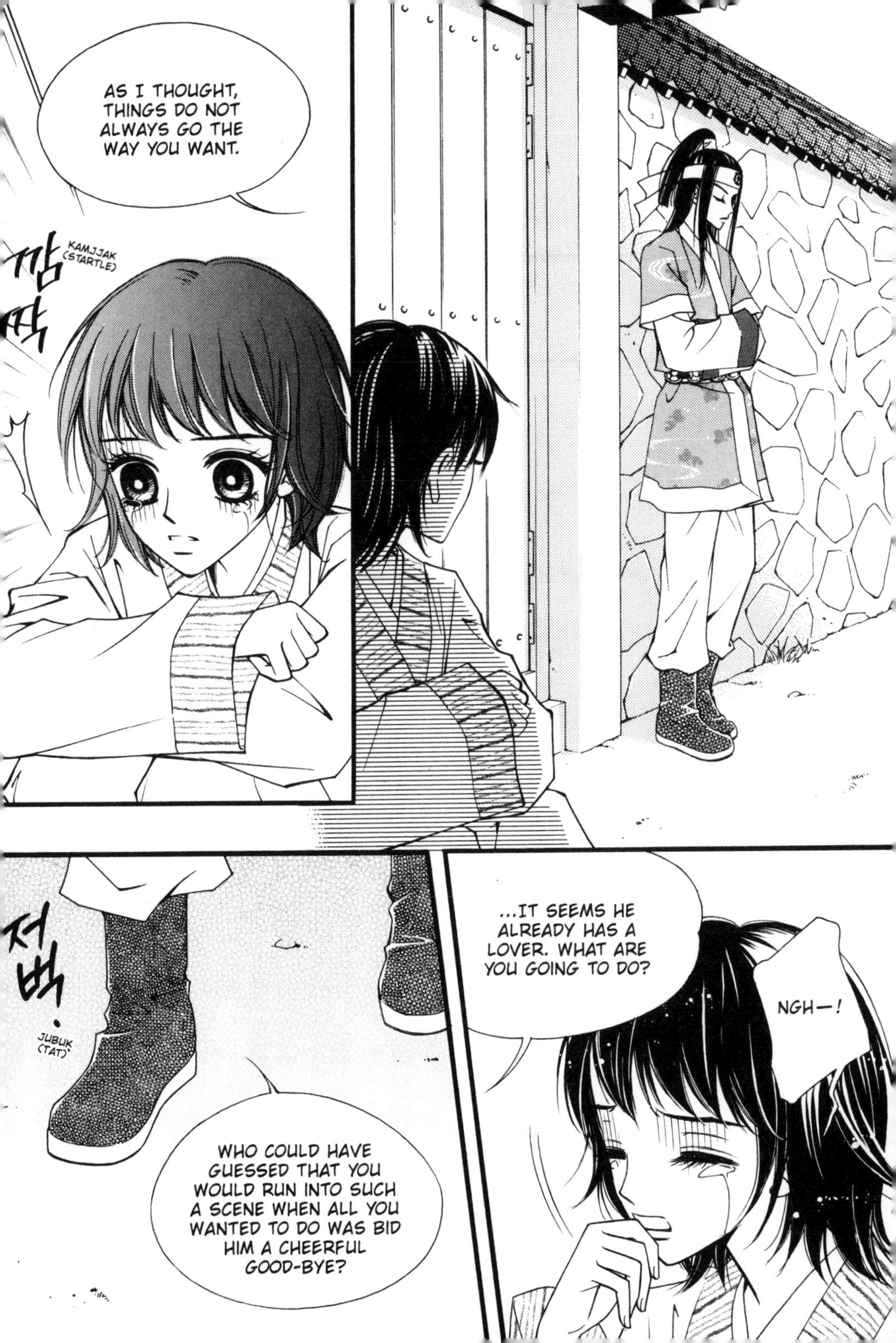
AS I THOUGHT, THINGS DO NOT ALWAYS GO THE WAY YOU WANT.
깜짝
KAMJJAK (STARTLE)
저벅
JUBUK (TAT)
WHO COULD HAVE GUESSED THAT YOU WOULD RUN INTO SUCH A SCENE WHEN ALL YOU WANTED TO DO WAS BID HIM A CHEERFUL GOOD-BYE?
...IT SEEMS HE ALREADY HAS A LOVER. WHAT ARE YOU GOING TO DO?
NGH—!

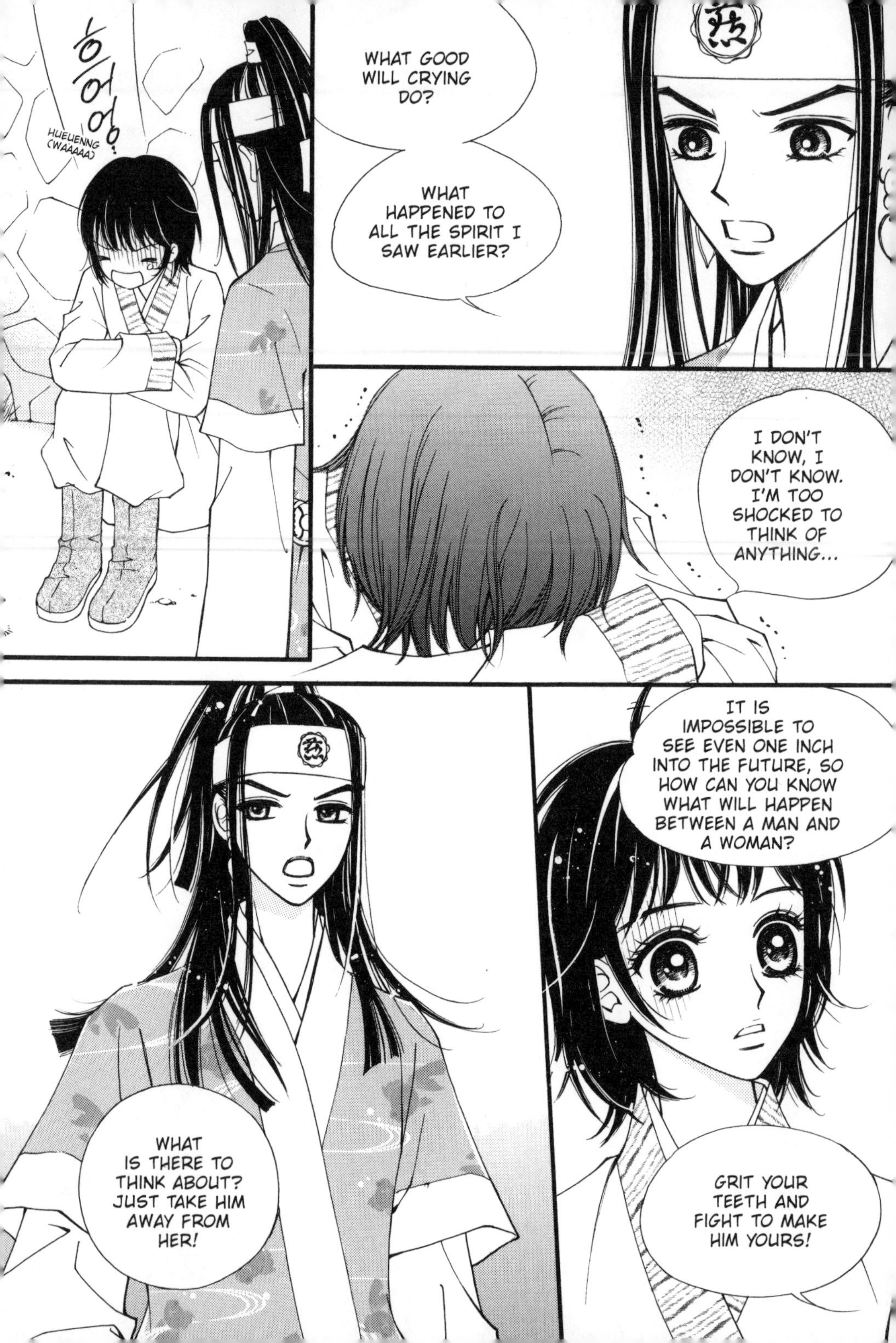

흐어엉
HUEUENNG (WAAAAA)
WHAT GOOD WILL CRYING DO?
WHAT HAPPENED TO ALL THE SPIRIT I SAW EARLIER?
I DON'T KNOW, I DON'T KNOW. I'M TOO SHOCKED TO THINK OF ANYTHING...
WHAT IS THERE TO THINK ABOUT? JUST TAKE HIM AWAY FROM HER!
IT IS IMPOSSIBLE TO SEE EVEN ONE INCH INTO THE FUTURE, SO HOW CAN YOU KNOW WHAT WILL HAPPEN BETWEEN A MAN AND A WOMAN?
GRIT YOUR TEETH AND FIGHT TO MAKE HIM YOURS!

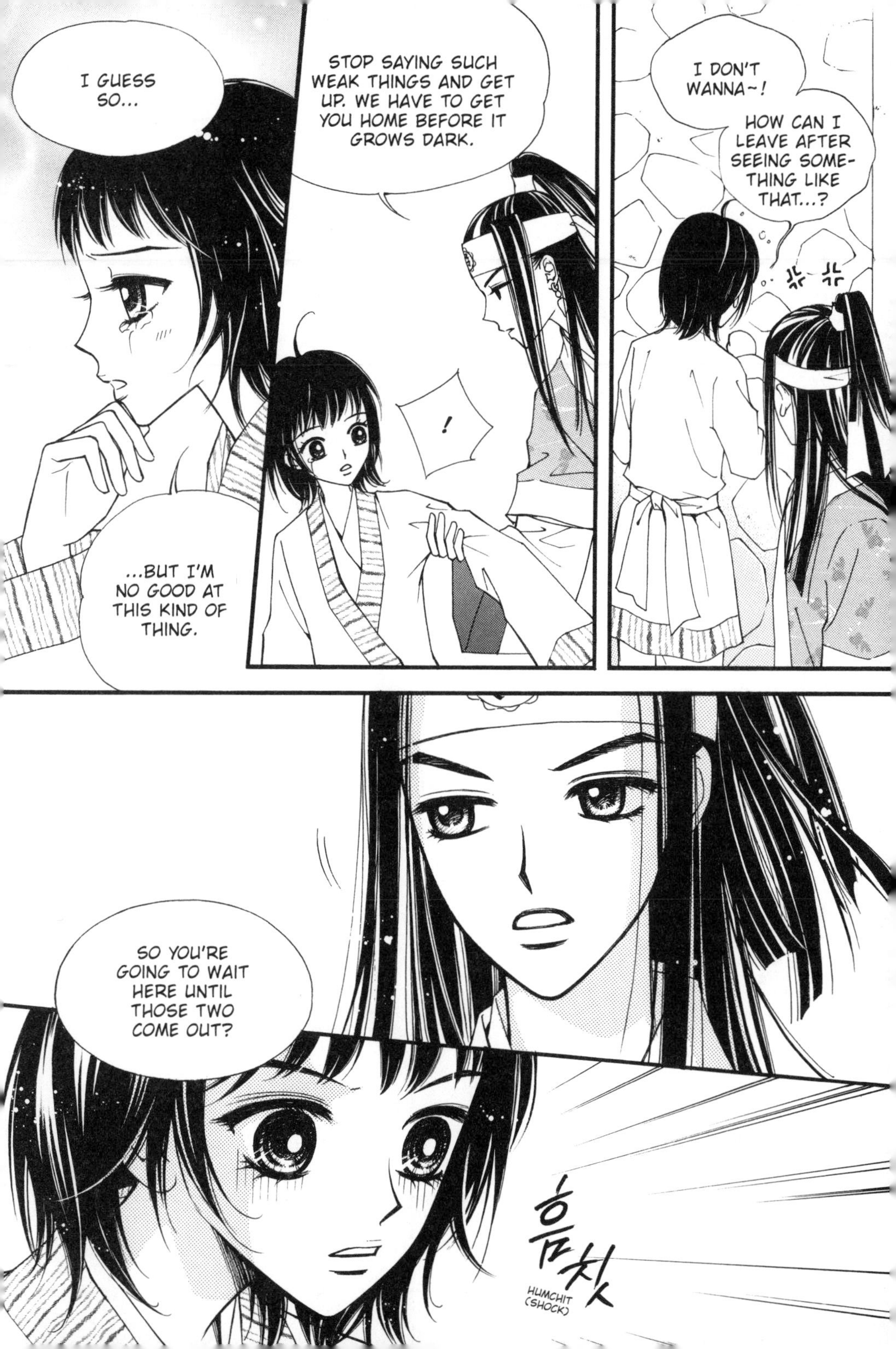
I GUESS SO...
...BUT I'M NO GOOD AT THIS KIND OF THING.
STOP SAYING SUCH WEAK THINGS AND GET UP. WE HAVE TO GET YOU HOME BEFORE IT GROWS DARK.
!
I DON'T WANNA~!
HOW CAN I LEAVE AFTER SEEING SOME-THING LIKE THAT...?
SO YOU'RE GOING TO WAIT HERE UNTIL THOSE TWO COME OUT?
흠칫
HUMCHIT (SHOCK)

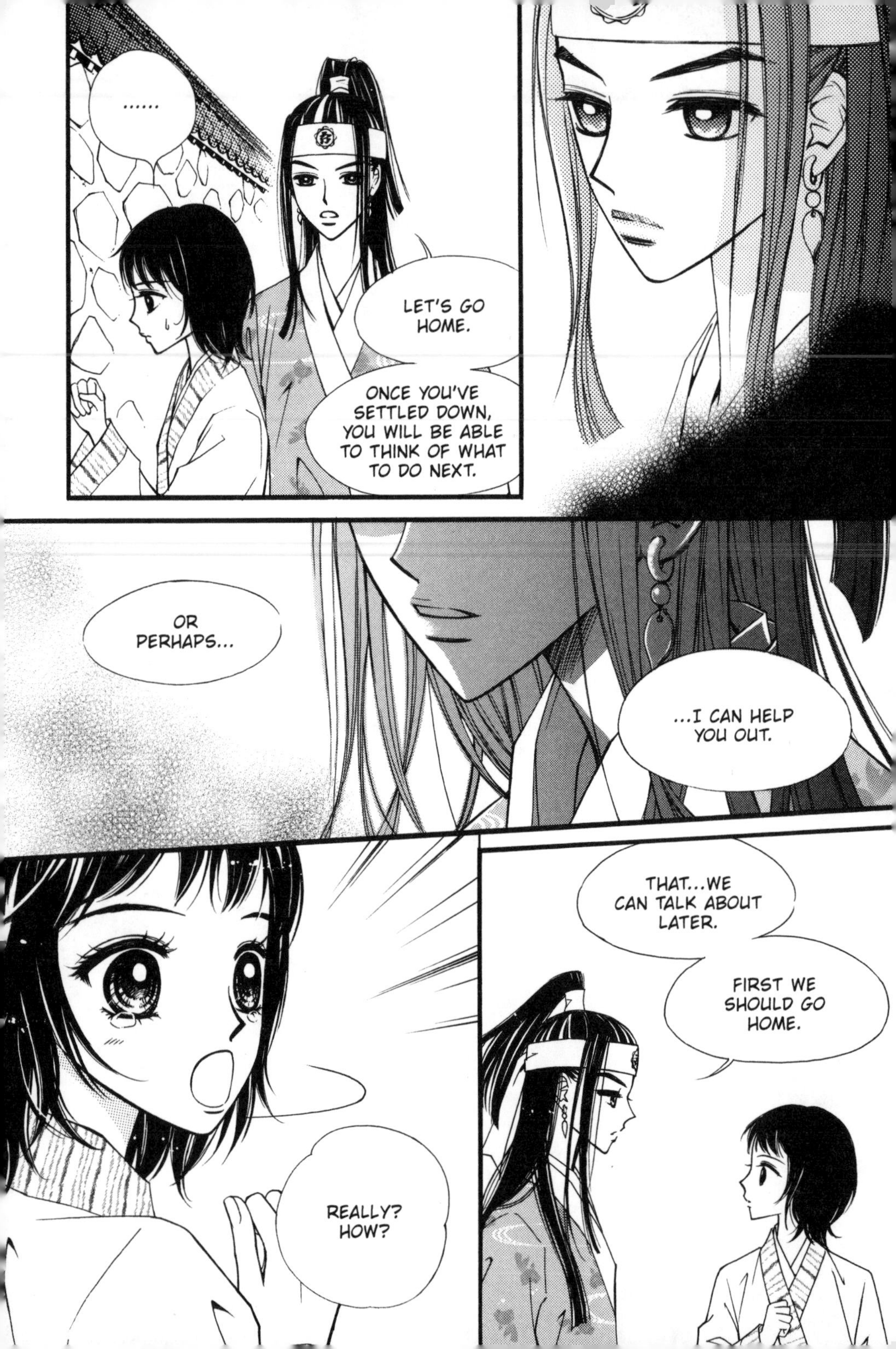
......
LET'S GO HOME.
ONCE YOU'VE SETTLED DOWN, YOU WILL BE ABLE TO THINK OF WHAT TO DO NEXT.
OR PERHAPS...
...I CAN HELP YOU OUT.
REALLY? HOW?
THAT...WE CAN TALK ABOUT LATER.
FIRST WE SHOULD GO HOME.

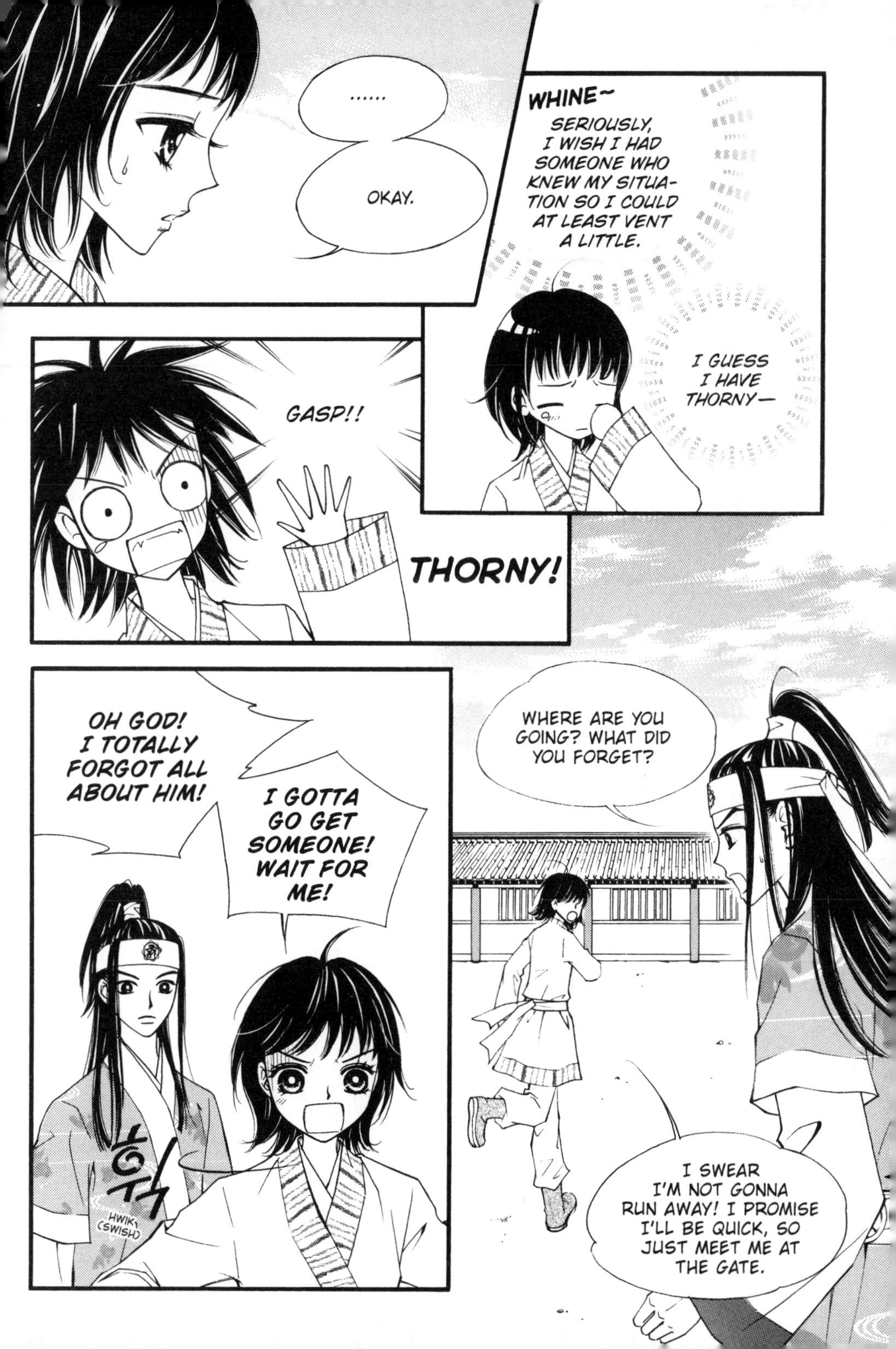
......
OKAY.
WHINE~
SERIOUSLY, I WISH I HAD SOMEONE WHO KNEW MY SITUATION SO I COULD AT LEAST VENT A LITTLE.
I GUESS I HAVE THORNY—
GASP!!
THORNY!
OH GOD! I TOTALLY FORGOT ALL ABOUT HIM!
I GOTTA GO GET SOMEONE! WAIT FOR ME!
HWIK (SWISH)
WHERE ARE YOU GOING? WHAT DID YOU FORGET?
I SWEAR I'M NOT GONNA RUN AWAY! I PROMISE I'LL BE QUICK, SO JUST MEET ME AT THE GATE.

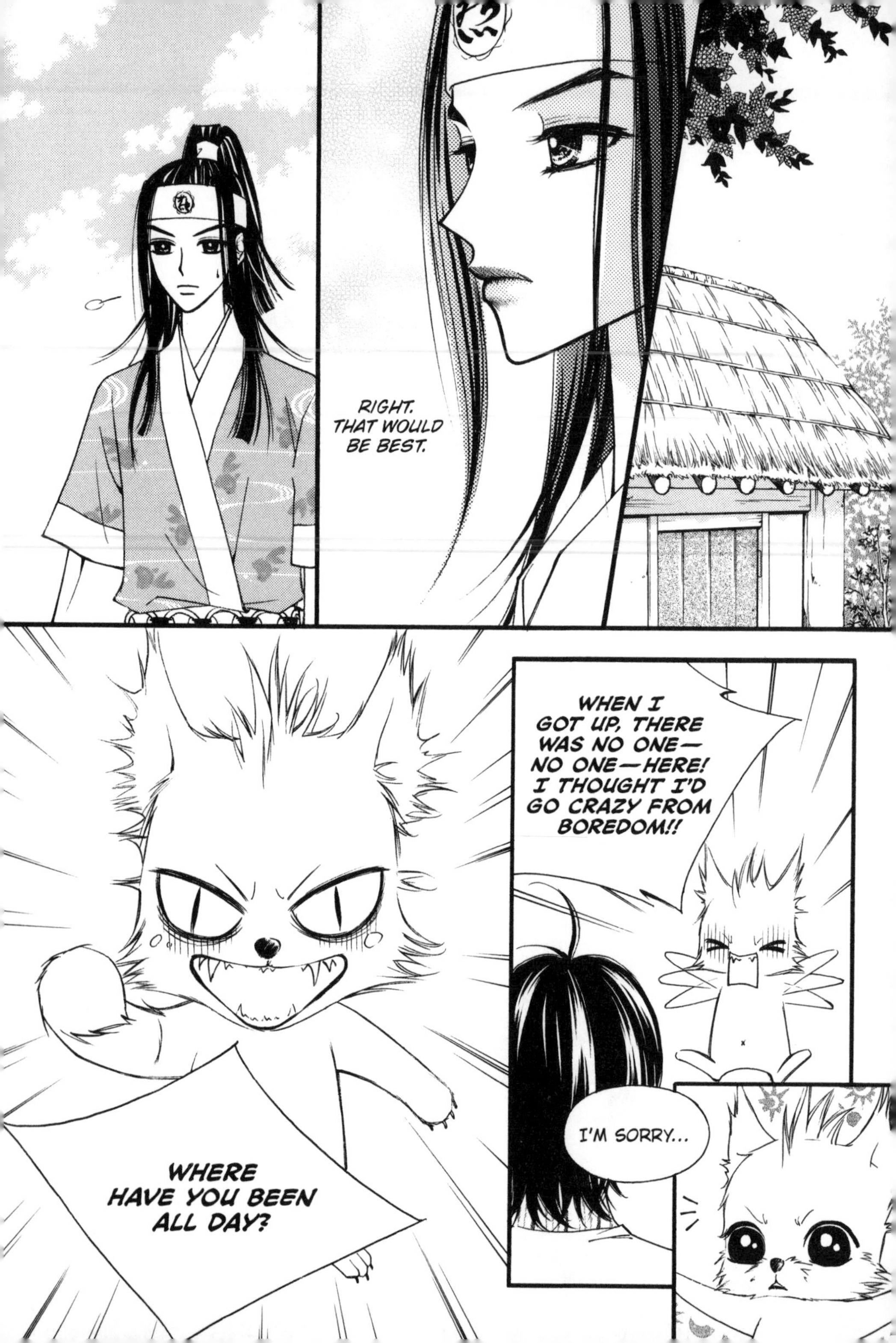
RIGHT. THAT WOULD BE BEST.
WHERE HAVE YOU BEEN ALL DAY?
WHEN I GOT UP, THERE WAS NO ONE— NO ONE—HERE! I THOUGHT I'D GO CRAZY FROM BOREDOM!!
I'M SORRY...

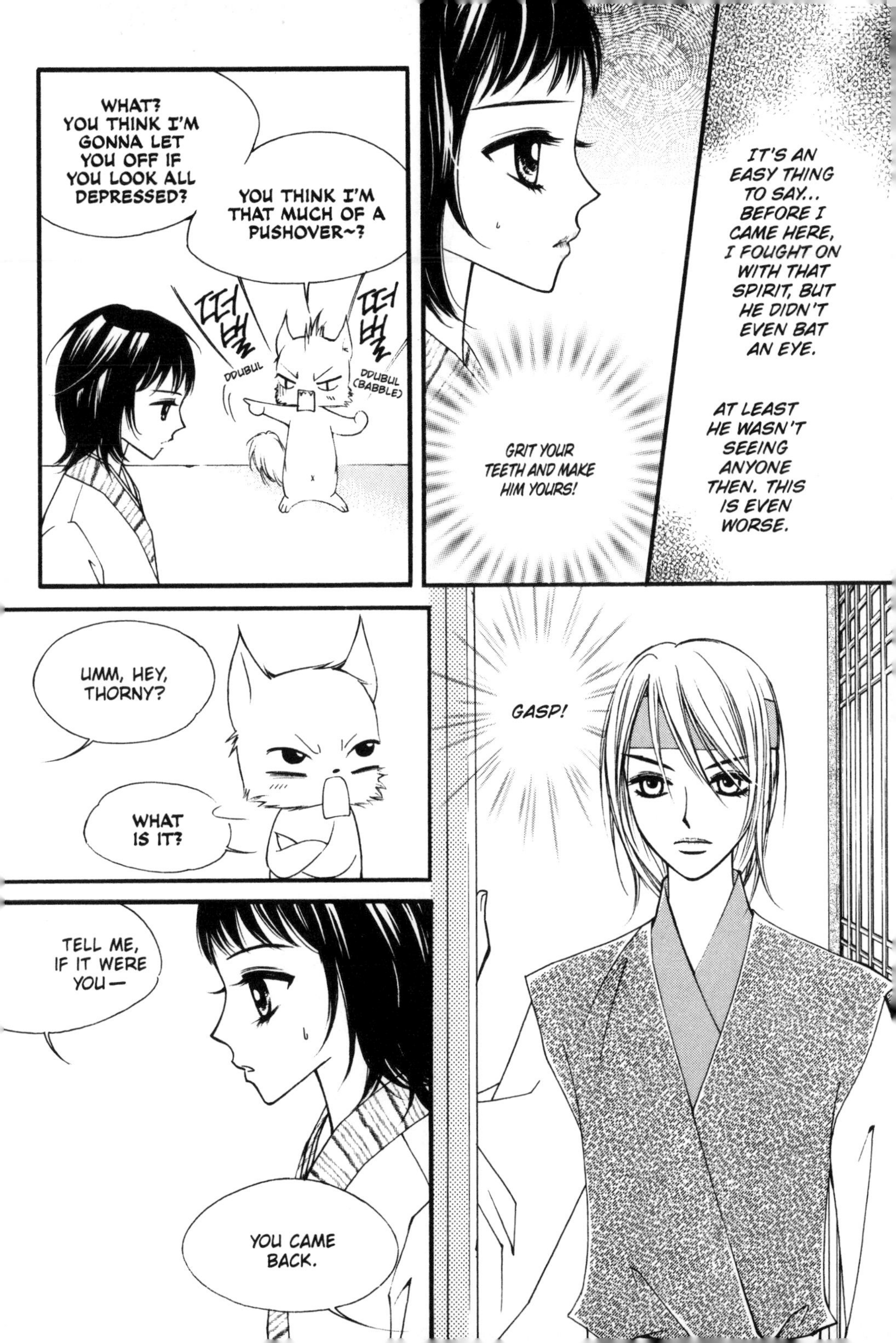
WHAT? YOU THINK I'M GONNA LET YOU OFF IF YOU LOOK ALL DEPRESSED?
YOU THINK I'M THAT MUCH OF A PUSHOVER~?
떠벌
DDUBUL
떠벌
DDUBUL (BABBLE)
IT'S AN EASY THING TO SAY... BEFORE I CAME HERE, I FOUGHT ON WITH THAT SPIRIT, BUT HE DIDN'T EVEN BAT AN EYE.
GRIT YOUR TEETH AND MAKE HIM YOURS!
AT LEAST HE WASN'T SEEING ANYONE THEN. THIS IS EVEN WORSE.
UMM, HEY, THORNY?
WHAT IS IT?
TELL ME, IF IT WERE YOU—
YOU CAME BACK.
GASP!

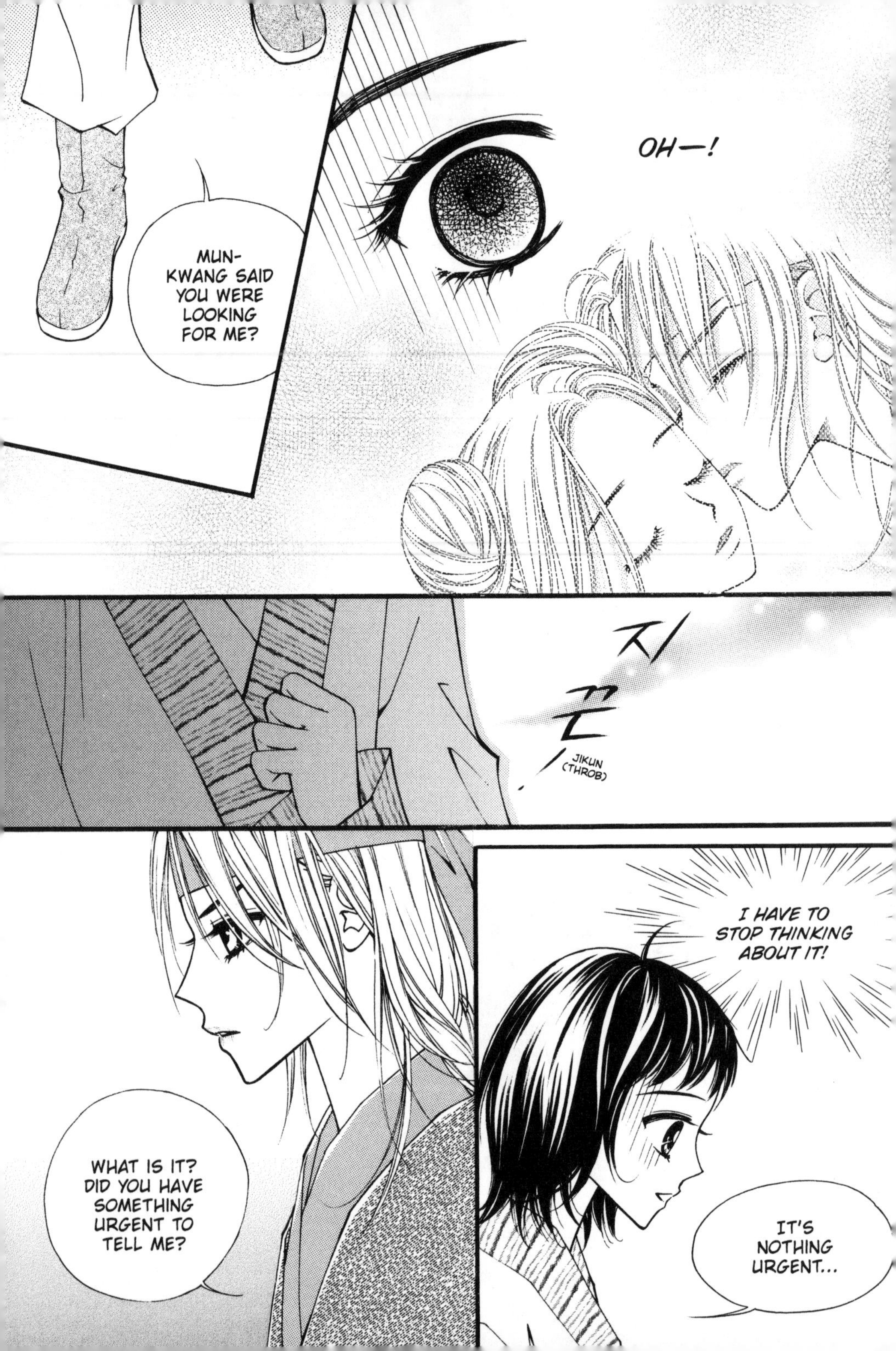
MUN-KWANG SAID YOU WERE LOOKING FOR ME?
OH—!
지끈!
JIKUN (THROB)
WHAT IS IT? DID YOU HAVE SOMETHING URGENT TO TELL ME?
I HAVE TO STOP THINKING ABOUT IT!
IT'S NOTHING URGENT...

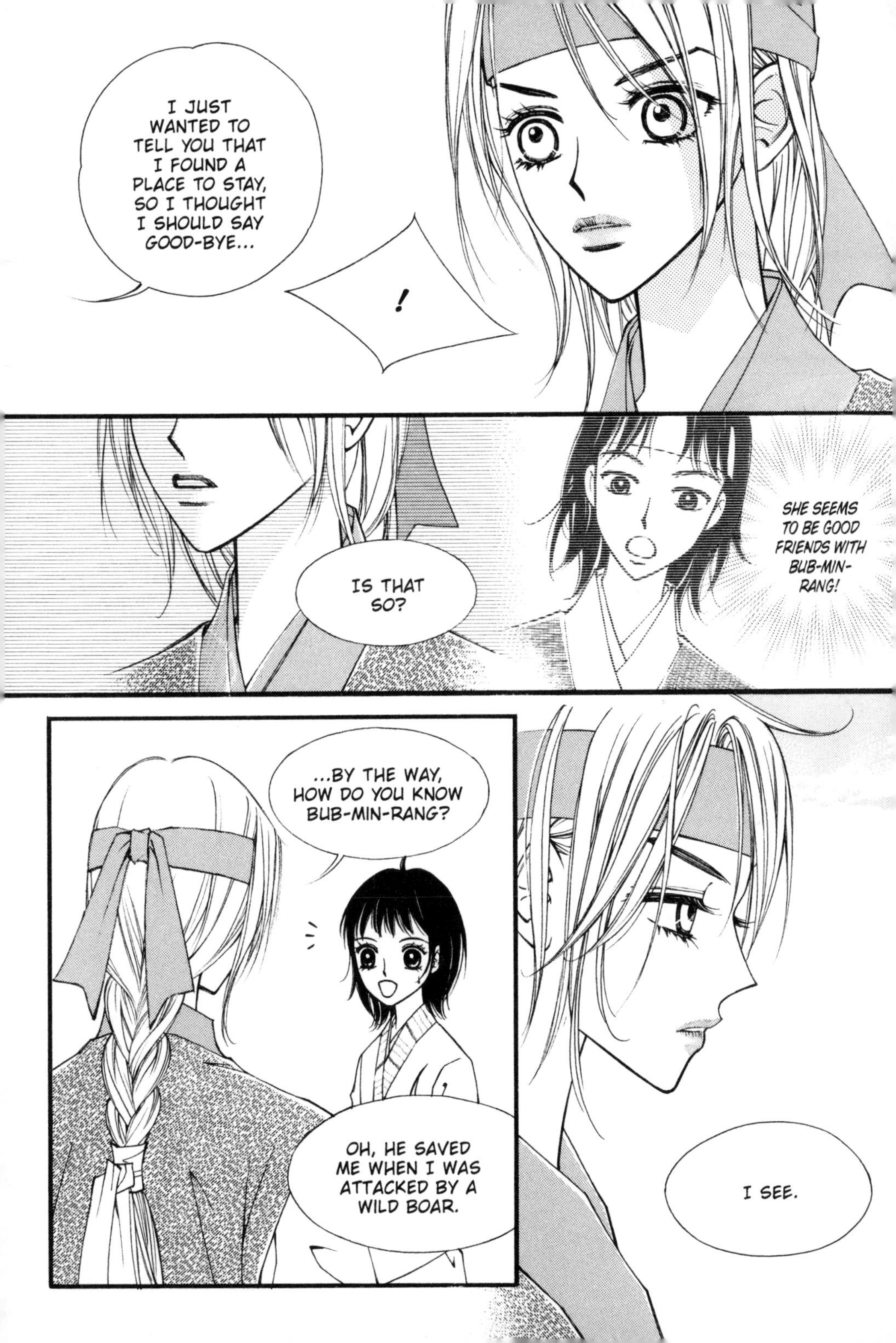
I JUST WANTED TO TELL YOU THAT I FOUND A PLACE TO STAY, SO I THOUGHT I SHOULD SAY GOOD-BYE...
!
IS THAT SO?
SHE SEEMS TO BE GOOD FRIENDS WITH BUB-MIN-RANG!
...BY THE WAY, HOW DO YOU KNOW BUB-MIN-RANG?
OH, HE SAVED ME WHEN I WAS ATTACKED BY A WILD BOAR.
I SEE.

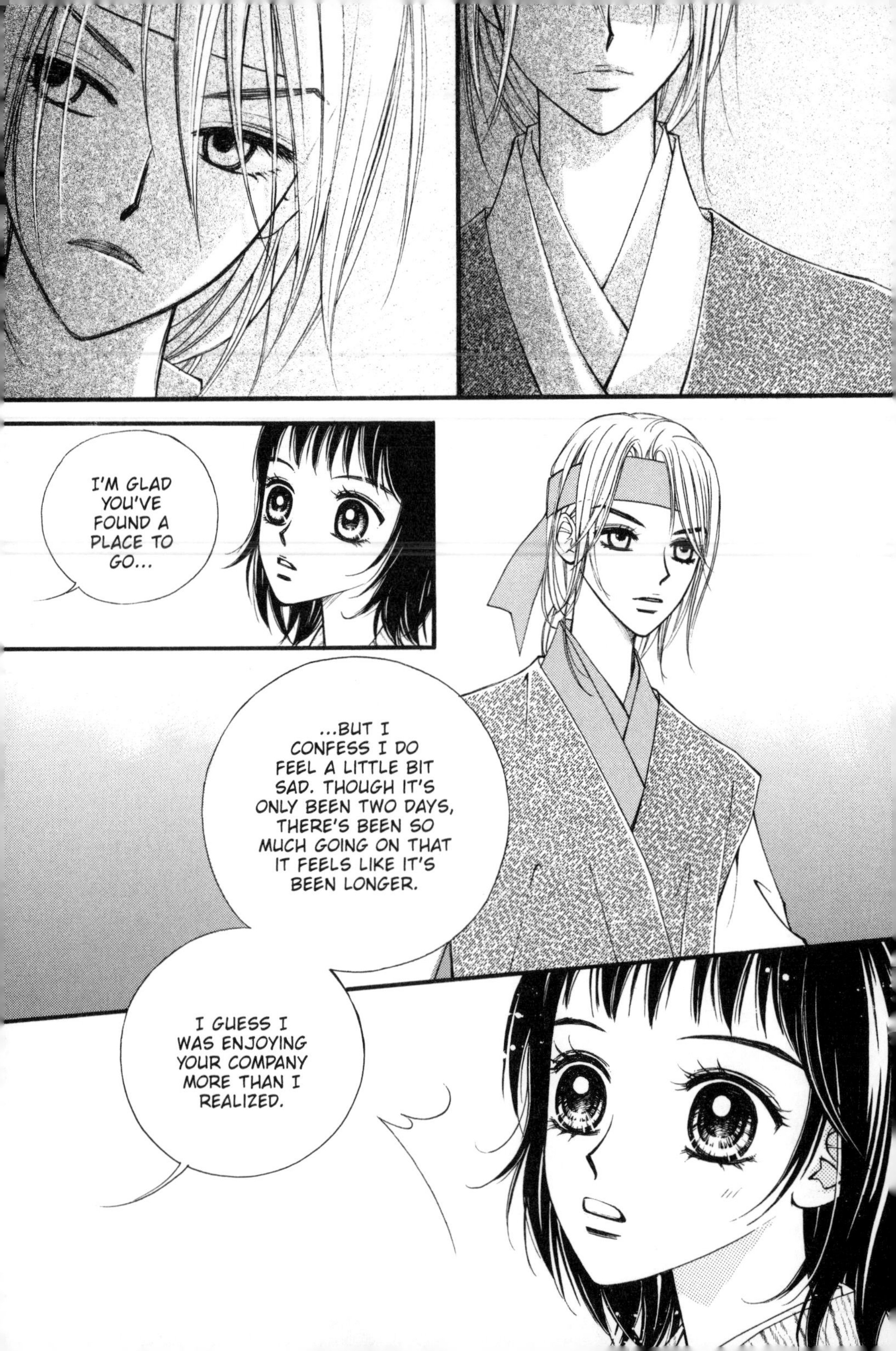
I'M GLAD YOU'VE FOUND A PLACE TO GO...
...BUT I CONFESS I DO FEEL A LITTLE BIT SAD. THOUGH IT'S ONLY BEEN TWO DAYS, THERE'S BEEN SO MUCH GOING ON THAT IT FEELS LIKE IT'S BEEN LONGER.
I GUESS I WAS ENJOYING YOUR COMPANY MORE THAN I REALIZED.

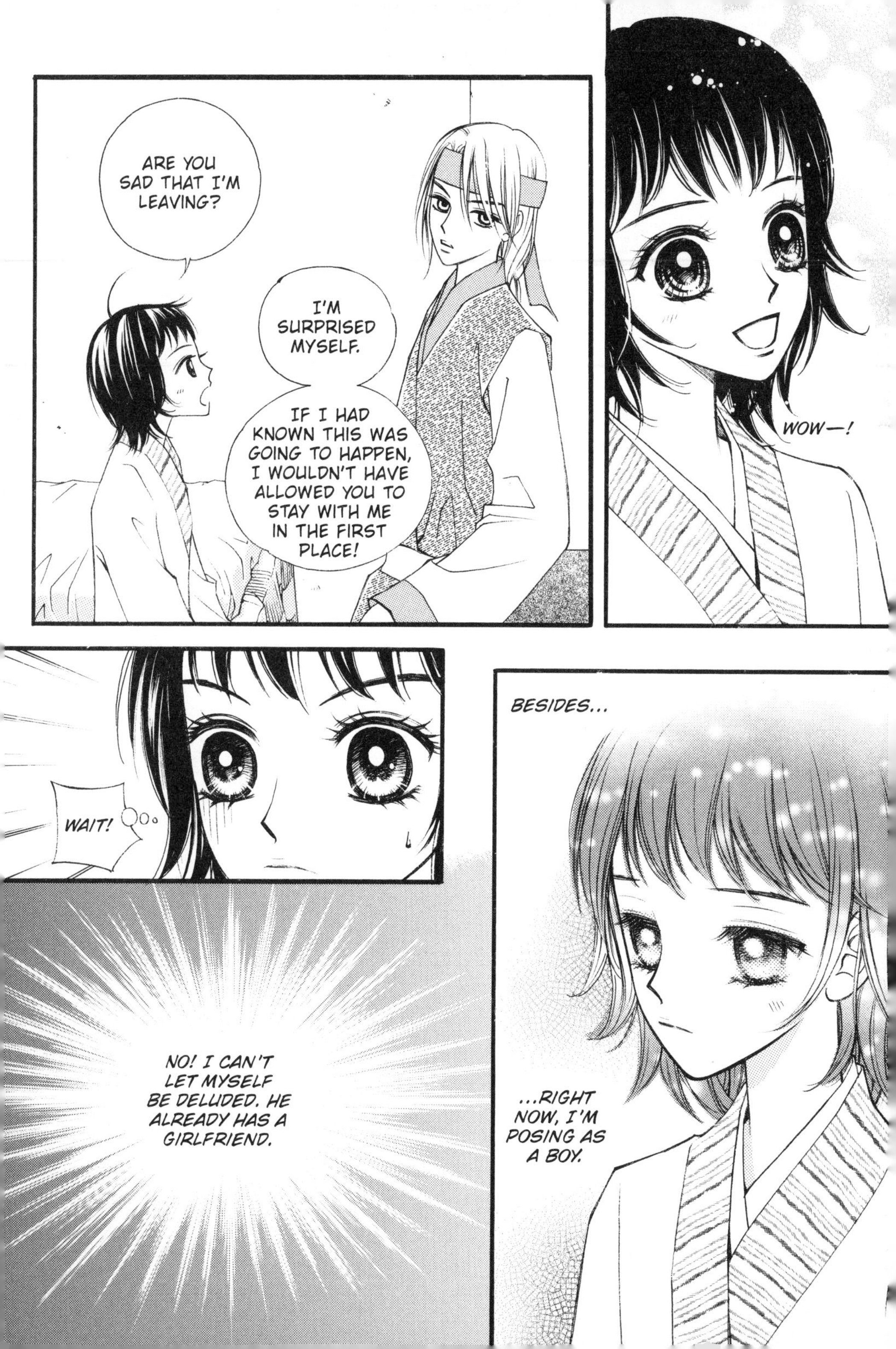
ARE YOU SAD THAT I'M LEAVING?
I'M SURPRISED MYSELF.
IF I HAD KNOWN THIS WAS GOING TO HAPPEN, I WOULDN'T HAVE ALLOWED YOU TO STAY WITH ME IN THE FIRST PLACE!
WOW—!
WAIT!
NO! I CAN'T LET MYSELF BE DELUDED. HE ALREADY HAS A GIRLFRIEND.
BESIDES...
...RIGHT NOW, I'M POSING AS A BOY.

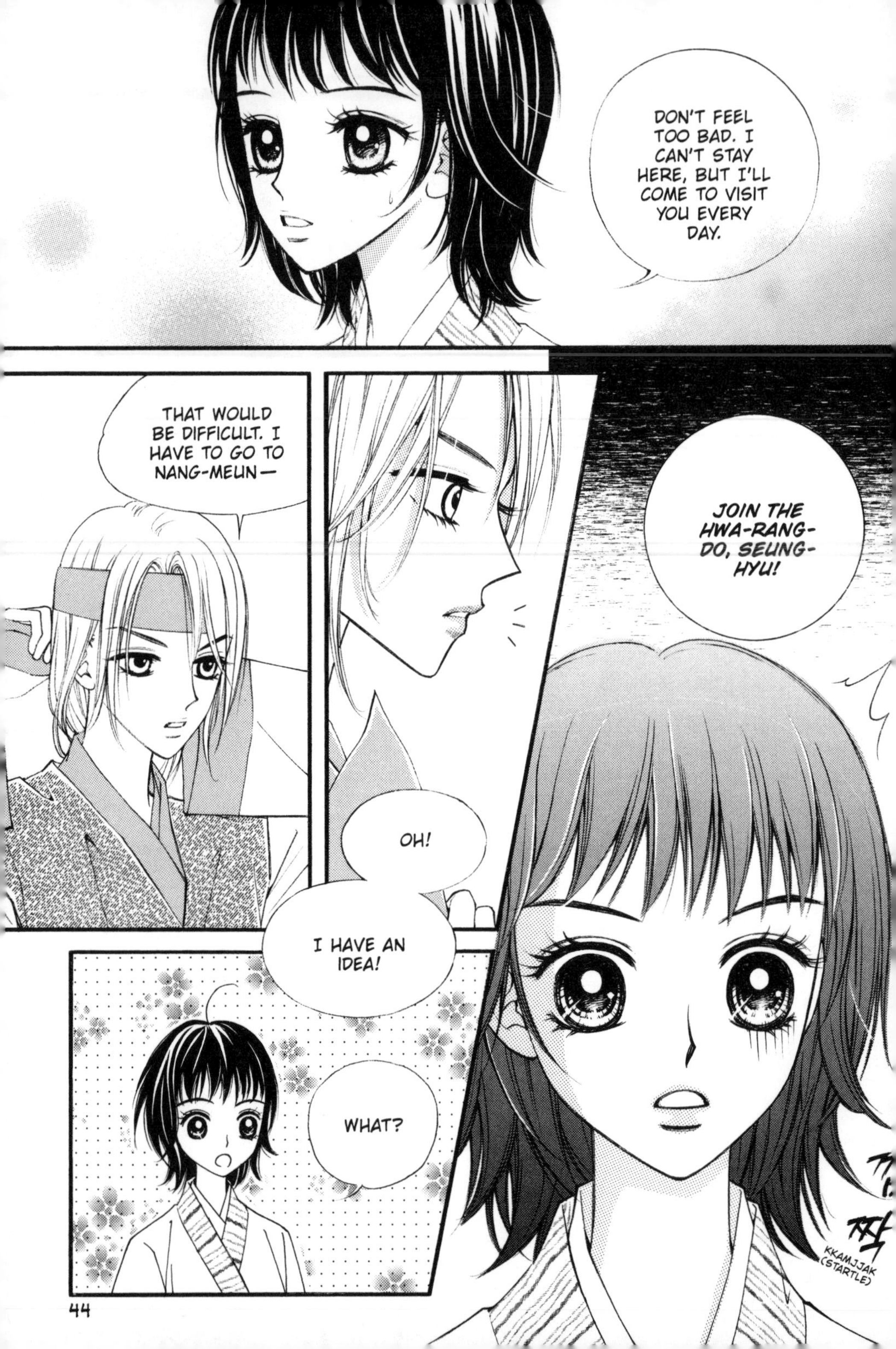
DON'T FEEL TOO BAD. I CAN'T STAY HERE, BUT I'LL COME TO VISIT YOU EVERY DAY.
THAT WOULD BE DIFFICULT. I HAVE TO GO TO NANG-MEUN—
OH!
I HAVE AN IDEA!
WHAT?
JOIN THE HWA-RANG-DO, SEUNG-HYU!
KKAMJJAK (STARTLE)

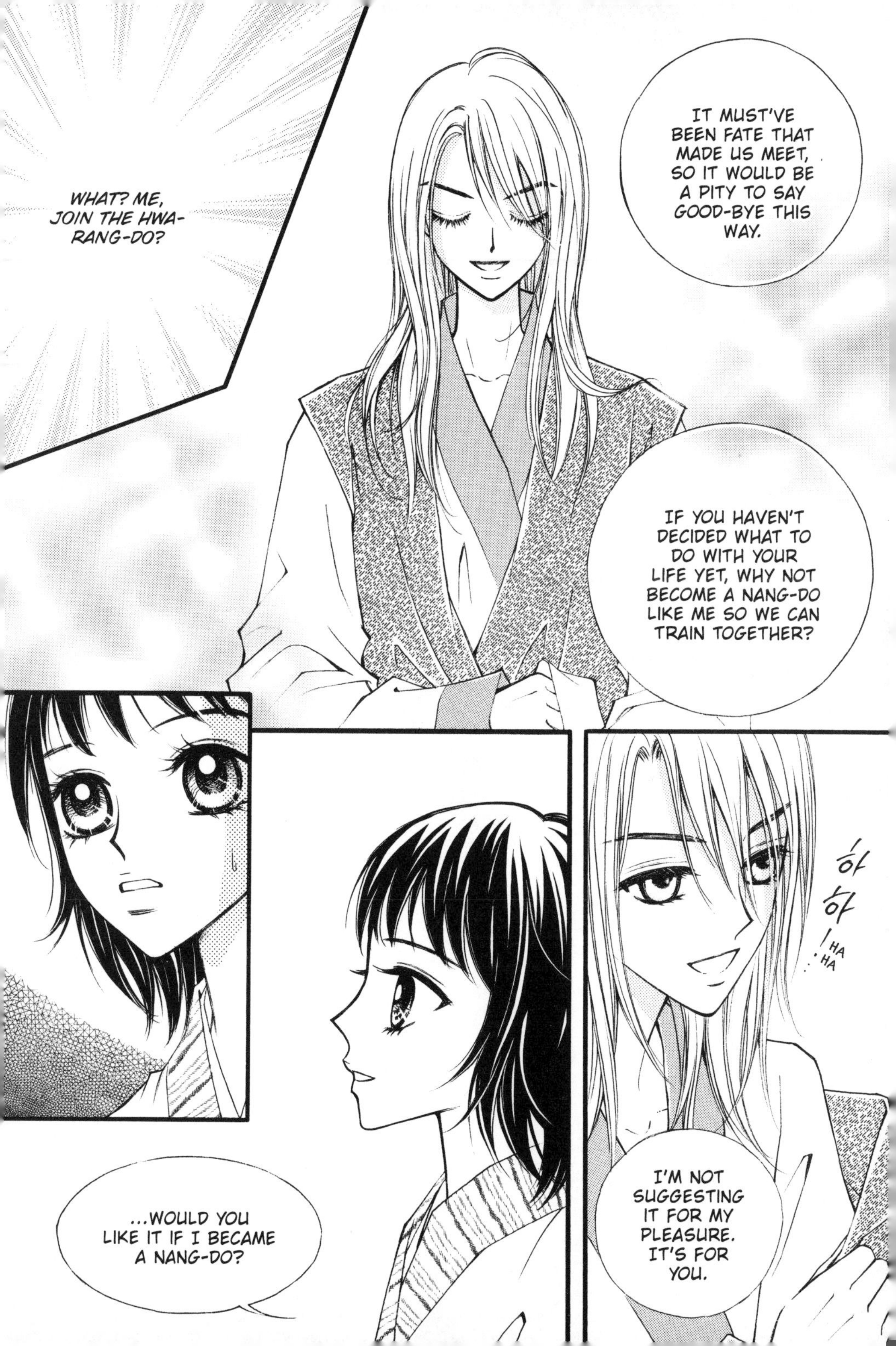
WHAT? ME, JOIN THE HWA-RANG-DO?
IT MUST'VE BEEN FATE THAT MADE US MEET, SO IT WOULD BE A PITY TO SAY GOOD-BYE THIS WAY.
IF YOU HAVEN'T DECIDED WHAT TO DO WITH YOUR LIFE YET, WHY NOT BECOME A NANG-DO LIKE ME SO WE CAN TRAIN TOGETHER?
...WOULD YOU LIKE IT IF I BECAME A NANG-DO?
하하
HA HA
I'M NOT SUGGESTING IT FOR MY PLEASURE. IT'S FOR YOU.

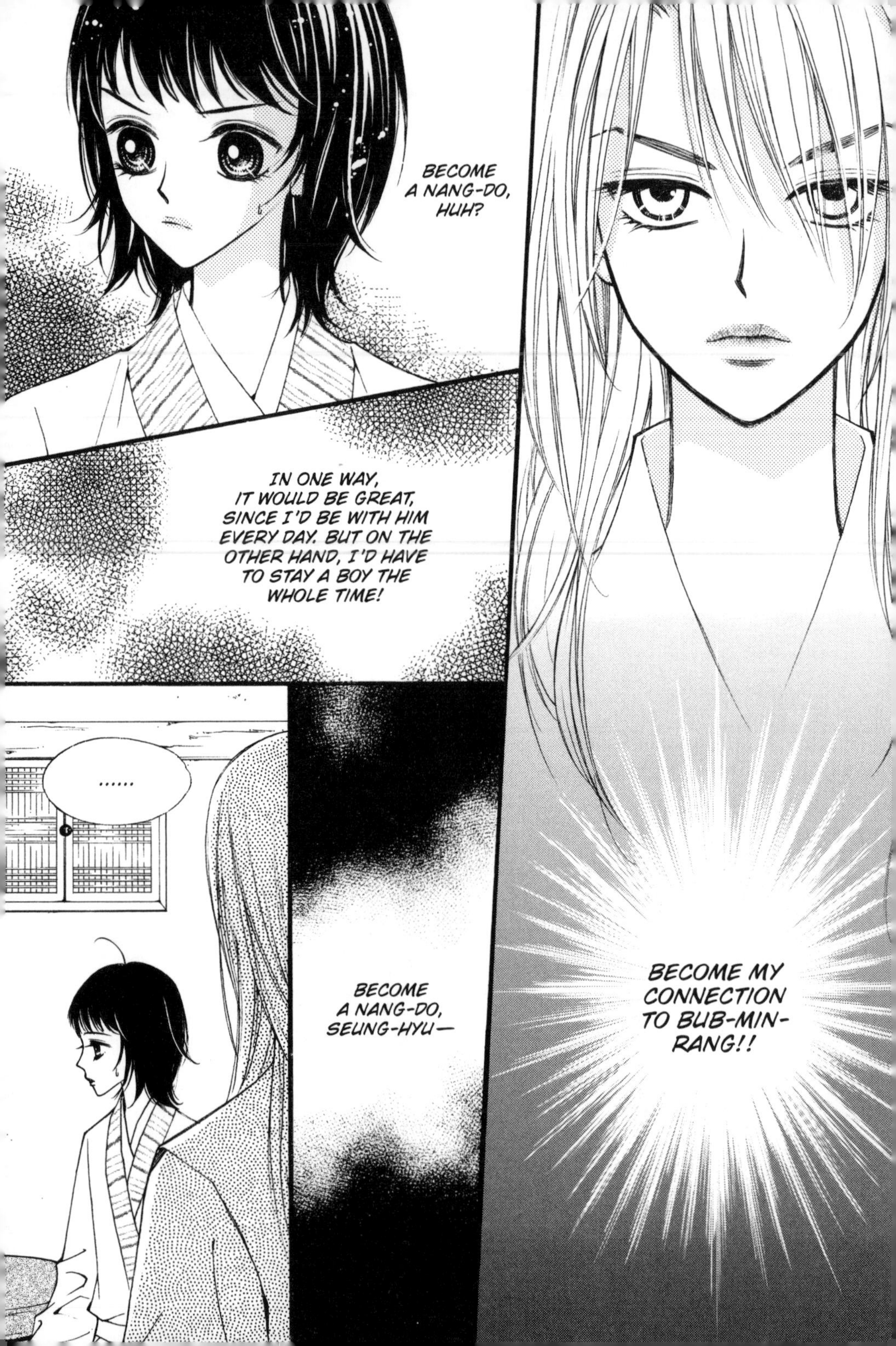
BECOME A NANG-DO, HUH?
IN ONE WAY, IT WOULD BE GREAT, SINCE I'D BE WITH HIM EVERY DAY. BUT ON THE OTHER HAND, I'D HAVE TO STAY A BOY THE WHOLE TIME!
......
BECOME A NANG-DO, SEUNG-HYU—
BECOME MY CONNECTION TO BUB-MIN-RANG!!

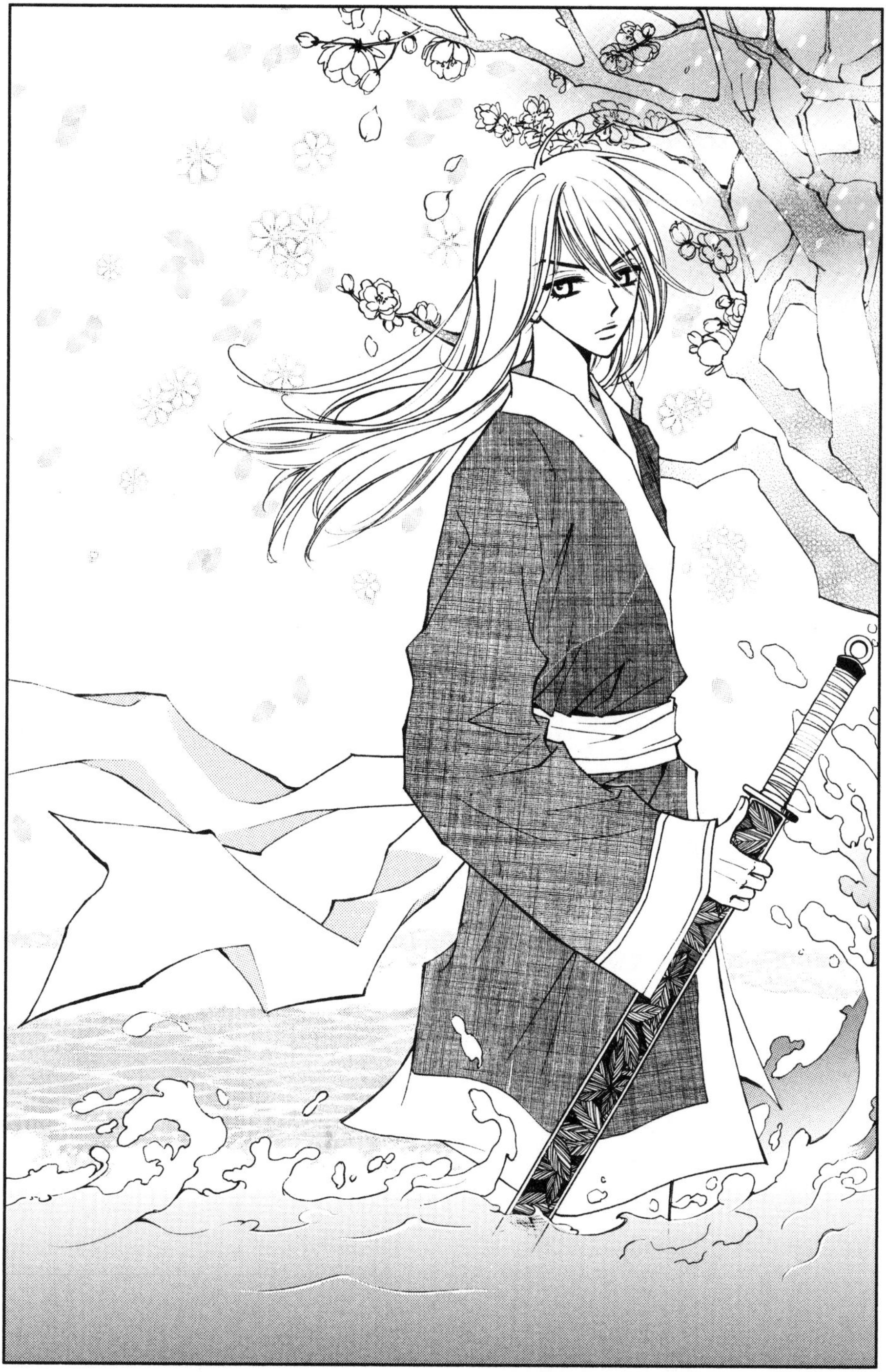

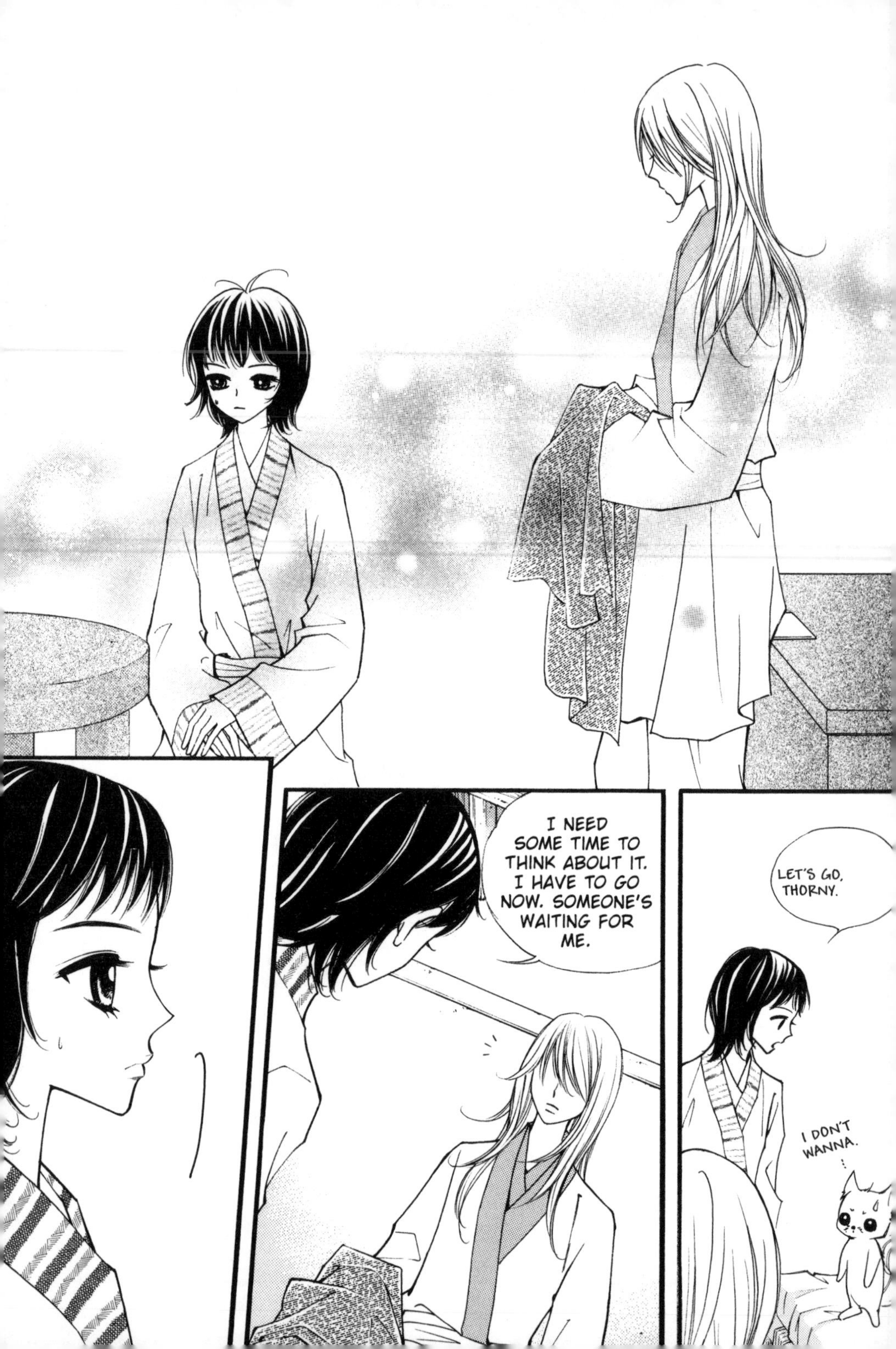
I NEED SOME TIME TO THINK ABOUT IT. I HAVE TO GO NOW. SOMEONE'S WAITING FOR ME.
LET'S GO, THORNY.
I DON'T WANNA.
...

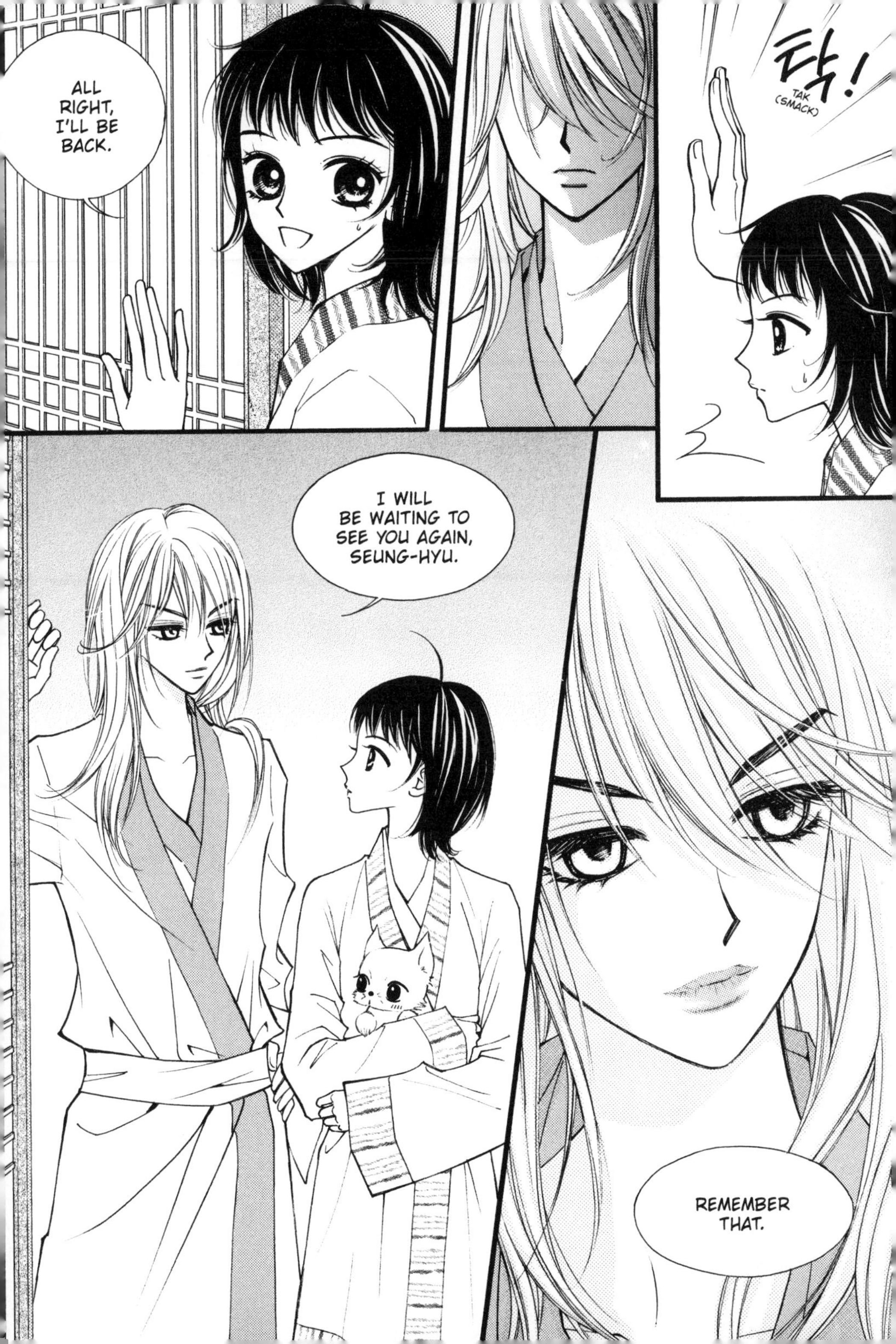
ALL RIGHT, I'LL BE BACK.
탁!
TAK (SMACK)
I WILL BE WAITING TO SEE YOU AGAIN, SEUNG-HYU.
REMEMBER THAT.

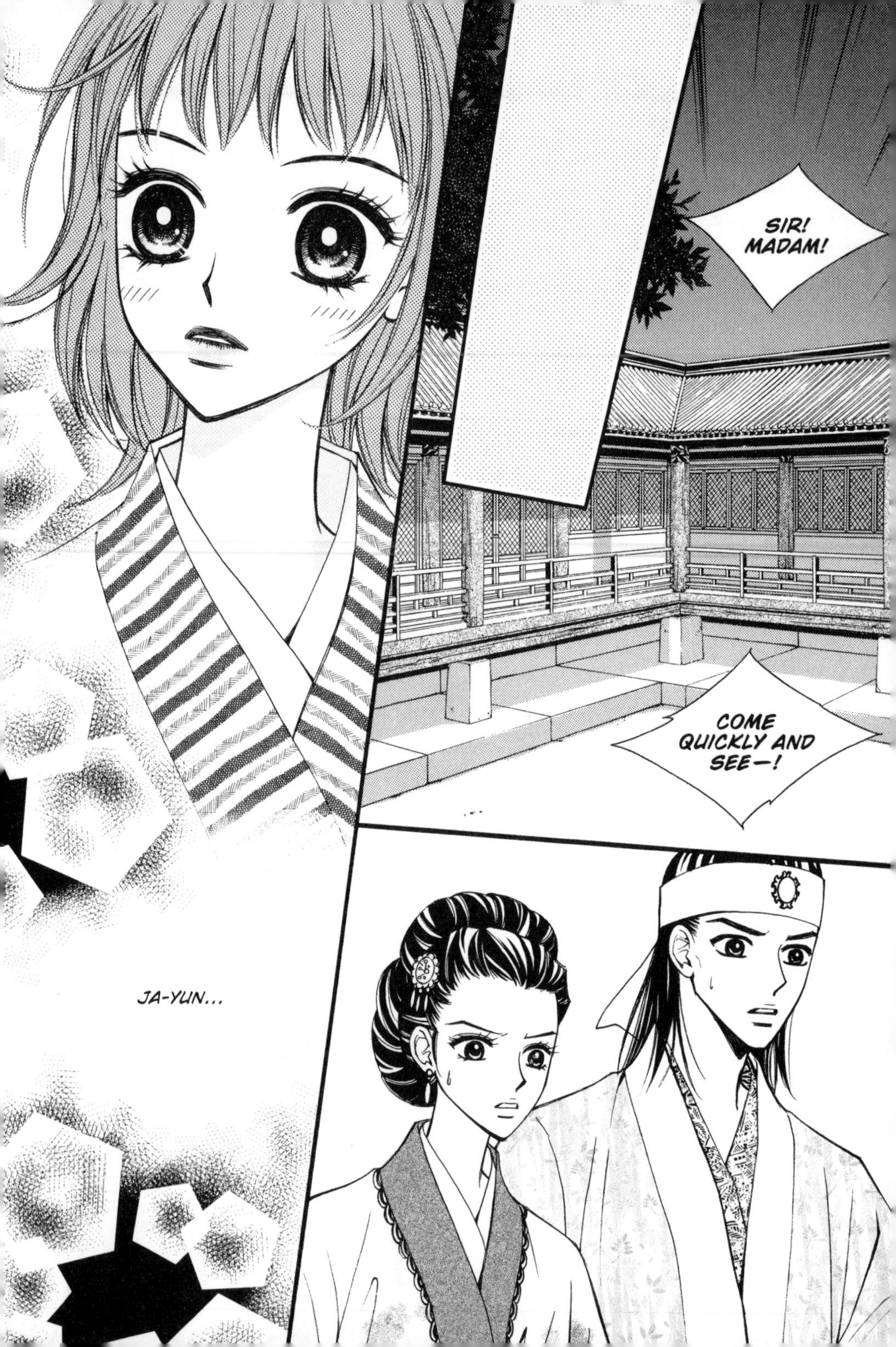
JA-YUN...
SIR! MADAM!
COME QUICKLY AND SEE—!

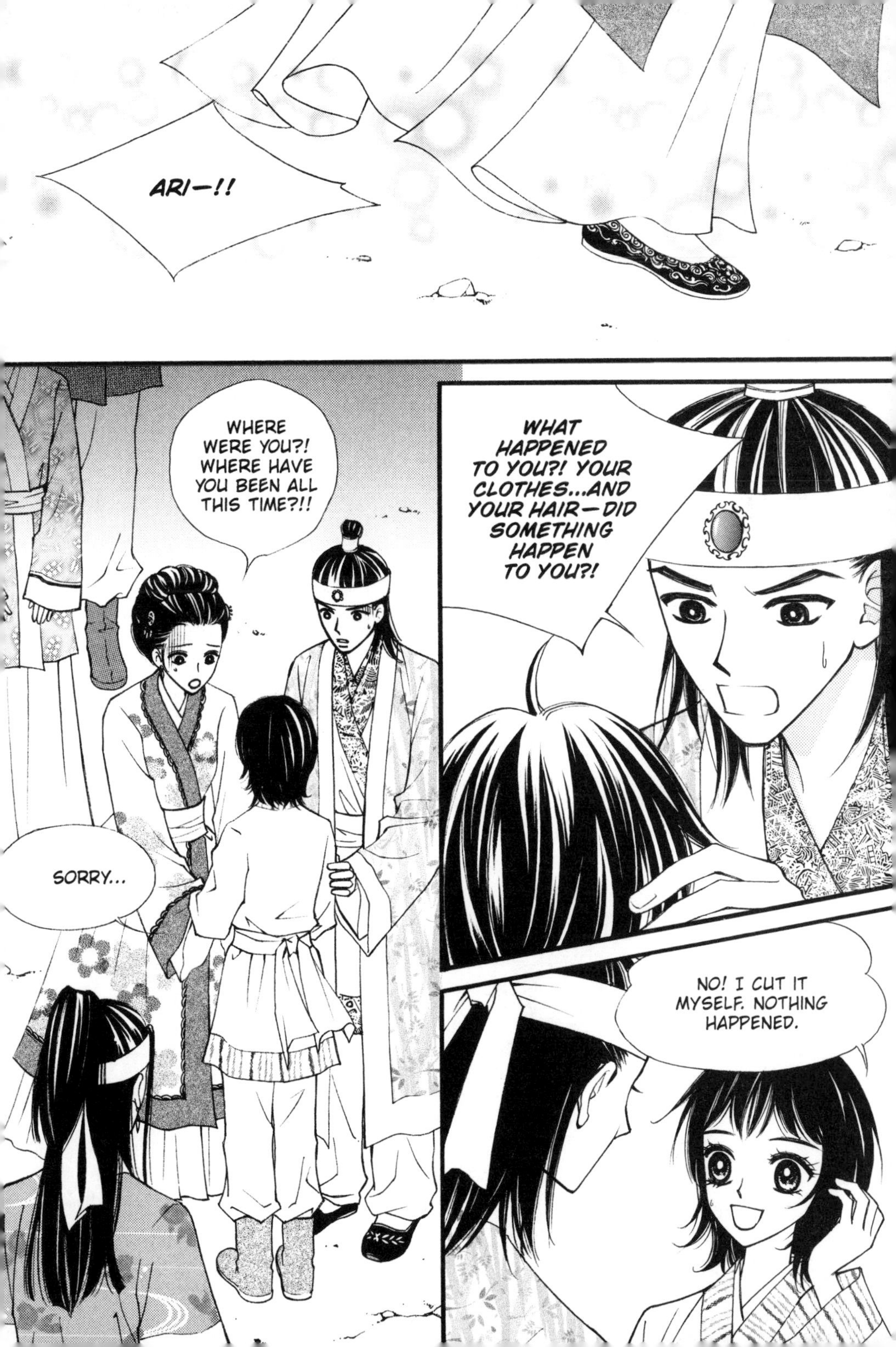
ARI—!!
WHERE WERE YOU?! WHERE HAVE YOU BEEN ALL THIS TIME?!!
SORRY...
WHAT HAPPENED TO YOU?! YOUR CLOTHES...AND YOUR HAIR—DID SOMETHING HAPPEN TO YOU?!
NO! I CUT IT MYSELF. NOTHING HAPPENED.

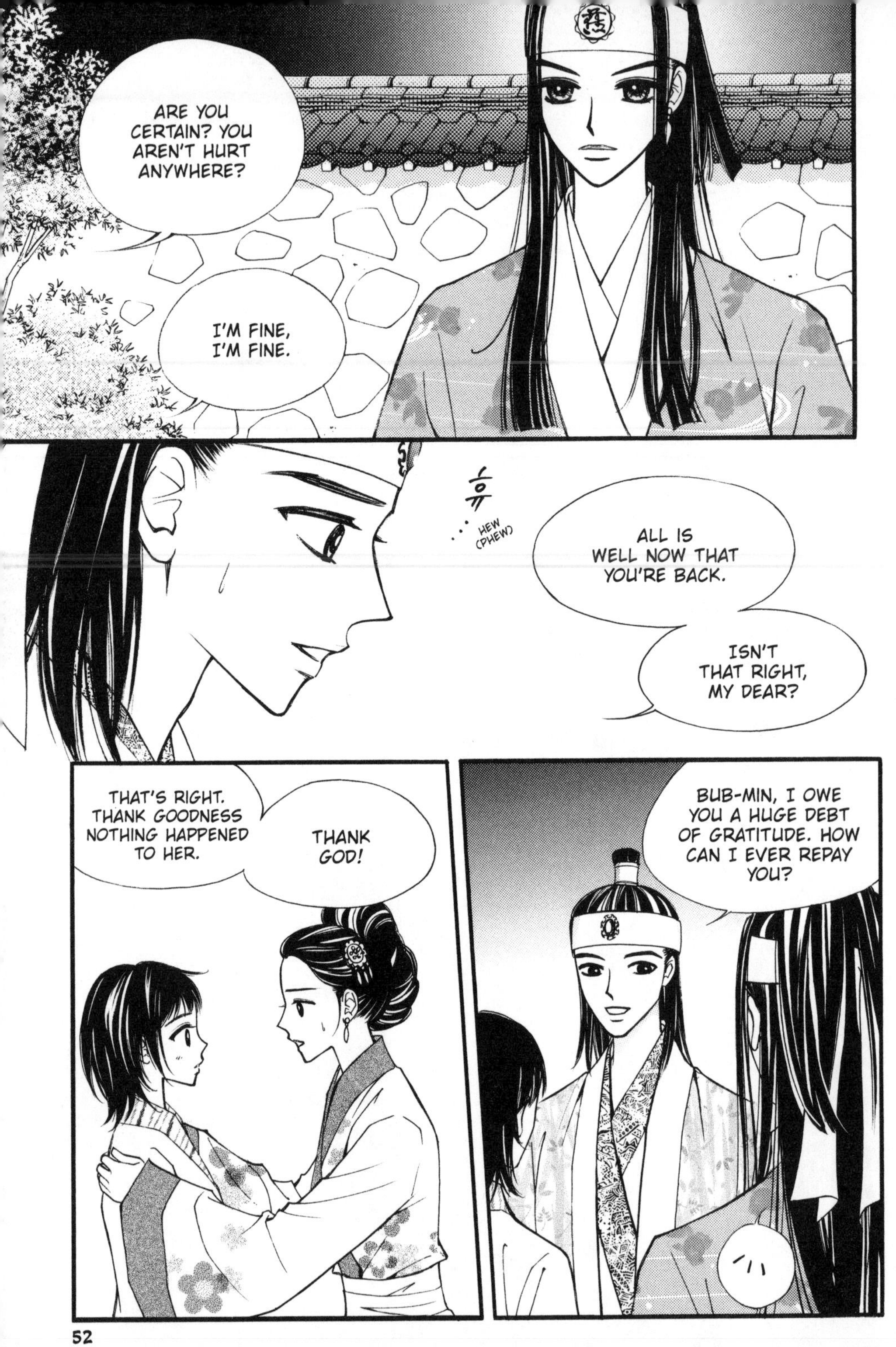
ARE YOU CERTAIN? YOU AREN'T HURT ANYWHERE?
I'M FINE, I'M FINE.
HEW (PHEW)
ALL IS WELL NOW THAT YOU'RE BACK.
ISN'T THAT RIGHT, MY DEAR?
THAT'S RIGHT. THANK GOODNESS NOTHING HAPPENED TO HER.
THANK GOD!
BUB-MIN, I OWE YOU A HUGE DEBT OF GRATITUDE. HOW CAN I EVER REPAY YOU?

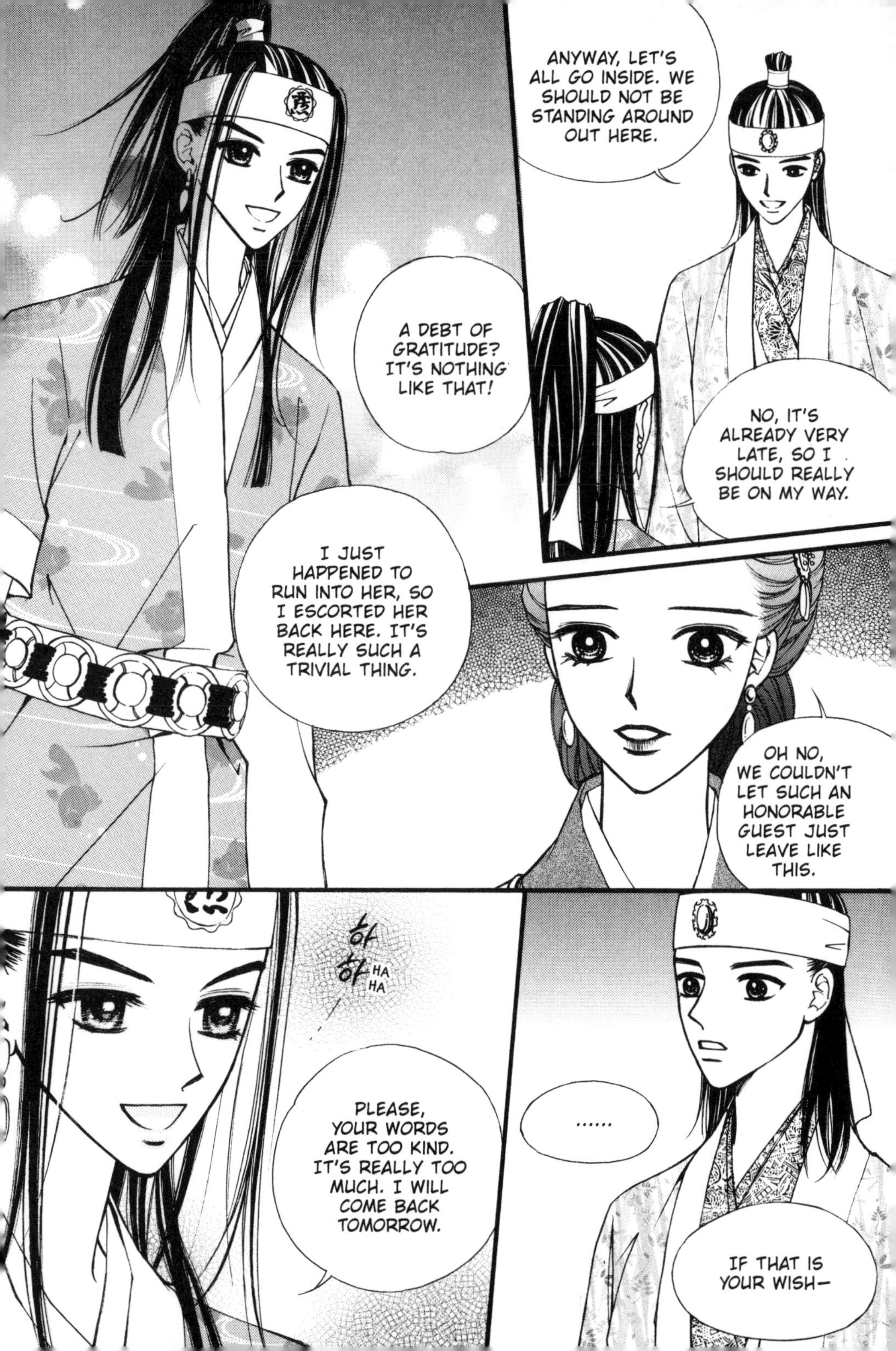

A DEBT OF GRATITUDE? IT'S NOTHING LIKE THAT!
I JUST HAPPENED TO RUN INTO HER, SO I ESCORTED HER BACK HERE. IT'S REALLY SUCH A TRIVIAL THING.
ANYWAY, LET'S ALL GO INSIDE. WE SHOULD NOT BE STANDING AROUND OUT HERE.
NO, IT'S ALREADY VERY LATE, SO I SHOULD REALLY BE ON MY WAY.
OH NO, WE COULDN'T LET SUCH AN HONORABLE GUEST JUST LEAVE LIKE THIS.
하하 HA HA
PLEASE, YOUR WORDS ARE TOO KIND. IT'S REALLY TOO MUCH. I WILL COME BACK TOMORROW.
......
IF THAT IS YOUR WISH—

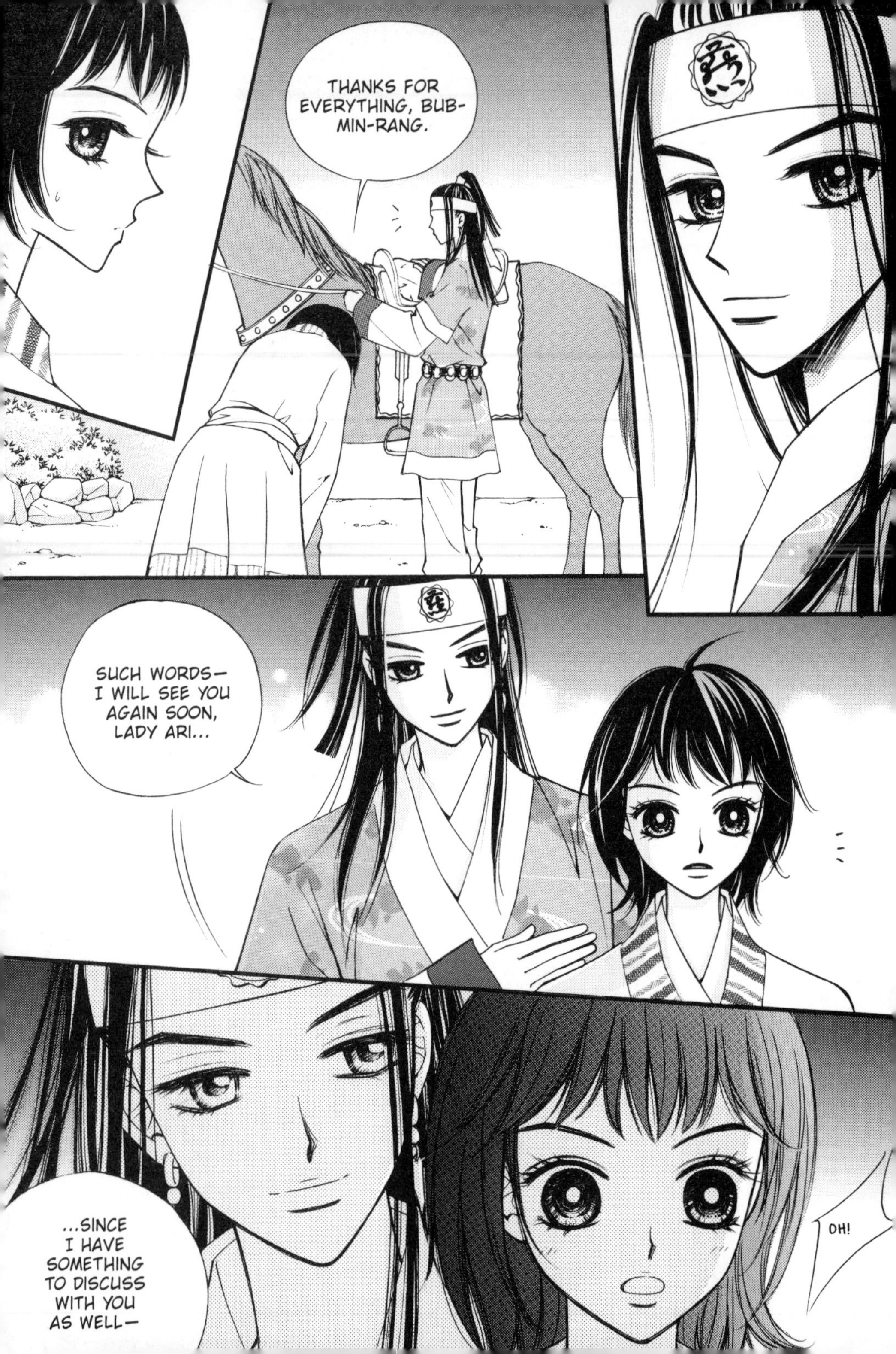
THANKS FOR EVERYTHING, BUB-MIN-RANG.
SUCH WORDS— I WILL SEE YOU AGAIN SOON, LADY ARI...
...SINCE I HAVE SOMETHING TO DISCUSS WITH YOU AS WELL—
OH!

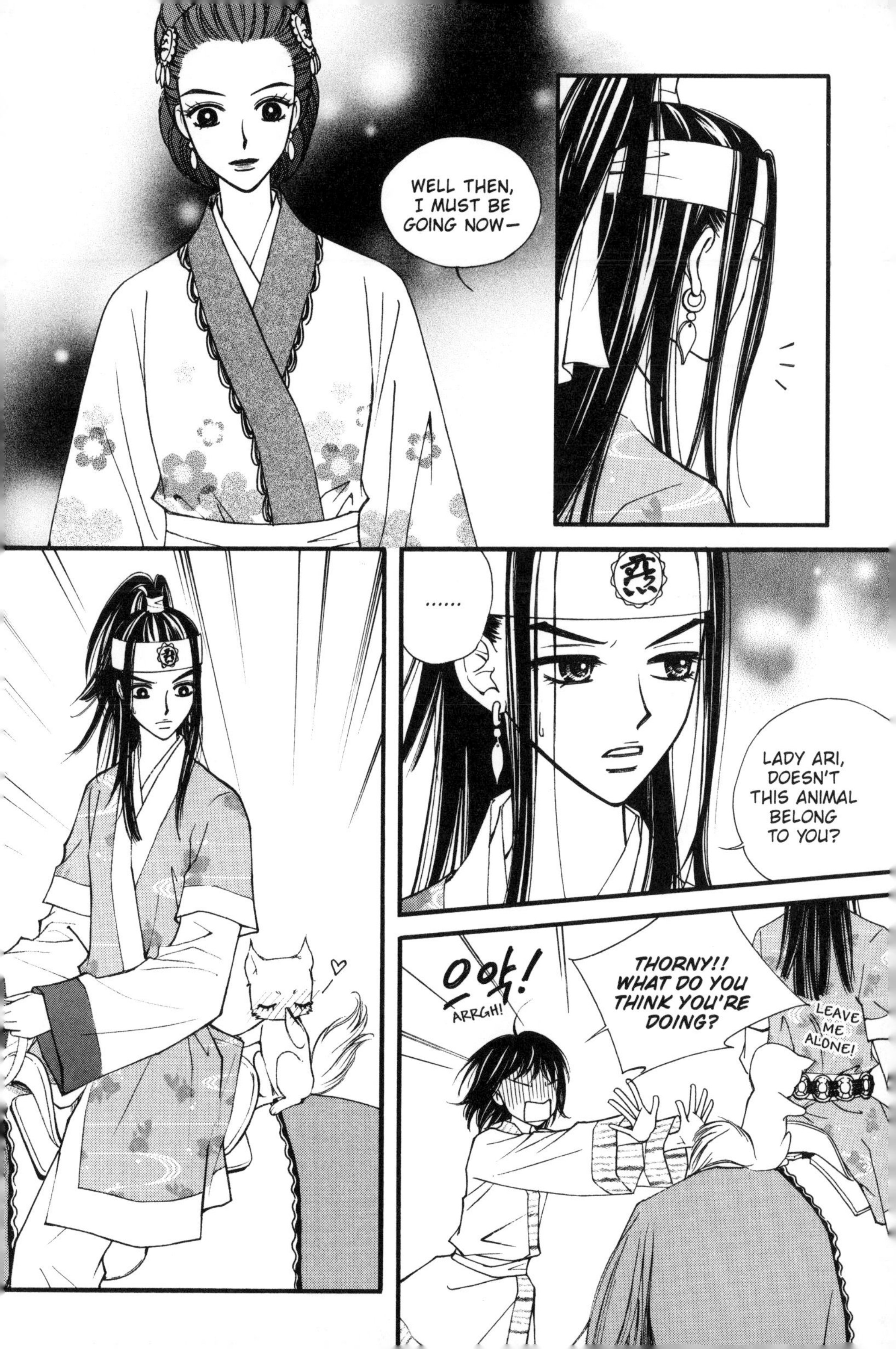
WELL THEN, I MUST BE GOING NOW—
......
LADY ARI, DOESN'T THIS ANIMAL BELONG TO YOU?
으악!
ARRGH!
THORNY!! WHAT DO YOU THINK YOU'RE DOING?
LEAVE ME ALONE!

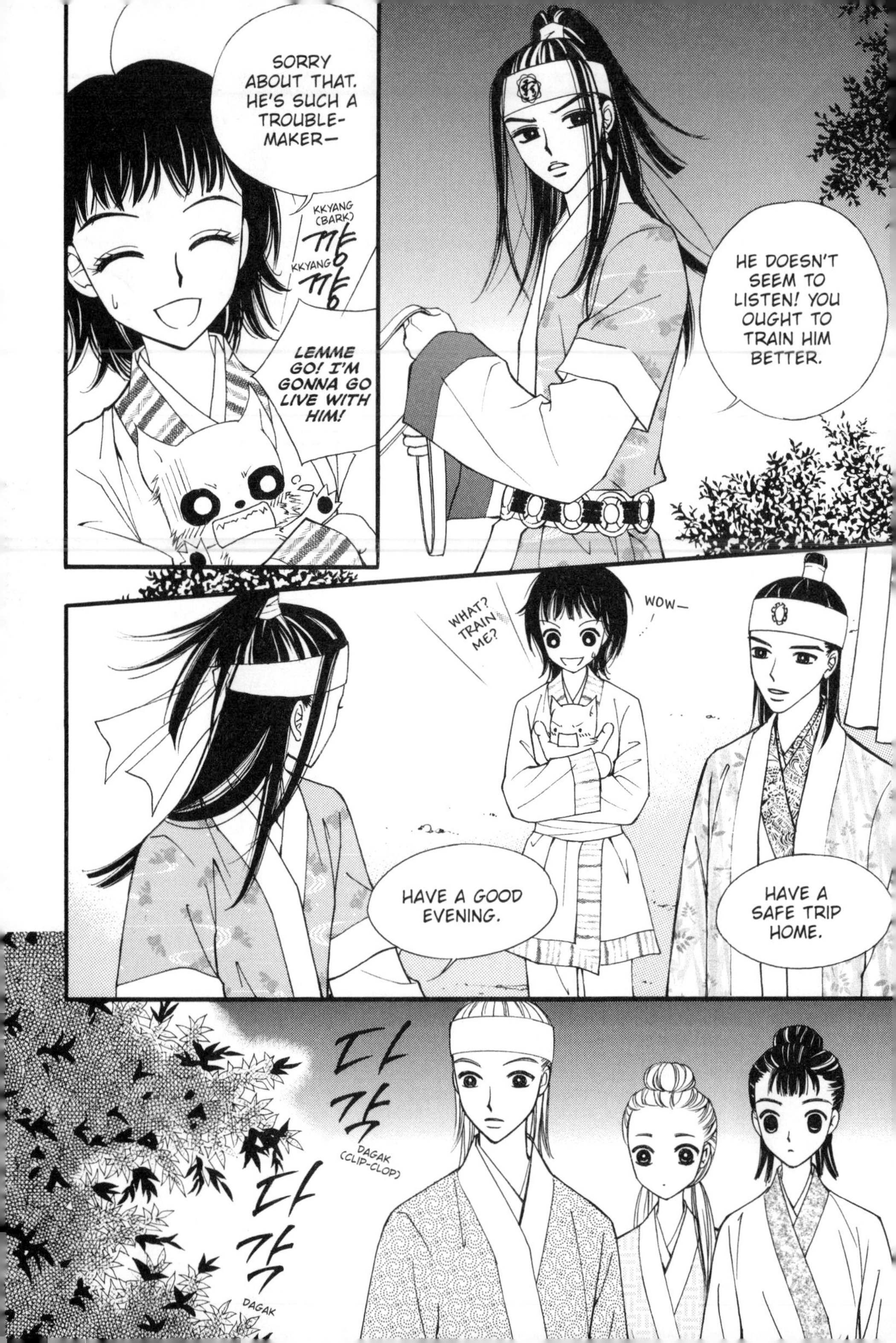
SORRY ABOUT THAT. HE'S SUCH A TROUBLE-MAKER—
KKYANG (BARK)
깡
KKYANG
깡
LEMME GO! I'M GONNA GO LIVE WITH HIM!
HE DOESN'T SEEM TO LISTEN! YOU OUGHT TO TRAIN HIM BETTER.
WHAT? TRAIN ME?
WOW—
HAVE A GOOD EVENING.
HAVE A SAFE TRIP HOME.
다각
DAGAK (CLIP-CLOP)
다각
DAGAK

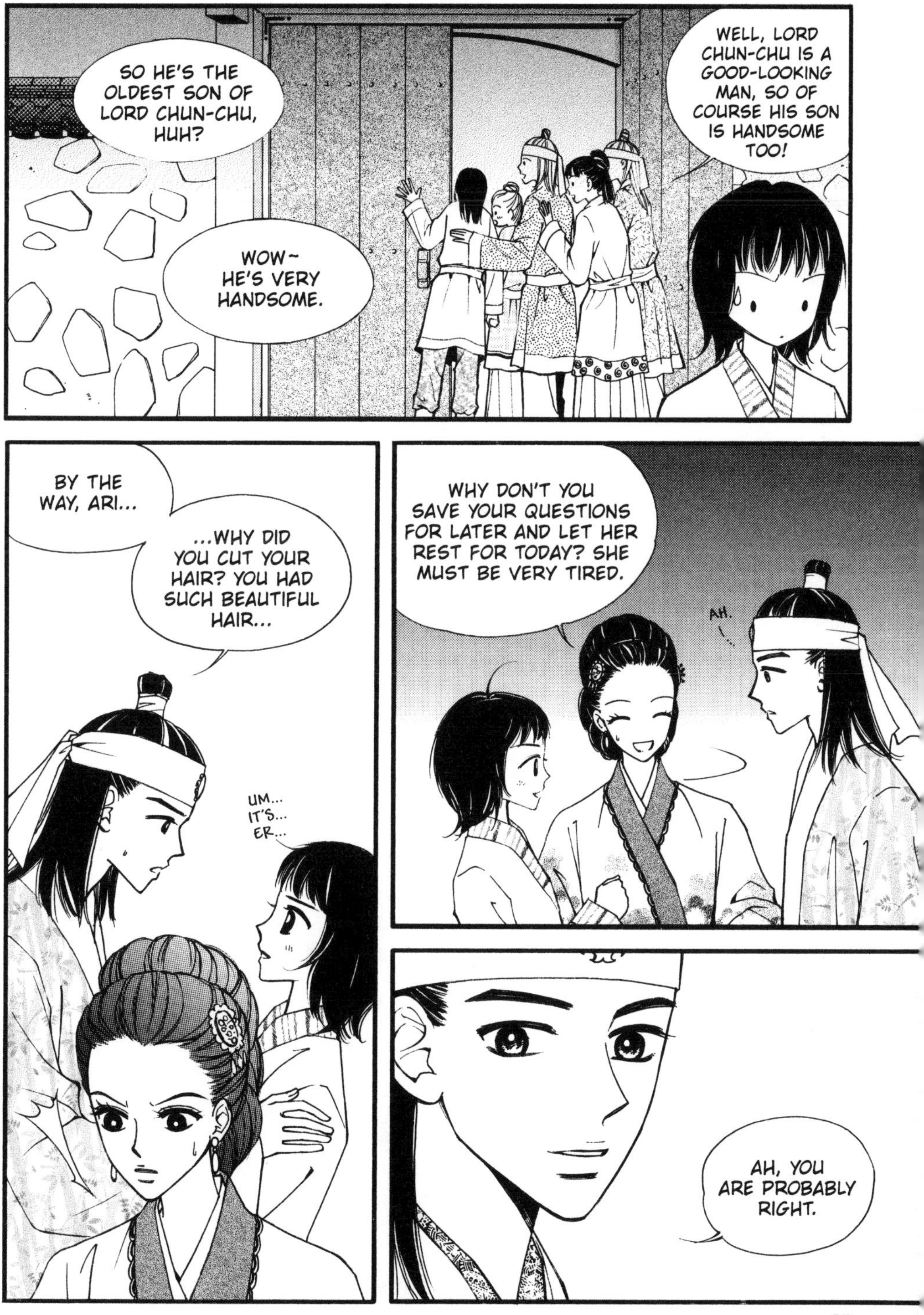
SO HE'S THE OLDEST SON OF LORD CHUN-CHU, HUH?
WOW~ HE'S VERY HANDSOME.
WELL, LORD CHUN-CHU IS A GOOD-LOOKING MAN, SO OF COURSE HIS SON IS HANDSOME TOO!
BY THE WAY, ARI...
...WHY DID YOU CUT YOUR HAIR? YOU HAD SUCH BEAUTIFUL HAIR...
UM... IT'S... ER...
WHY DON'T YOU SAVE YOUR QUESTIONS FOR LATER AND LET HER REST FOR TODAY? SHE MUST BE VERY TIRED.
AH.
AH, YOU ARE PROBABLY RIGHT.

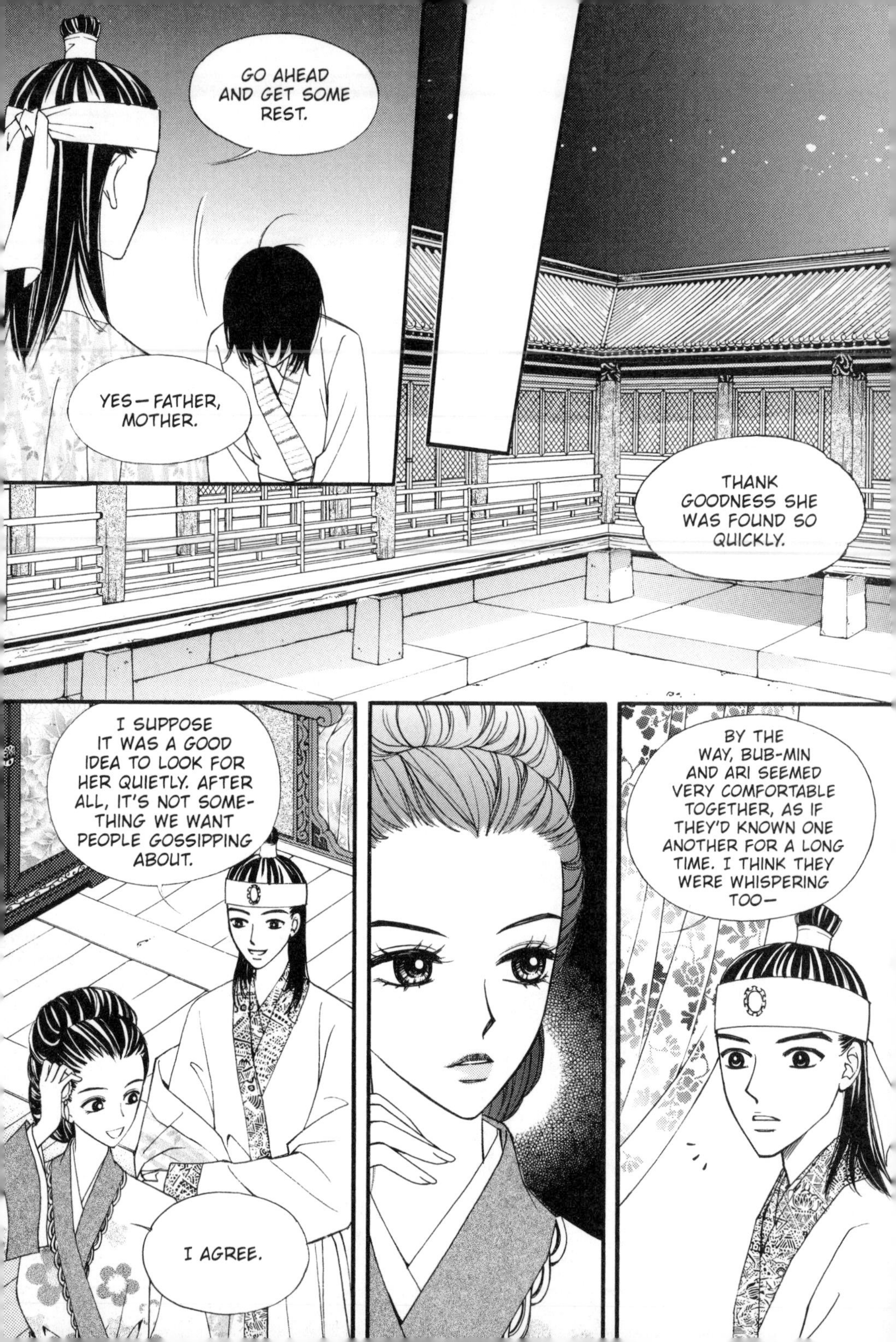
GO AHEAD AND GET SOME REST.
YES—FATHER, MOTHER.
THANK GOODNESS SHE WAS FOUND SO QUICKLY.
I SUPPOSE IT WAS A GOOD IDEA TO LOOK FOR HER QUIETLY. AFTER ALL, IT'S NOT SOME-THING WE WANT PEOPLE GOSSIPPING ABOUT.
I AGREE.
BY THE WAY, BUB-MIN AND ARI SEEMED VERY COMFORTABLE TOGETHER, AS IF THEY'D KNOWN ONE ANOTHER FOR A LONG TIME. I THINK THEY WERE WHISPERING TOO—

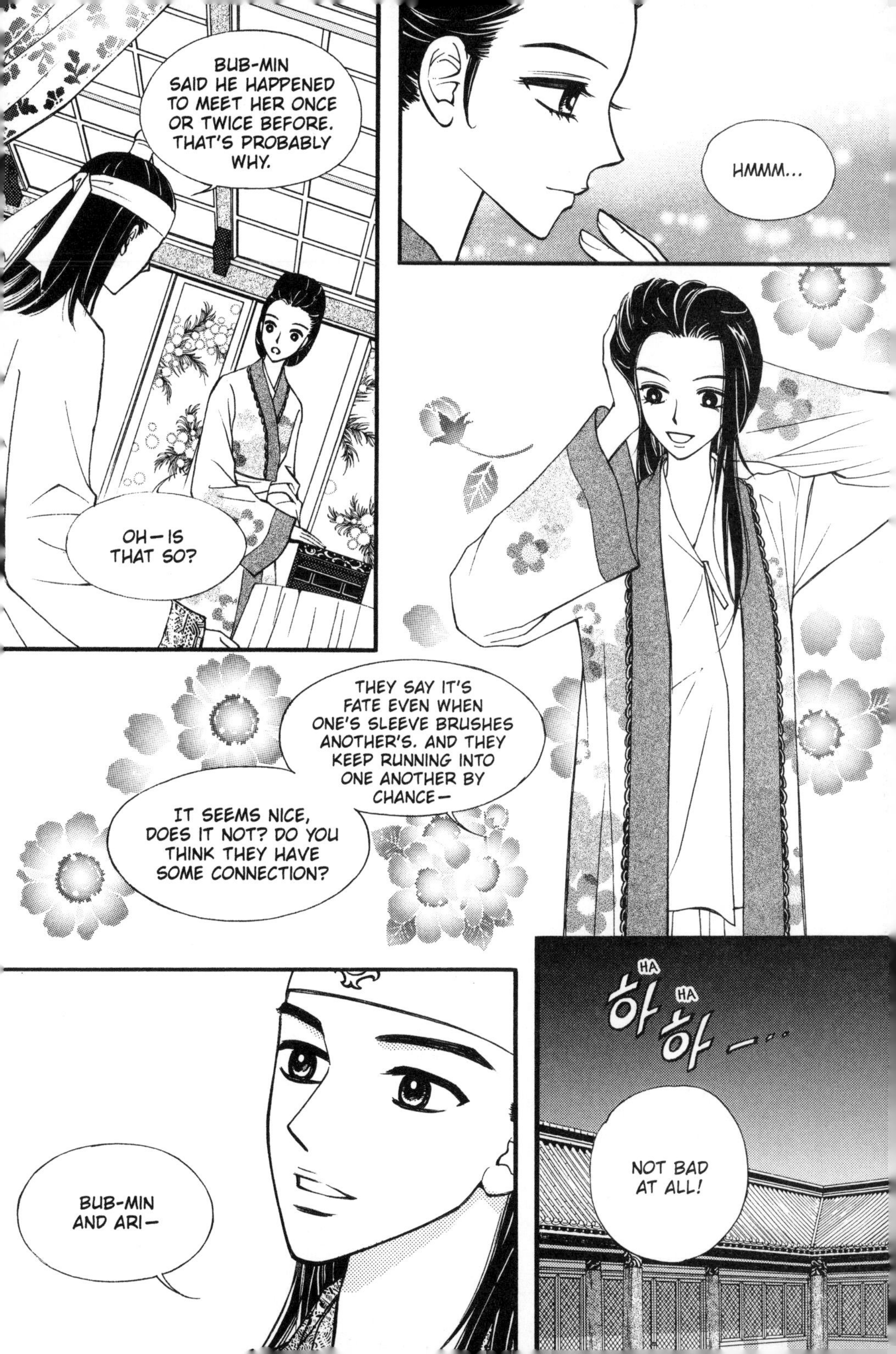
BUB-MIN SAID HE HAPPENED TO MEET HER ONCE OR TWICE BEFORE. THAT'S PROBABLY WHY.
OH—IS THAT SO?
HMMM...
THEY SAY IT'S FATE EVEN WHEN ONE'S SLEEVE BRUSHES ANOTHER'S. AND THEY KEEP RUNNING INTO ONE ANOTHER BY CHANCE—
IT SEEMS NICE, DOES IT NOT? DO YOU THINK THEY HAVE SOME CONNECTION?
BUB-MIN AND ARI—
HA HA
하 하—...
NOT BAD AT ALL!

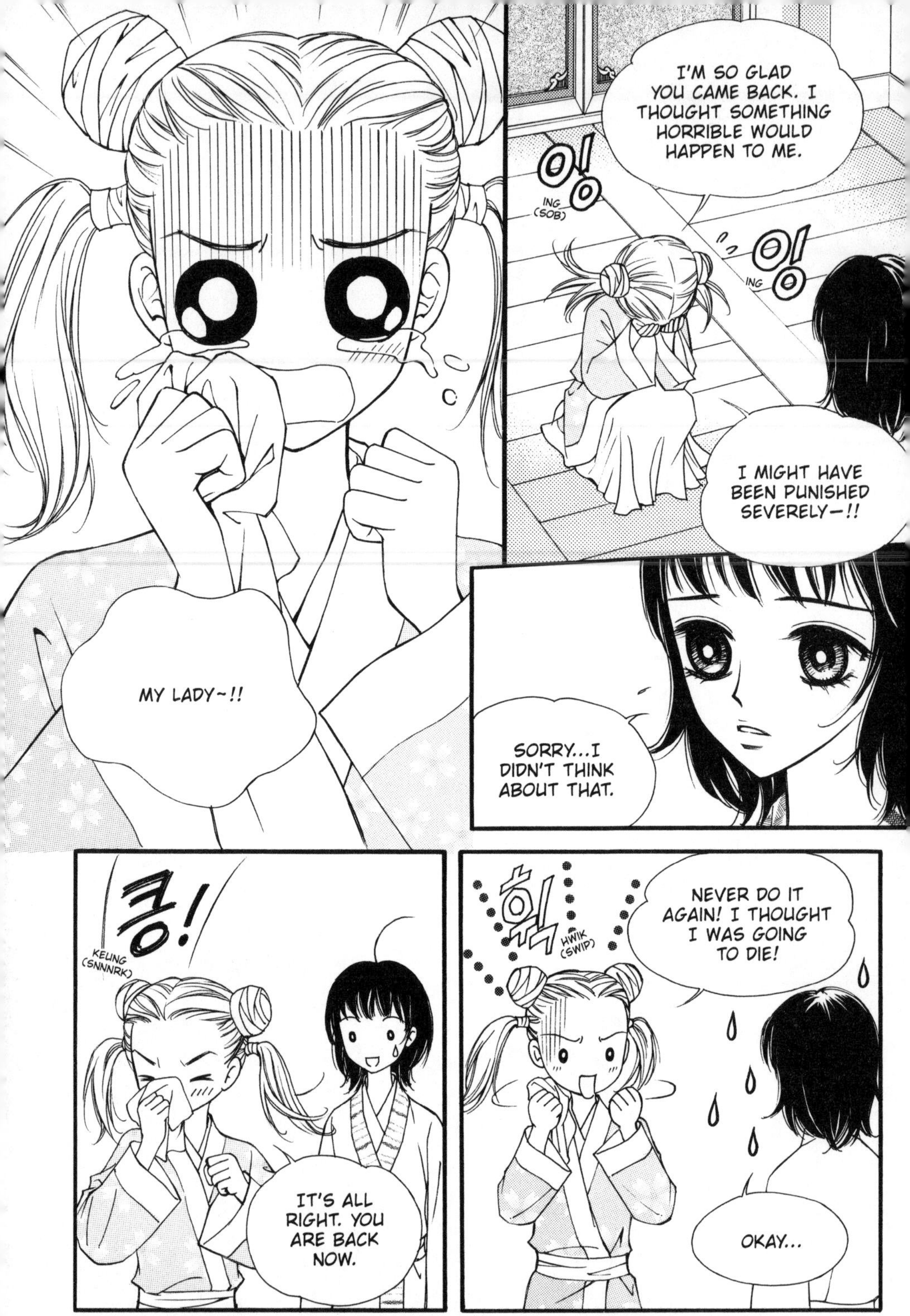
MY LADY~!!
이 ING (SOB)
I'M SO GLAD YOU CAME BACK. I THOUGHT SOMETHING HORRIBLE WOULD HAPPEN TO ME.
잉 ING
I MIGHT HAVE BEEN PUNISHED SEVERELY—!!
SORRY...I DIDN'T THINK ABOUT THAT.
쿵! KEUNG (SNNNRK)
IT'S ALL RIGHT. YOU ARE BACK NOW.
휙 HWIK (SWIP)
NEVER DO IT AGAIN! I THOUGHT I WAS GOING TO DIE!
OKAY...

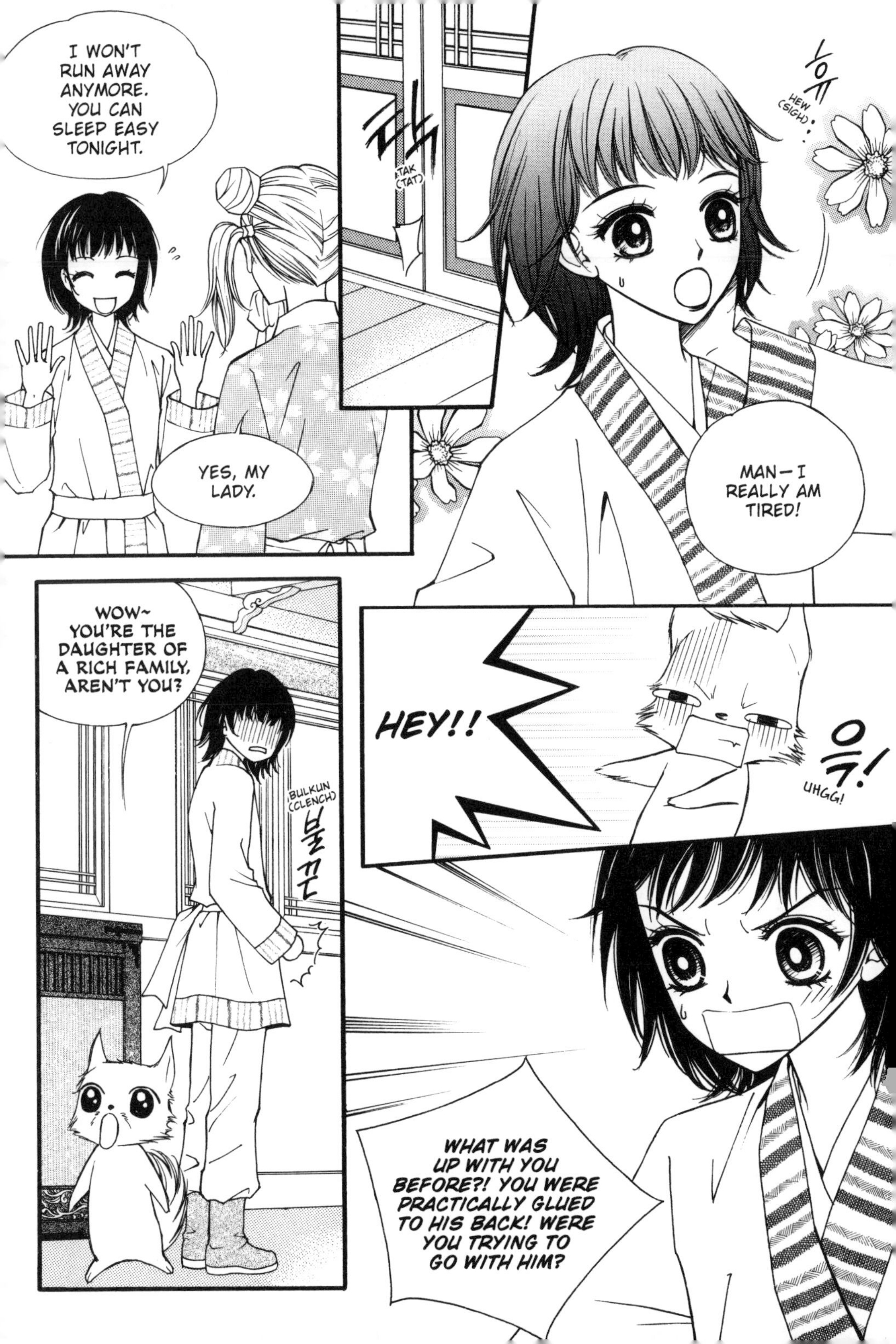
I WON'T RUN AWAY ANYMORE. YOU CAN SLEEP EASY TONIGHT.
YES, MY LADY.
TAK (TAT)
HEW (SIGH)
MAN— I REALLY AM TIRED!
WOW~ YOU'RE THE DAUGHTER OF A RICH FAMILY, AREN'T YOU?
BULKUN (CLENCH)
불끈
HEY!!
UHGG!
WHAT WAS UP WITH YOU BEFORE?! YOU WERE PRACTICALLY GLUED TO HIS BACK! WERE YOU TRYING TO GO WITH HIM?

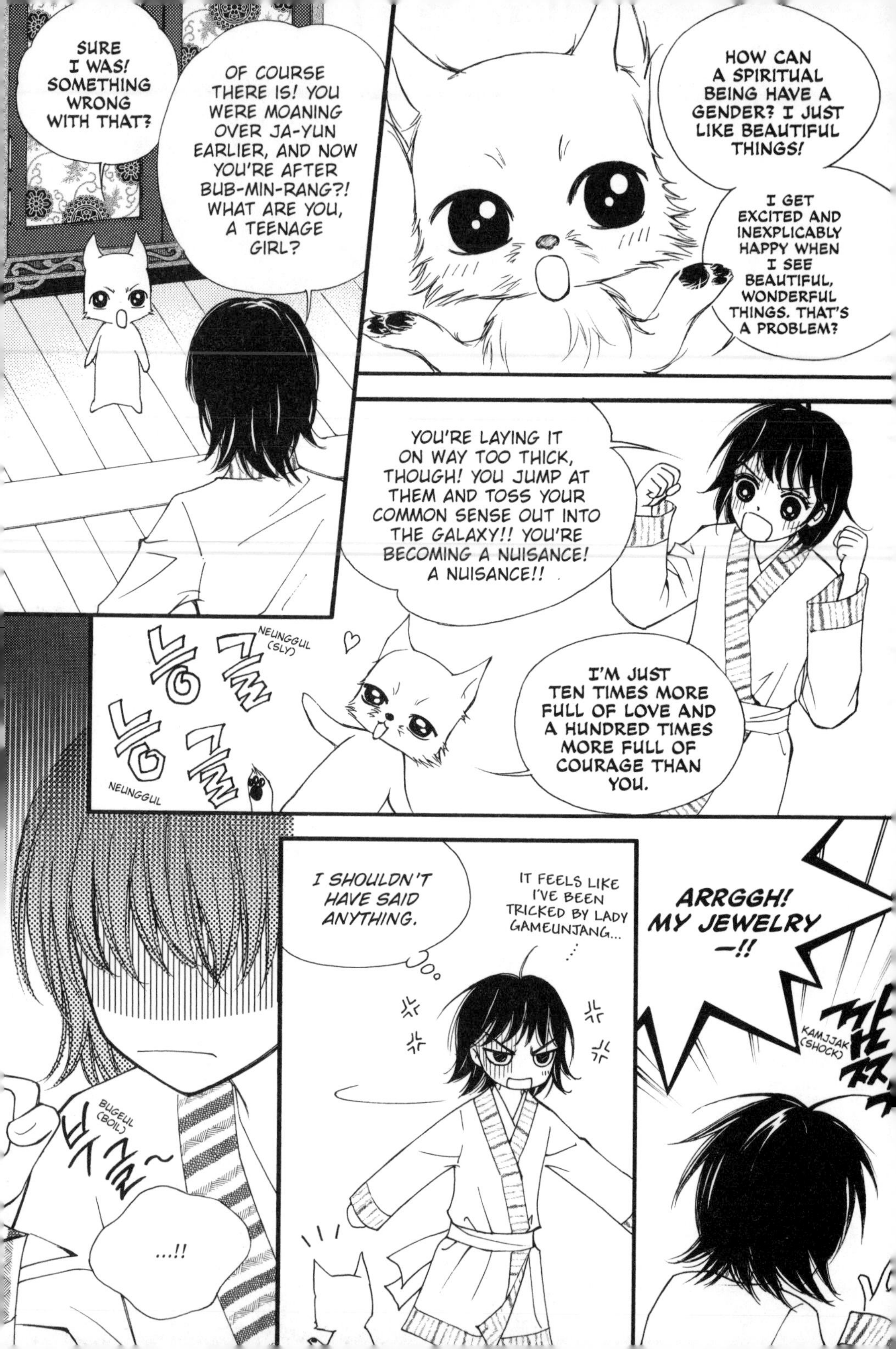
SURE I WAS! SOMETHING WRONG WITH THAT?
OF COURSE THERE IS! YOU WERE MOANING OVER JA-YUN EARLIER, AND NOW YOU'RE AFTER BUB-MIN-RANG?! WHAT ARE YOU, A TEENAGE GIRL?
HOW CAN A SPIRITUAL BEING HAVE A GENDER? I JUST LIKE BEAUTIFUL THINGS!
I GET EXCITED AND INEXPLICABLY HAPPY WHEN I SEE BEAUTIFUL, WONDERFUL THINGS. THAT'S A PROBLEM?
YOU'RE LAYING IT ON WAY TOO THICK, THOUGH! YOU JUMP AT THEM AND TOSS YOUR COMMON SENSE OUT INTO THE GALAXY!! YOU'RE BECOMING A NUISANCE! A NUISANCE!!
능글
NEUNGGUL (SLY)
능글
NEUNGGUL
I'M JUST TEN TIMES MORE FULL OF LOVE AND A HUNDRED TIMES MORE FULL OF COURAGE THAN YOU.
부글~
BUGEUL (BOIL)
...!!
I SHOULDN'T HAVE SAID ANYTHING.
IT FEELS LIKE I'VE BEEN TRICKED BY LADY GAMEUNJANG...
ARRGGH! MY JEWELRY—!!
깜짝
KAMJJAK (SHOCK)

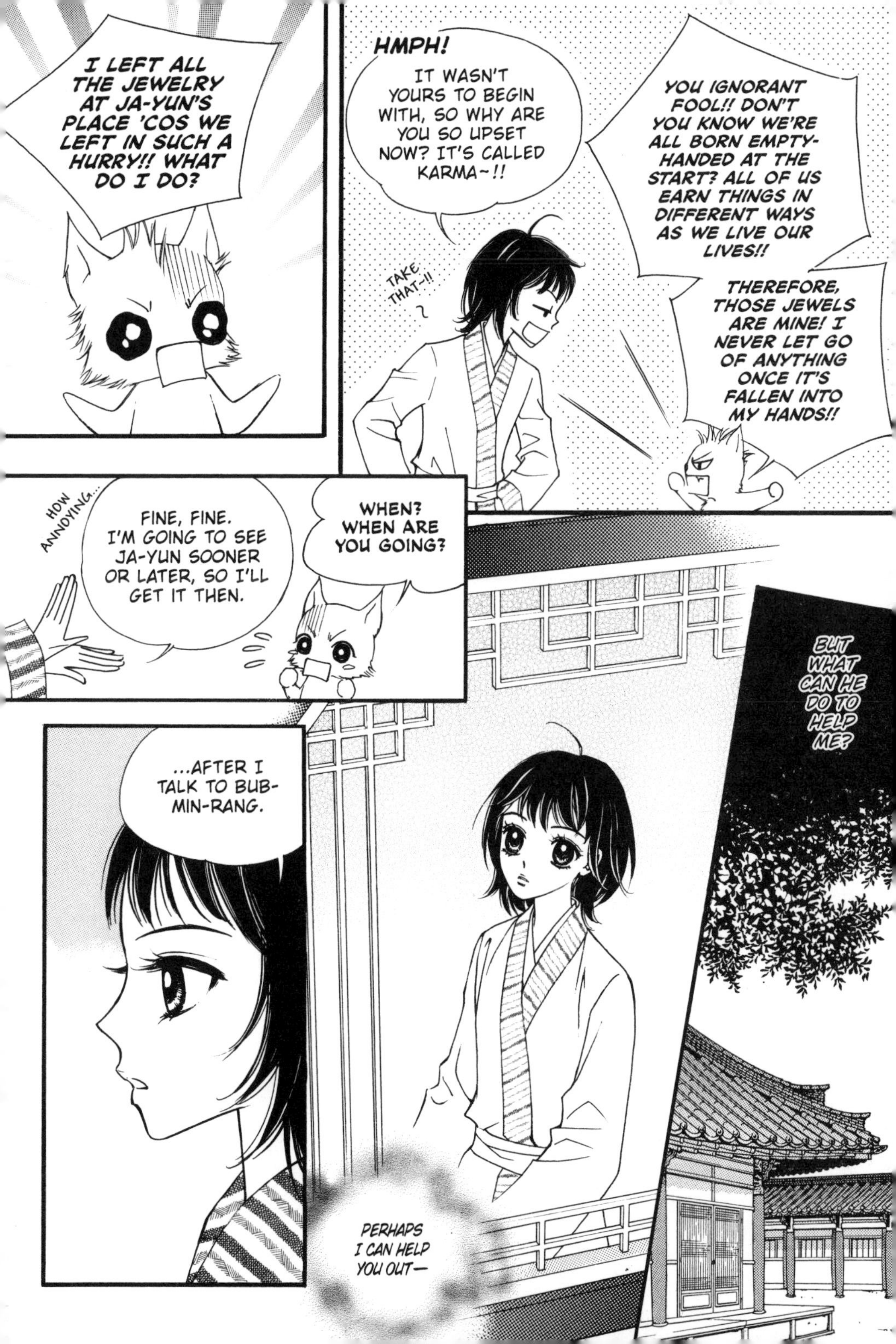
I LEFT ALL THE JEWELRY AT JA-YUN'S PLACE 'COS WE LEFT IN SUCH A HURRY!! WHAT DO I DO?
HMPH!
IT WASN'T YOURS TO BEGIN WITH, SO WHY ARE YOU SO UPSET NOW? IT'S CALLED KARMA~!!
TAKE THAT~!!
YOU IGNORANT FOOL!! DON'T YOU KNOW WE'RE ALL BORN EMPTY-HANDED AT THE START? ALL OF US EARN THINGS IN DIFFERENT WAYS AS WE LIVE OUR LIVES!!
THEREFORE, THOSE JEWELS ARE MINE! I NEVER LET GO OF ANYTHING ONCE IT'S FALLEN INTO MY HANDS!!
HOW ANNOYING...
FINE, FINE. I'M GOING TO SEE JA-YUN SOONER OR LATER, SO I'LL GET IT THEN.
WHEN? WHEN ARE YOU GOING?
...AFTER I TALK TO BUB-MIN-RANG.
BUT WHAT CAN HE DO TO HELP ME?
PERHAPS I CAN HELP YOU OUT—

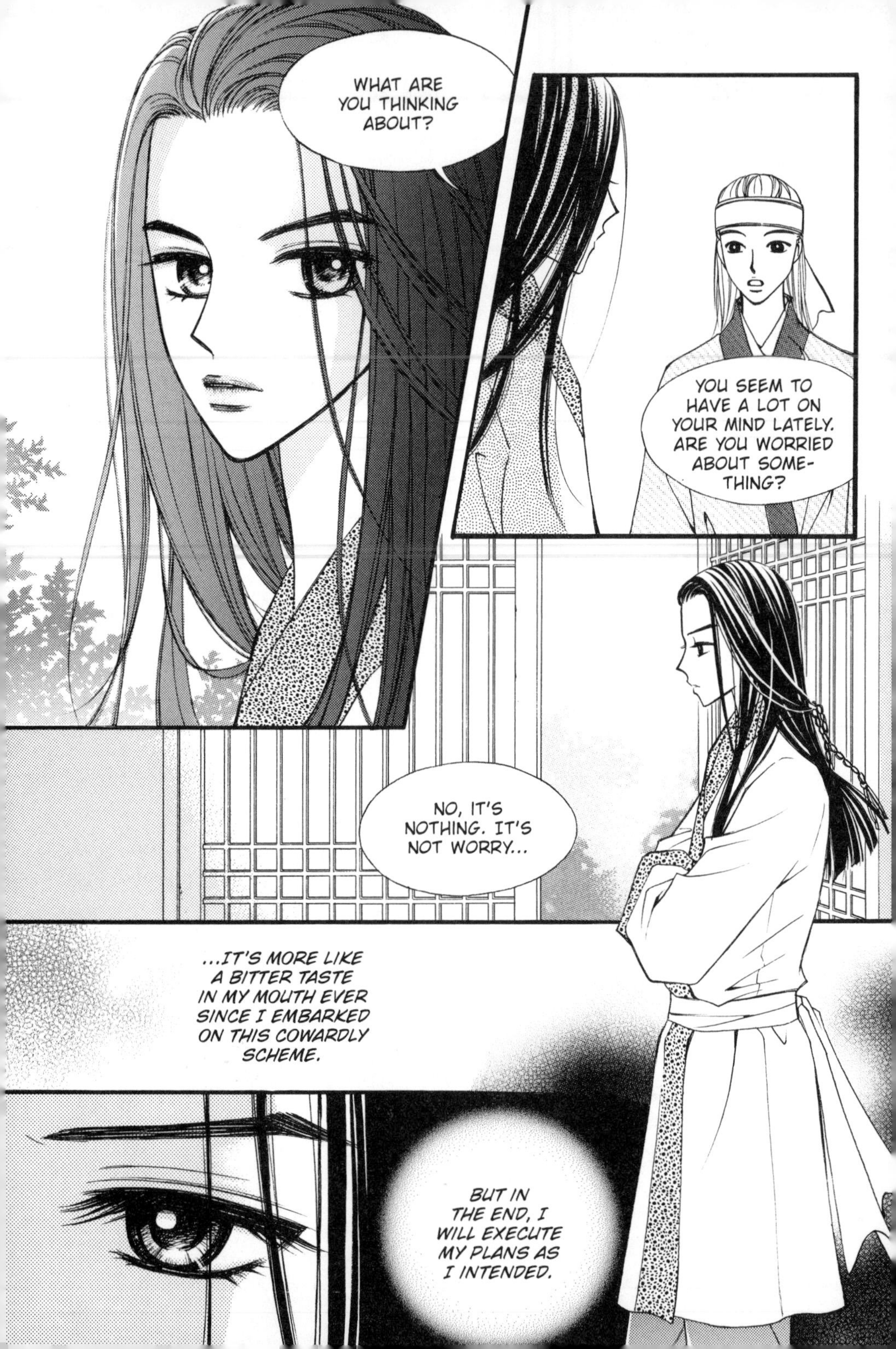
WHAT ARE YOU THINKING ABOUT?
YOU SEEM TO HAVE A LOT ON YOUR MIND LATELY. ARE YOU WORRIED ABOUT SOME-THING?
NO, IT'S NOTHING. IT'S NOT WORRY...
...IT'S MORE LIKE A BITTER TASTE IN MY MOUTH EVER SINCE I EMBARKED ON THIS COWARDLY SCHEME.
BUT IN THE END, I WILL EXECUTE MY PLANS AS I INTENDED.

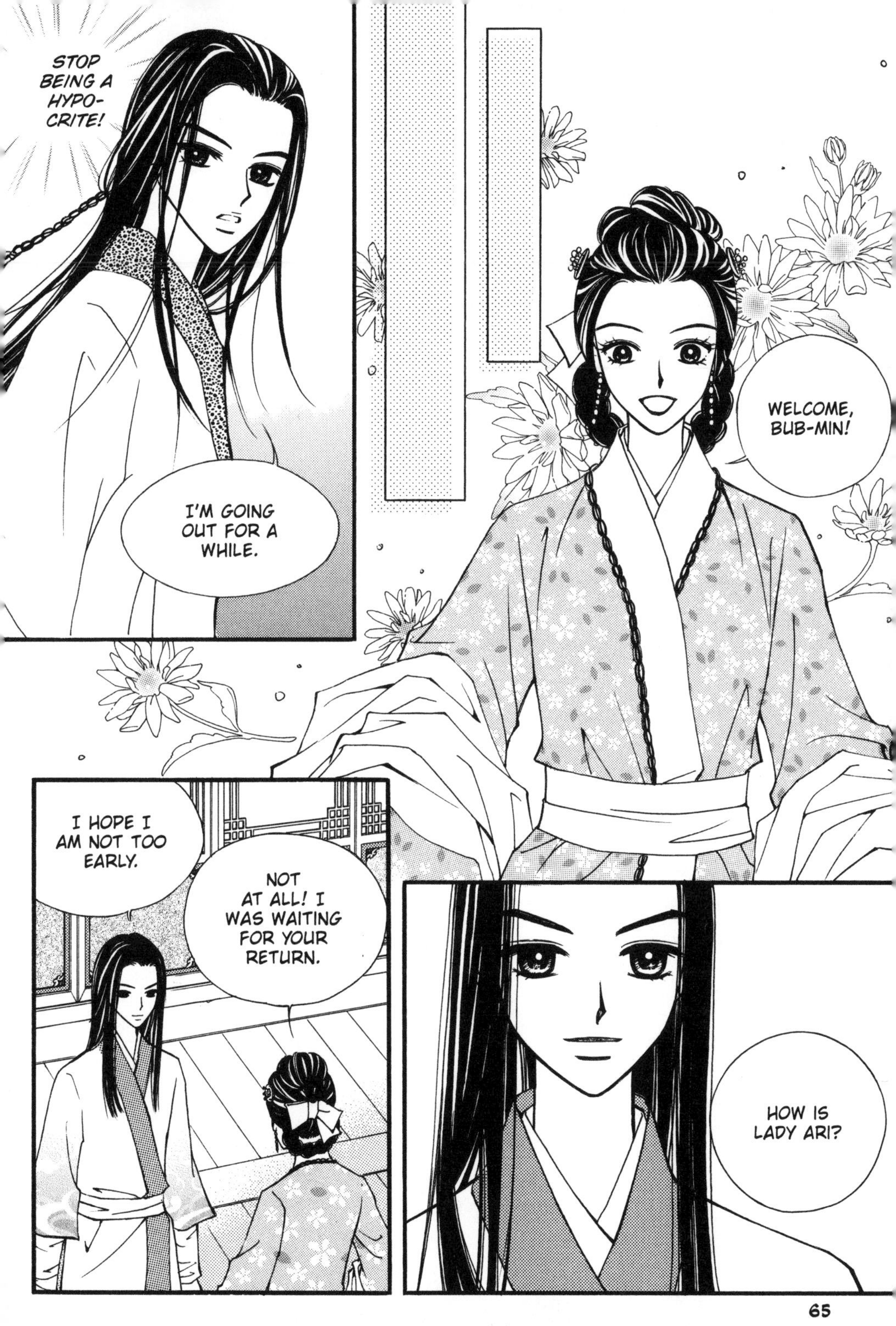
STOP BEING A HYPO-CRITE!
I'M GOING OUT FOR A WHILE.
WELCOME, BUB-MIN!
I HOPE I AM NOT TOO EARLY.
NOT AT ALL! I WAS WAITING FOR YOUR RETURN.
HOW IS LADY ARI?

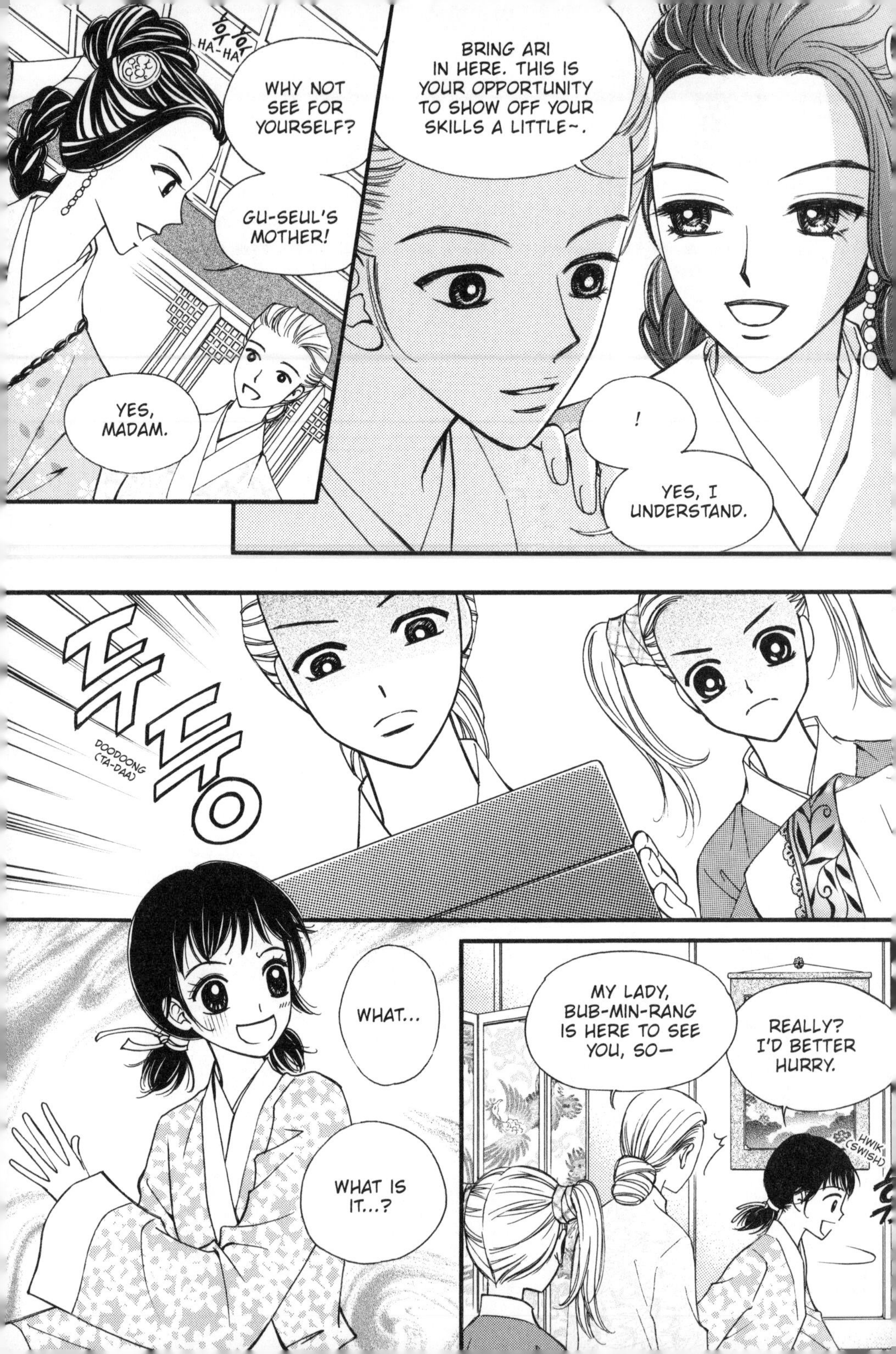
HA-HA
WHY NOT SEE FOR YOURSELF?
GU-SEUL'S MOTHER!
YES, MADAM.
BRING ARI IN HERE. THIS IS YOUR OPPORTUNITY TO SHOW OFF YOUR SKILLS A LITTLE~.
!
YES, I UNDERSTAND.
DOODOONG (TA-DAA)
WHAT...
WHAT IS IT...?
MY LADY, BUB-MIN-RANG IS HERE TO SEE YOU, SO—
REALLY? I'D BETTER HURRY.
HWIK (SWISH)

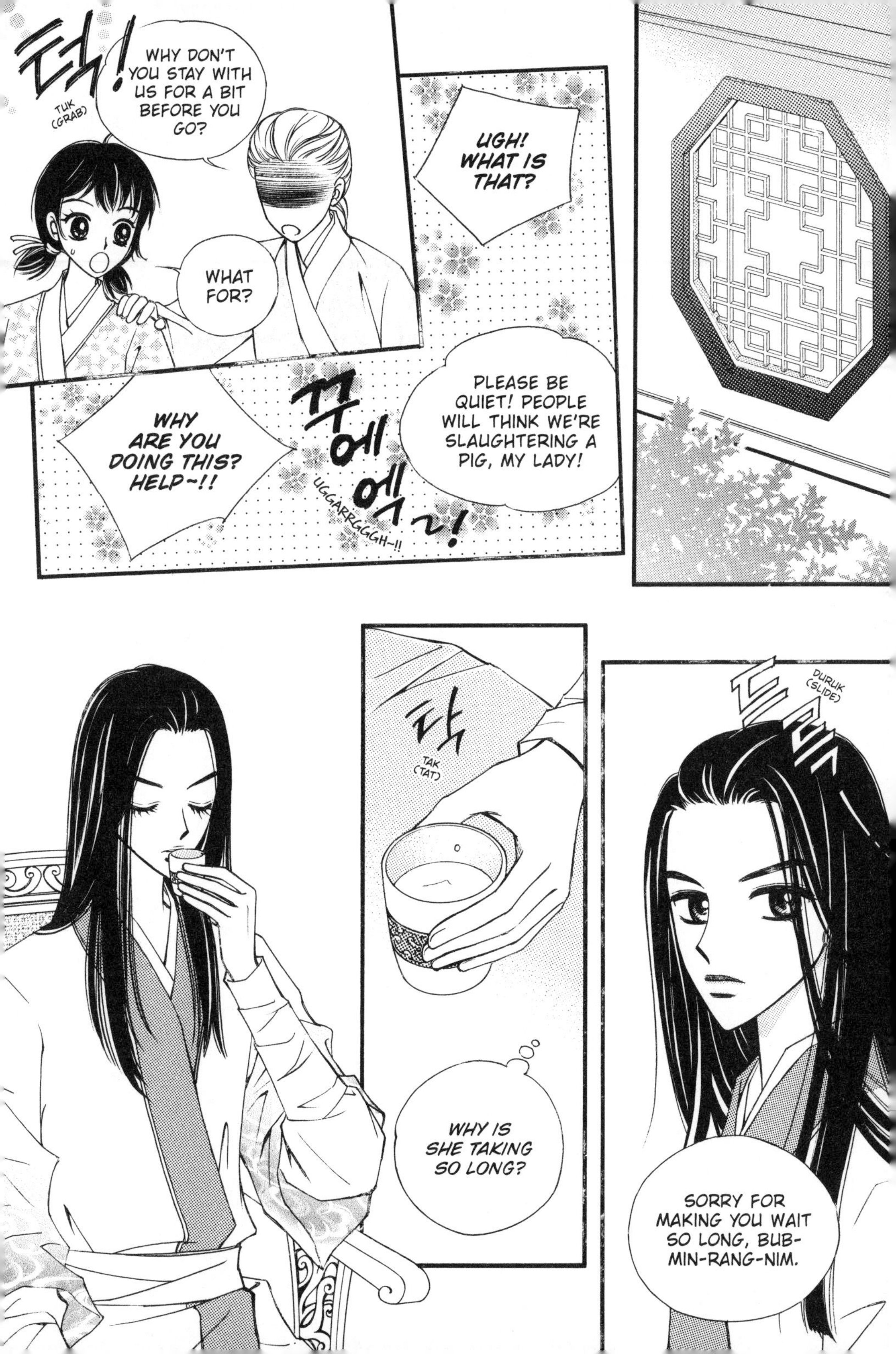

턱!
TUK (GRAB)
WHY DON'T YOU STAY WITH US FOR A BIT BEFORE YOU GO?
WHAT FOR?
UGH! WHAT IS THAT?
WHY ARE YOU DOING THIS? HELP~!!
꾸에엑~!
UGGARRGGGH~!!
PLEASE BE QUIET! PEOPLE WILL THINK WE'RE SLAUGHTERING A PIG, MY LADY!
탁
TAK (TAT)
WHY IS SHE TAKING SO LONG?
드르륵
DURUK (SLIDE)
SORRY FOR MAKING YOU WAIT SO LONG, BUB-MIN-RANG-NIM.

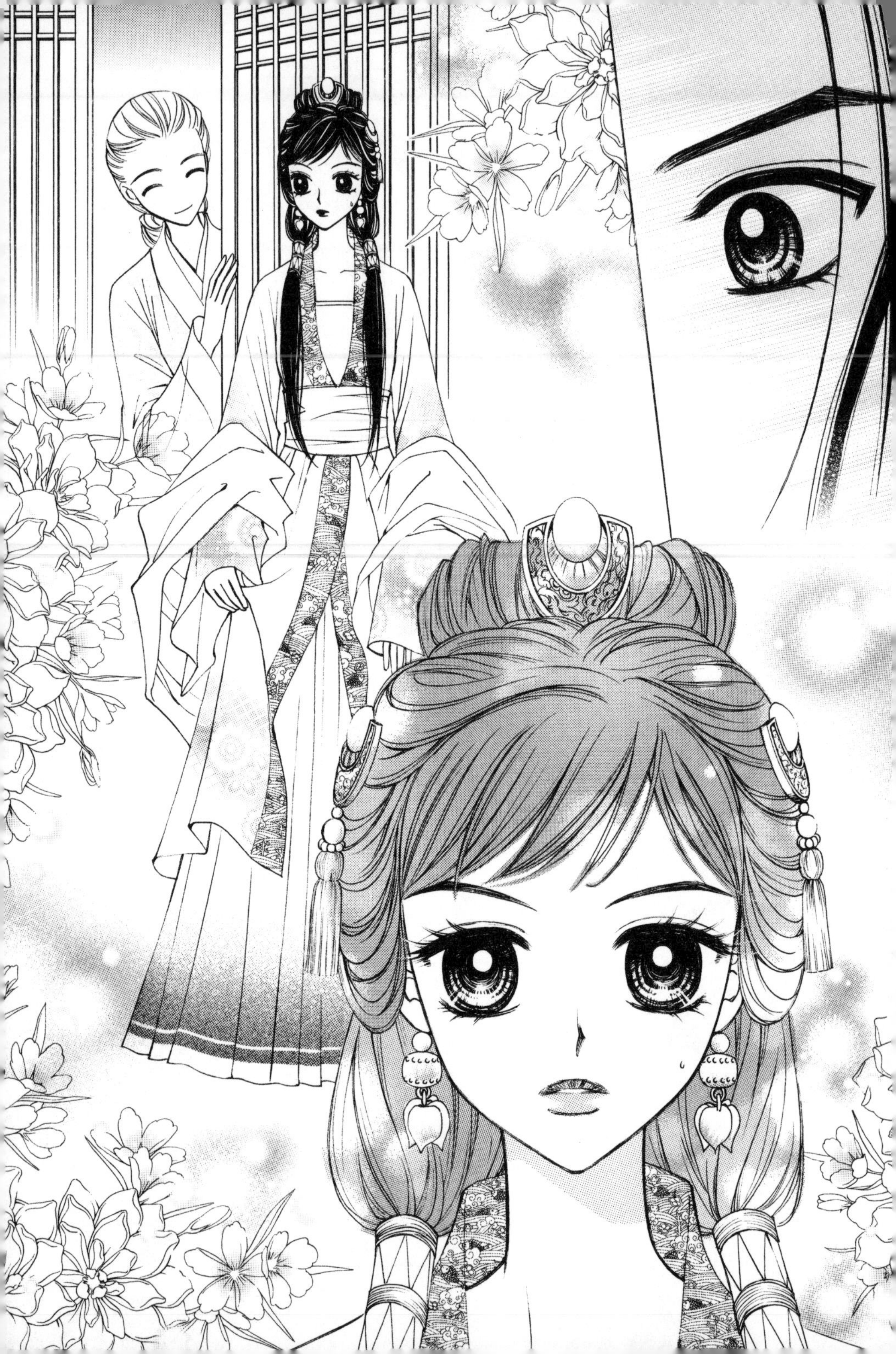

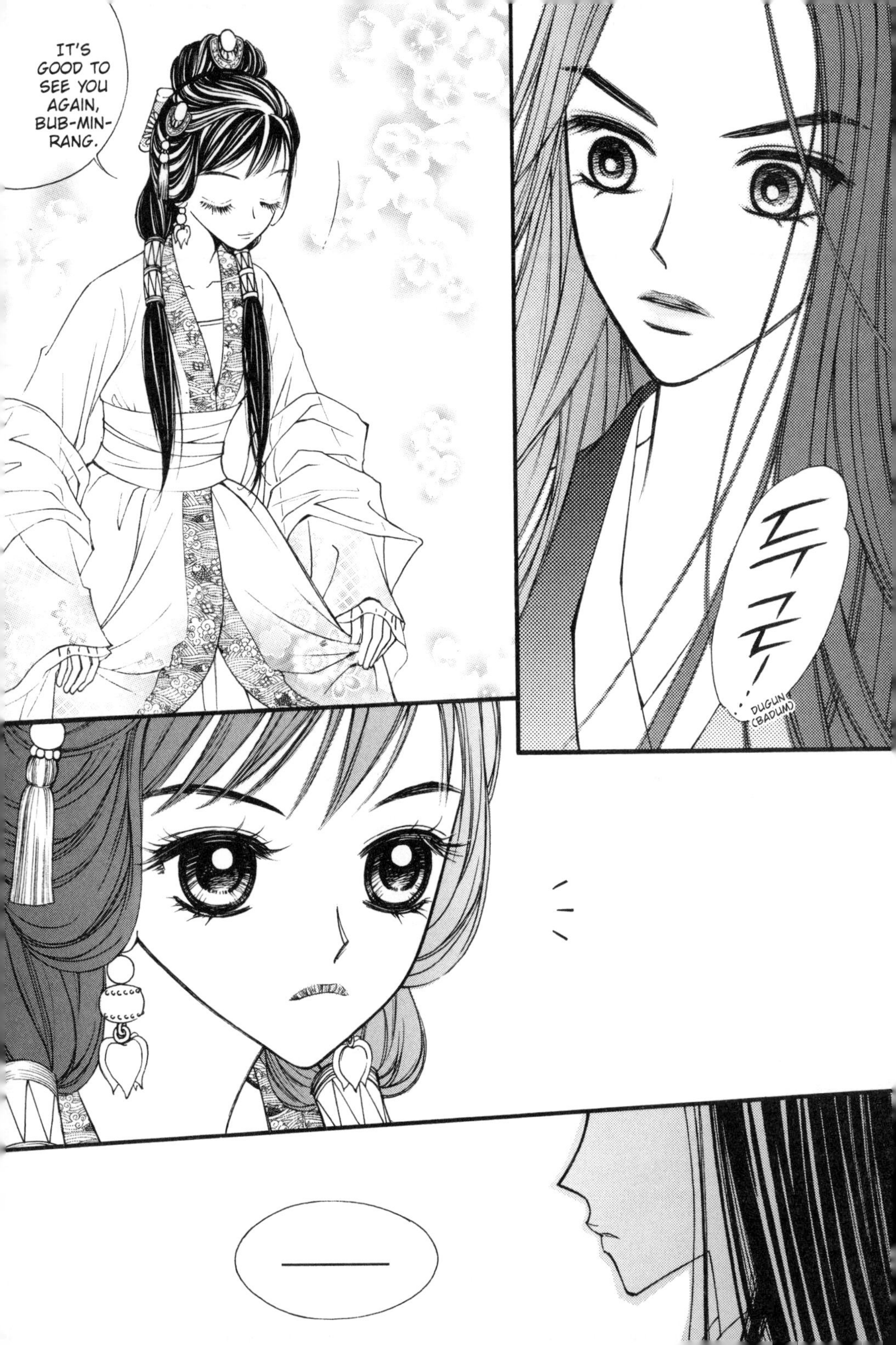
IT'S GOOD TO SEE YOU AGAIN, BUB-MIN-RANG.
DUGUN (BADUM)
—

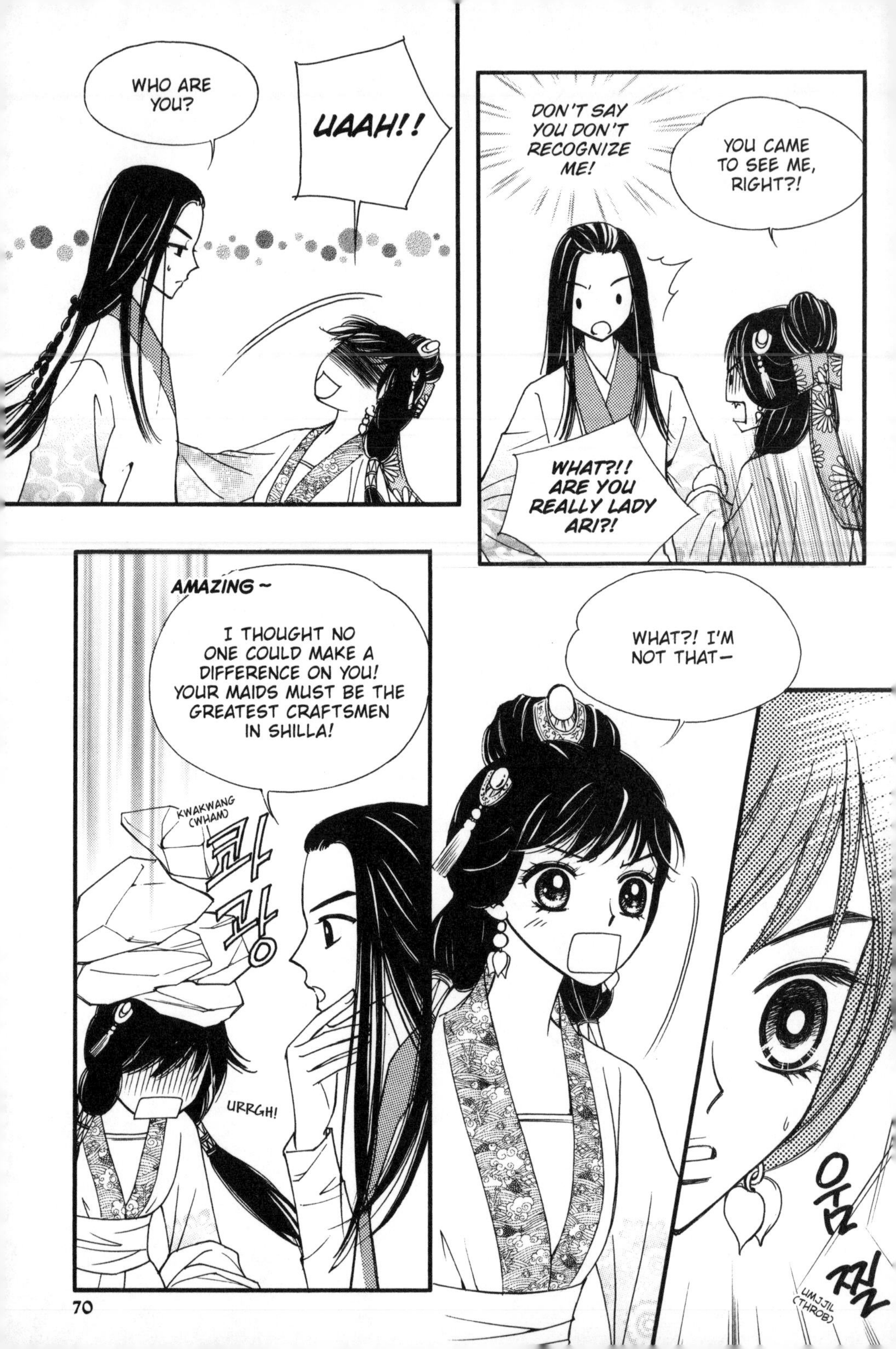
WHO ARE YOU?
UAAH!!
DON'T SAY YOU DON'T RECOGNIZE ME!
YOU CAME TO SEE ME, RIGHT?!
WHAT?!! ARE YOU REALLY LADY ARI?!
AMAZING~
I THOUGHT NO ONE COULD MAKE A DIFFERENCE ON YOU! YOUR MAIDS MUST BE THE GREATEST CRAFTSMEN IN SHILLA!
KWAKWANG (WHAM)
콰광
URRGH!
WHAT?! I'M NOT THAT—
움찔
UMJJIL (THROB)

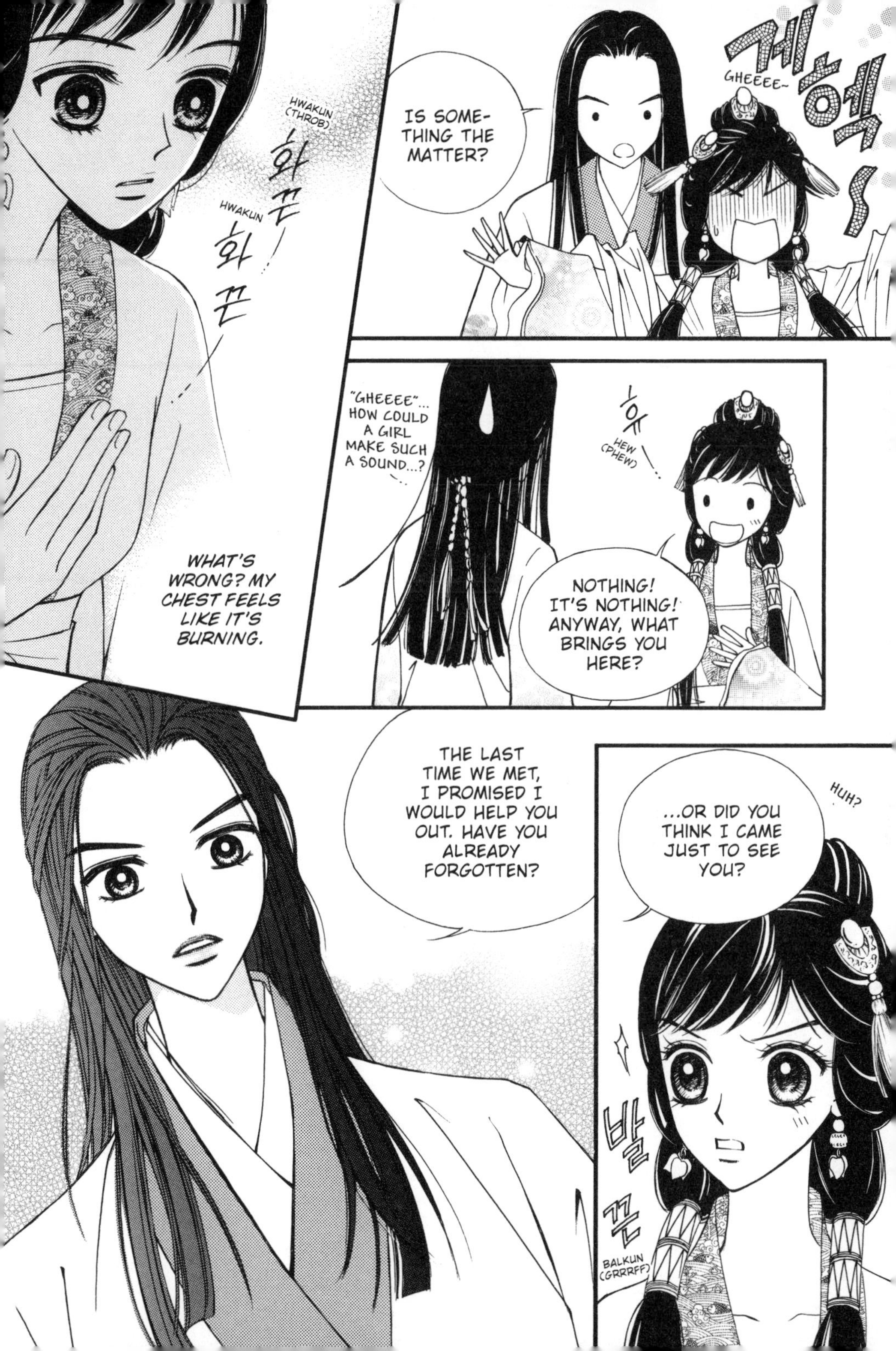
HWAKUN (THROB)
화끈...
HWAKUN
화끈
WHAT'S WRONG? MY CHEST FEELS LIKE IT'S BURNING.
IS SOME-THING THE MATTER?
게헥~
GHEEEE~
"GHEEEE"... HOW COULD A GIRL MAKE SUCH A SOUND...?
휴...
HEW (PHEW)
NOTHING! IT'S NOTHING! ANYWAY, WHAT BRINGS YOU HERE?
THE LAST TIME WE MET, I PROMISED I WOULD HELP YOU OUT. HAVE YOU ALREADY FORGOTTEN?
...OR DID YOU THINK I CAME JUST TO SEE YOU?
HUH?
발끈
BALKUN (GRRRFF)

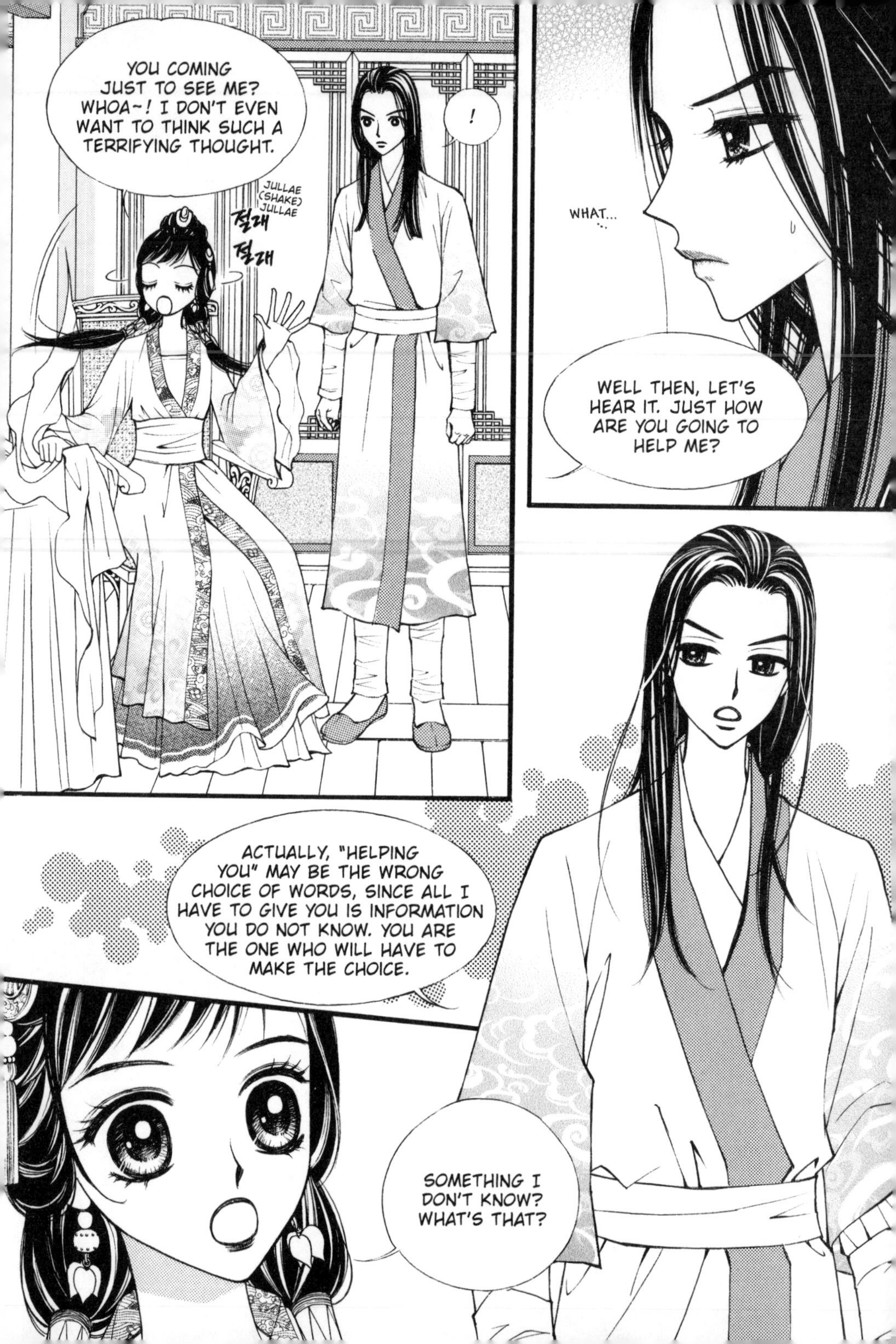

YOU COMING JUST TO SEE ME? WHOA~! I DON'T EVEN WANT TO THINK SUCH A TERRIFYING THOUGHT.
!
JULLAE (SHAKE) JULLAE
절래
절래
WHAT...
WELL THEN, LET'S HEAR IT. JUST HOW ARE YOU GOING TO HELP ME?
ACTUALLY, "HELPING YOU" MAY BE THE WRONG CHOICE OF WORDS, SINCE ALL I HAVE TO GIVE YOU IS INFORMATION YOU DO NOT KNOW. YOU ARE THE ONE WHO WILL HAVE TO MAKE THE CHOICE.
SOMETHING I DON'T KNOW? WHAT'S THAT?

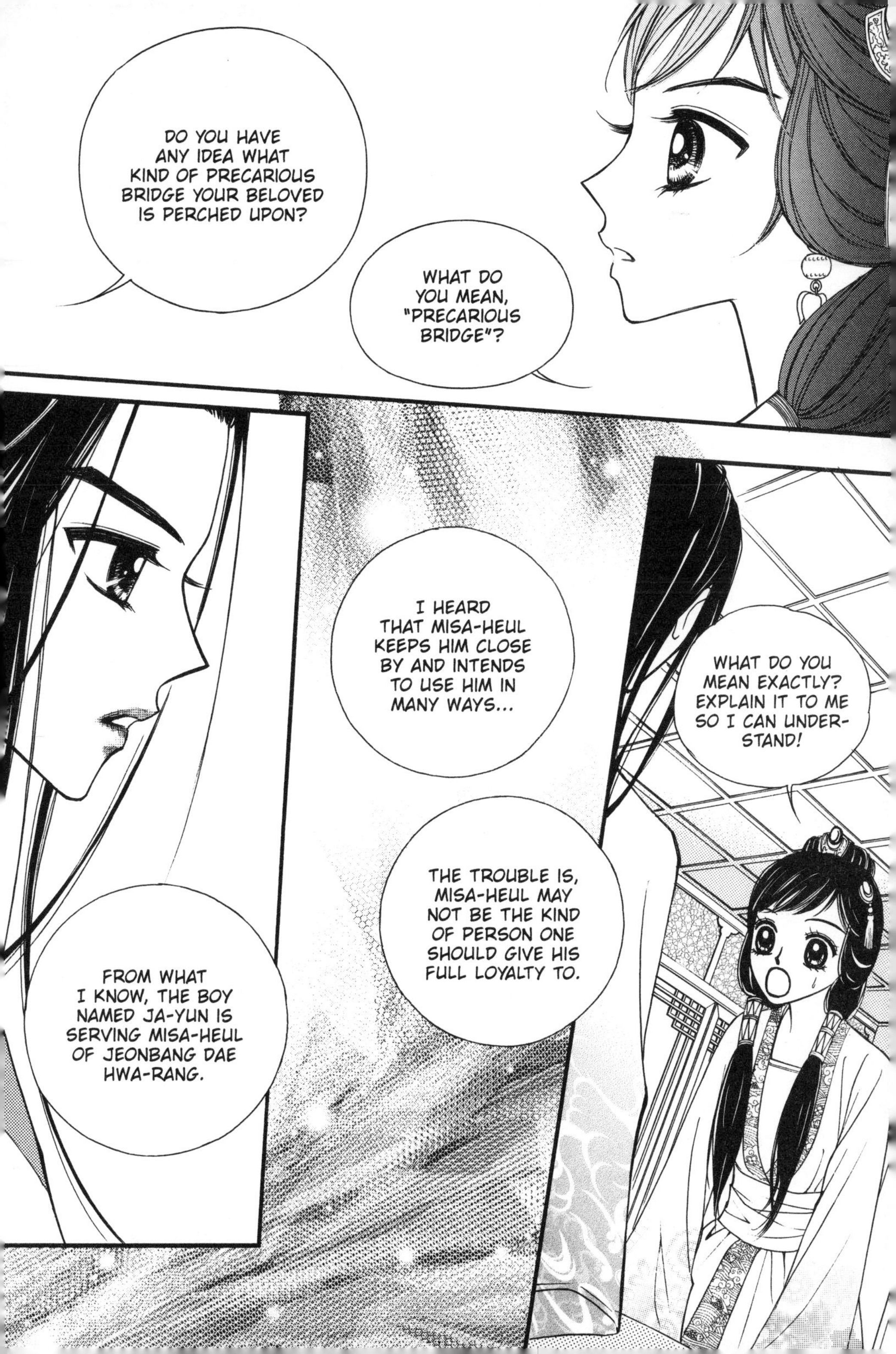
DO YOU HAVE ANY IDEA WHAT KIND OF PRECARIOUS BRIDGE YOUR BELOVED IS PERCHED UPON?
WHAT DO YOU MEAN, "PRECARIOUS BRIDGE"?
FROM WHAT I KNOW, THE BOY NAMED JA-YUN IS SERVING MISA-HEUL OF JEONBANG DAE HWA-RANG.
I HEARD THAT MISA-HEUL KEEPS HIM CLOSE BY AND INTENDS TO USE HIM IN MANY WAYS...
THE TROUBLE IS, MISA-HEUL MAY NOT BE THE KIND OF PERSON ONE SHOULD GIVE HIS FULL LOYALTY TO.
WHAT DO YOU MEAN EXACTLY? EXPLAIN IT TO ME SO I CAN UNDERSTAND!

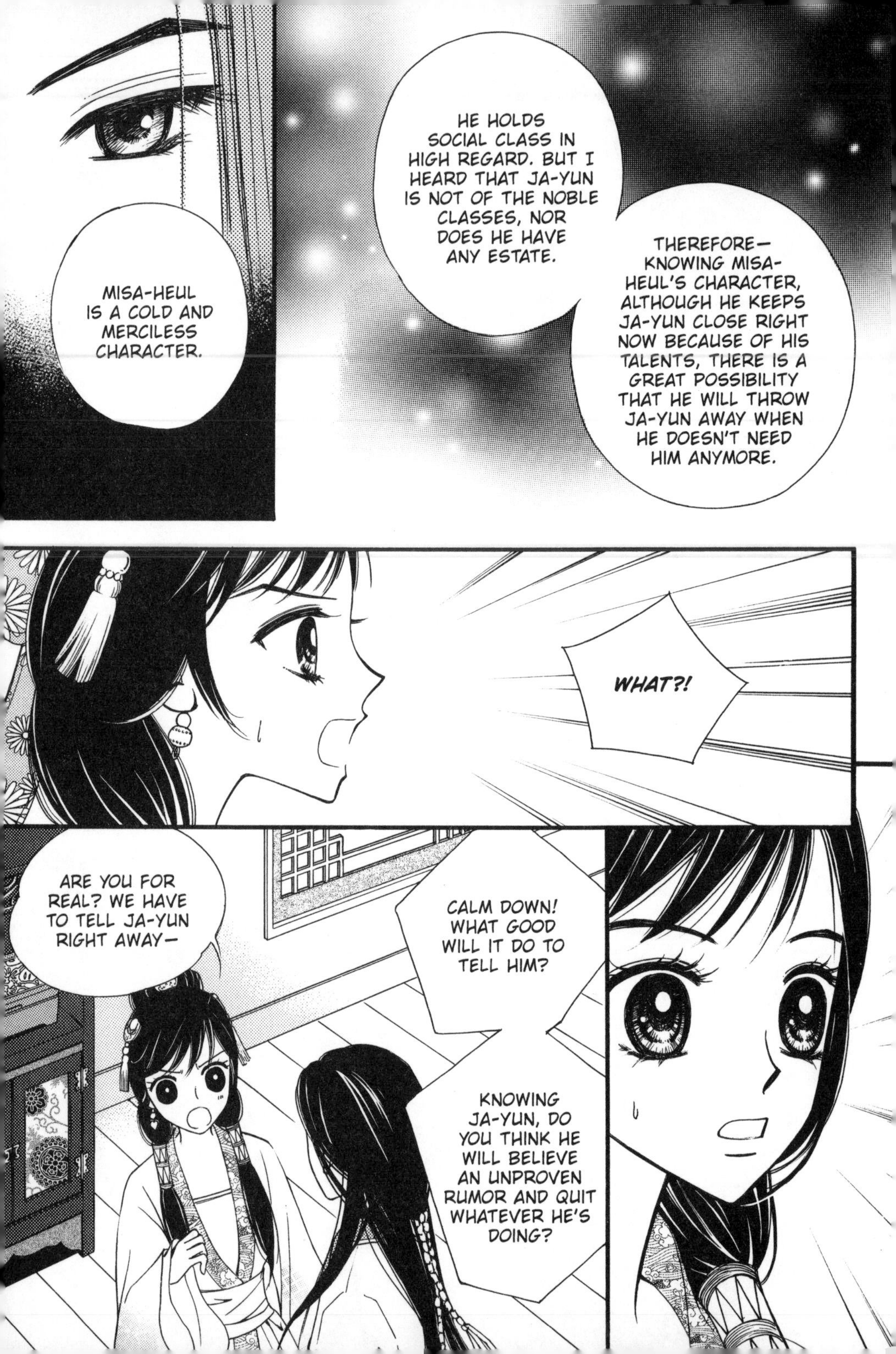
MISA-HEUL IS A COLD AND MERCILESS CHARACTER.
HE HOLDS SOCIAL CLASS IN HIGH REGARD. BUT I HEARD THAT JA-YUN IS NOT OF THE NOBLE CLASSES, NOR DOES HE HAVE ANY ESTATE.
THEREFORE— KNOWING MISA-HEUL'S CHARACTER, ALTHOUGH HE KEEPS JA-YUN CLOSE RIGHT NOW BECAUSE OF HIS TALENTS, THERE IS A GREAT POSSIBILITY THAT HE WILL THROW JA-YUN AWAY WHEN HE DOESN'T NEED HIM ANYMORE.
WHAT?!
ARE YOU FOR REAL? WE HAVE TO TELL JA-YUN RIGHT AWAY—
CALM DOWN! WHAT GOOD WILL IT DO TO TELL HIM?
KNOWING JA-YUN, DO YOU THINK HE WILL BELIEVE AN UNPROVEN RUMOR AND QUIT WHATEVER HE'S DOING?

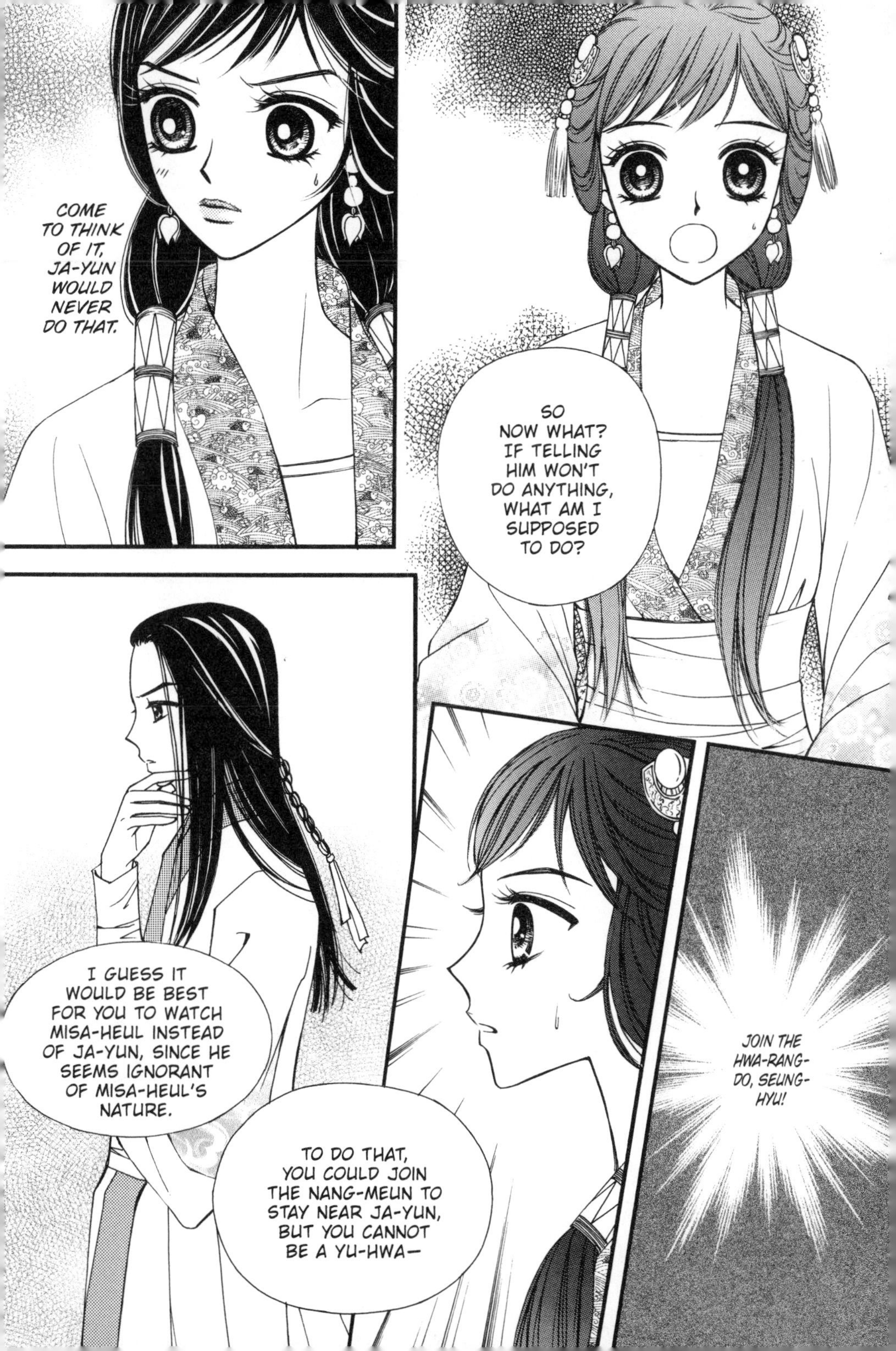
COME TO THINK OF IT, JA-YUN WOULD NEVER DO THAT.
SO NOW WHAT? IF TELLING HIM WON'T DO ANYTHING, WHAT AM I SUPPOSED TO DO?
I GUESS IT WOULD BE BEST FOR YOU TO WATCH MISA-HEUL INSTEAD OF JA-YUN, SINCE HE SEEMS IGNORANT OF MISA-HEUL'S NATURE.
TO DO THAT, YOU COULD JOIN THE NANG-MEUN TO STAY NEAR JA-YUN, BUT YOU CANNOT BE A YU-HWA—
JOIN THE HWA-RANG-DO, SEUNG-HYU!

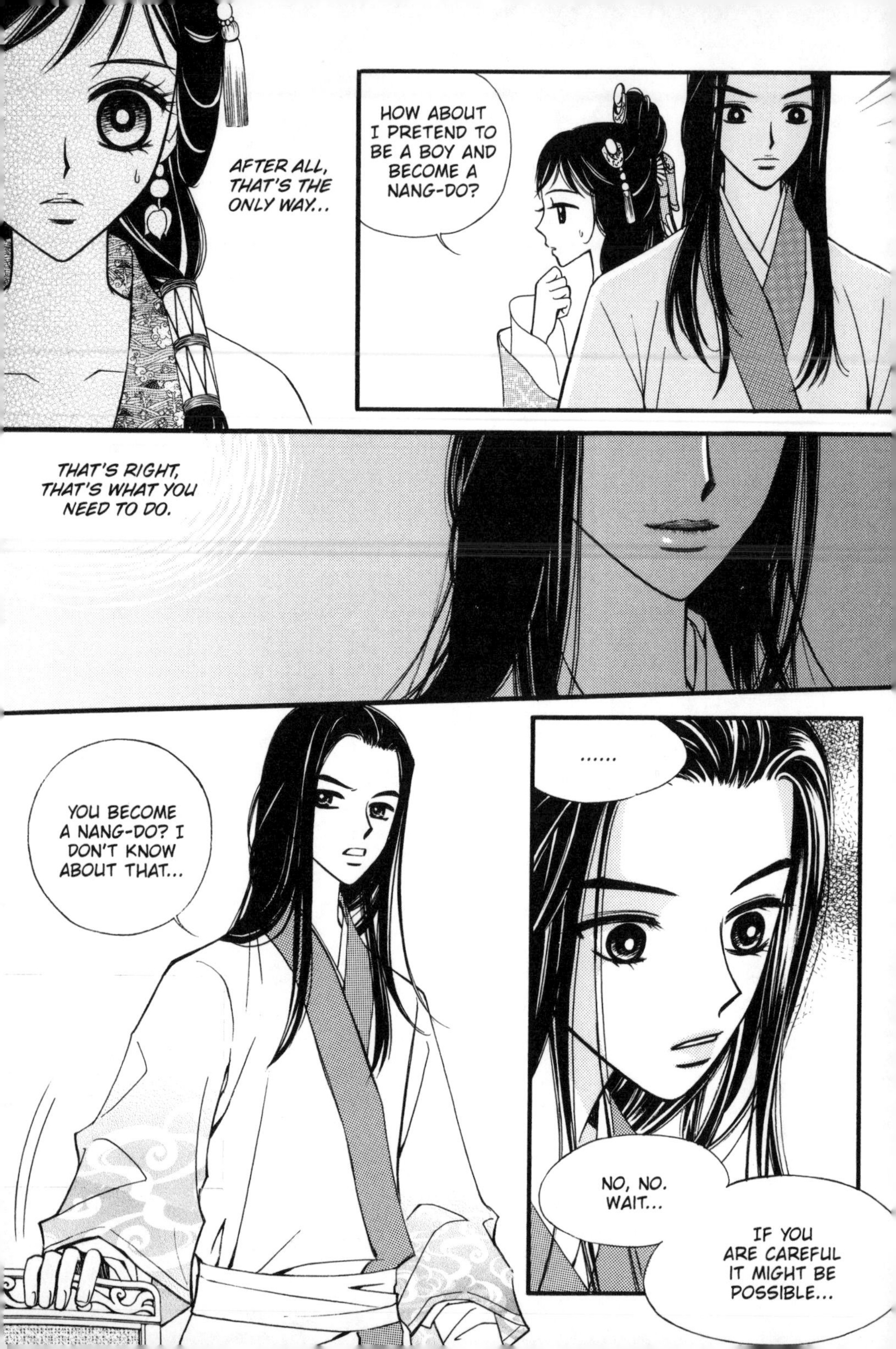
AFTER ALL, THAT'S THE ONLY WAY...
HOW ABOUT I PRETEND TO BE A BOY AND BECOME A NANG-DO?
THAT'S RIGHT, THAT'S WHAT YOU NEED TO DO.
YOU BECOME A NANG-DO? I DON'T KNOW ABOUT THAT...
......
NO, NO. WAIT...
IF YOU ARE CAREFUL IT MIGHT BE POSSIBLE...

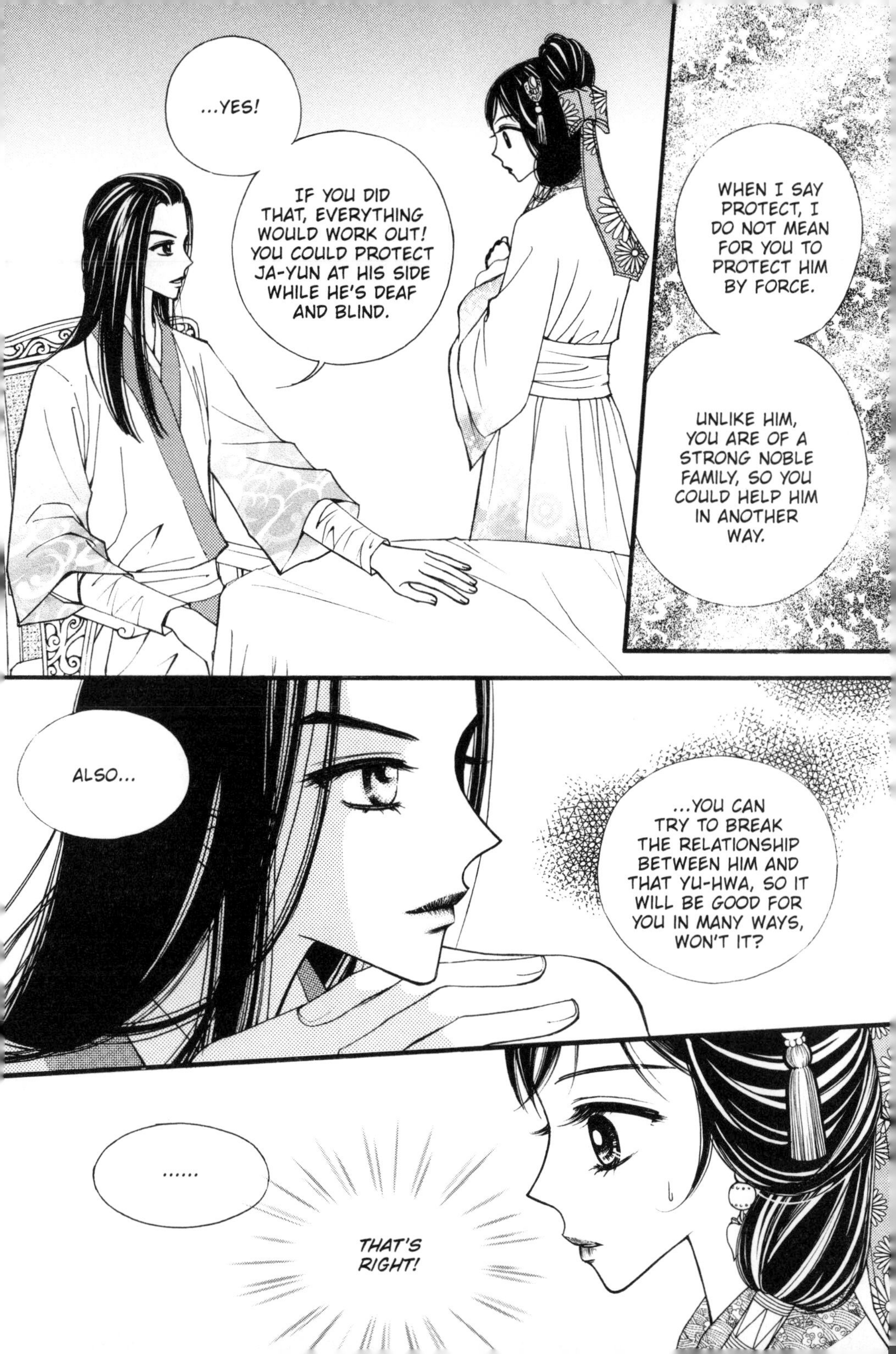
...YES!
IF YOU DID THAT, EVERYTHING WOULD WORK OUT! YOU COULD PROTECT JA-YUN AT HIS SIDE WHILE HE'S DEAF AND BLIND.
WHEN I SAY PROTECT, I DO NOT MEAN FOR YOU TO PROTECT HIM BY FORCE.
UNLIKE HIM, YOU ARE OF A STRONG NOBLE FAMILY, SO YOU COULD HELP HIM IN ANOTHER WAY.
ALSO...
...YOU CAN TRY TO BREAK THE RELATIONSHIP BETWEEN HIM AND THAT YU-HWA, SO IT WILL BE GOOD FOR YOU IN MANY WAYS, WON'T IT?
......
THAT'S RIGHT!

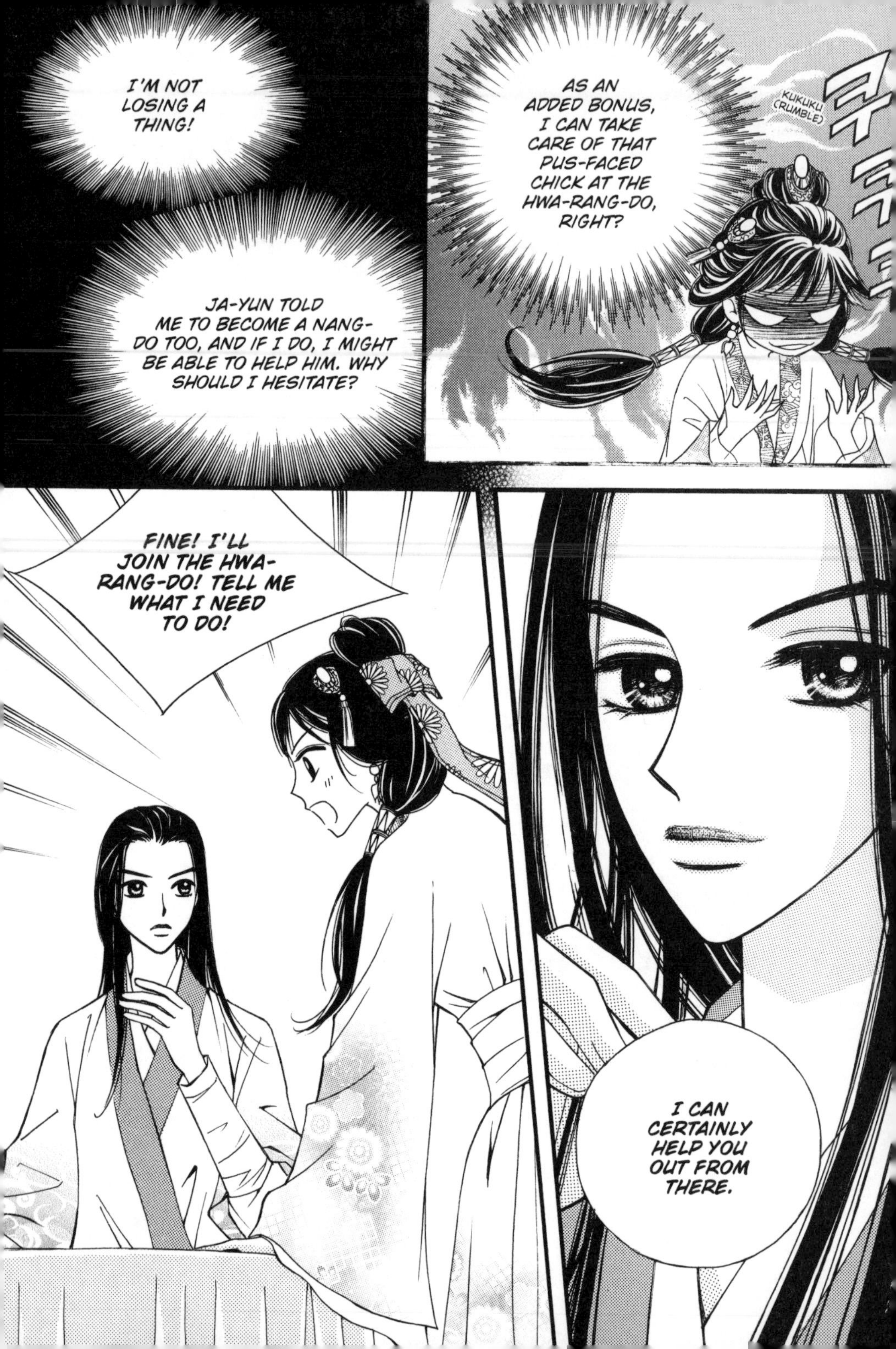

I'M NOT LOSING A THING!
JA-YUN TOLD ME TO BECOME A NANG-DO TOO, AND IF I DO, I MIGHT BE ABLE TO HELP HIM. WHY SHOULD I HESITATE?
AS AN ADDED BONUS, I CAN TAKE CARE OF THAT PUS-FACED CHICK AT THE HWA-RANG-DO, RIGHT?
KUKUKU (RUMBLE)
FINE! I'LL JOIN THE HWA-RANG-DO! TELL ME WHAT I NEED TO DO!
I CAN CERTAINLY HELP YOU OUT FROM THERE.

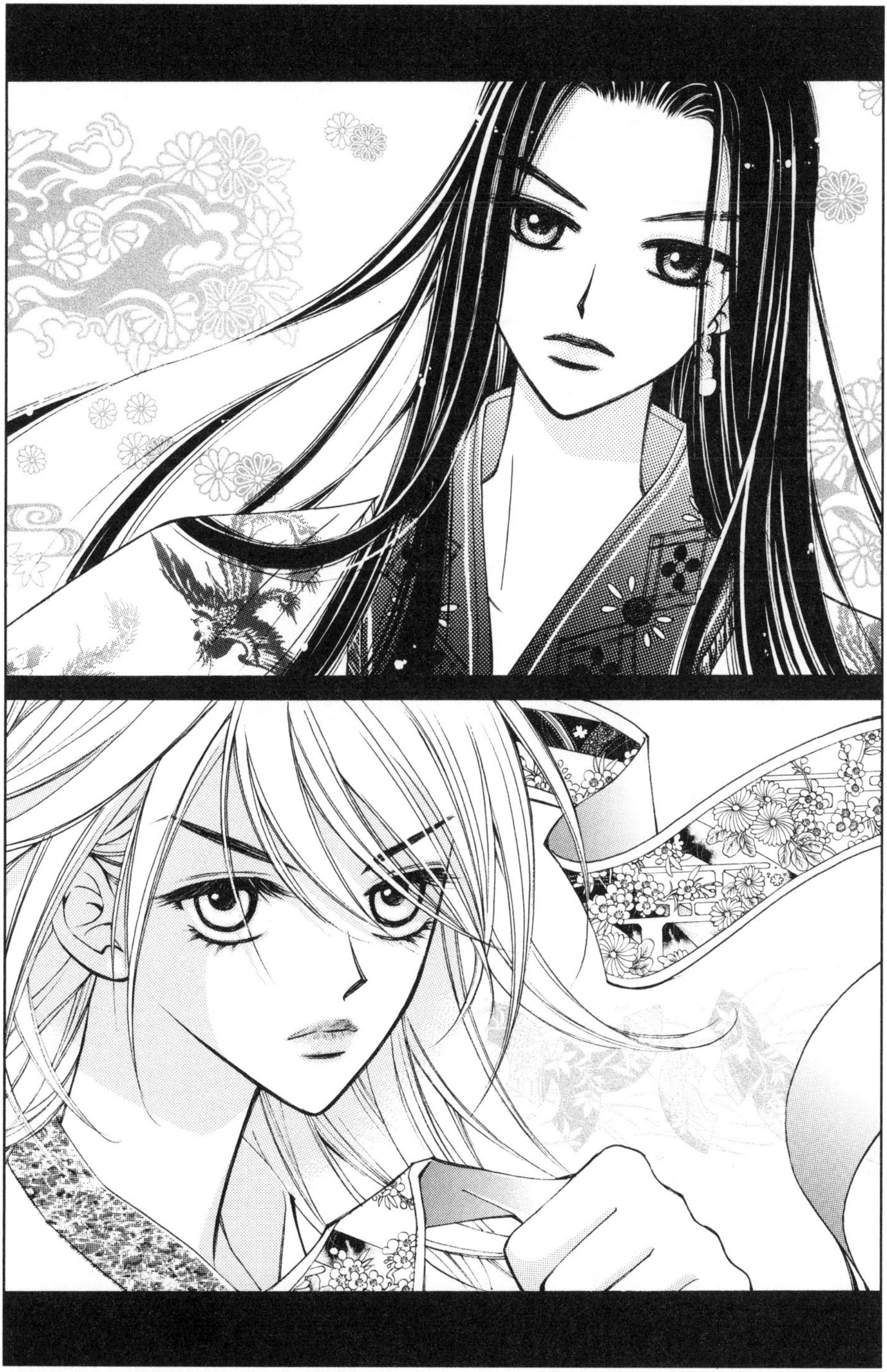

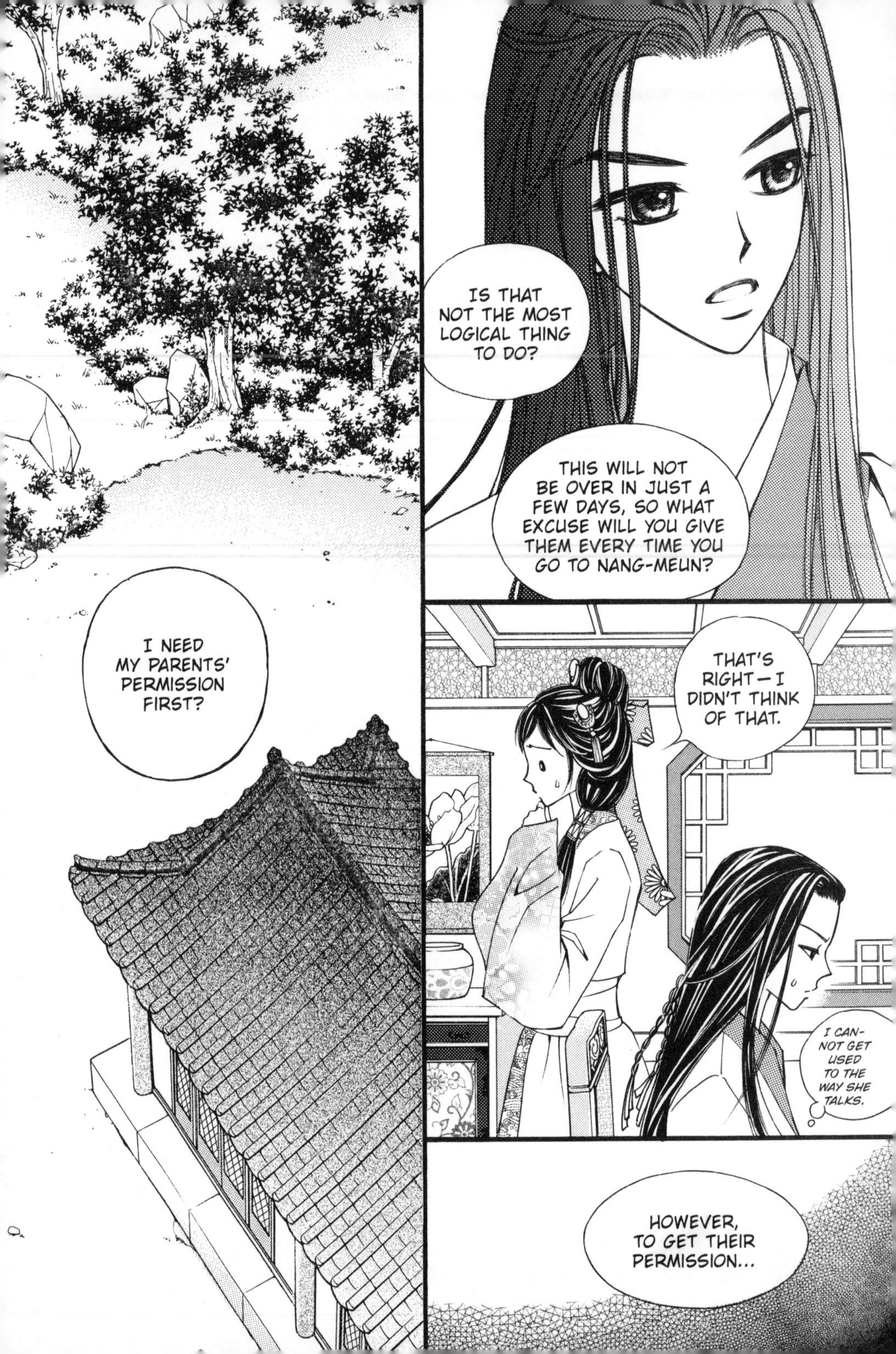
I NEED MY PARENTS' PERMISSION FIRST?
IS THAT NOT THE MOST LOGICAL THING TO DO?
THIS WILL NOT BE OVER IN JUST A FEW DAYS, SO WHAT EXCUSE WILL YOU GIVE THEM EVERY TIME YOU GO TO NANG-MEUN?
THAT'S RIGHT—I DIDN'T THINK OF THAT.
I CAN-NOT GET USED TO THE WAY SHE TALKS.
HOWEVER, TO GET THEIR PERMISSION...

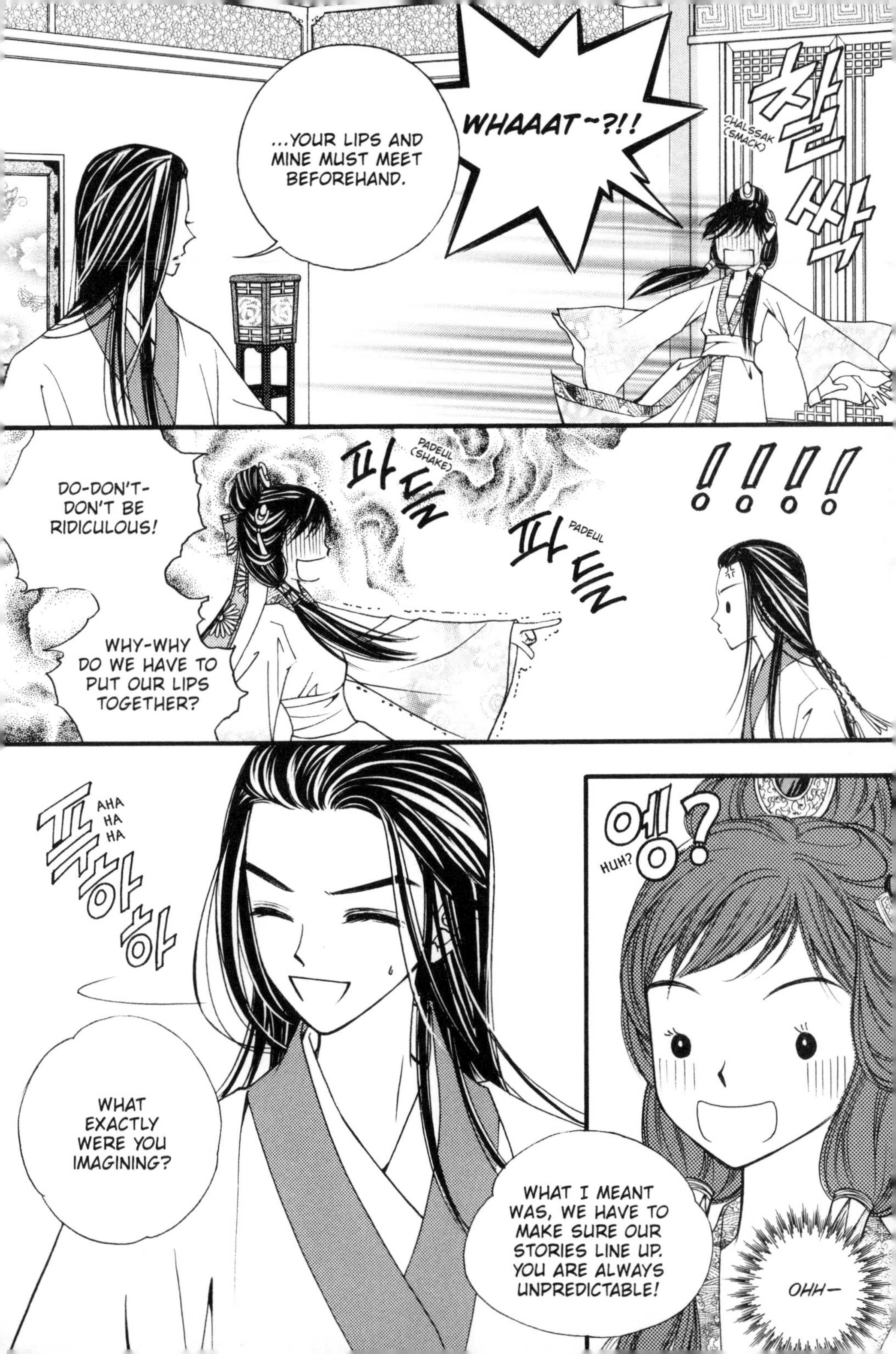
...YOUR LIPS AND MINE MUST MEET BEFOREHAND.
WHAAAT~?!!
CHALSSAK (SMACK)
DO-DON'T-DON'T BE RIDICULOUS!
PADEUL (SHAKE)
PADEUL
WHY-WHY DO WE HAVE TO PUT OUR LIPS TOGETHER?
!!!!
AHA HA HA
WHAT EXACTLY WERE YOU IMAGINING?
WHAT I MEANT WAS, WE HAVE TO MAKE SURE OUR STORIES LINE UP. YOU ARE ALWAYS UNPREDICTABLE!
HUH?
OHH—

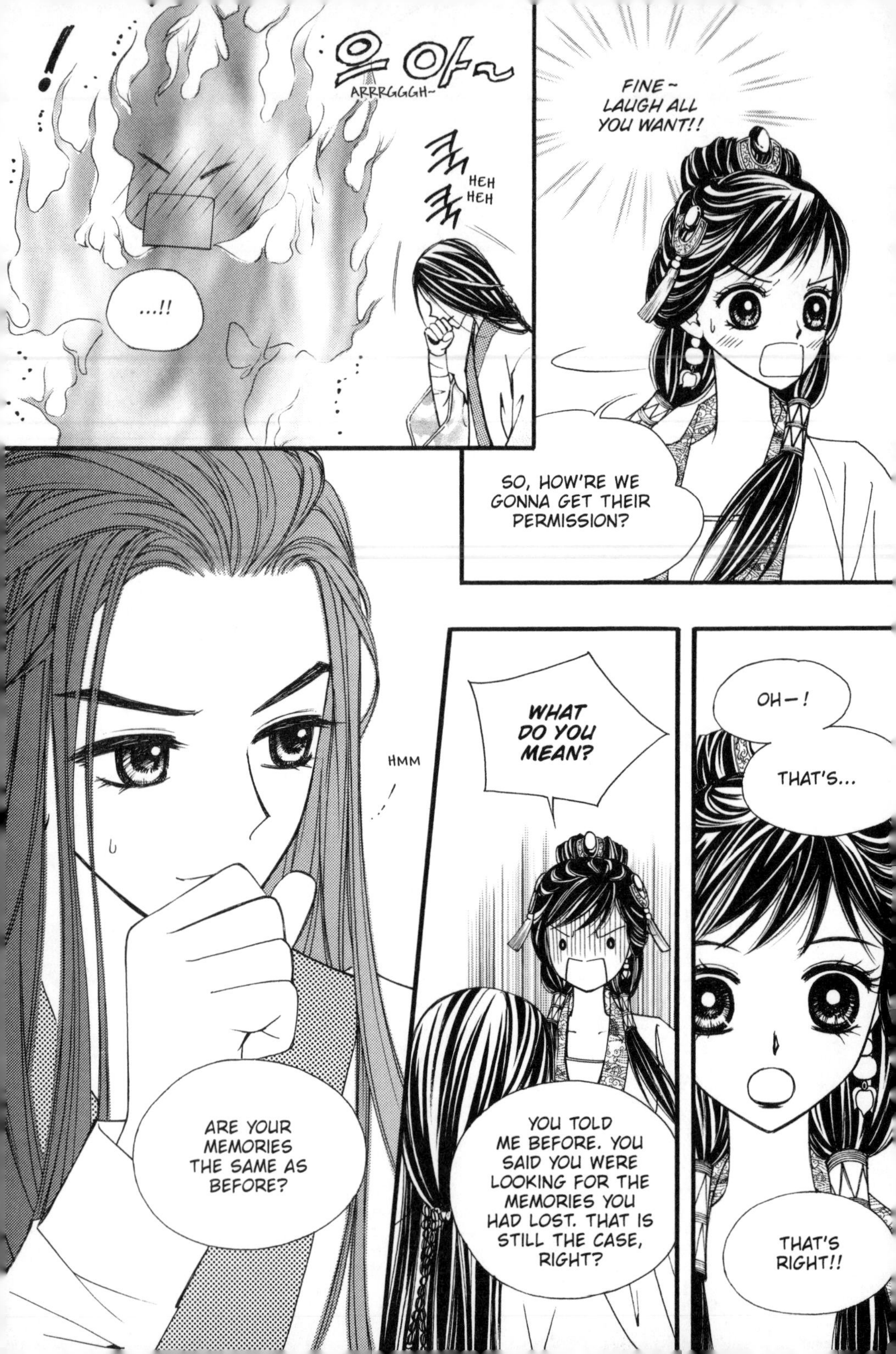
!
...!!
으아~
ARRRGGGH~
쿡
쿡
HEH HEH
FINE~ LAUGH ALL YOU WANT!!
HMM
ARE YOUR MEMORIES THE SAME AS BEFORE?
SO, HOW'RE WE GONNA GET THEIR PERMISSION?
WHAT DO YOU MEAN?
YOU TOLD ME BEFORE. YOU SAID YOU WERE LOOKING FOR THE MEMORIES YOU HAD LOST. THAT IS STILL THE CASE, RIGHT?
OH—!
THAT'S...
THAT'S RIGHT!!

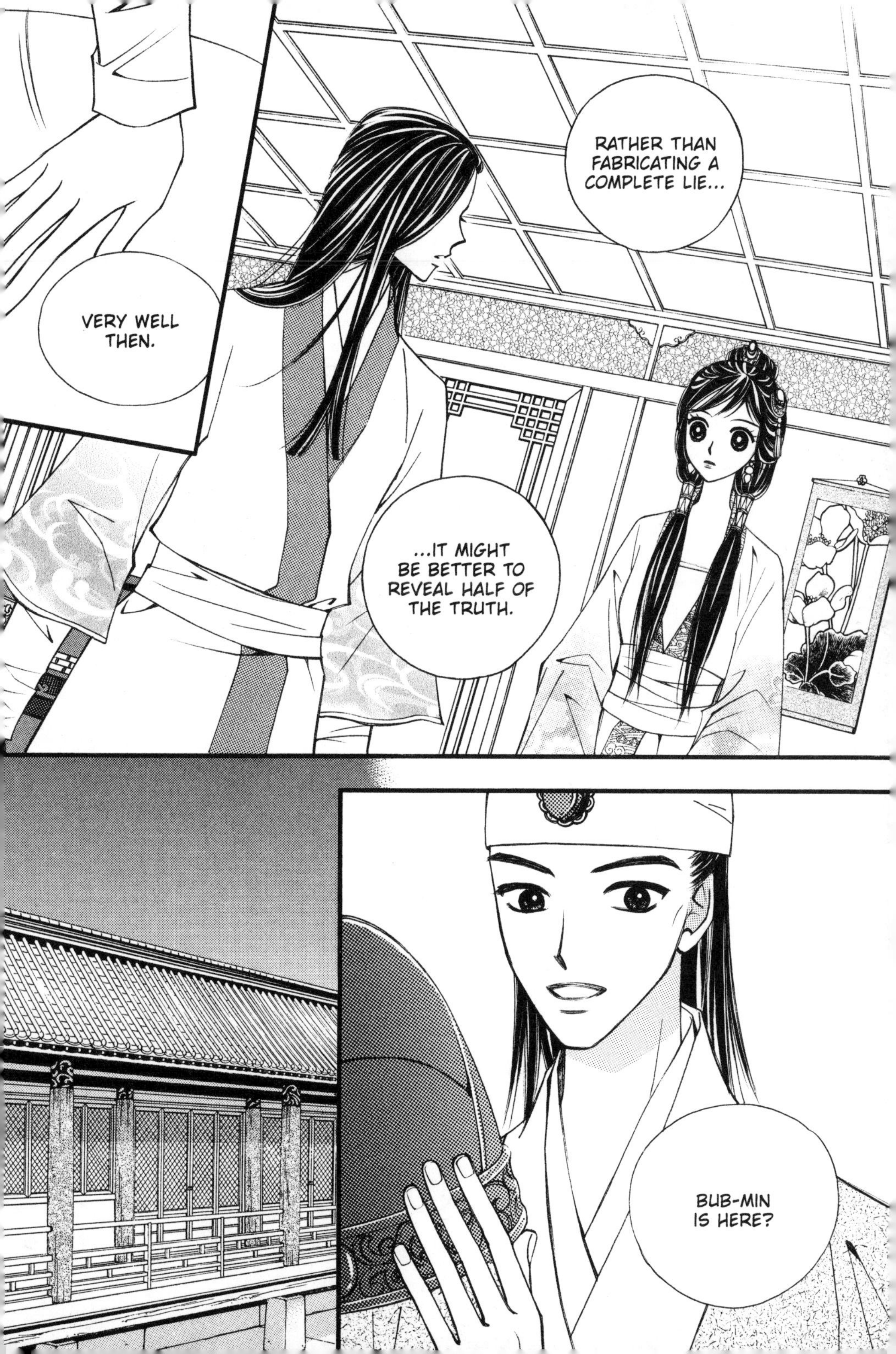
VERY WELL THEN.
RATHER THAN FABRICATING A COMPLETE LIE...
...IT MIGHT BE BETTER TO REVEAL HALF OF THE TRUTH.
BUB-MIN IS HERE?

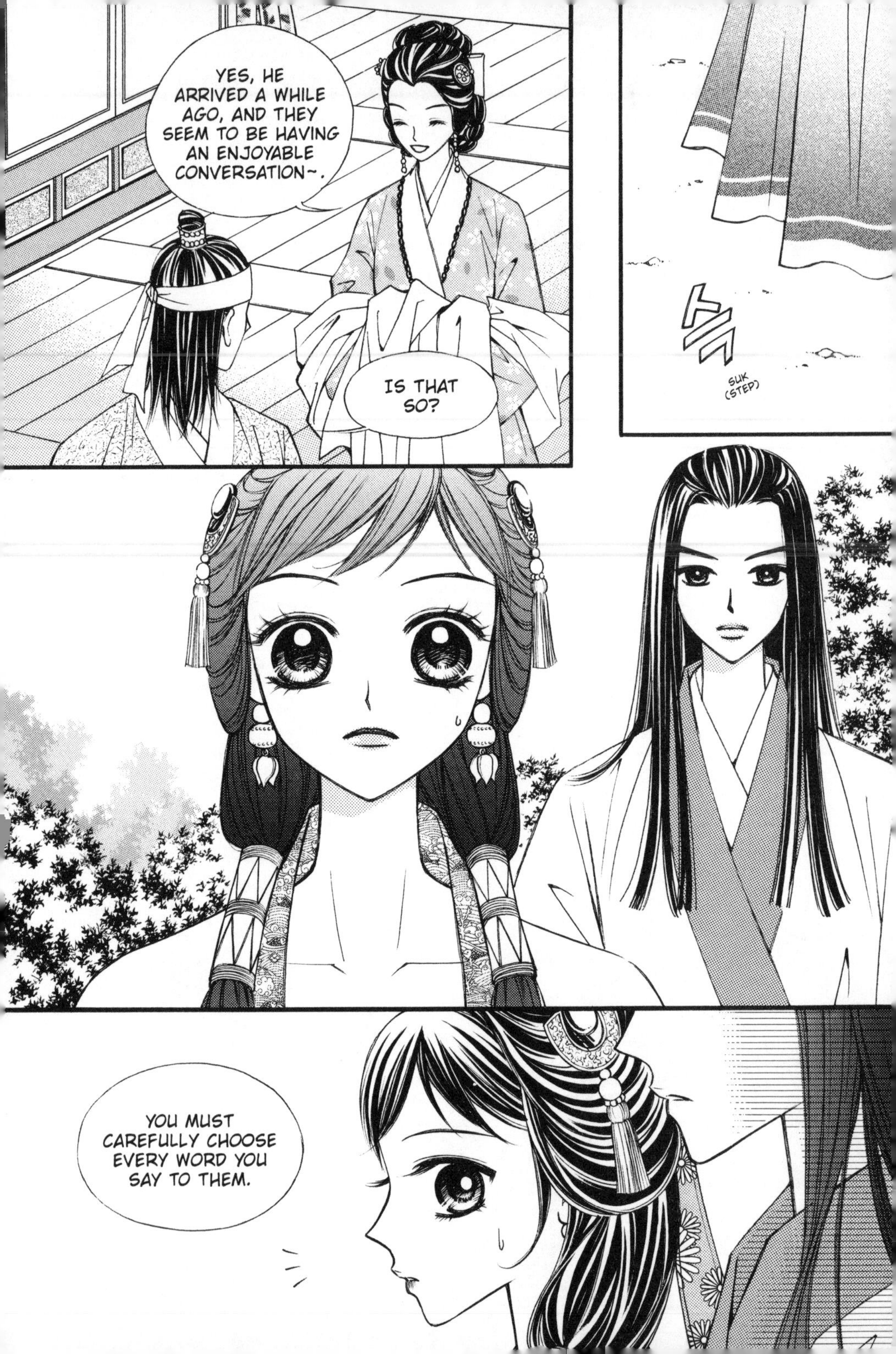
YES, HE ARRIVED A WHILE AGO, AND THEY SEEM TO BE HAVING AN ENJOYABLE CONVERSATION~.
IS THAT SO?
SUK (STEP)
YOU MUST CAREFULLY CHOOSE EVERY WORD YOU SAY TO THEM.

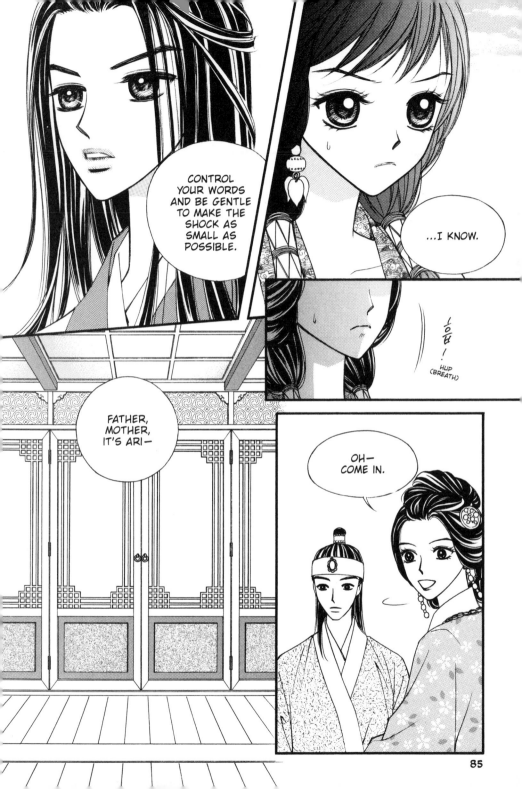

CONTROL YOUR WORDS AND BE GENTLE TO MAKE THE SHOCK AS SMALL AS POSSIBLE.

...I KNOW.

ㅎㅂ
!
HUP (BREATH)

FATHER, MOTHER, IT'S ARI—

OH— COME IN.

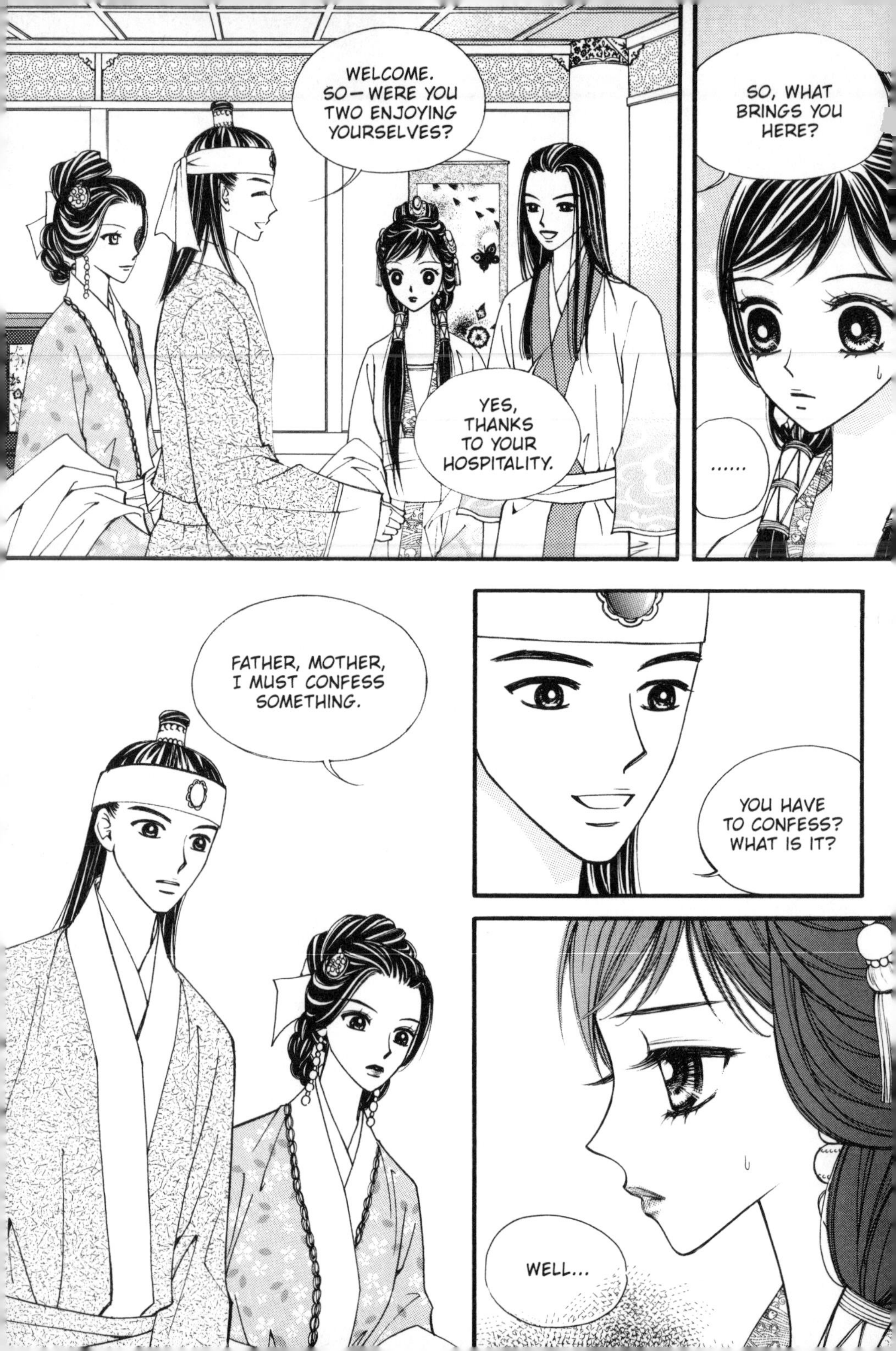
WELCOME. SO—WERE YOU TWO ENJOYING YOURSELVES?
YES, THANKS TO YOUR HOSPITALITY.
SO, WHAT BRINGS YOU HERE?
......
FATHER, MOTHER, I MUST CONFESS SOMETHING.
YOU HAVE TO CONFESS? WHAT IS IT?
WELL...

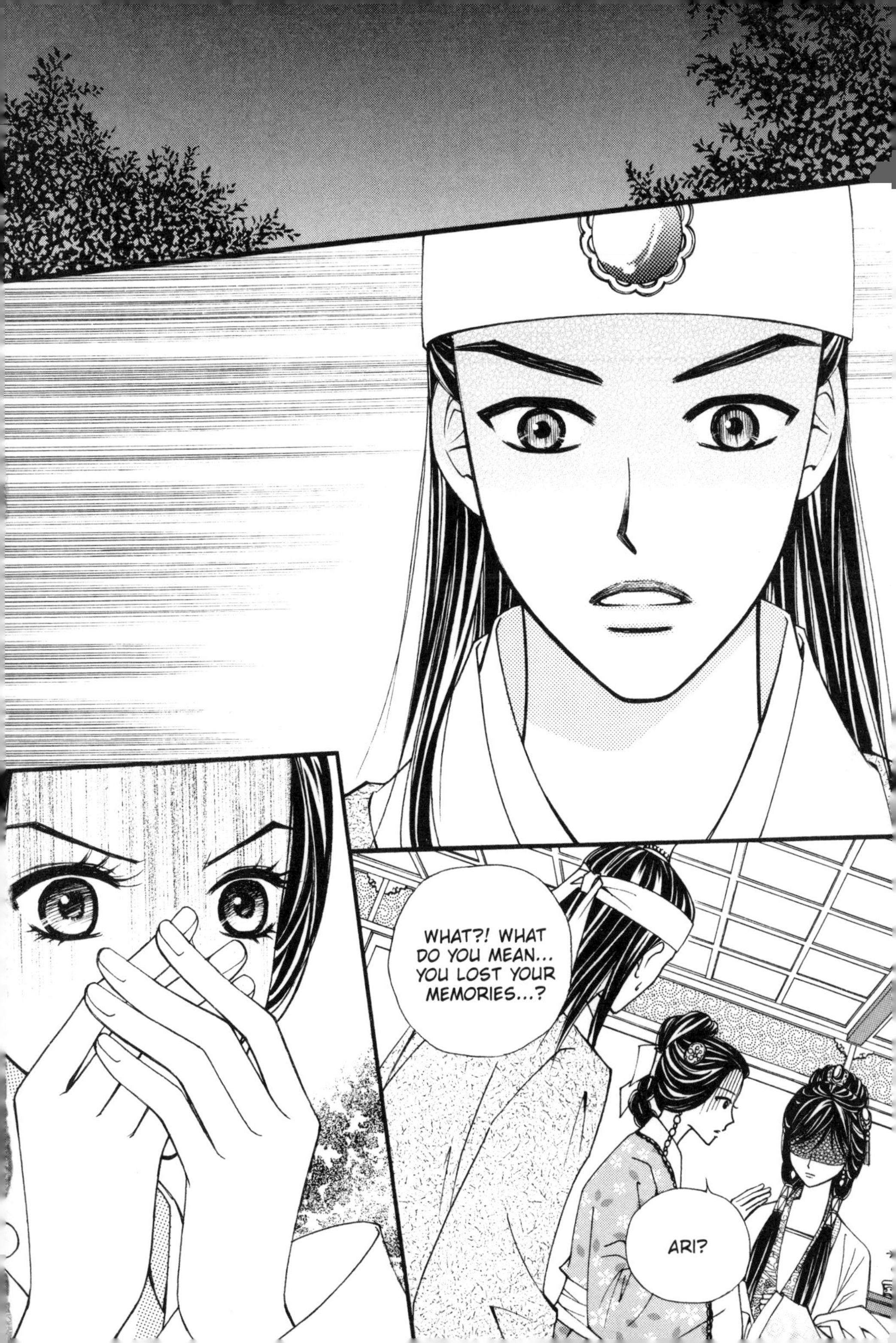
WHAT?! WHAT DO YOU MEAN... YOU LOST YOUR MEMORIES...?
ARI?

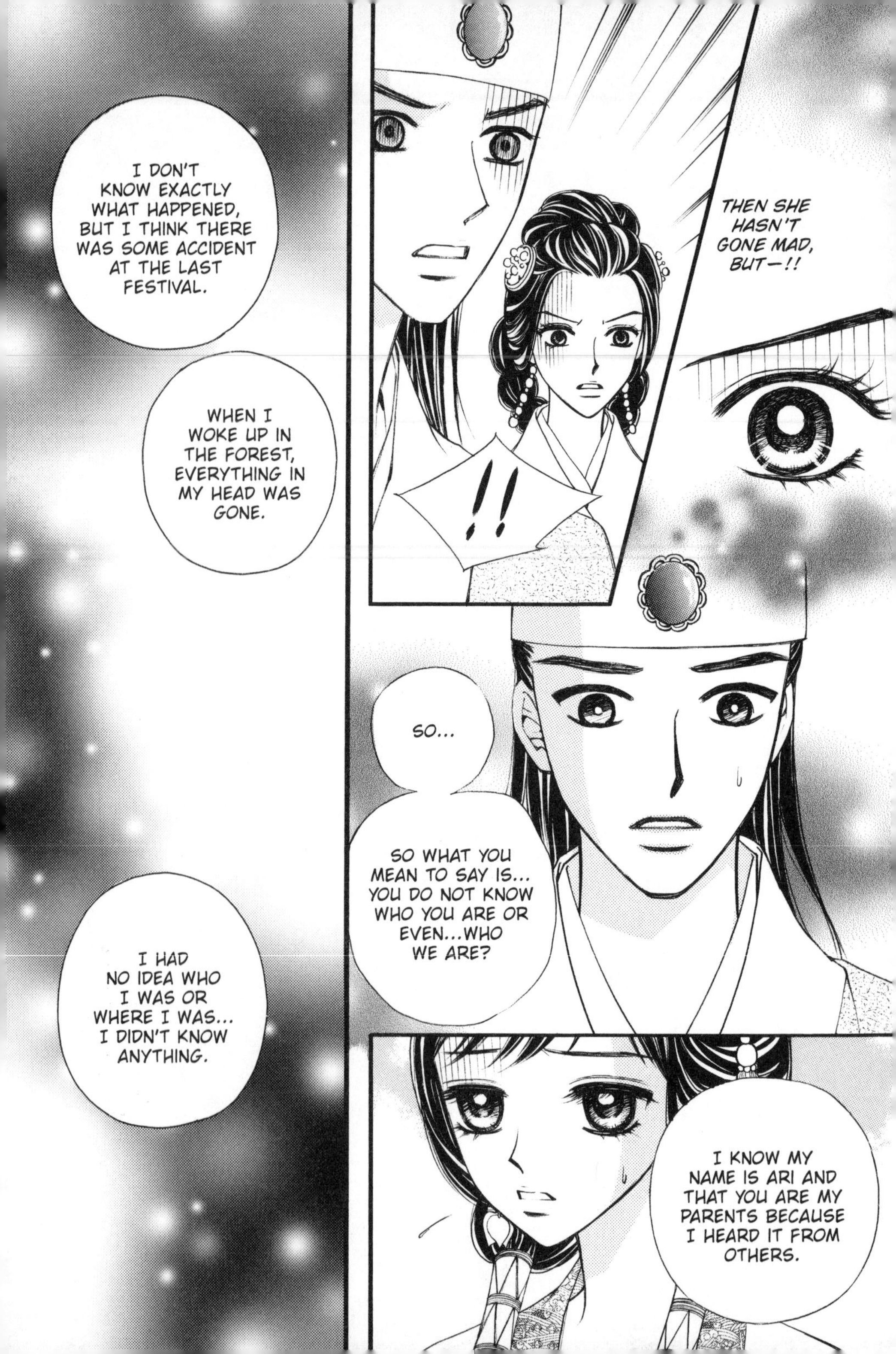
I DON'T KNOW EXACTLY WHAT HAPPENED, BUT I THINK THERE WAS SOME ACCIDENT AT THE LAST FESTIVAL.
WHEN I WOKE UP IN THE FOREST, EVERYTHING IN MY HEAD WAS GONE.
I HAD NO IDEA WHO I WAS OR WHERE I WAS... I DIDN'T KNOW ANYTHING.
THEN SHE HASN'T GONE MAD, BUT—!!
!!
SO...
SO WHAT YOU MEAN TO SAY IS... YOU DO NOT KNOW WHO YOU ARE OR EVEN...WHO WE ARE?
I KNOW MY NAME IS ARI AND THAT YOU ARE MY PARENTS BECAUSE I HEARD IT FROM OTHERS.

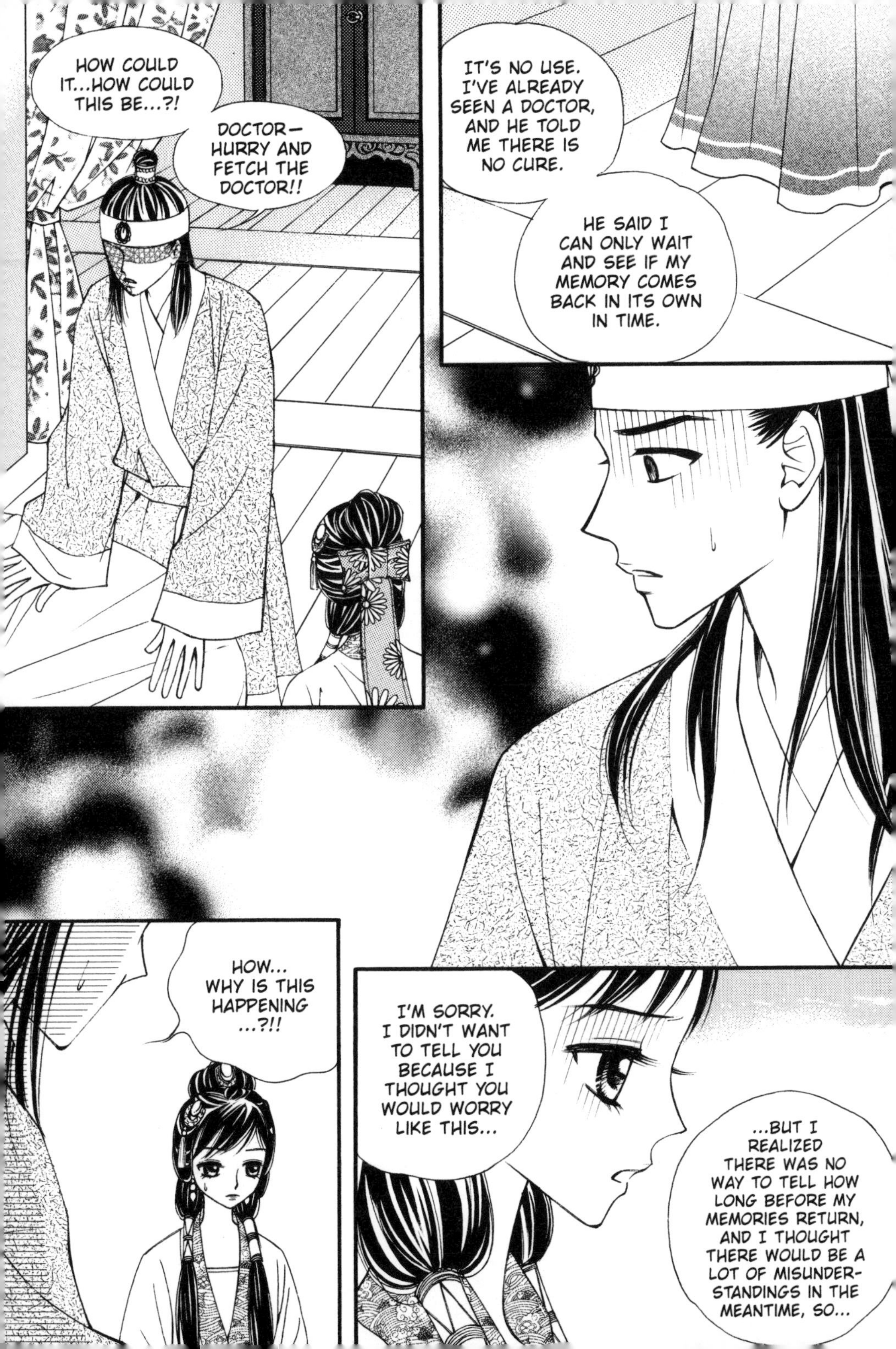
HOW COULD IT...HOW COULD THIS BE...?!
DOCTOR—HURRY AND FETCH THE DOCTOR!!
IT'S NO USE. I'VE ALREADY SEEN A DOCTOR, AND HE TOLD ME THERE IS NO CURE.
HE SAID I CAN ONLY WAIT AND SEE IF MY MEMORY COMES BACK IN ITS OWN IN TIME.
HOW... WHY IS THIS HAPPENING ...?!!
I'M SORRY. I DIDN'T WANT TO TELL YOU BECAUSE I THOUGHT YOU WOULD WORRY LIKE THIS...
...BUT I REALIZED THERE WAS NO WAY TO TELL HOW LONG BEFORE MY MEMORIES RETURN, AND I THOUGHT THERE WOULD BE A LOT OF MISUNDER-STANDINGS IN THE MEANTIME, SO...

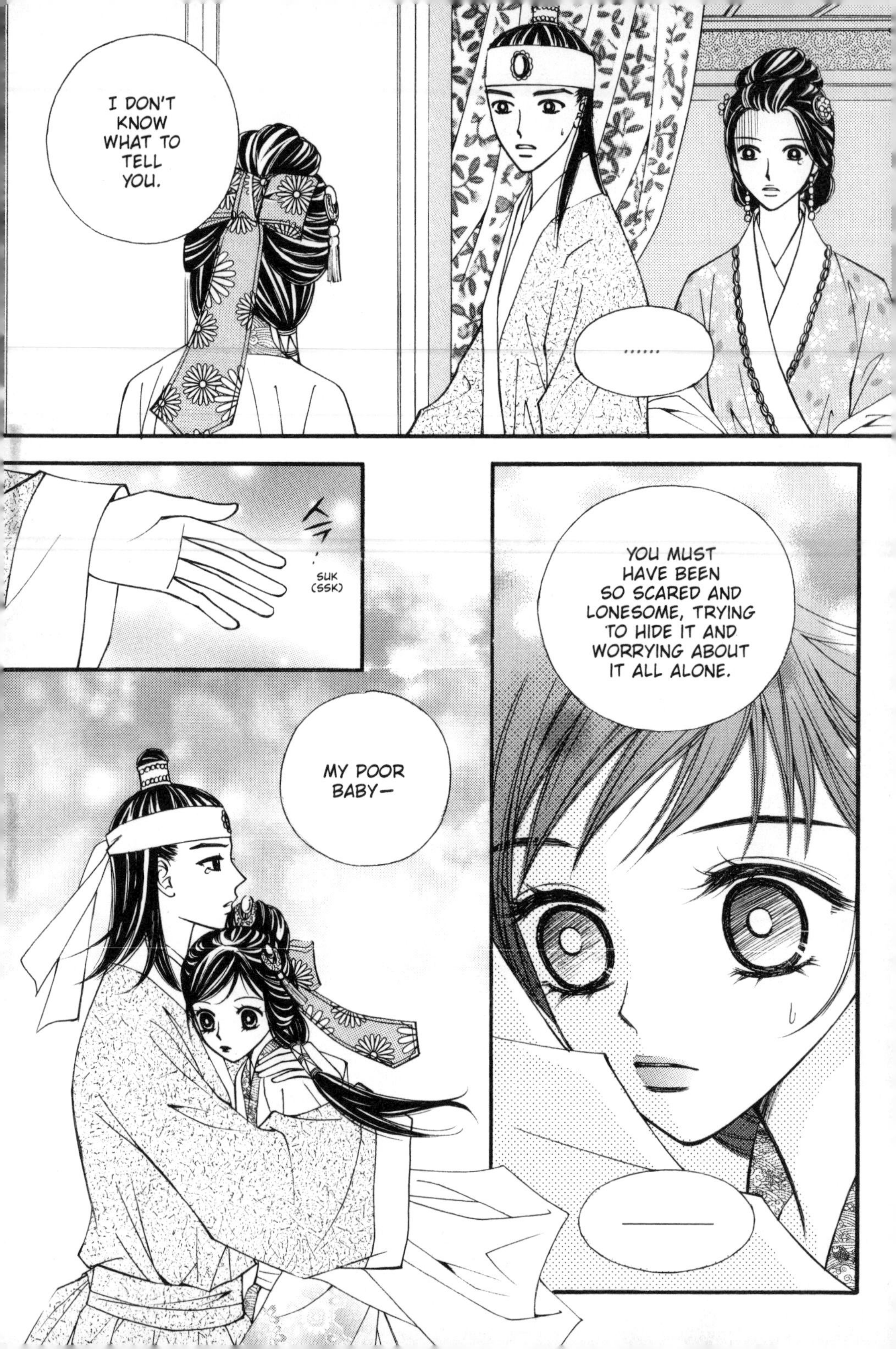
I DON'T KNOW WHAT TO TELL YOU.
......
SUK (SSK)
YOU MUST HAVE BEEN SO SCARED AND LONESOME, TRYING TO HIDE IT AND WORRYING ABOUT IT ALL ALONE.
MY POOR BABY—
———

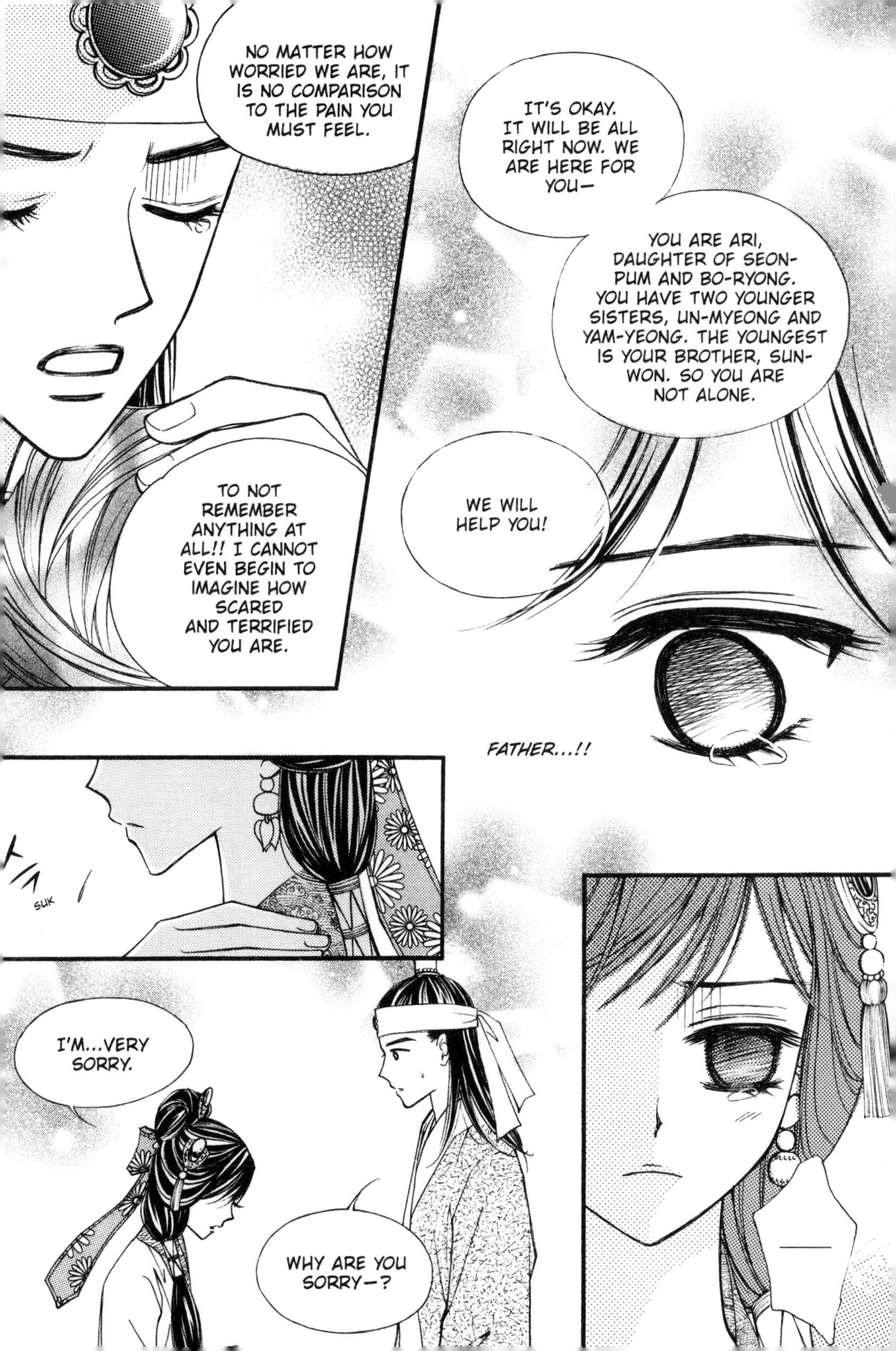
NO MATTER HOW WORRIED WE ARE, IT IS NO COMPARISON TO THE PAIN YOU MUST FEEL.
TO NOT REMEMBER ANYTHING AT ALL!! I CANNOT EVEN BEGIN TO IMAGINE HOW SCARED AND TERRIFIED YOU ARE.
IT'S OKAY. IT WILL BE ALL RIGHT NOW. WE ARE HERE FOR YOU—
YOU ARE ARI, DAUGHTER OF SEON-PUM AND BO-RYONG. YOU HAVE TWO YOUNGER SISTERS, UN-MYEONG AND YAM-YEONG. THE YOUNGEST IS YOUR BROTHER, SUN-WON. SO YOU ARE NOT ALONE.
WE WILL HELP YOU!
FATHER...!!
SUK
I'M...VERY SORRY.
WHY ARE YOU SORRY—?

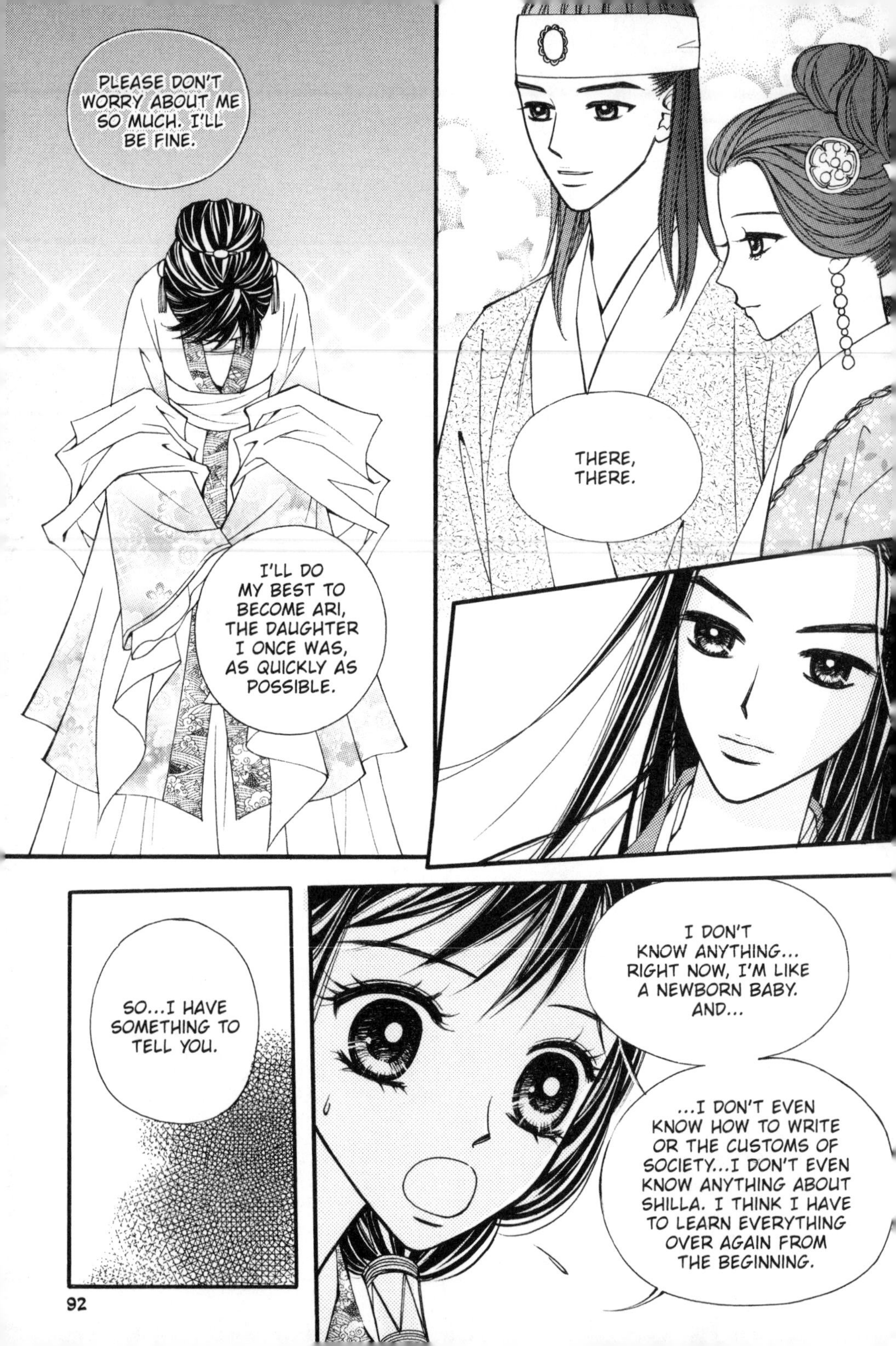
PLEASE DON'T WORRY ABOUT ME SO MUCH. I'LL BE FINE.
I'LL DO MY BEST TO BECOME ARI, THE DAUGHTER I ONCE WAS, AS QUICKLY AS POSSIBLE.
THERE, THERE.
SO...I HAVE SOMETHING TO TELL YOU.
I DON'T KNOW ANYTHING... RIGHT NOW, I'M LIKE A NEWBORN BABY. AND...
...I DON'T EVEN KNOW HOW TO WRITE OR THE CUSTOMS OF SOCIETY...I DON'T EVEN KNOW ANYTHING ABOUT SHILLA. I THINK I HAVE TO LEARN EVERYTHING OVER AGAIN FROM THE BEGINNING.

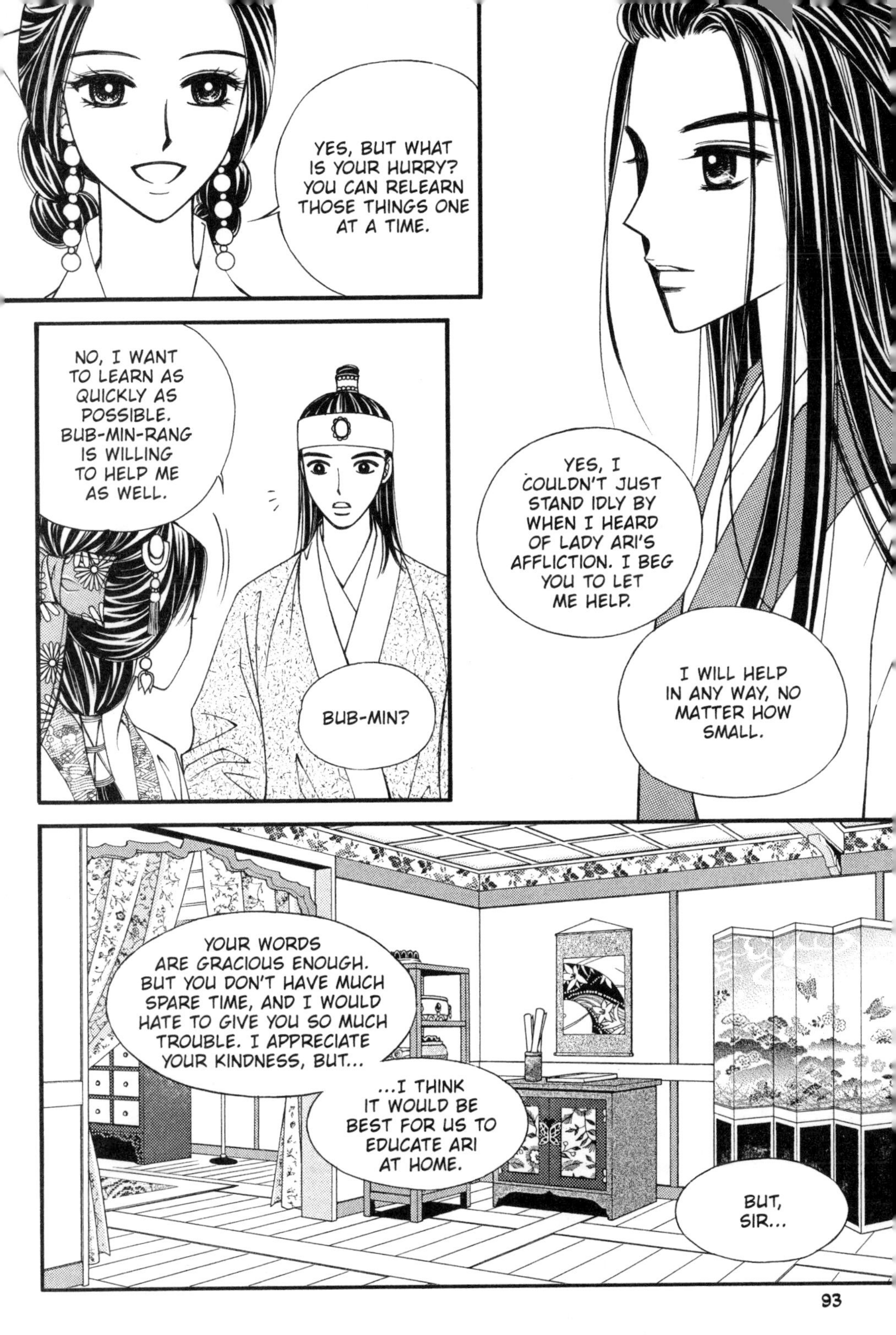
YES, BUT WHAT IS YOUR HURRY? YOU CAN RELEARN THOSE THINGS ONE AT A TIME.
NO, I WANT TO LEARN AS QUICKLY AS POSSIBLE. BUB-MIN-RANG IS WILLING TO HELP ME AS WELL.
BUB-MIN?
YES, I COULDN'T JUST STAND IDLY BY WHEN I HEARD OF LADY ARI'S AFFLICTION. I BEG YOU TO LET ME HELP.
I WILL HELP IN ANY WAY, NO MATTER HOW SMALL.
YOUR WORDS ARE GRACIOUS ENOUGH. BUT YOU DON'T HAVE MUCH SPARE TIME, AND I WOULD HATE TO GIVE YOU SO MUCH TROUBLE. I APPRECIATE YOUR KINDNESS, BUT...
...I THINK IT WOULD BE BEST FOR US TO EDUCATE ARI AT HOME.
BUT, SIR...

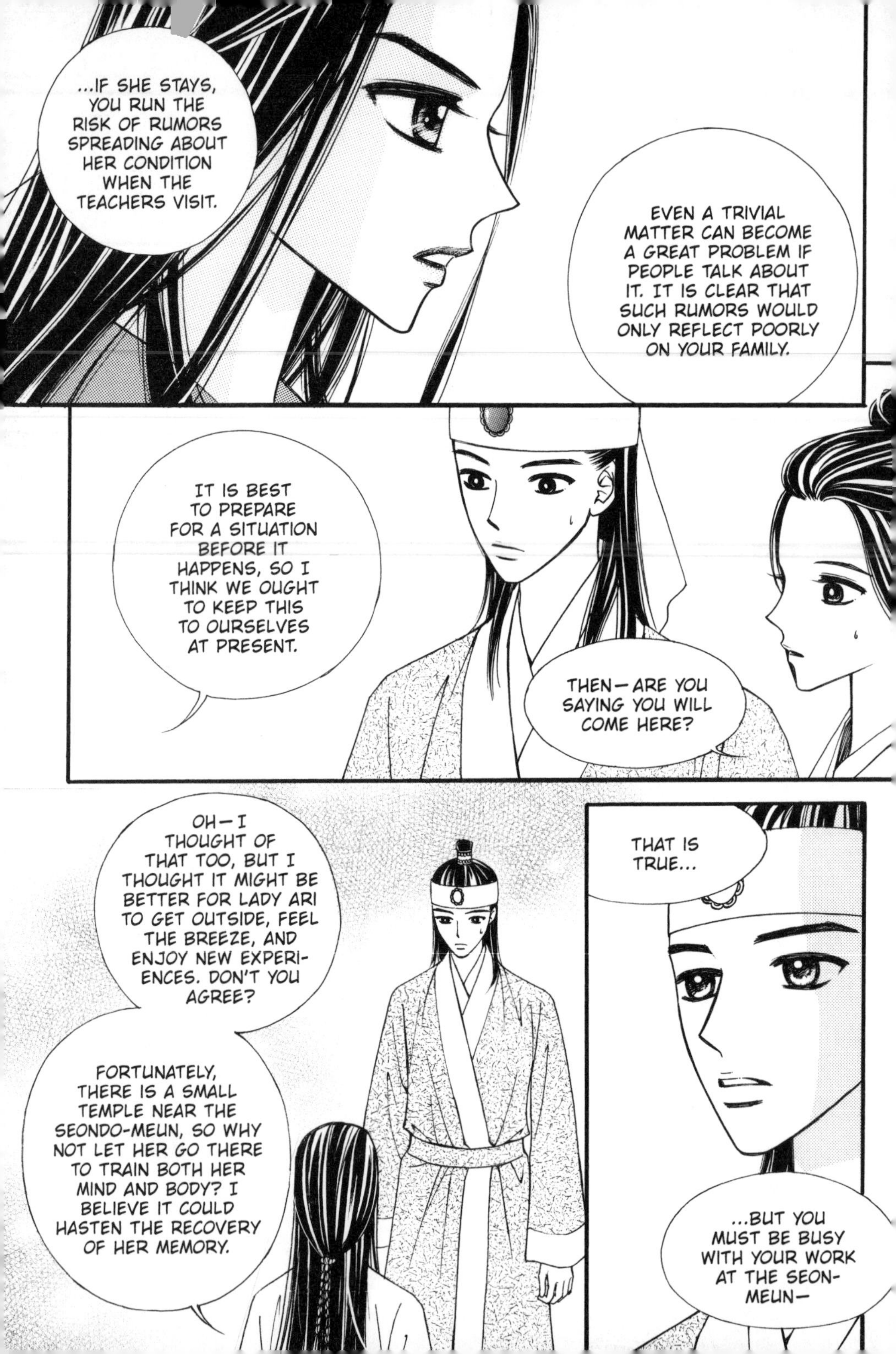
...IF SHE STAYS, YOU RUN THE RISK OF RUMORS SPREADING ABOUT HER CONDITION WHEN THE TEACHERS VISIT.
EVEN A TRIVIAL MATTER CAN BECOME A GREAT PROBLEM IF PEOPLE TALK ABOUT IT. IT IS CLEAR THAT SUCH RUMORS WOULD ONLY REFLECT POORLY ON YOUR FAMILY.
IT IS BEST TO PREPARE FOR A SITUATION BEFORE IT HAPPENS, SO I THINK WE OUGHT TO KEEP THIS TO OURSELVES AT PRESENT.
THEN—ARE YOU SAYING YOU WILL COME HERE?
OH—I THOUGHT OF THAT TOO, BUT I THOUGHT IT MIGHT BE BETTER FOR LADY ARI TO GET OUTSIDE, FEEL THE BREEZE, AND ENJOY NEW EXPERI-ENCES. DON'T YOU AGREE?
FORTUNATELY, THERE IS A SMALL TEMPLE NEAR THE SEONDO-MEUN, SO WHY NOT LET HER GO THERE TO TRAIN BOTH HER MIND AND BODY? I BELIEVE IT COULD HASTEN THE RECOVERY OF HER MEMORY.
THAT IS TRUE...
...BUT YOU MUST BE BUSY WITH YOUR WORK AT THE SEON-MEUN—

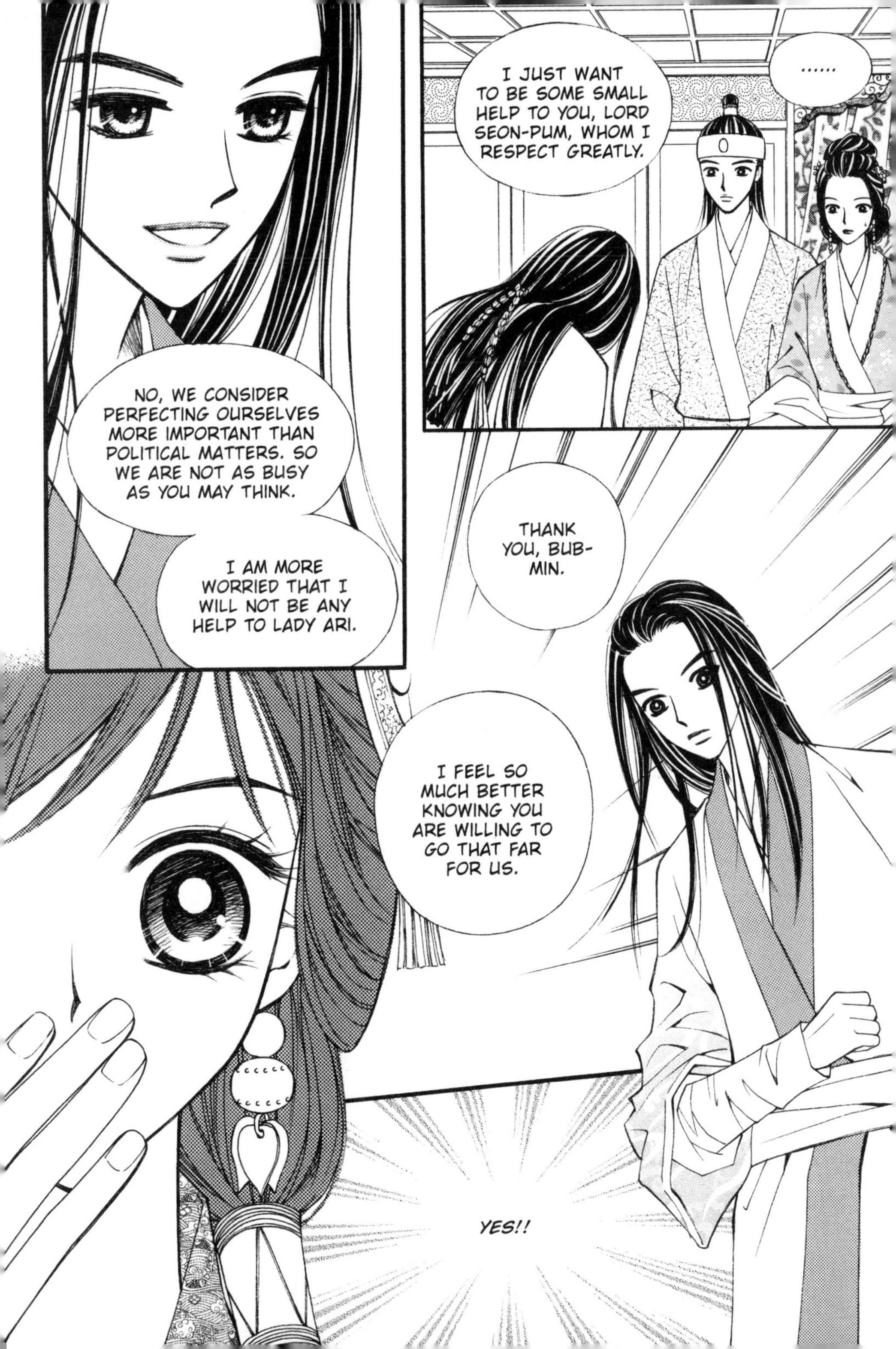
NO, WE CONSIDER PERFECTING OURSELVES MORE IMPORTANT THAN POLITICAL MATTERS. SO WE ARE NOT AS BUSY AS YOU MAY THINK.
I AM MORE WORRIED THAT I WILL NOT BE ANY HELP TO LADY ARI.
I JUST WANT TO BE SOME SMALL HELP TO YOU, LORD SEON-PUM, WHOM I RESPECT GREATLY.
......
THANK YOU, BUB-MIN.
I FEEL SO MUCH BETTER KNOWING YOU ARE WILLING TO GO THAT FAR FOR US.
YES!!

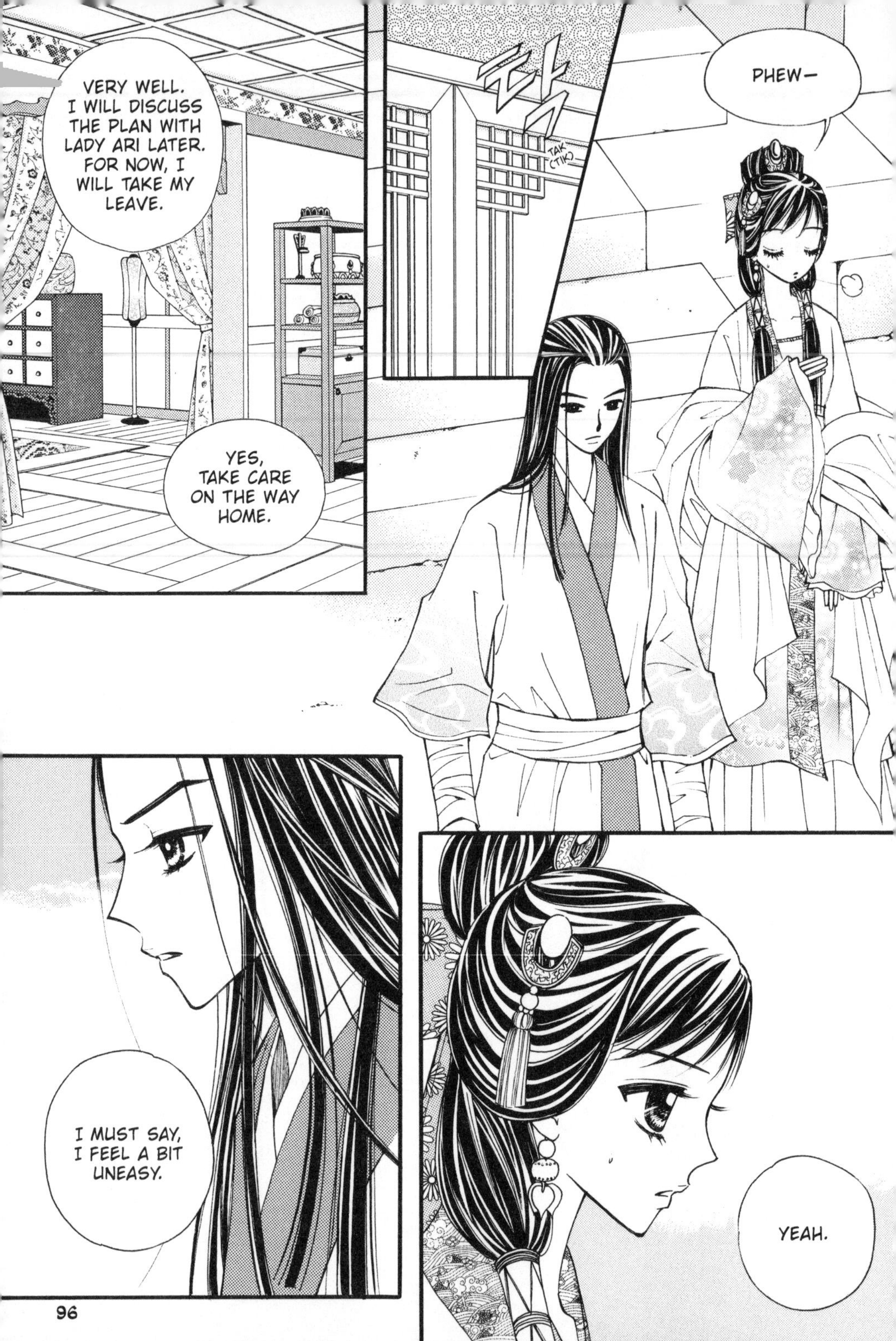

VERY WELL. I WILL DISCUSS THE PLAN WITH LADY ARI LATER. FOR NOW, I WILL TAKE MY LEAVE.
YES, TAKE CARE ON THE WAY HOME.
TAK (TIK)
PHEW—
I MUST SAY, I FEEL A BIT UNEASY.
YEAH.

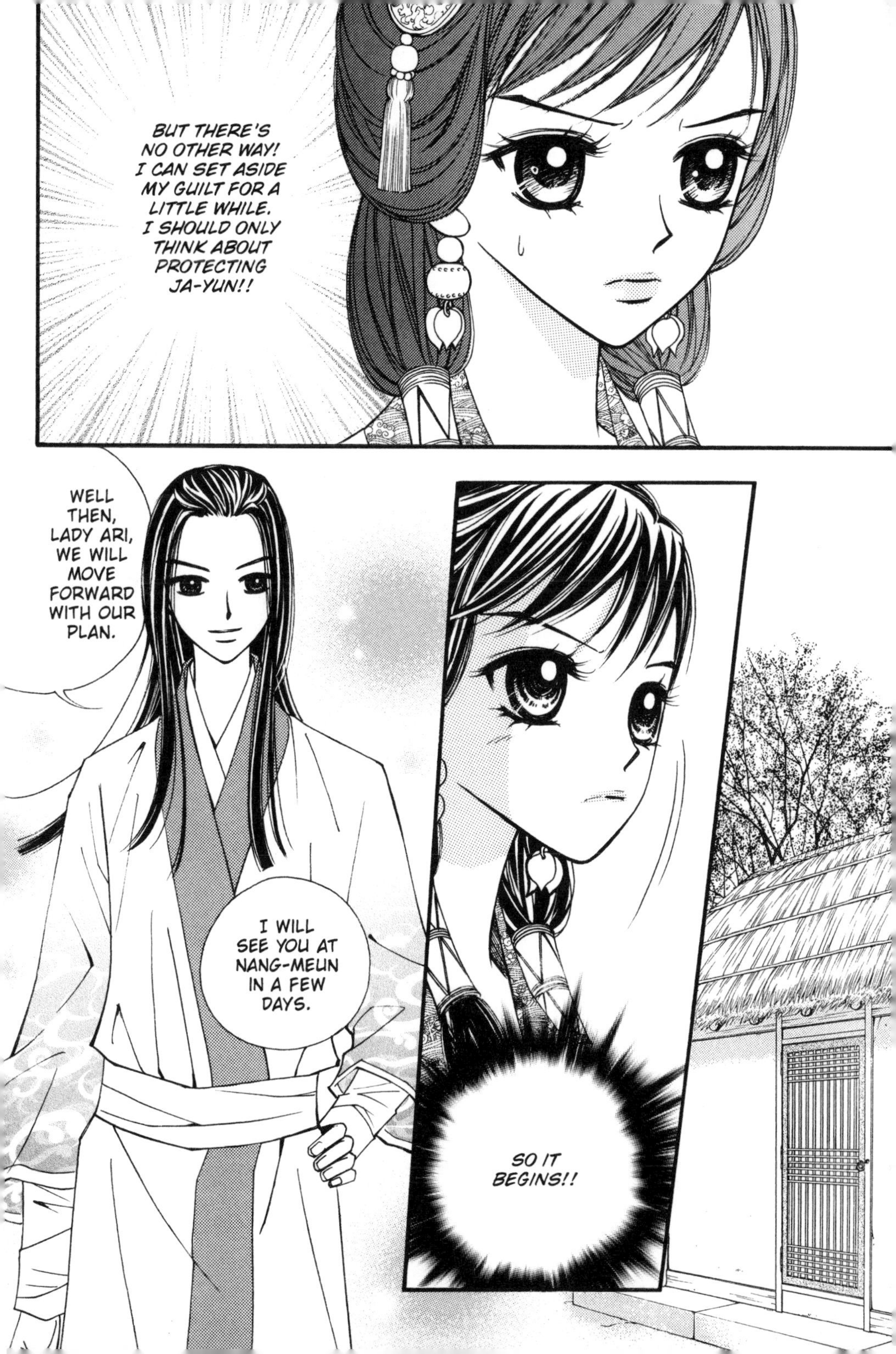
BUT THERE'S NO OTHER WAY! I CAN SET ASIDE MY GUILT FOR A LITTLE WHILE. I SHOULD ONLY THINK ABOUT PROTECTING JA-YUN!!
WELL THEN, LADY ARI, WE WILL MOVE FORWARD WITH OUR PLAN.
I WILL SEE YOU AT NANG-MEUN IN A FEW DAYS.
SO IT BEGINS!!

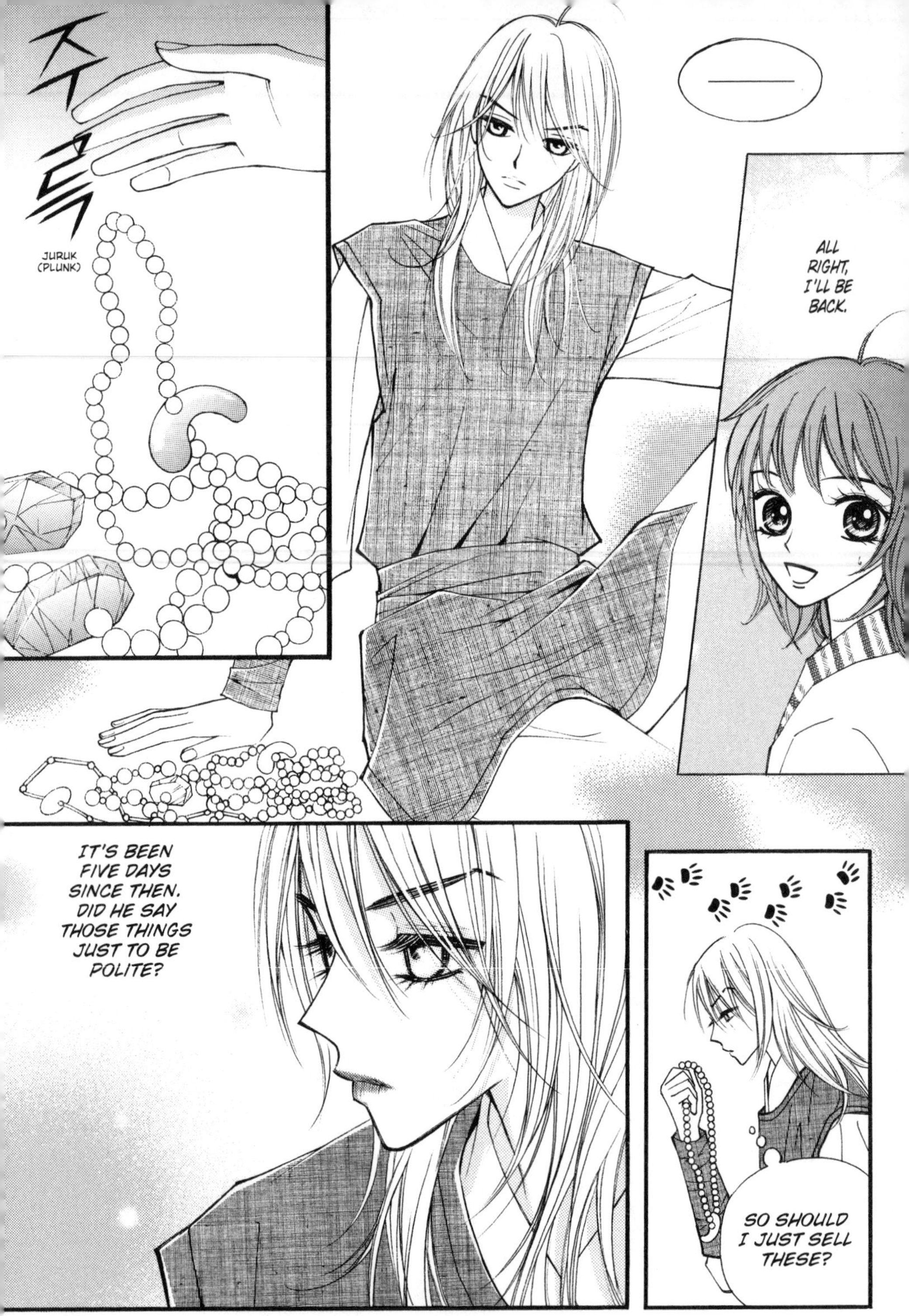
JURUK
(PLUNK)
——
ALL RIGHT, I'LL BE BACK.
IT'S BEEN FIVE DAYS SINCE THEN. DID HE SAY THOSE THINGS JUST TO BE POLITE?
SO SHOULD I JUST SELL THESE?

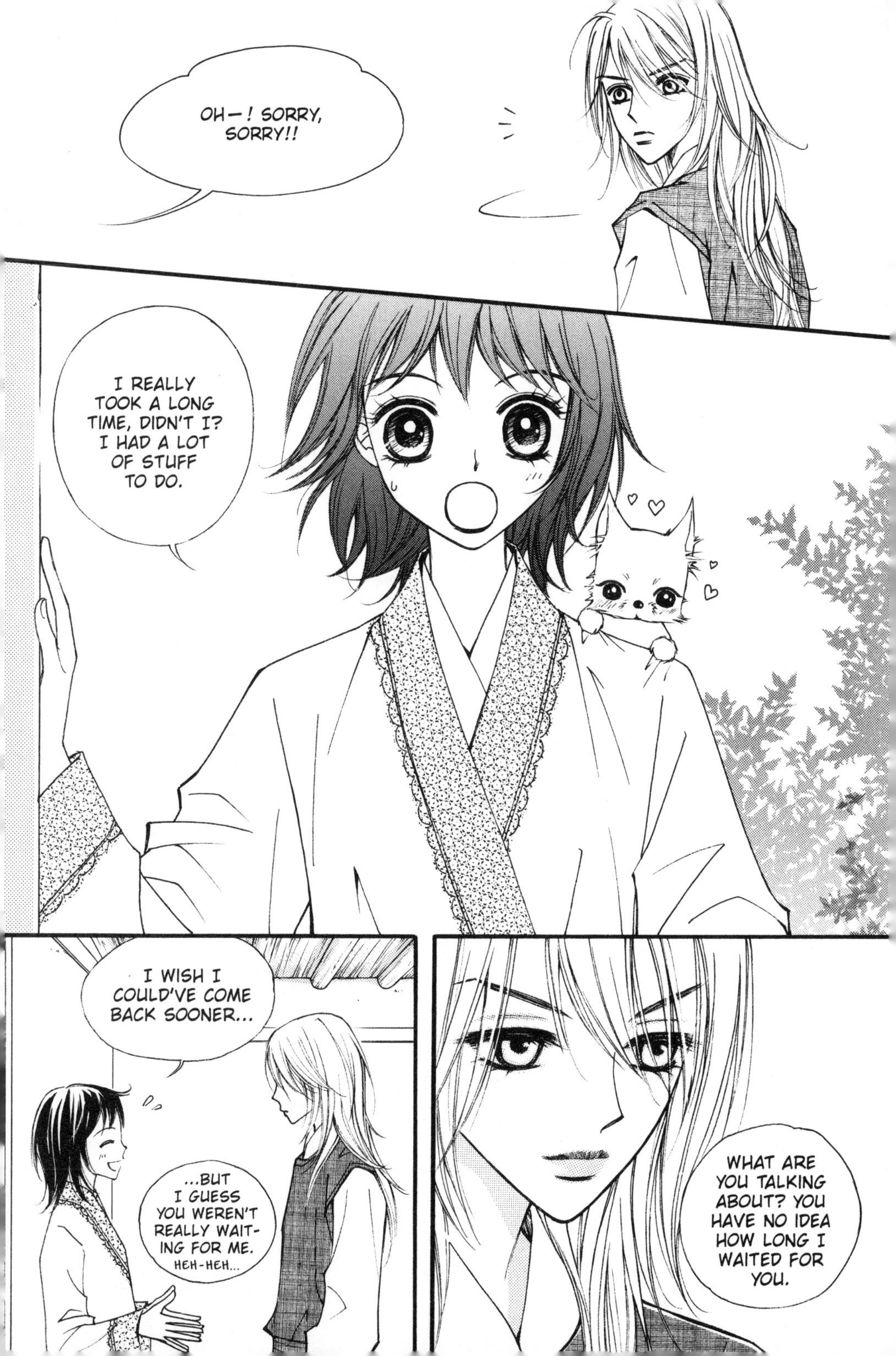
OH—! SORRY, SORRY!!
I REALLY TOOK A LONG TIME, DIDN'T I? I HAD A LOT OF STUFF TO DO.
I WISH I COULD'VE COME BACK SOONER...
...BUT I GUESS YOU WEREN'T REALLY WAIT-ING FOR ME.
HEH-HEH...
WHAT ARE YOU TALKING ABOUT? YOU HAVE NO IDEA HOW LONG I WAITED FOR YOU.

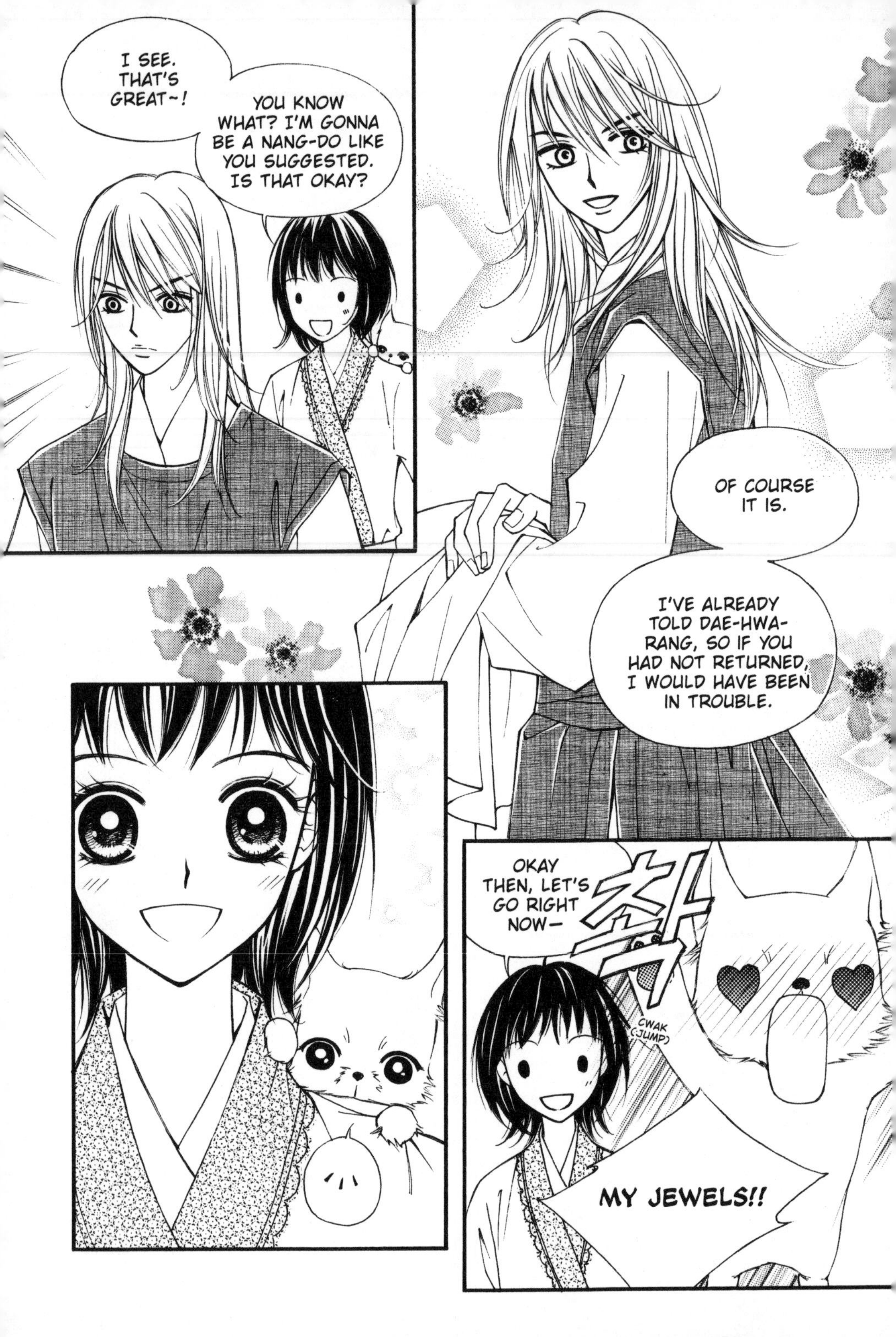
I SEE. THAT'S GREAT~!
YOU KNOW WHAT? I'M GONNA BE A NANG-DO LIKE YOU SUGGESTED. IS THAT OKAY?
OF COURSE IT IS.
I'VE ALREADY TOLD DAE-HWA-RANG, SO IF YOU HAD NOT RETURNED, I WOULD HAVE BEEN IN TROUBLE.
OKAY THEN, LET'S GO RIGHT NOW—
CWAK (JUMP)
MY JEWELS!!

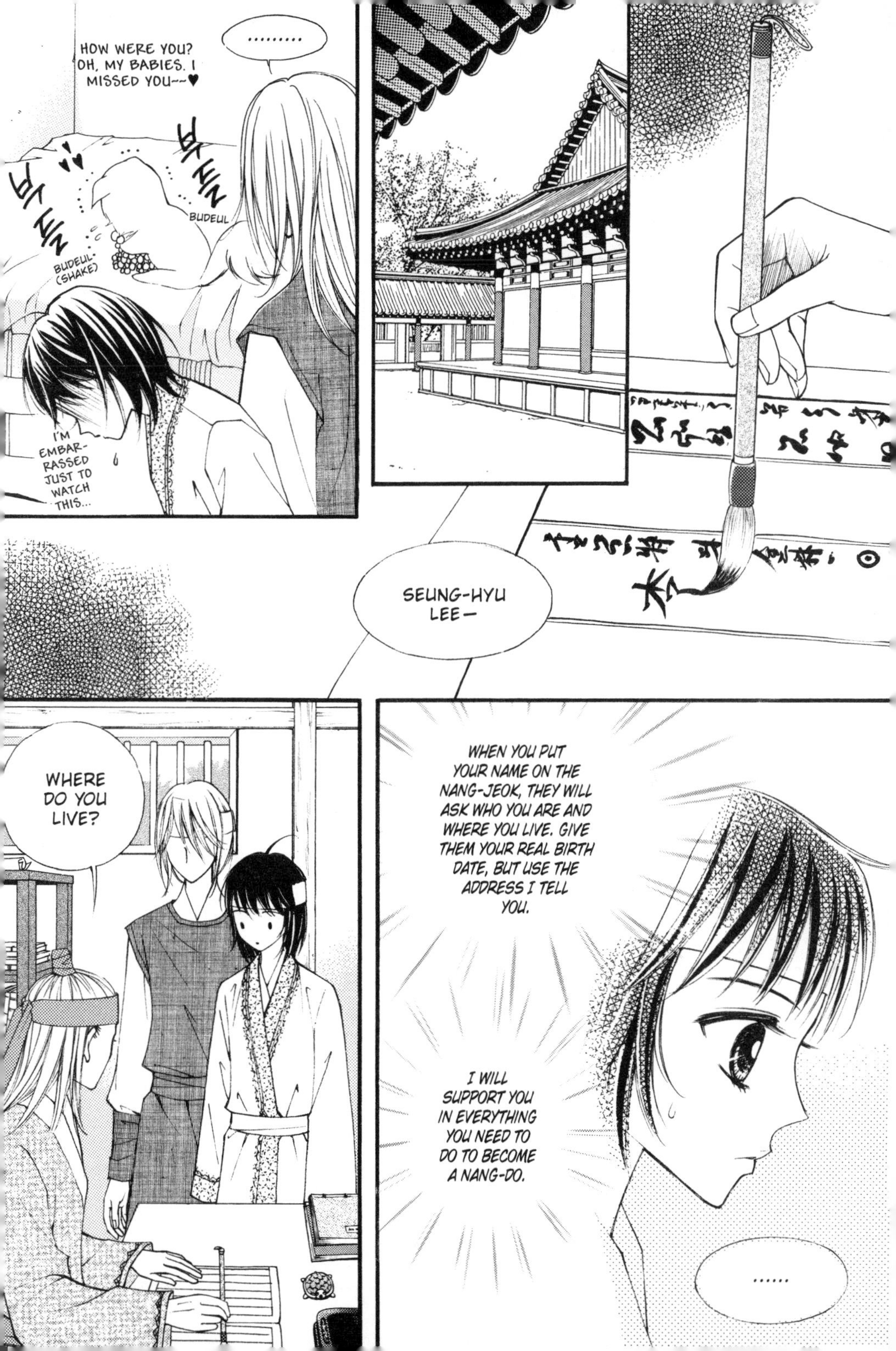
HOW WERE YOU? OH, MY BABIES. I MISSED YOU~~♥
....
BUDEUL
BUDEUL- (SHAKE)
I'M EMBARRASSED JUST TO WATCH THIS...
SEUNG-HYU LEE—
WHERE DO YOU LIVE?
WHEN YOU PUT YOUR NAME ON THE NANG-JEOK, THEY WILL ASK WHO YOU ARE AND WHERE YOU LIVE. GIVE THEM YOUR REAL BIRTH DATE, BUT USE THE ADDRESS I TELL YOU.
I WILL SUPPORT YOU IN EVERYTHING YOU NEED TO DO TO BECOME A NANG-DO.
......

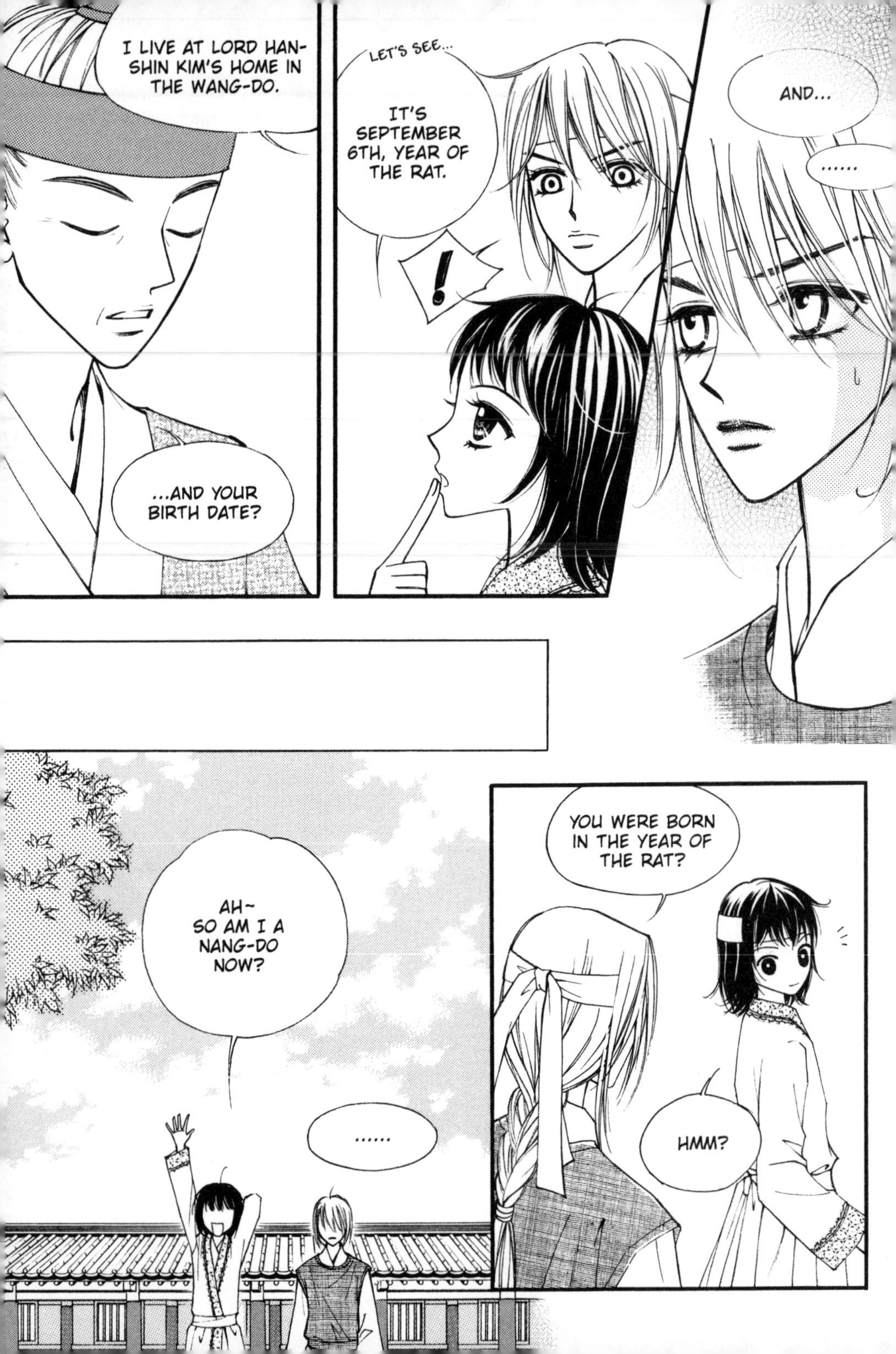
I LIVE AT LORD HAN-SHIN KIM'S HOME IN THE WANG-DO.
...AND YOUR BIRTH DATE?
LET'S SEE...
IT'S SEPTEMBER 6TH, YEAR OF THE RAT.
!
AND...
......
AH~ SO AM I A NANG-DO NOW?
......
YOU WERE BORN IN THE YEAR OF THE RAT?
HMM?

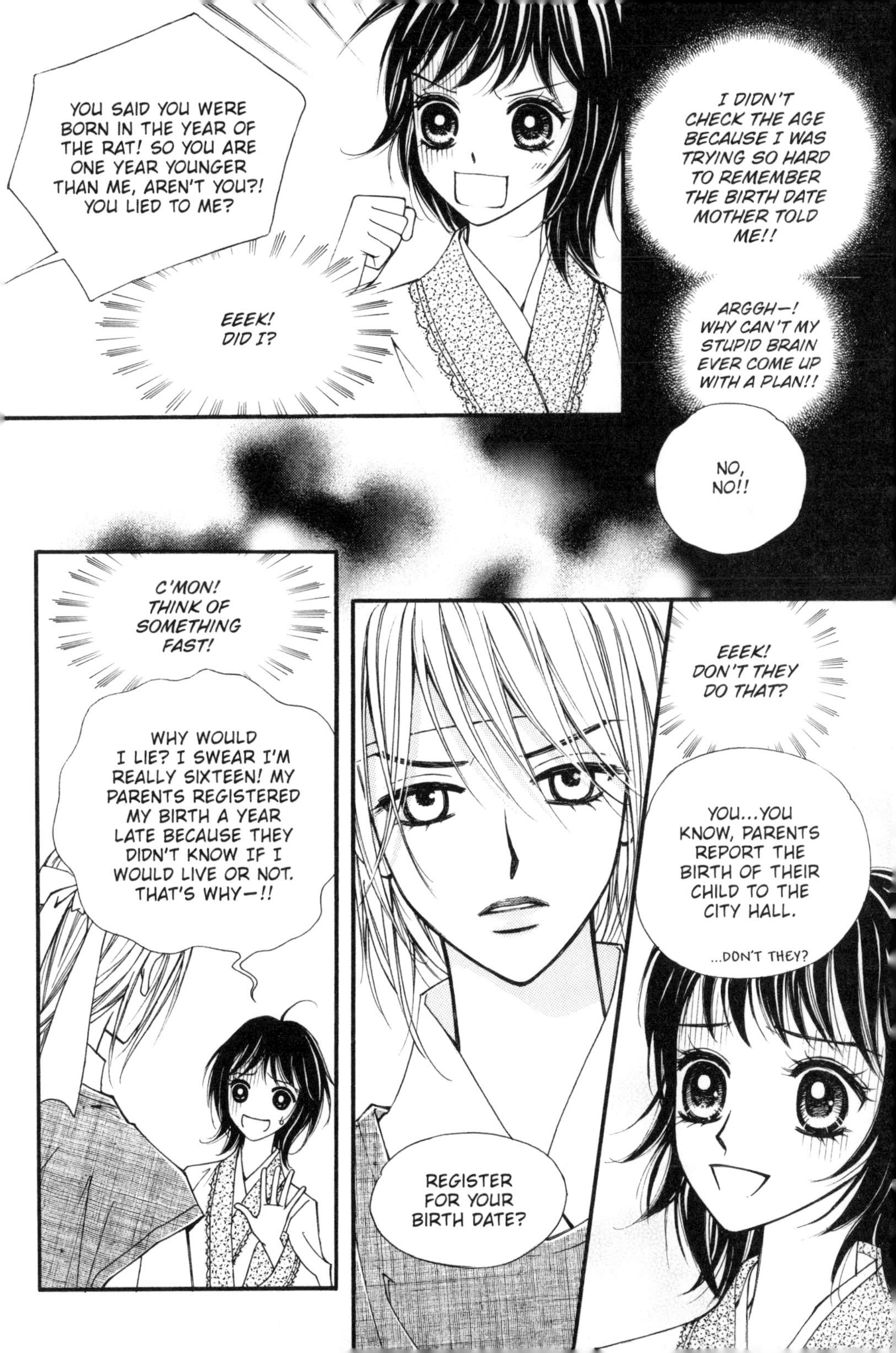
YOU SAID YOU WERE BORN IN THE YEAR OF THE RAT! SO YOU ARE ONE YEAR YOUNGER THAN ME, AREN'T YOU?! YOU LIED TO ME?
EEEK! DID I?
I DIDN'T CHECK THE AGE BECAUSE I WAS TRYING SO HARD TO REMEMBER THE BIRTH DATE MOTHER TOLD ME!!
ARGGH—! WHY CAN'T MY STUPID BRAIN EVER COME UP WITH A PLAN!!
NO, NO!!
C'MON! THINK OF SOMETHING FAST!
WHY WOULD I LIE? I SWEAR I'M REALLY SIXTEEN! MY PARENTS REGISTERED MY BIRTH A YEAR LATE BECAUSE THEY DIDN'T KNOW IF I WOULD LIVE OR NOT. THAT'S WHY—!!
REGISTER FOR YOUR BIRTH DATE?
YOU...YOU KNOW, PARENTS REPORT THE BIRTH OF THEIR CHILD TO THE CITY HALL.
...DON'T THEY?
EEEK! DON'T THEY DO THAT?

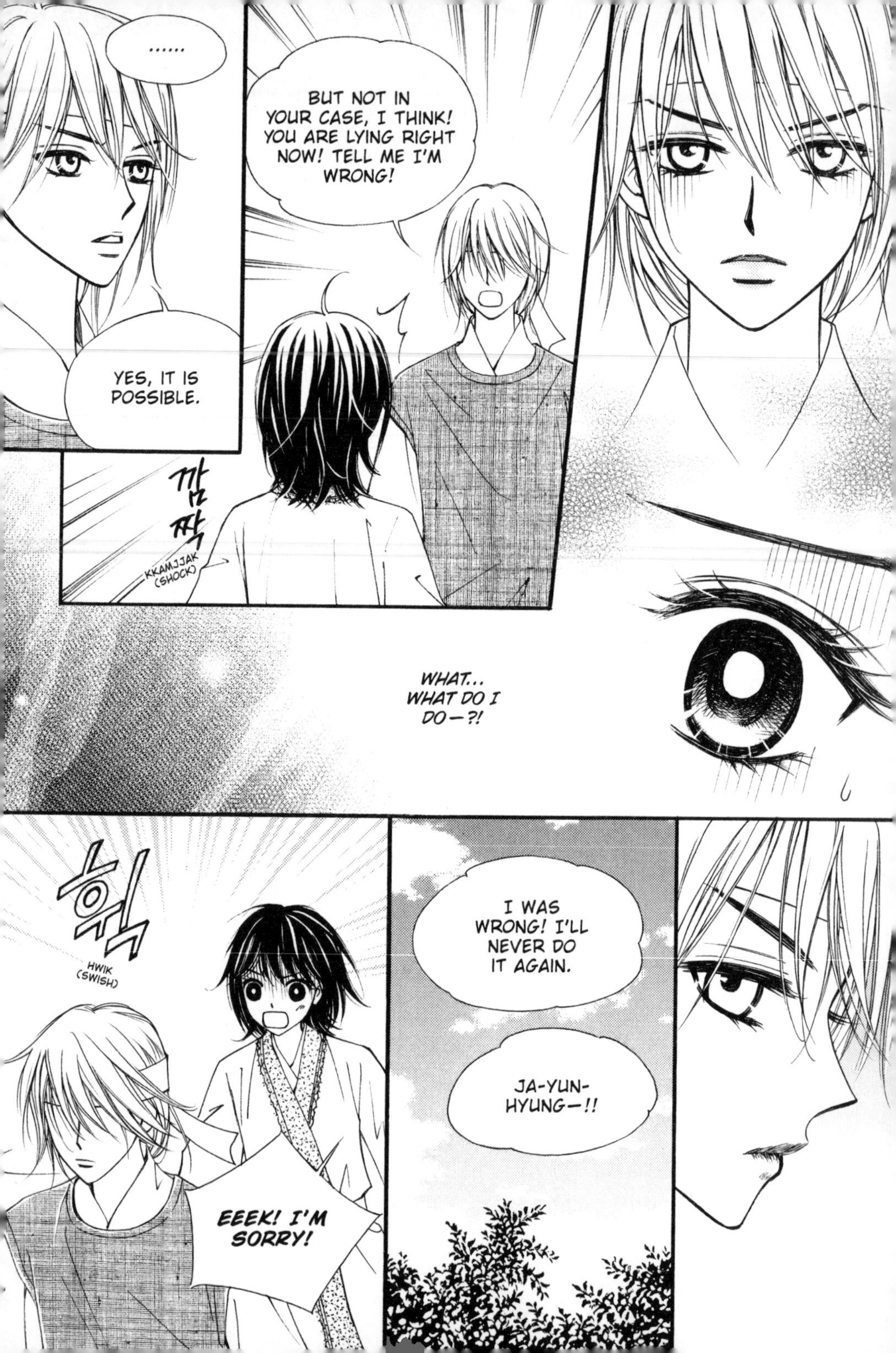
......
YES, IT IS POSSIBLE.
BUT NOT IN YOUR CASE, I THINK! YOU ARE LYING RIGHT NOW! TELL ME I'M WRONG!
깜짝
KKAMJJAK (SHOCK)
WHAT... WHAT DO I DO—?!
휙
HWIK (SWISH)
EEEK! I'M SORRY!
I WAS WRONG! I'LL NEVER DO IT AGAIN.
JA-YUN-HYUNG—!!

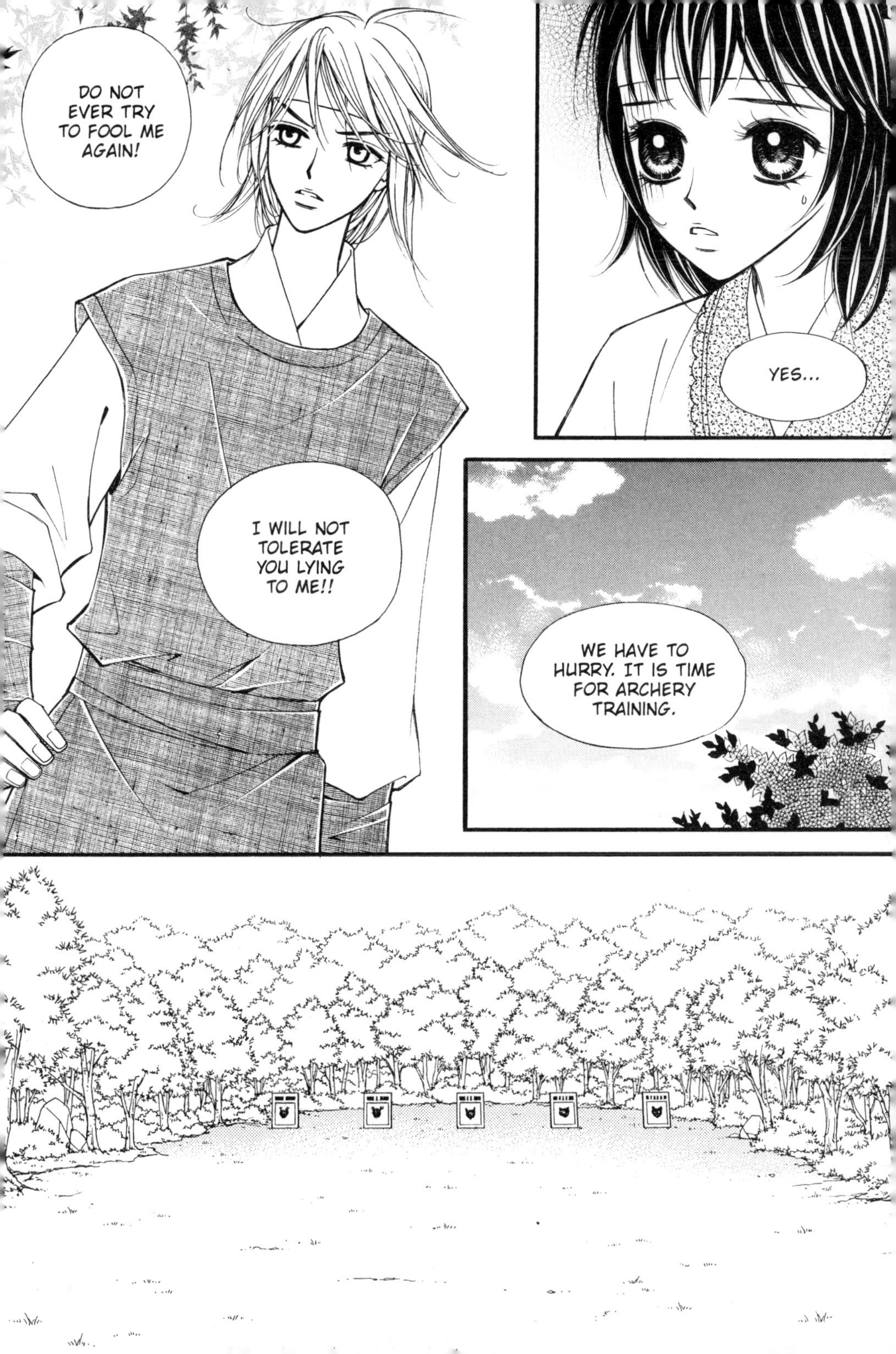
DO NOT EVER TRY TO FOOL ME AGAIN!
YES...
I WILL NOT TOLERATE YOU LYING TO ME!!
WE HAVE TO HURRY. IT IS TIME FOR ARCHERY TRAINING.

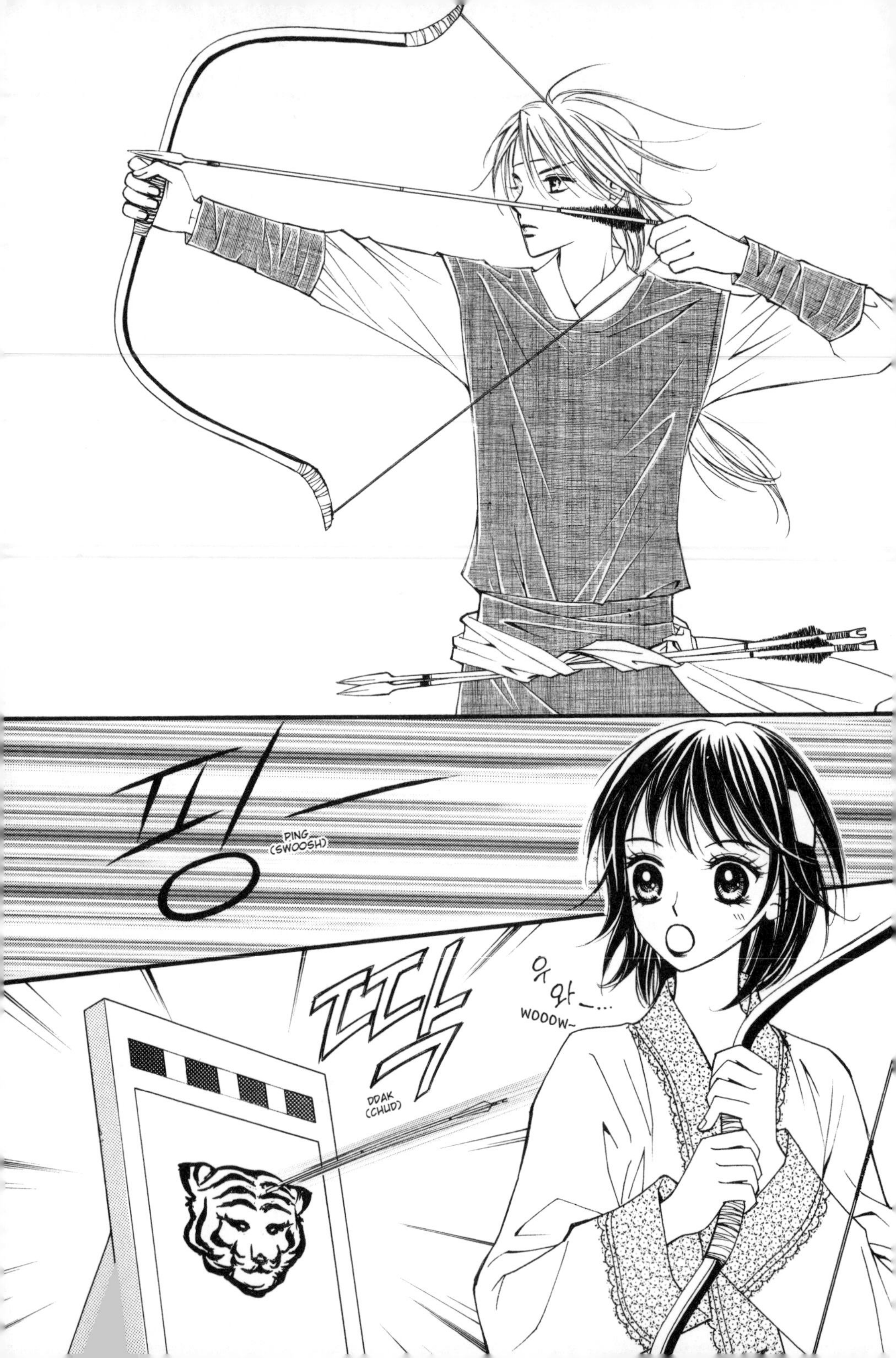

핑
PING (SWOOSH)
딱
DDAK (CHUD)
와아~...
WOOOW~

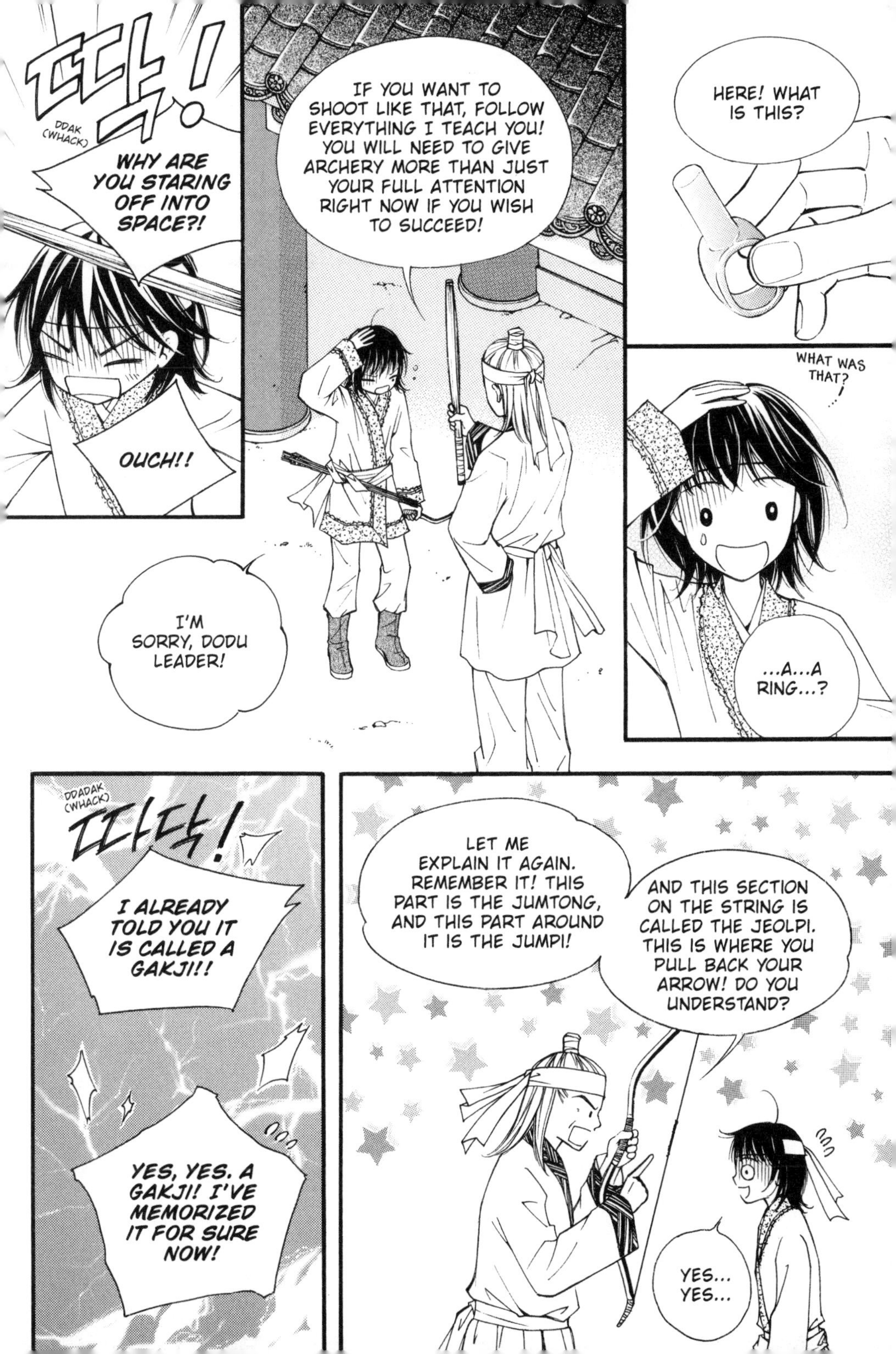
딱!
DDAK (WHACK)
WHY ARE YOU STARING OFF INTO SPACE?!
OUCH!!
IF YOU WANT TO SHOOT LIKE THAT, FOLLOW EVERYTHING I TEACH YOU! YOU WILL NEED TO GIVE ARCHERY MORE THAN JUST YOUR FULL ATTENTION RIGHT NOW IF YOU WISH TO SUCCEED!
I'M SORRY, DODU LEADER!
HERE! WHAT IS THIS?
WHAT WAS THAT?
...A...A RING...?
DDADAK (WHACK)
따닥!
I ALREADY TOLD YOU IT IS CALLED A GAKJI!!
YES, YES. A GAKJI! I'VE MEMORIZED IT FOR SURE NOW!
LET ME EXPLAIN IT AGAIN. REMEMBER IT! THIS PART IS THE JUMTONG, AND THIS PART AROUND IT IS THE JUMPI!
AND THIS SECTION ON THE STRING IS CALLED THE JEOLPI. THIS IS WHERE YOU PULL BACK YOUR ARROW! DO YOU UNDERSTAND?
YES... YES...

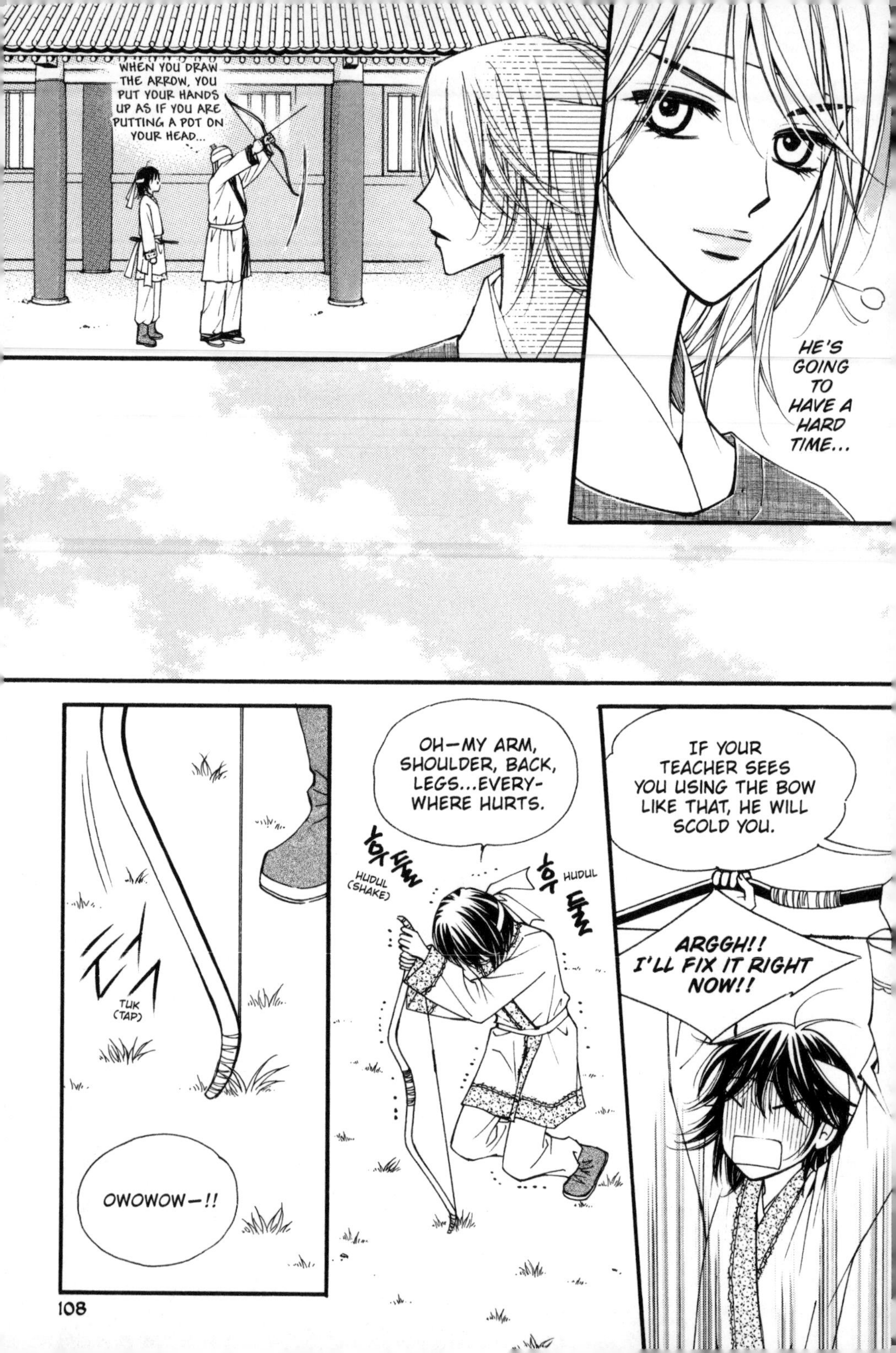
WHEN YOU DRAW THE ARROW, YOU PUT YOUR HANDS UP AS IF YOU ARE PUTTING A POT ON YOUR HEAD...
HE'S GOING TO HAVE A HARD TIME...
TUK (TAP)
OWOWOW—!!
OH—MY ARM, SHOULDER, BACK, LEGS...EVERY-WHERE HURTS.
HUDUL (SHAKE)
HUDUL
IF YOUR TEACHER SEES YOU USING THE BOW LIKE THAT, HE WILL SCOLD YOU.
ARGGH!! I'LL FIX IT RIGHT NOW!!

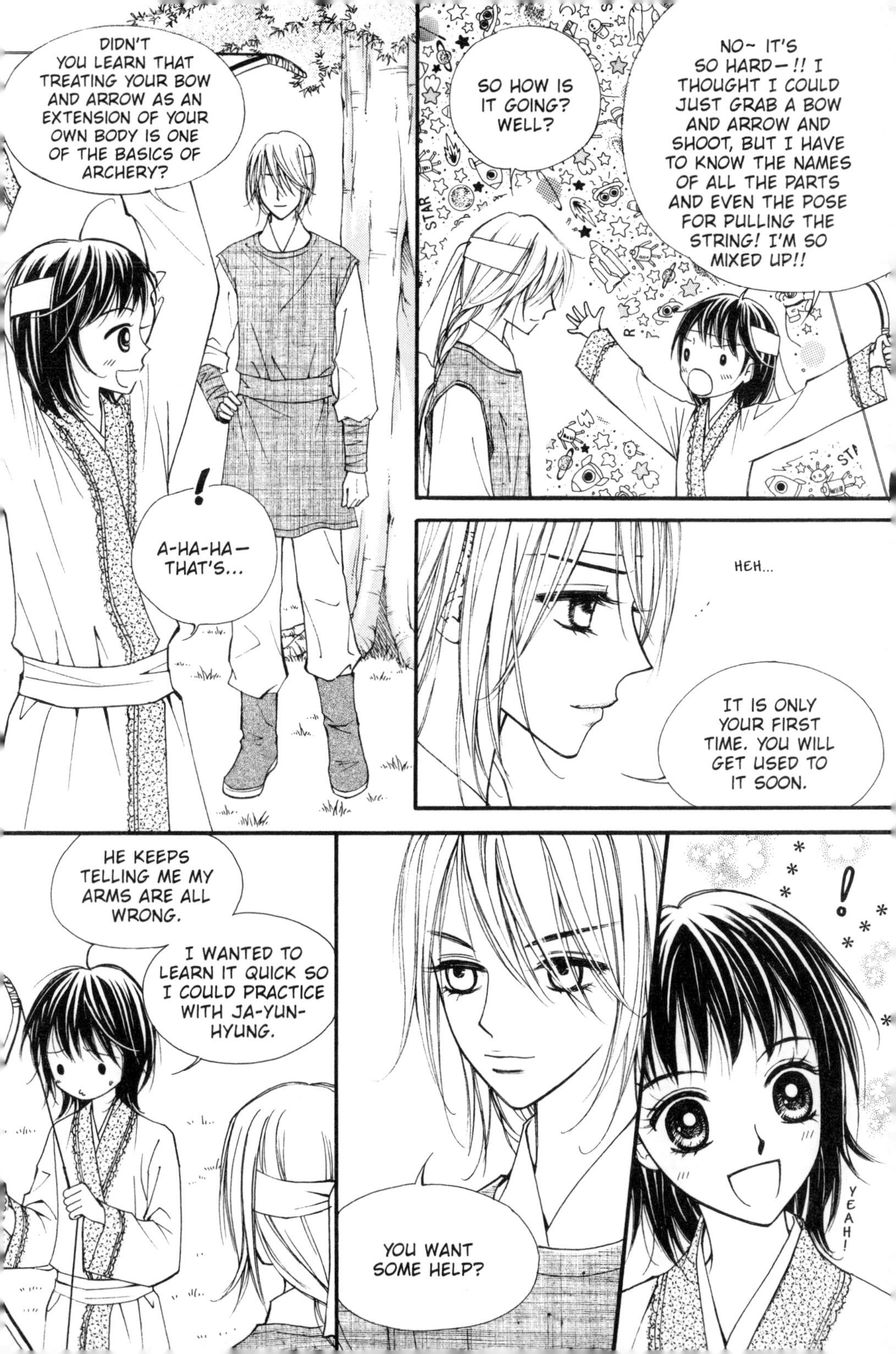
DIDN'T YOU LEARN THAT TREATING YOUR BOW AND ARROW AS AN EXTENSION OF YOUR OWN BODY IS ONE OF THE BASICS OF ARCHERY?
!
A-HA-HA— THAT'S...
SO HOW IS IT GOING? WELL?
NO~ IT'S SO HARD—!! I THOUGHT I COULD JUST GRAB A BOW AND ARROW AND SHOOT, BUT I HAVE TO KNOW THE NAMES OF ALL THE PARTS AND EVEN THE POSE FOR PULLING THE STRING! I'M SO MIXED UP!!
HEH...
IT IS ONLY YOUR FIRST TIME. YOU WILL GET USED TO IT SOON.
HE KEEPS TELLING ME MY ARMS ARE ALL WRONG.
I WANTED TO LEARN IT QUICK SO I COULD PRACTICE WITH JA-YUN-HYUNG.
YOU WANT SOME HELP?
!
YEAH!

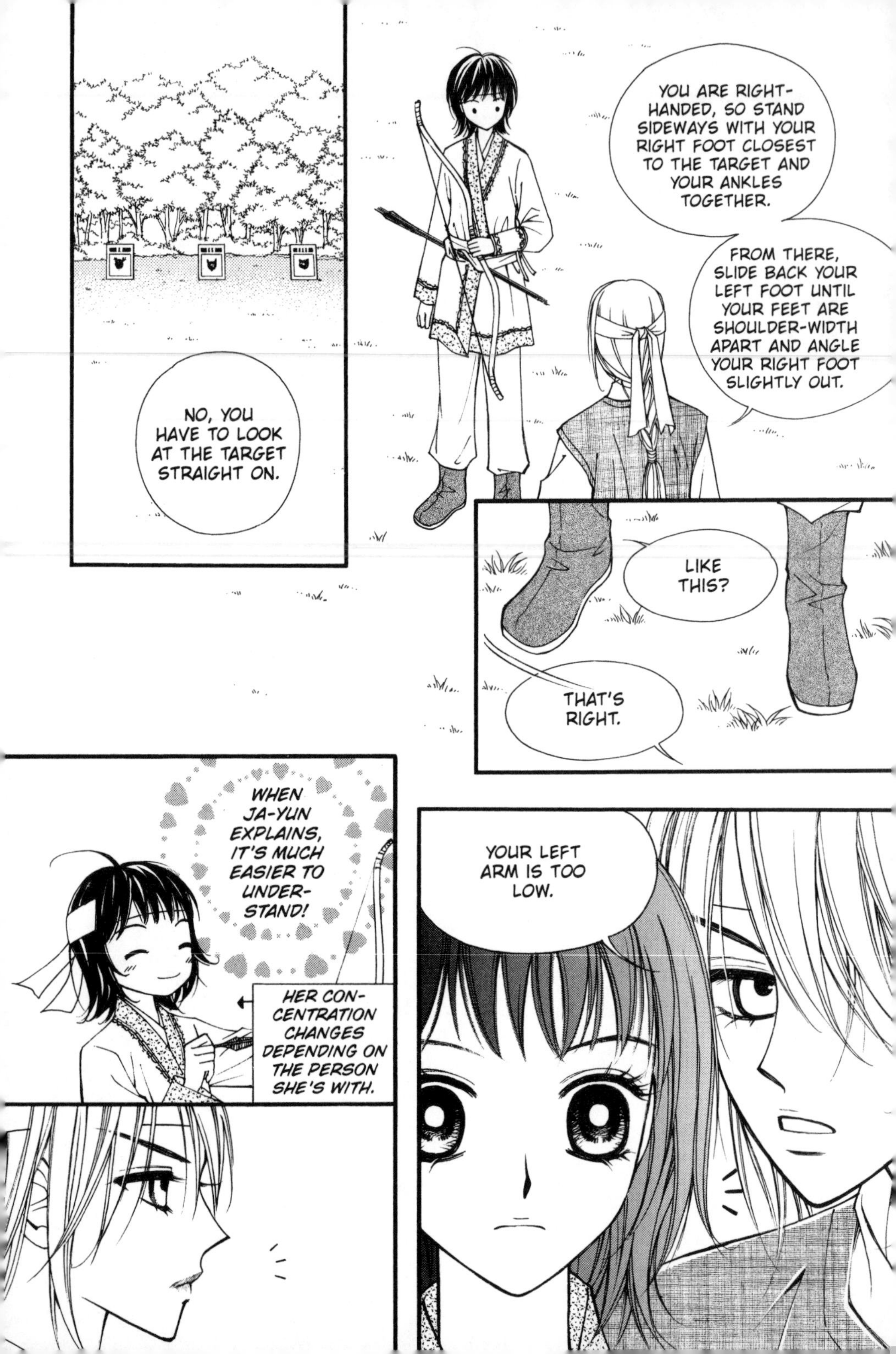
NO, YOU HAVE TO LOOK AT THE TARGET STRAIGHT ON.
YOU ARE RIGHT-HANDED, SO STAND SIDEWAYS WITH YOUR RIGHT FOOT CLOSEST TO THE TARGET AND YOUR ANKLES TOGETHER.
FROM THERE, SLIDE BACK YOUR LEFT FOOT UNTIL YOUR FEET ARE SHOULDER-WIDTH APART AND ANGLE YOUR RIGHT FOOT SLIGHTLY OUT.
LIKE THIS?
THAT'S RIGHT.
WHEN JA-YUN EXPLAINS, IT'S MUCH EASIER TO UNDER-STAND!
HER CON-CENTRATION CHANGES DEPENDING ON THE PERSON SHE'S WITH.
YOUR LEFT ARM IS TOO LOW.

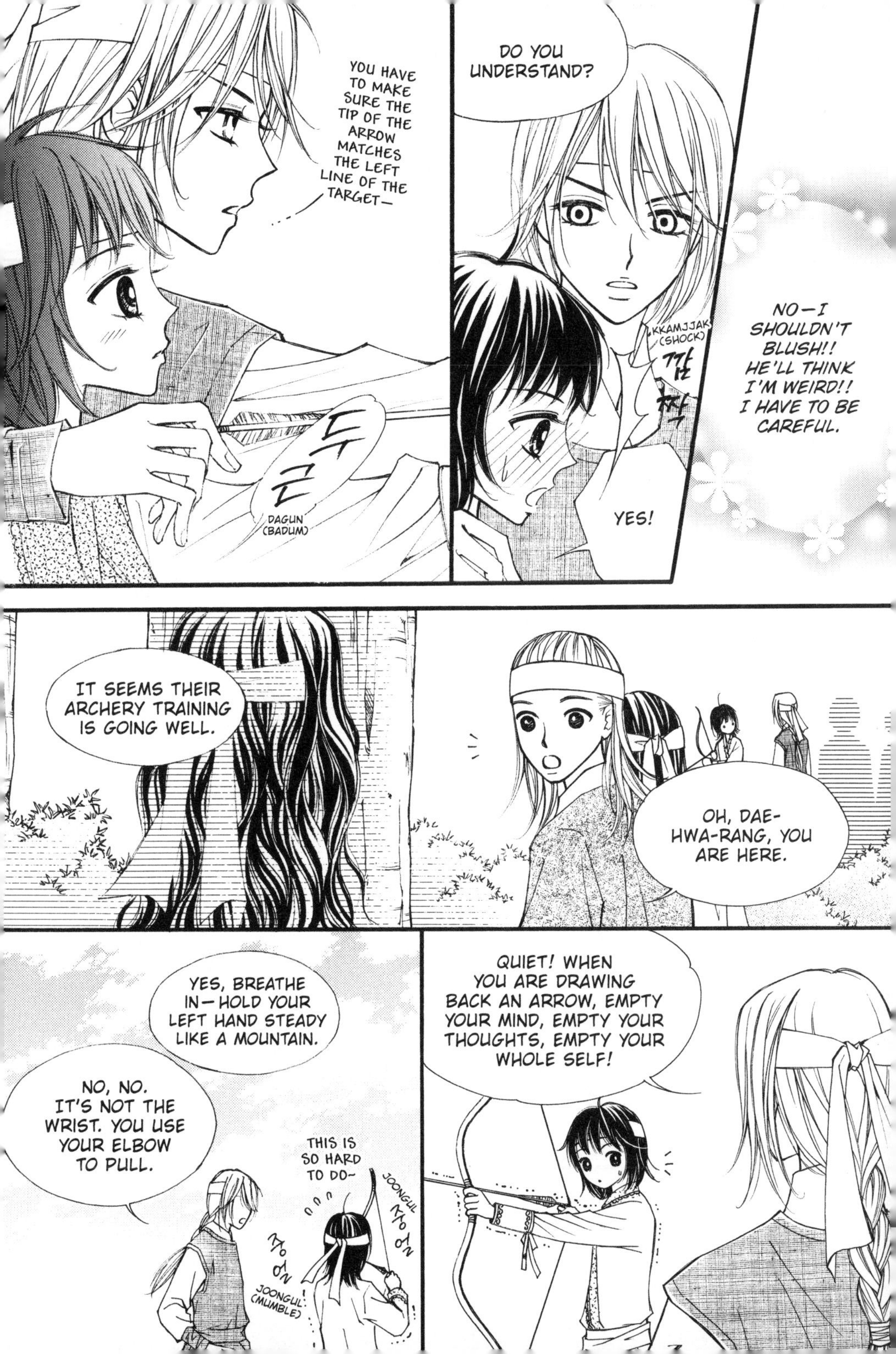
YOU HAVE TO MAKE SURE THE TIP OF THE ARROW MATCHES THE LEFT LINE OF THE TARGET—
...
두근
DAGUN (BADUM)
DO YOU UNDERSTAND?
KKAMJJAK (SHOCK)
깜짝
NO—I SHOULDN'T BLUSH!! HE'LL THINK I'M WEIRD!! I HAVE TO BE CAREFUL.
YES!
IT SEEMS THEIR ARCHERY TRAINING IS GOING WELL.
OH, DAE-HWA-RANG, YOU ARE HERE.
YES, BREATHE IN—HOLD YOUR LEFT HAND STEADY LIKE A MOUNTAIN.
NO, NO. IT'S NOT THE WRIST. YOU USE YOUR ELBOW TO PULL.
THIS IS SO HARD TO DO~
JOONGUL
중얼
중얼
JOONGUL (MUMBLE)
QUIET! WHEN YOU ARE DRAWING BACK AN ARROW, EMPTY YOUR MIND, EMPTY YOUR THOUGHTS, EMPTY YOUR WHOLE SELF!

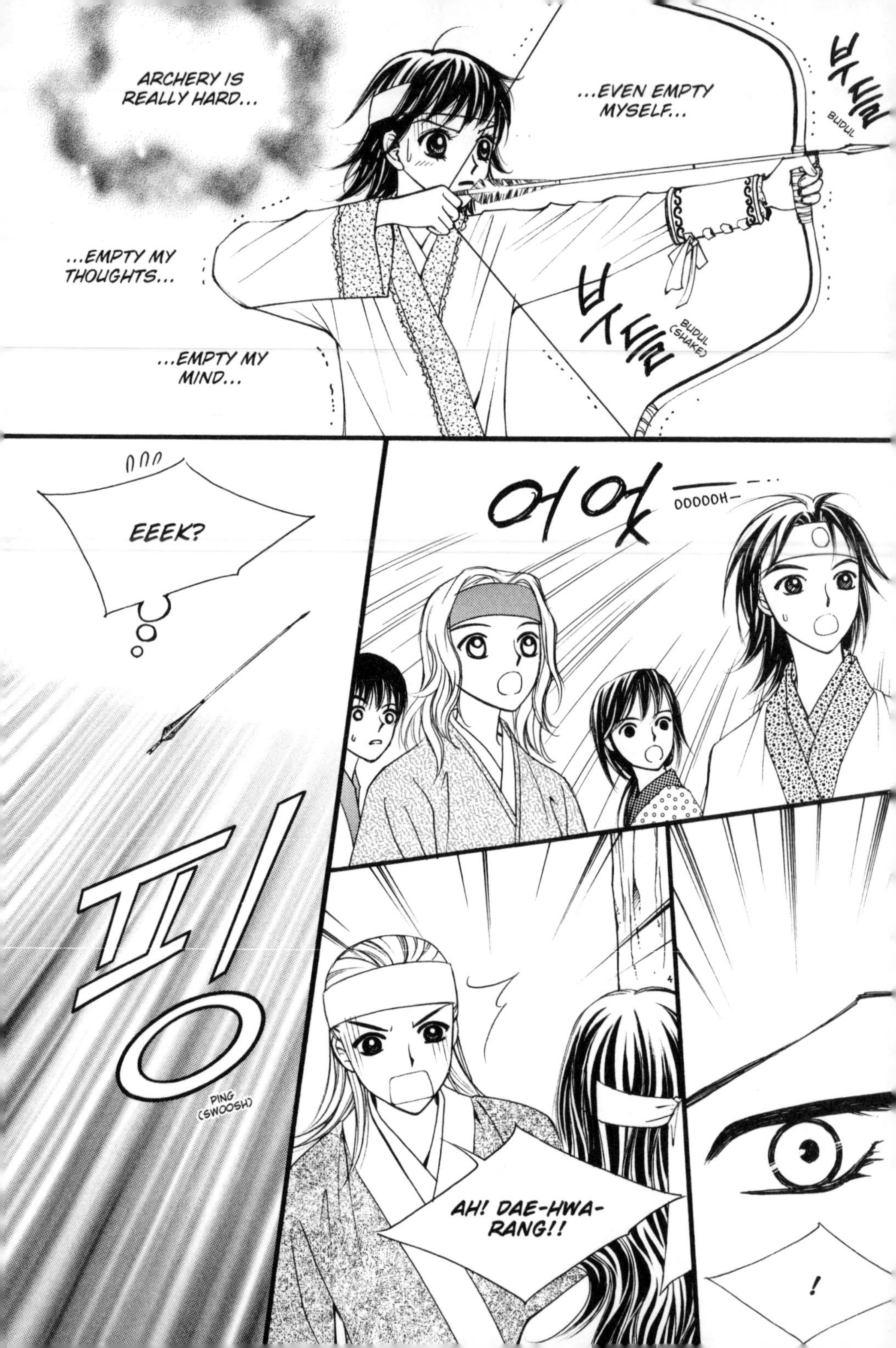
ARCHERY IS REALLY HARD...
...EMPTY MY THOUGHTS...
...EMPTY MY MIND...
...EVEN EMPTY MYSELF...
부들
BUDUL
부들
BUDUL (SHAKE)
EEEK?
피잉
PING (SWOOSH)
어억
OOOOOH—
AH! DAE-HWA-RANG!!
!

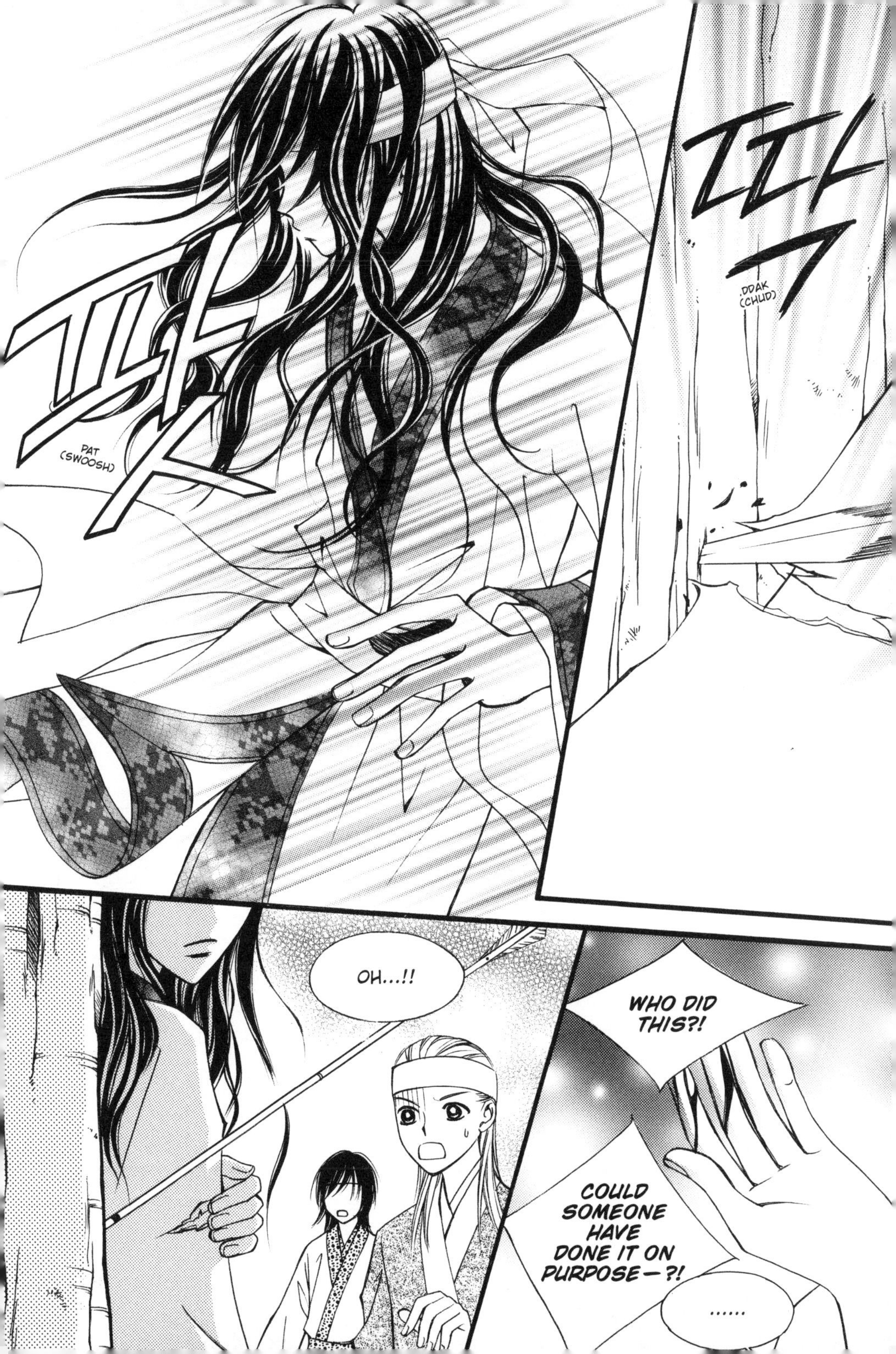
PAT
(SWOOSH)
DDAK
(CHUD)
OH...!!
WHO DID THIS?!
COULD SOMEONE HAVE DONE IT ON PURPOSE—?!
......

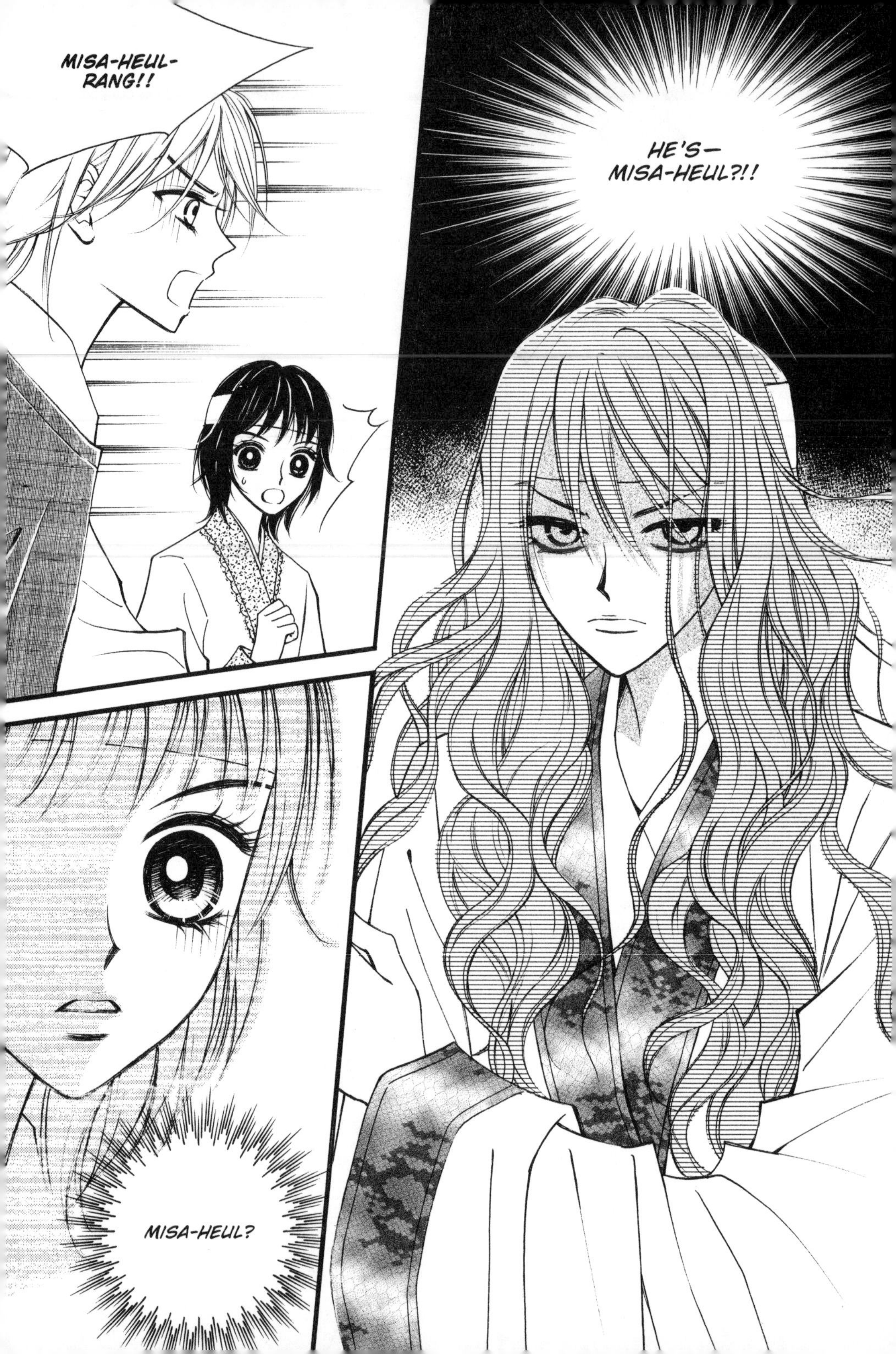
MISA-HEUL-RANG!!
MISA-HEUL?
HE'S—MISA-HEUL?!!

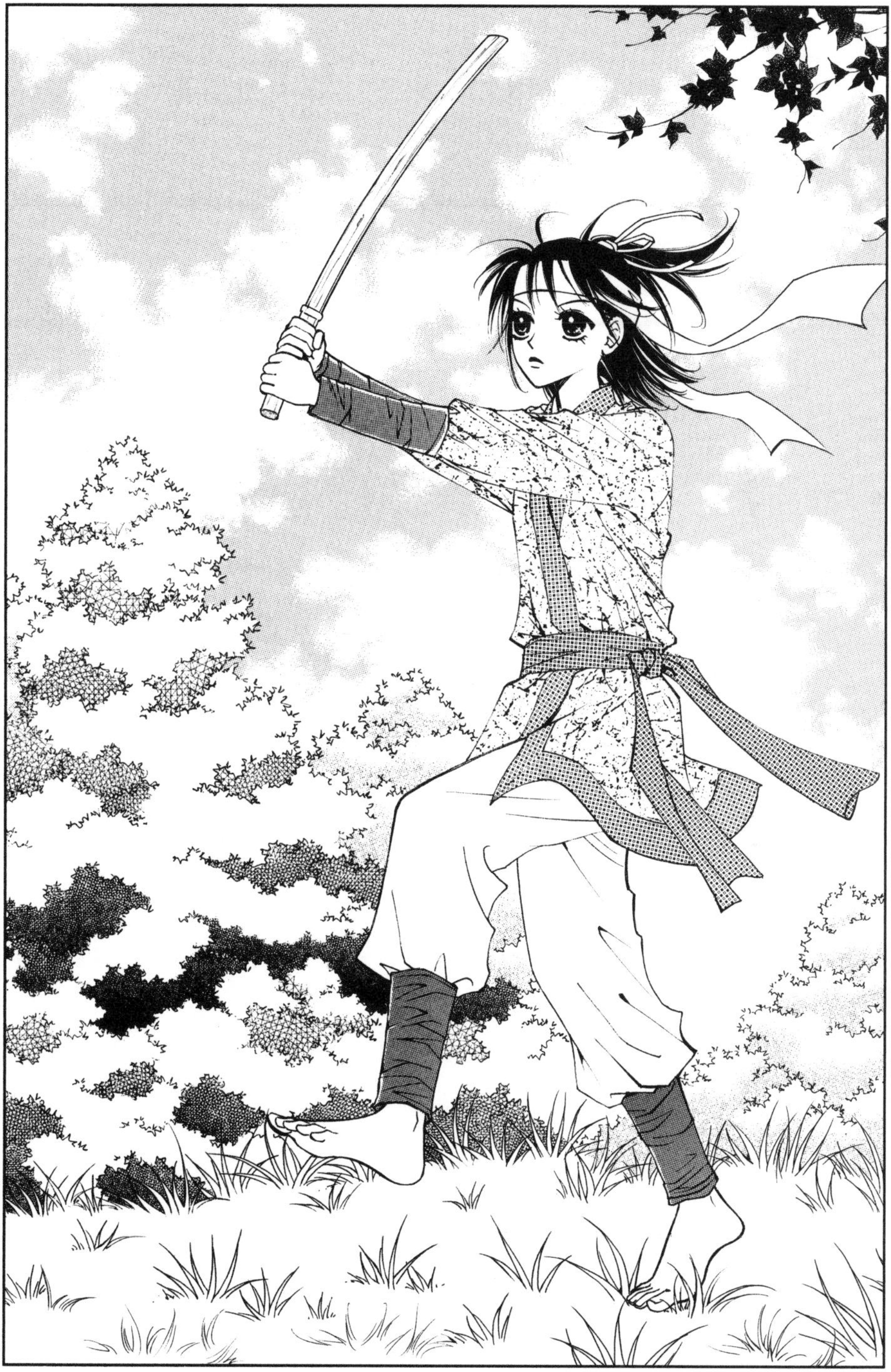

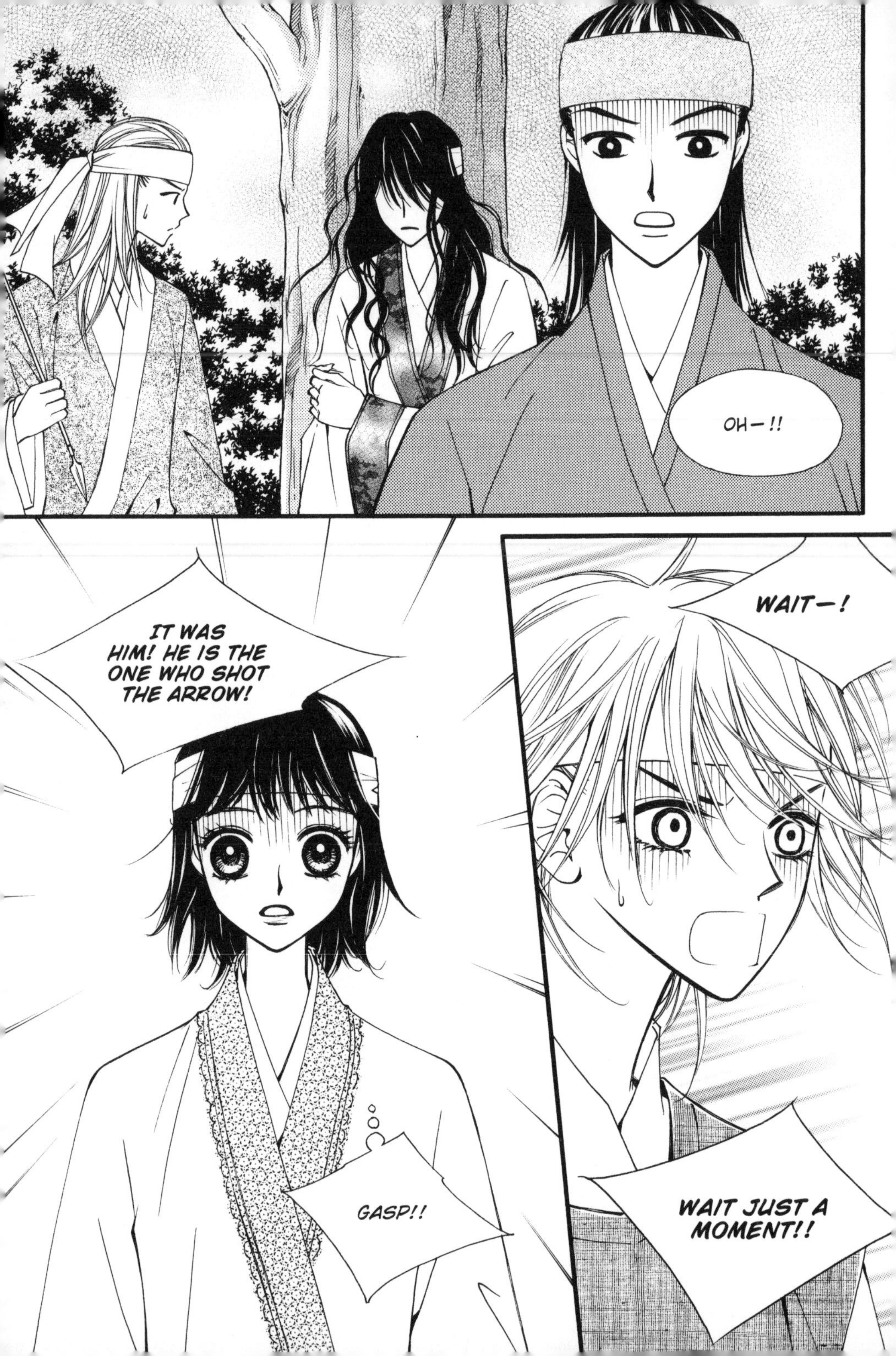
OH—!!
IT WAS HIM! HE IS THE ONE WHO SHOT THE ARROW!
GASP!!
WAIT—!
WAIT JUST A MOMENT!!

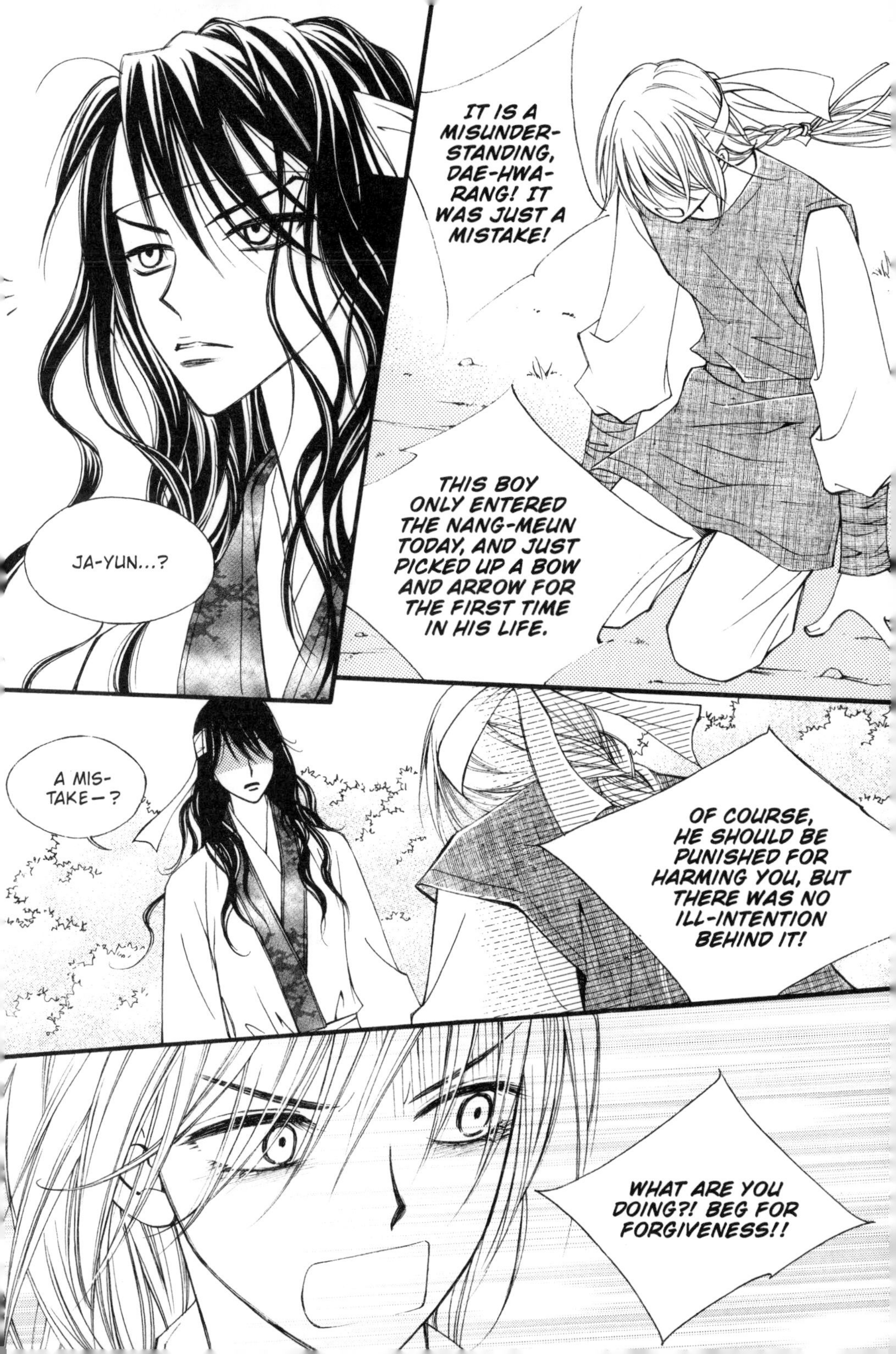
JA-YUN...?
IT IS A MISUNDERSTANDING, DAE-HWA-RANG! IT WAS JUST A MISTAKE!
THIS BOY ONLY ENTERED THE NANG-MEUN TODAY, AND JUST PICKED UP A BOW AND ARROW FOR THE FIRST TIME IN HIS LIFE.
A MIS-TAKE—?
OF COURSE, HE SHOULD BE PUNISHED FOR HARMING YOU, BUT THERE WAS NO ILL-INTENTION BEHIND IT!
WHAT ARE YOU DOING?! BEG FOR FORGIVENESS!!

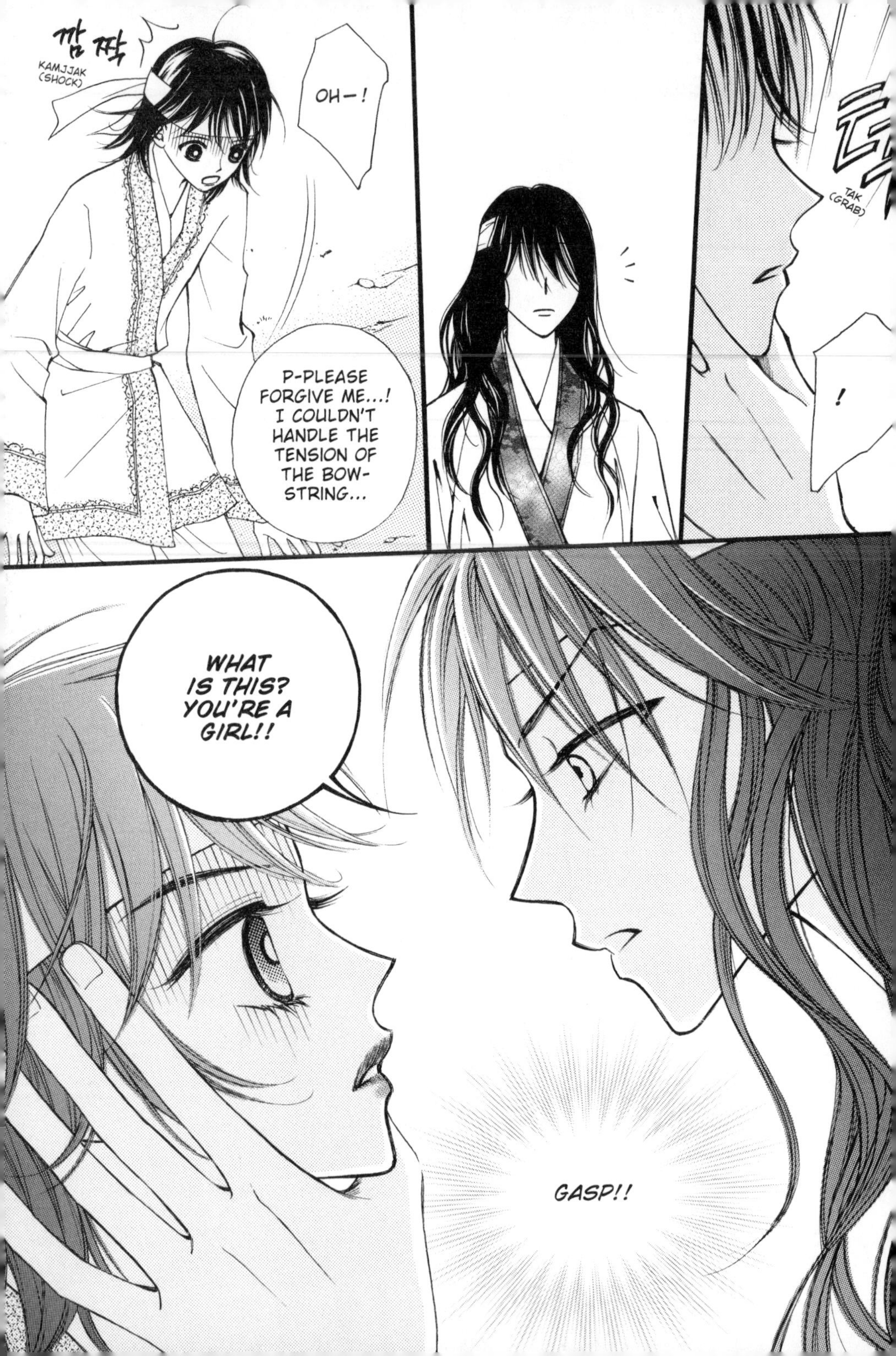
깜짝
KAMJJAK (SHOCK)
OH—!
P-PLEASE FORGIVE ME...! I COULDN'T HANDLE THE TENSION OF THE BOW-STRING...
TAK (GRAB)
!
WHAT IS THIS? YOU'RE A GIRL!!
GASP!!

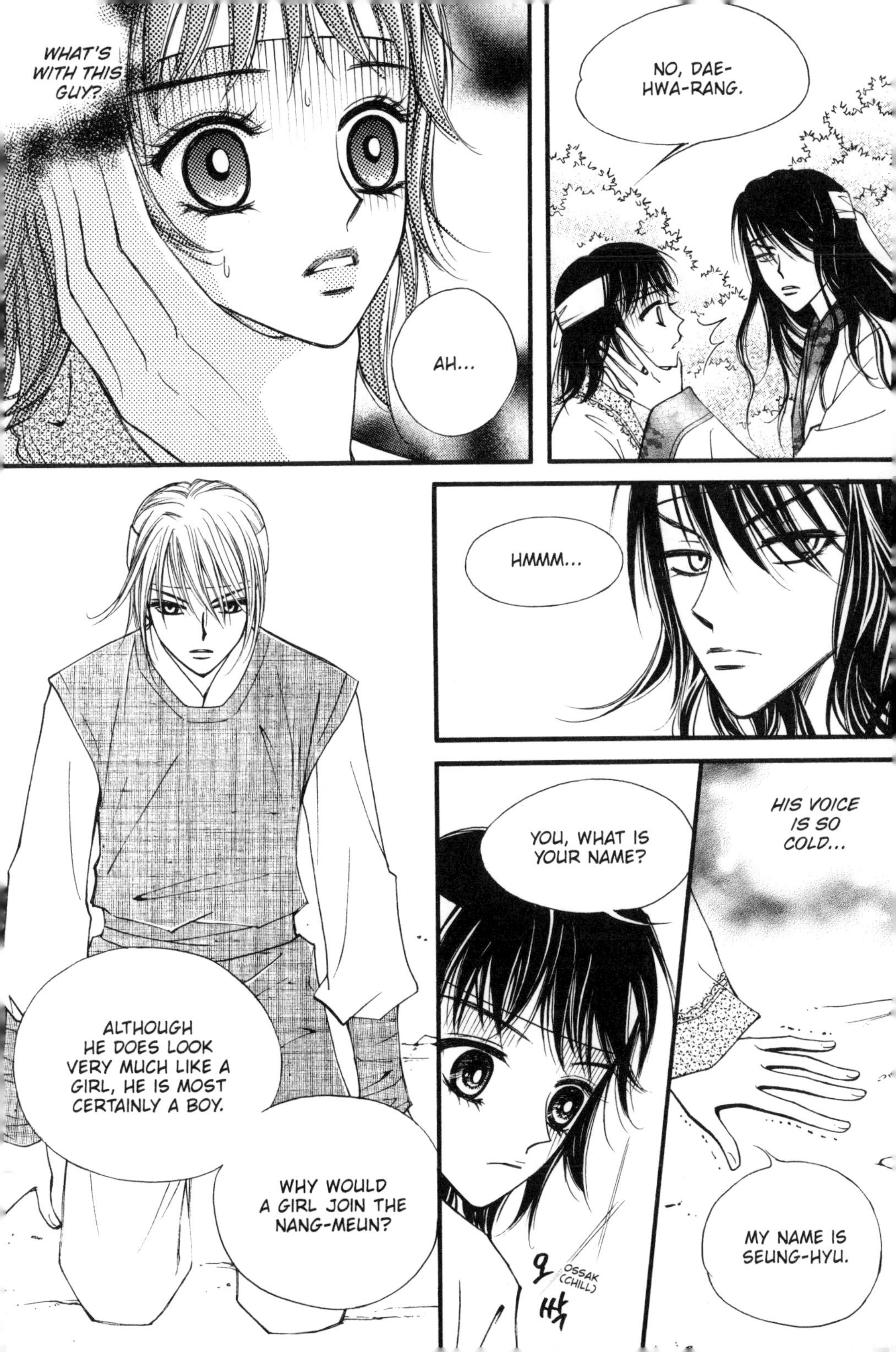
WHAT'S WITH THIS GUY?
AH...
NO, DAE-HWA-RANG.
ALTHOUGH HE DOES LOOK VERY MUCH LIKE A GIRL, HE IS MOST CERTAINLY A BOY.
WHY WOULD A GIRL JOIN THE NANG-MEUN?
HMMM...
YOU, WHAT IS YOUR NAME?
HIS VOICE IS SO COLD...
OSSAK (CHILL)
MY NAME IS SEUNG-HYU.

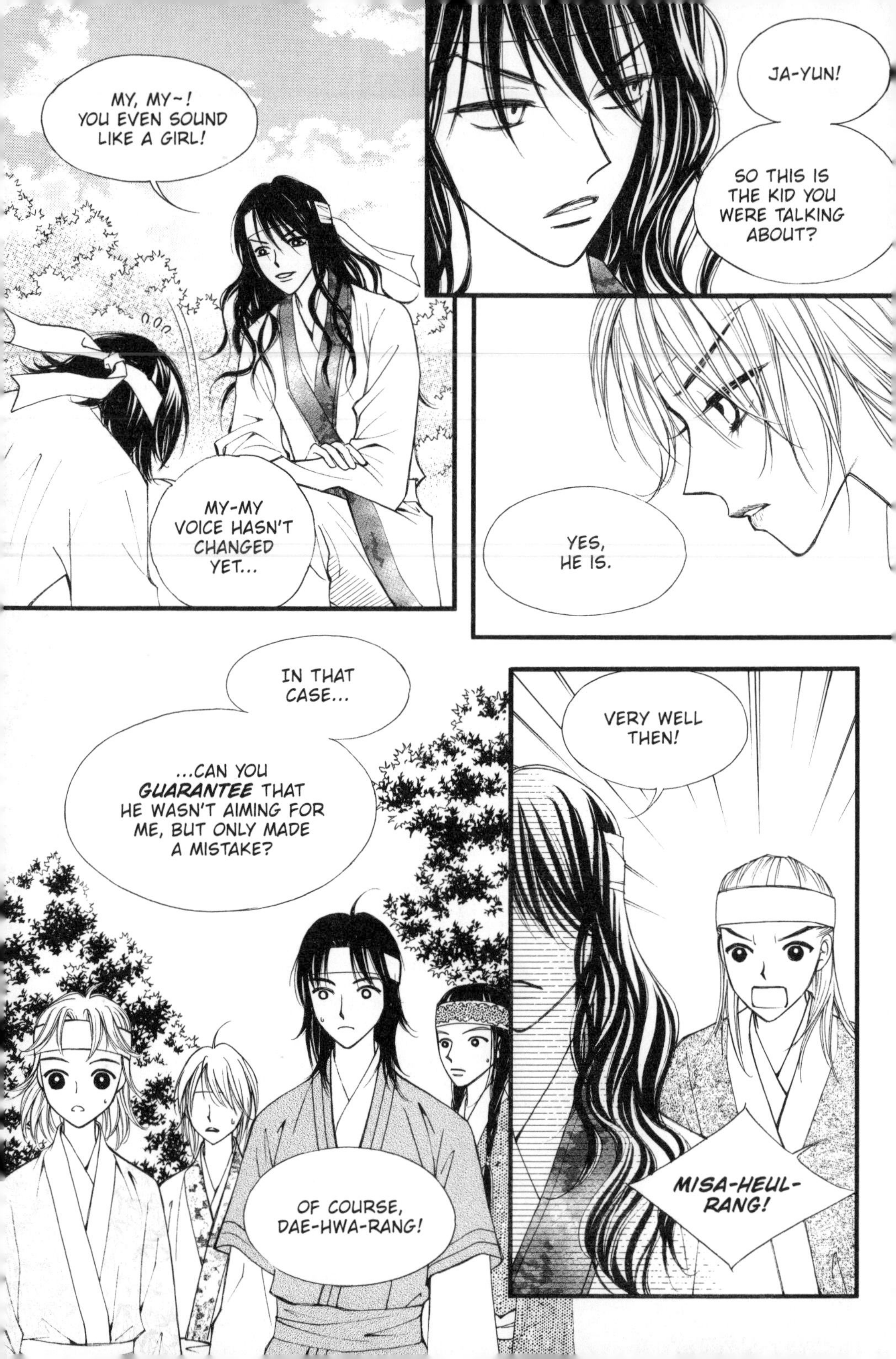
MY, MY~! YOU EVEN SOUND LIKE A GIRL!
MY-MY VOICE HASN'T CHANGED YET...
JA-YUN!
SO THIS IS THE KID YOU WERE TALKING ABOUT?
YES, HE IS.
IN THAT CASE...
...CAN YOU GUARANTEE THAT HE WASN'T AIMING FOR ME, BUT ONLY MADE A MISTAKE?
OF COURSE, DAE-HWA-RANG!
VERY WELL THEN!
MISA-HEUL-RANG!

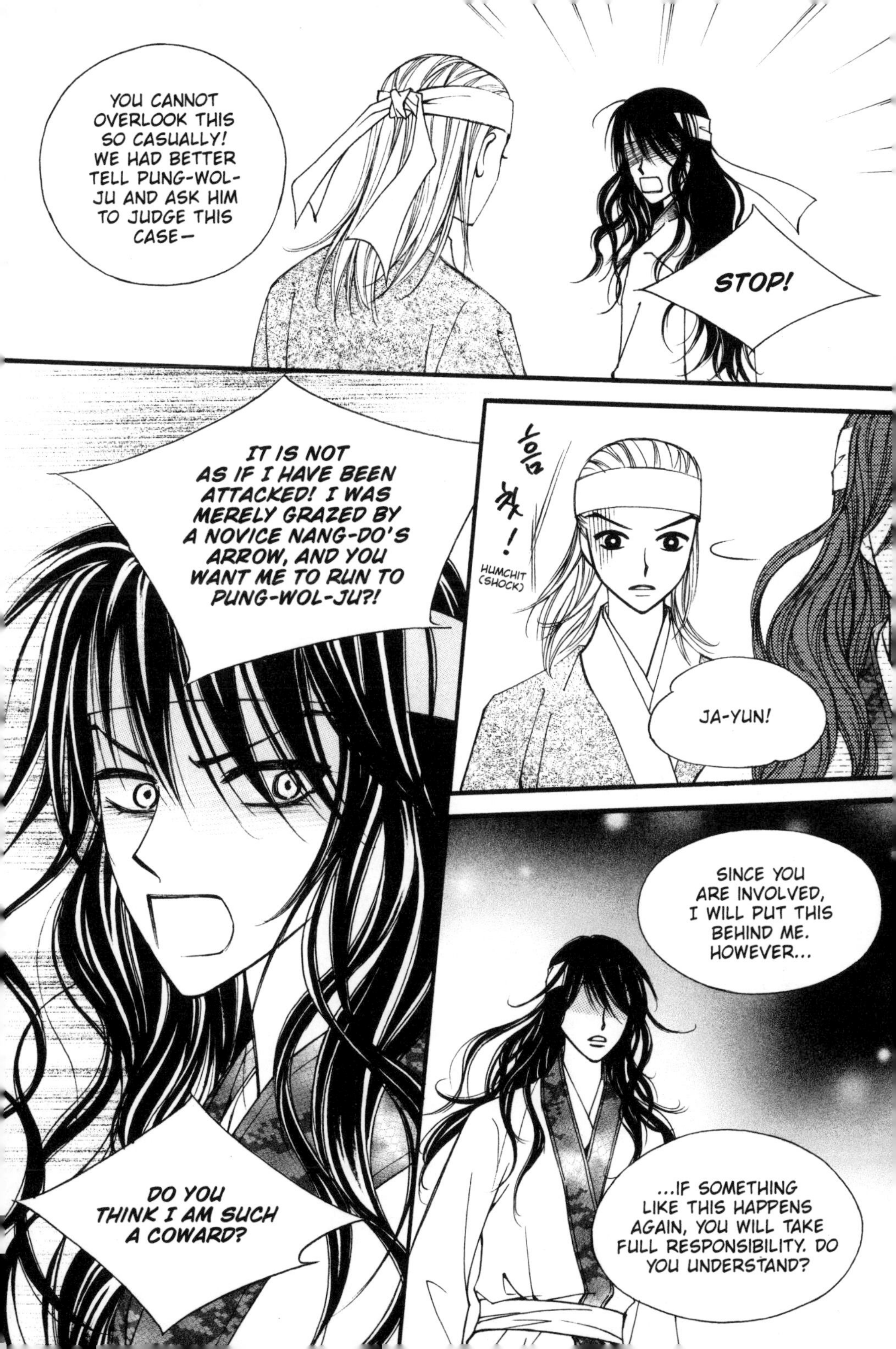
YOU CANNOT OVERLOOK THIS SO CASUALLY! WE HAD BETTER TELL PUNG-WOL-JU AND ASK HIM TO JUDGE THIS CASE—
STOP!
IT IS NOT AS IF I HAVE BEEN ATTACKED! I WAS MERELY GRAZED BY A NOVICE NANG-DO'S ARROW, AND YOU WANT ME TO RUN TO PUNG-WOL-JU?!
DO YOU THINK I AM SUCH A COWARD?
흠칫!
HUMCHIT (SHOCK)
JA-YUN!
SINCE YOU ARE INVOLVED, I WILL PUT THIS BEHIND ME. HOWEVER...
...IF SOMETHING LIKE THIS HAPPENS AGAIN, YOU WILL TAKE FULL RESPONSIBILITY. DO YOU UNDERSTAND?

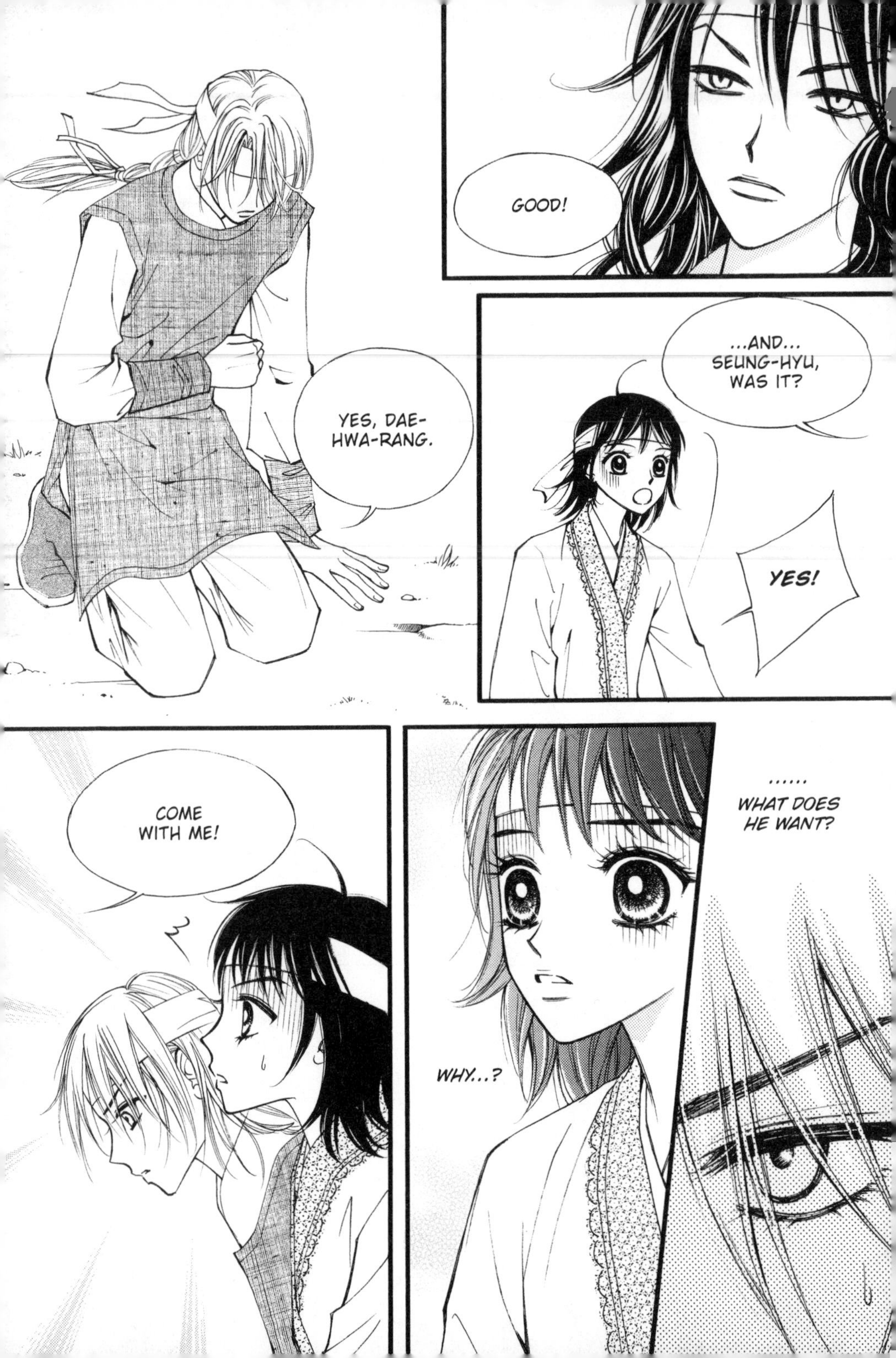
YES, DAE-HWA-RANG.
GOOD!
...AND... SEUNG-HYU, WAS IT?
YES!
COME WITH ME!
......
WHAT DOES HE WANT?
WHY...?

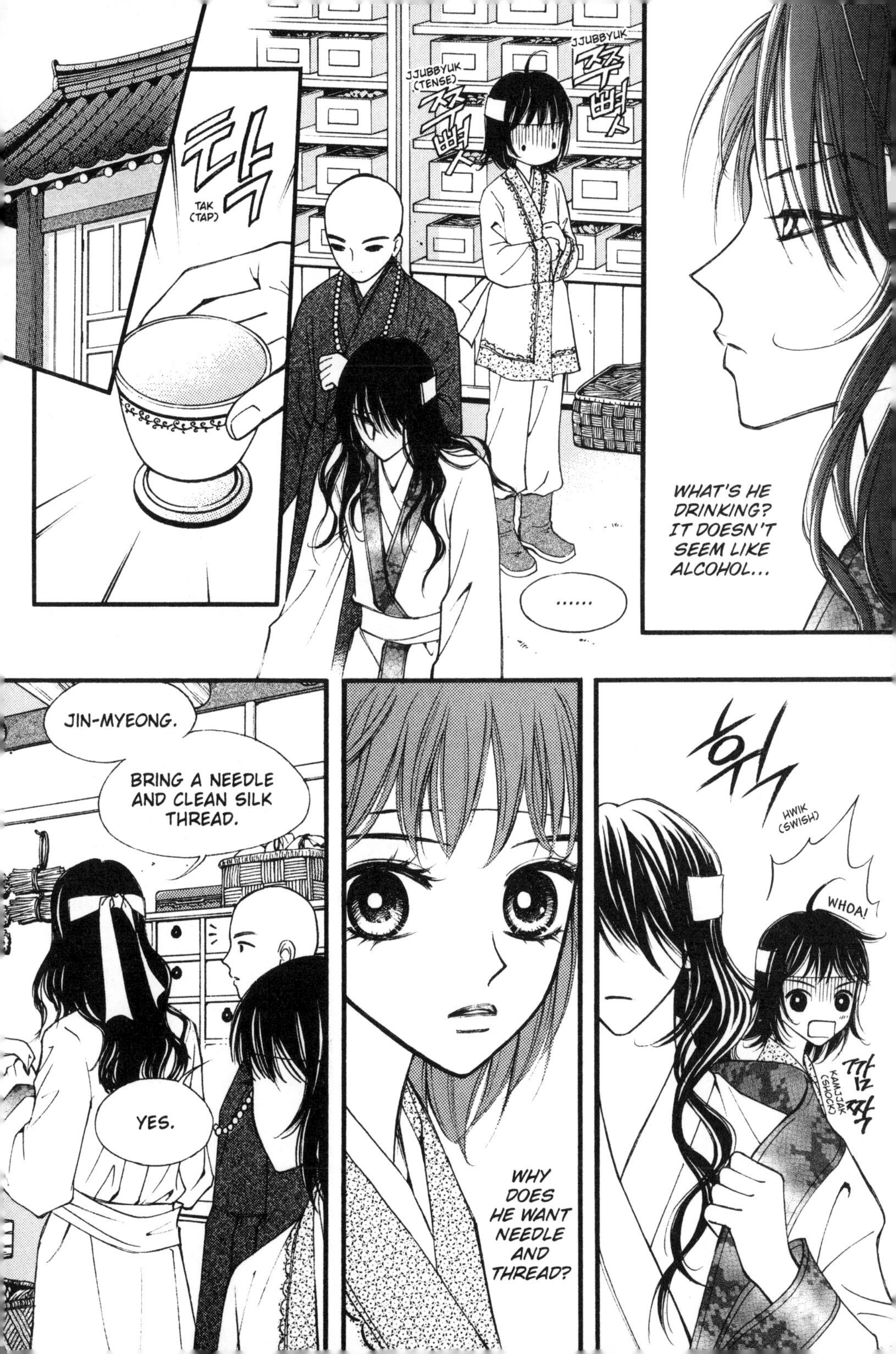
TAK (TAP)
JJUBBYUK (TENSE)
JJUBBYUK
......
WHAT'S HE DRINKING? IT DOESN'T SEEM LIKE ALCOHOL...
JIN-MYEONG.
BRING A NEEDLE AND CLEAN SILK THREAD.
YES.
WHY DOES HE WANT NEEDLE AND THREAD?
HWIK (SWISH)
WHOA!
KAMJJAK (SHOCK)

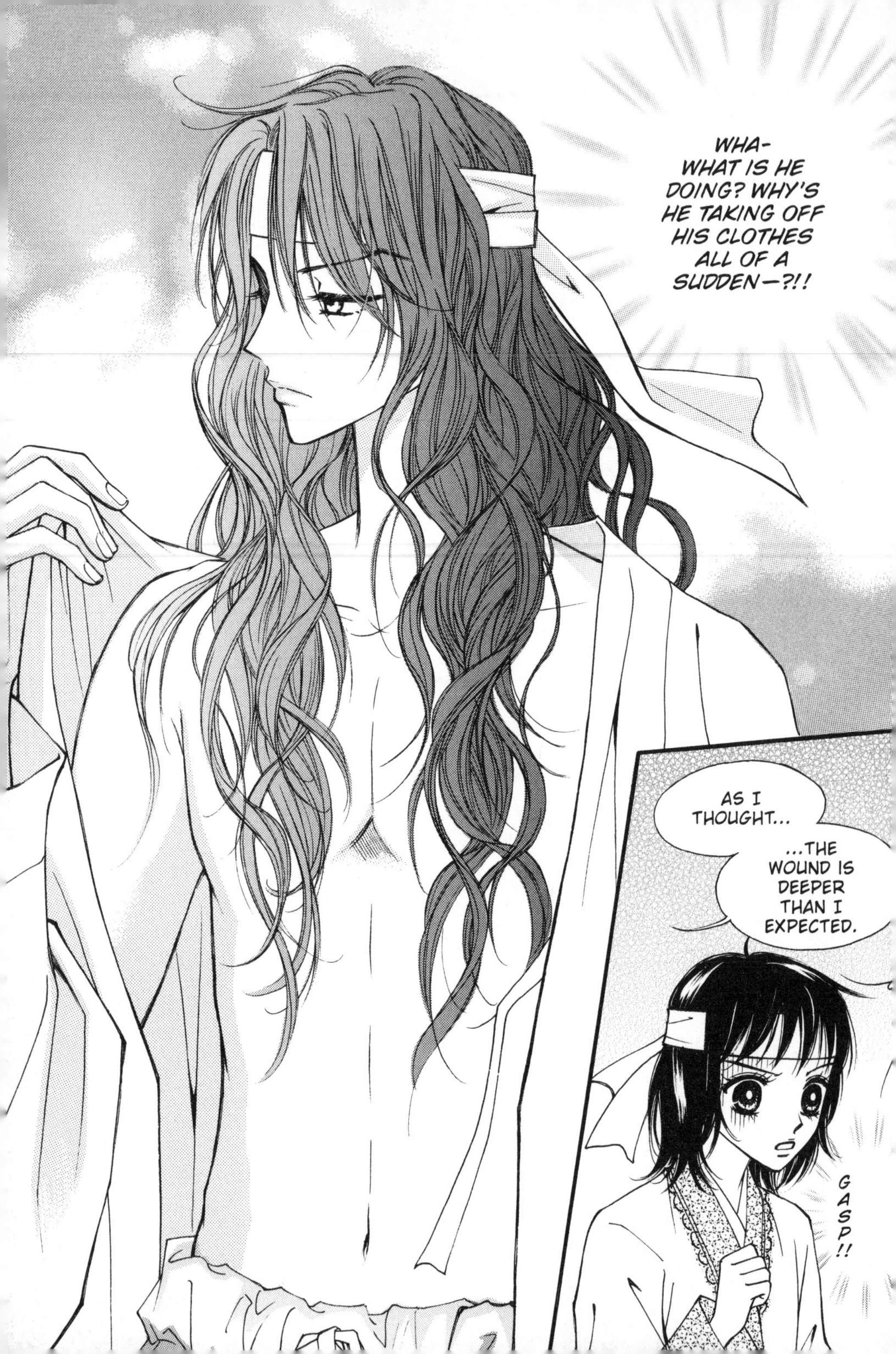
WHA- WHAT IS HE DOING? WHY'S HE TAKING OFF HIS CLOTHES ALL OF A SUDDEN—?!!
AS I THOUGHT...
...THE WOUND IS DEEPER THAN I EXPECTED.
GASP!!

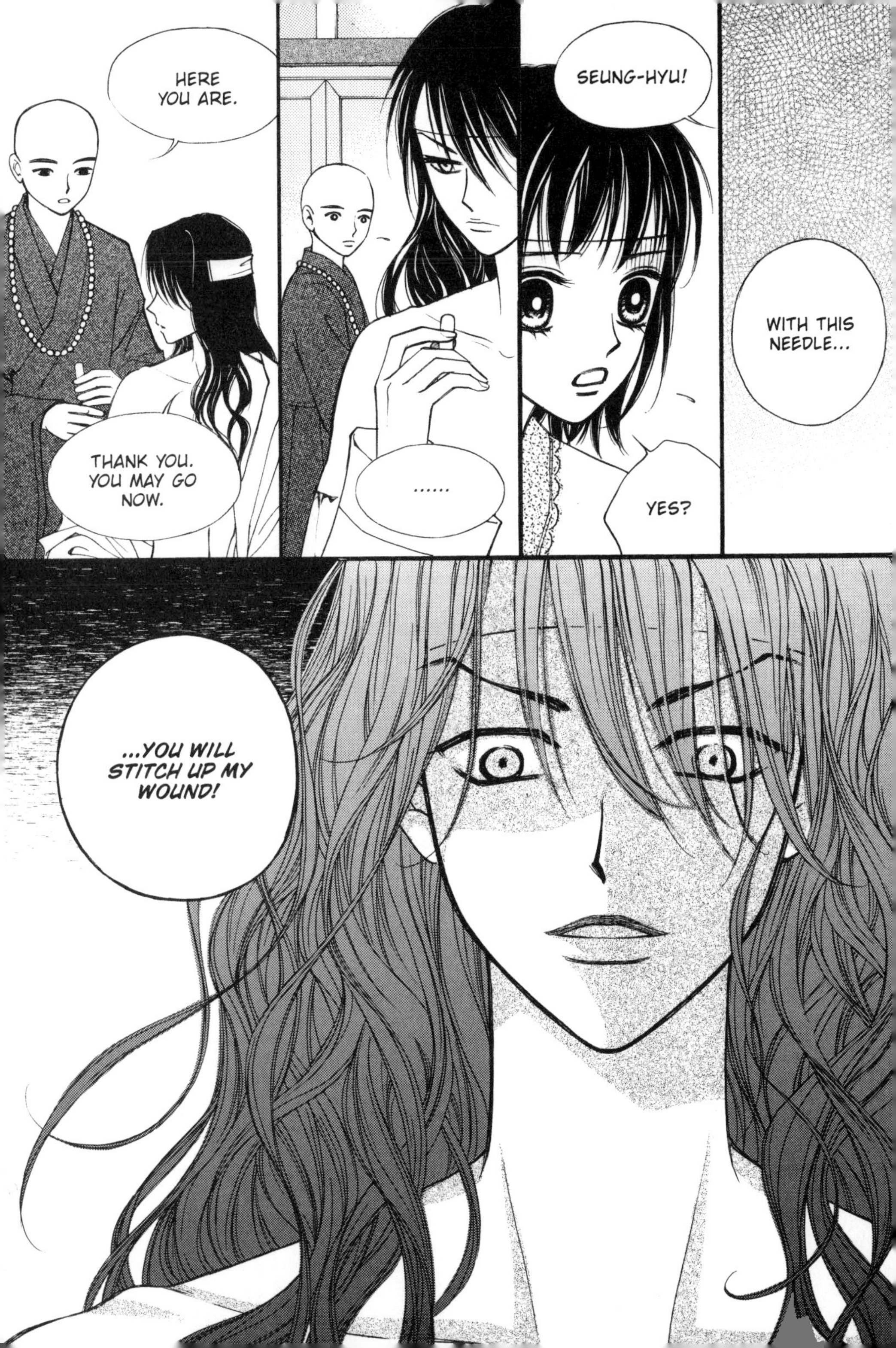
HERE YOU ARE.
THANK YOU. YOU MAY GO NOW.
......
SEUNG-HYU!
YES?
WITH THIS NEEDLE...
...YOU WILL STITCH UP MY WOUND!

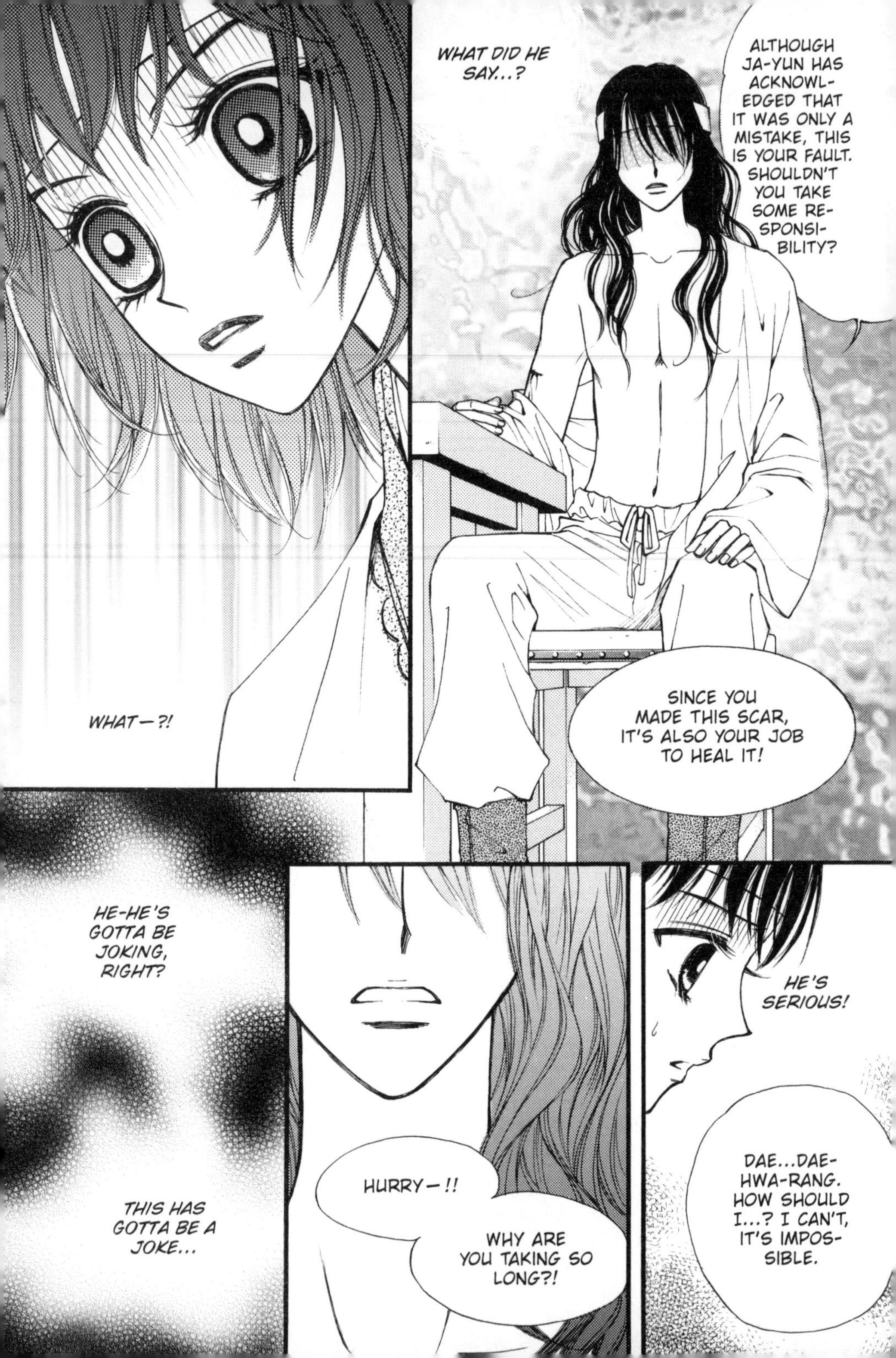
WHAT—?!
WHAT DID HE SAY...?
ALTHOUGH JA-YUN HAS ACKNOWLEDGED THAT IT WAS ONLY A MISTAKE, THIS IS YOUR FAULT. SHOULDN'T YOU TAKE SOME RESPONSIBILITY?
SINCE YOU MADE THIS SCAR, IT'S ALSO YOUR JOB TO HEAL IT!
HE-HE'S GOTTA BE JOKING, RIGHT?
THIS HAS GOTTA BE A JOKE...
HURRY—!!
WHY ARE YOU TAKING SO LONG?!
HE'S SERIOUS!
DAE...DAE-HWA-RANG. HOW SHOULD I...? I CAN'T, IT'S IMPOSSIBLE.

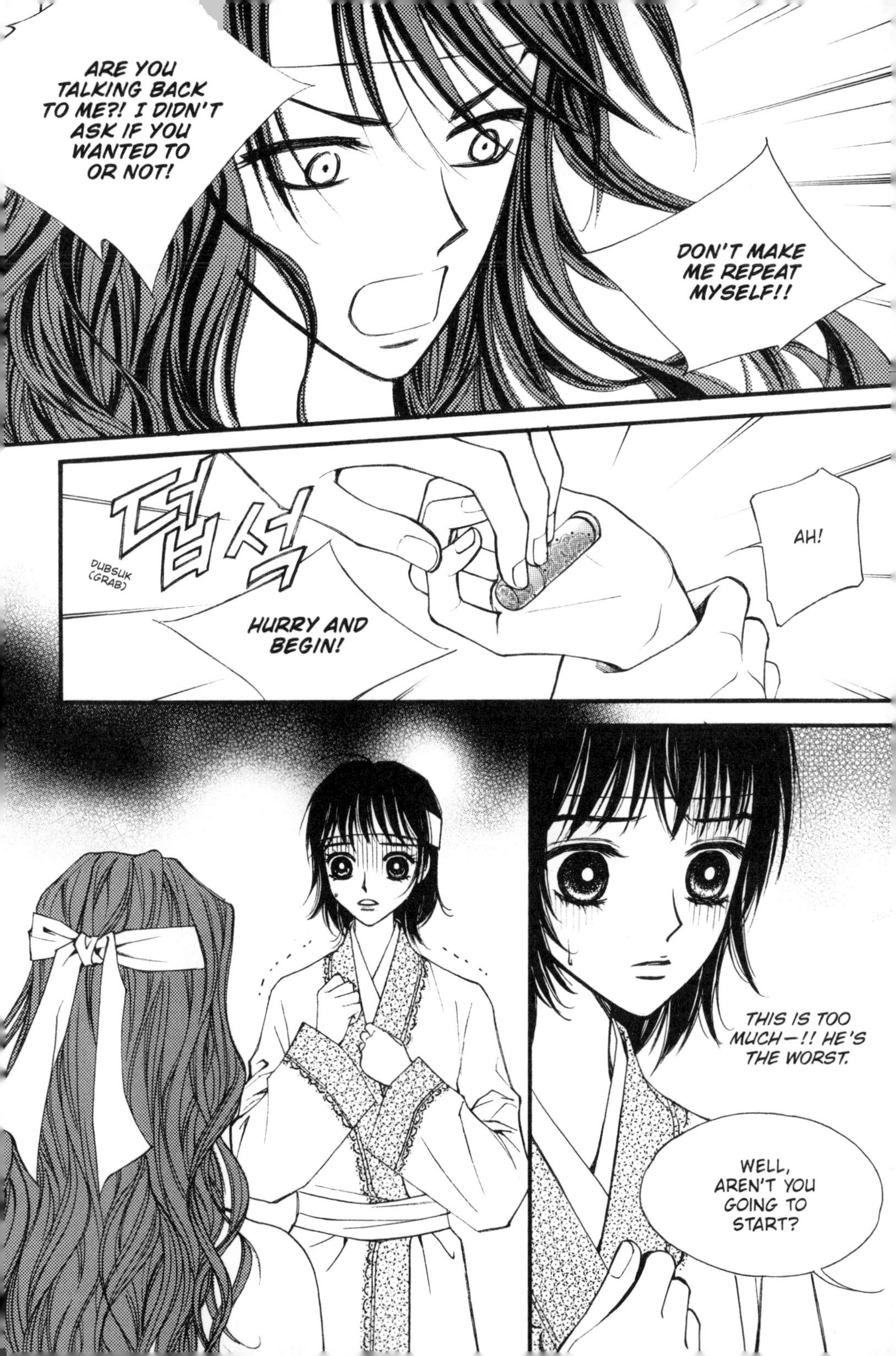
ARE YOU TALKING BACK TO ME?! I DIDN'T ASK IF YOU WANTED TO OR NOT!
DON'T MAKE ME REPEAT MYSELF!!
덥석
DUBSUK (GRAB)
HURRY AND BEGIN!
AH!
THIS IS TOO MUCH—!! HE'S THE WORST.
WELL, AREN'T YOU GOING TO START?

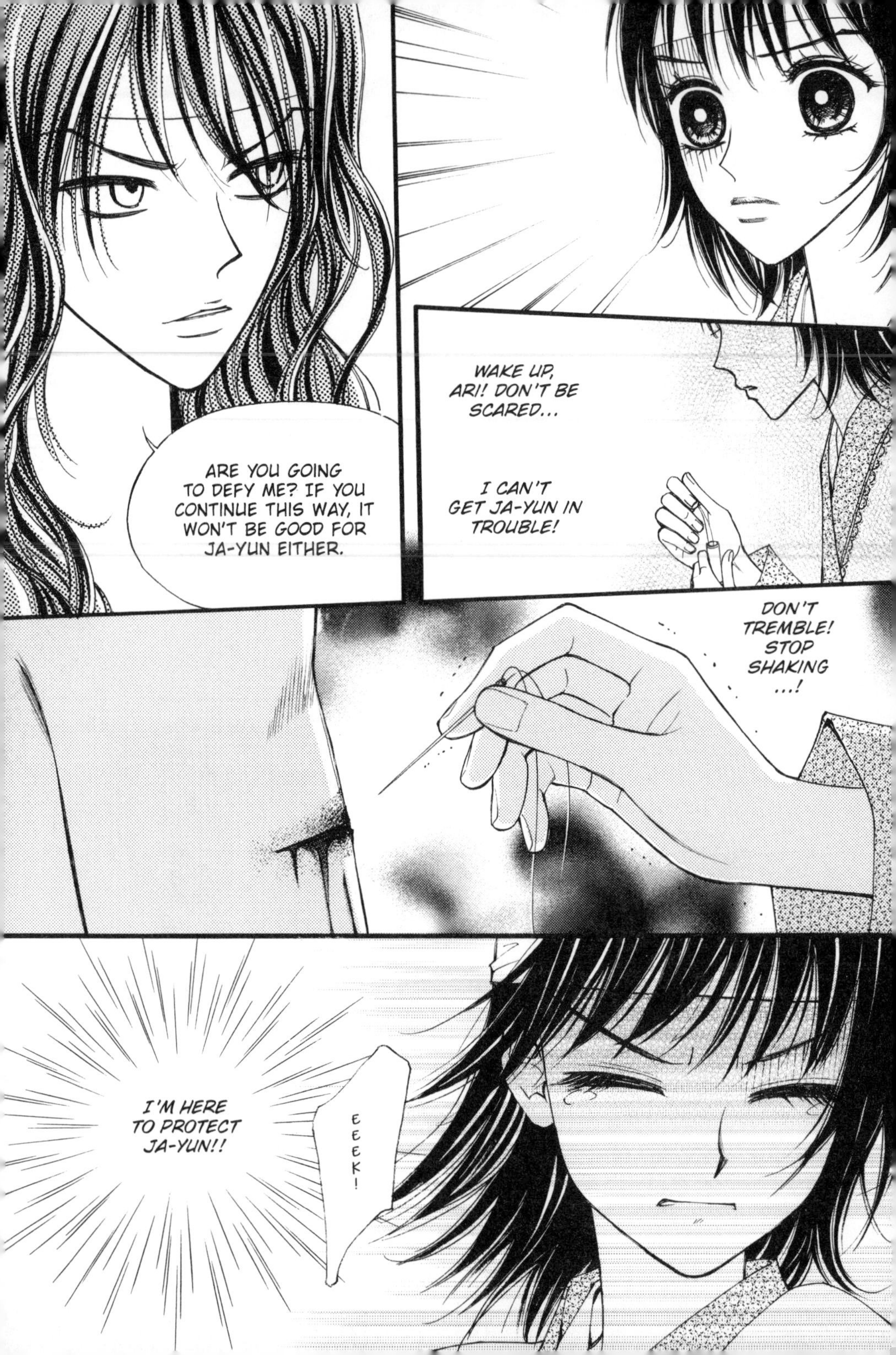
ARE YOU GOING TO DEFY ME? IF YOU CONTINUE THIS WAY, IT WON'T BE GOOD FOR JA-YUN EITHER.
WAKE UP, ARI! DON'T BE SCARED...
I CAN'T GET JA-YUN IN TROUBLE!
DON'T TREMBLE! STOP SHAKING ...!
I'M HERE TO PROTECT JA-YUN!!
EEEK!

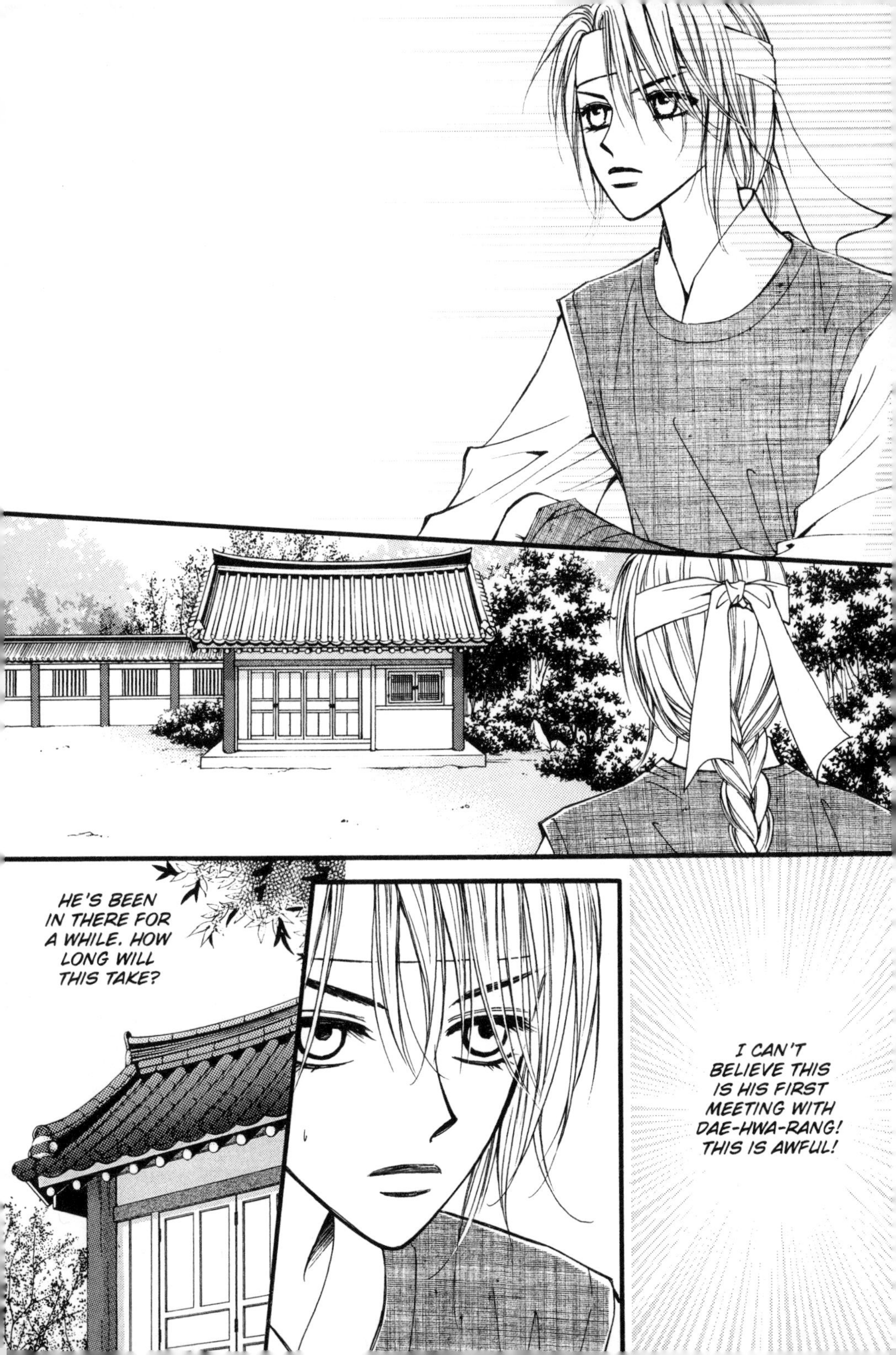
HE'S BEEN IN THERE FOR A WHILE. HOW LONG WILL THIS TAKE?
I CAN'T BELIEVE THIS IS HIS FIRST MEETING WITH DAE-HWA-RANG! THIS IS AWFUL!

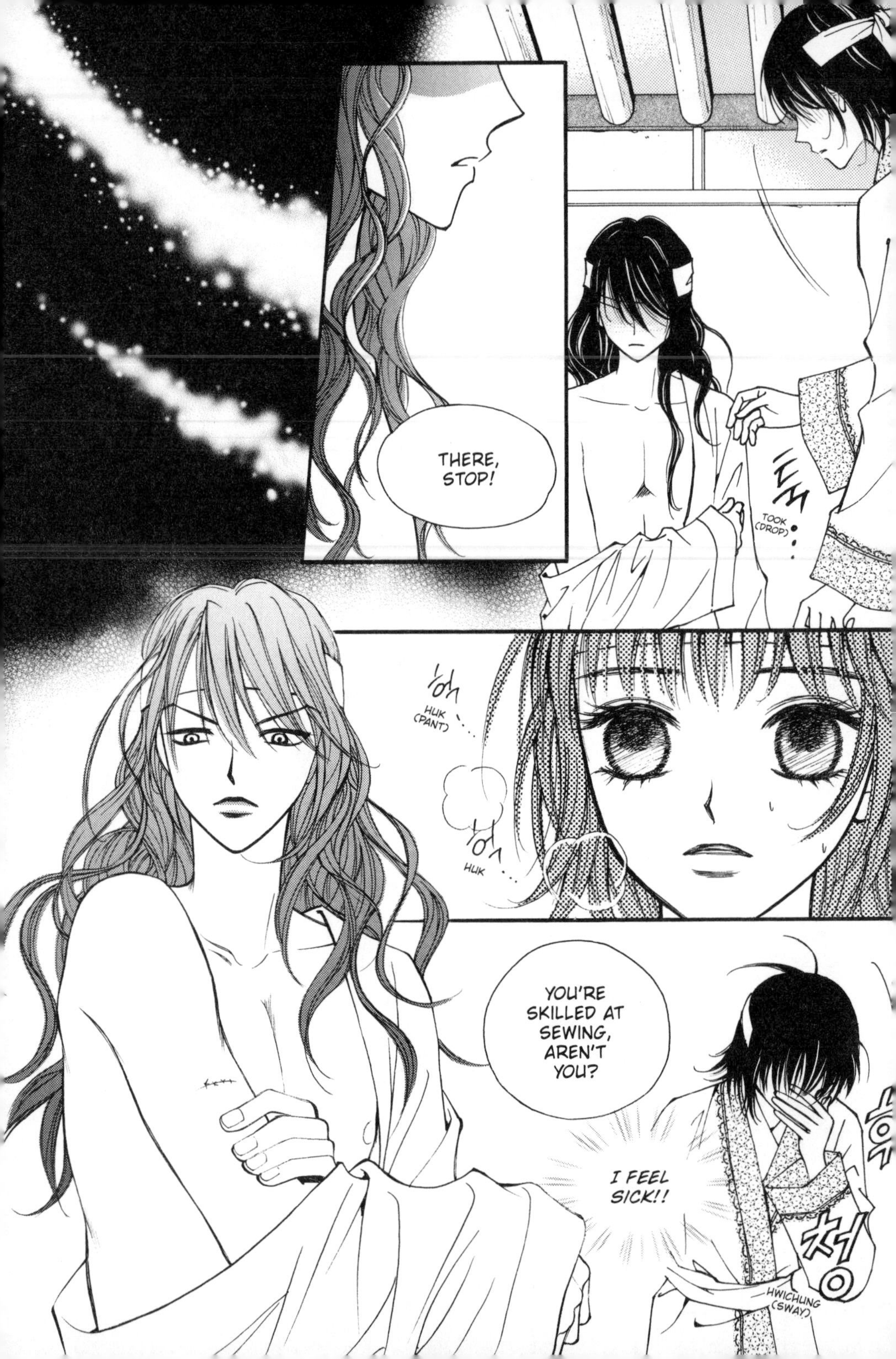
THERE, STOP!
TOOK (DROP)
헉
HUK (PANT)
헉
HUK
YOU'RE SKILLED AT SEWING, AREN'T YOU?
I FEEL SICK!!
HWICHUNG (SWAY)

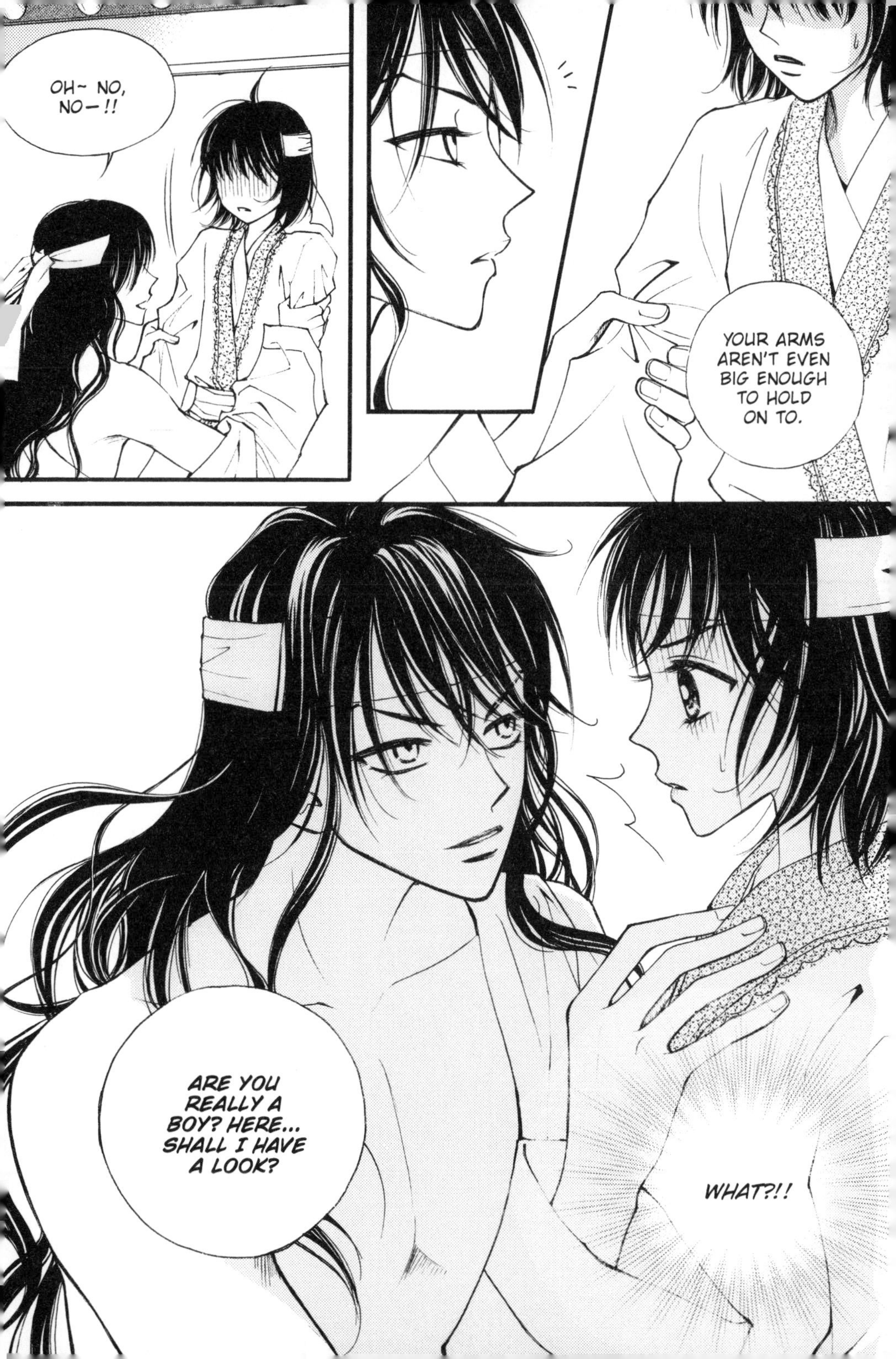
OH~ NO, NO—!!
YOUR ARMS AREN'T EVEN BIG ENOUGH TO HOLD ON TO.
ARE YOU REALLY A BOY? HERE... SHALL I HAVE A LOOK?
WHAT?!!

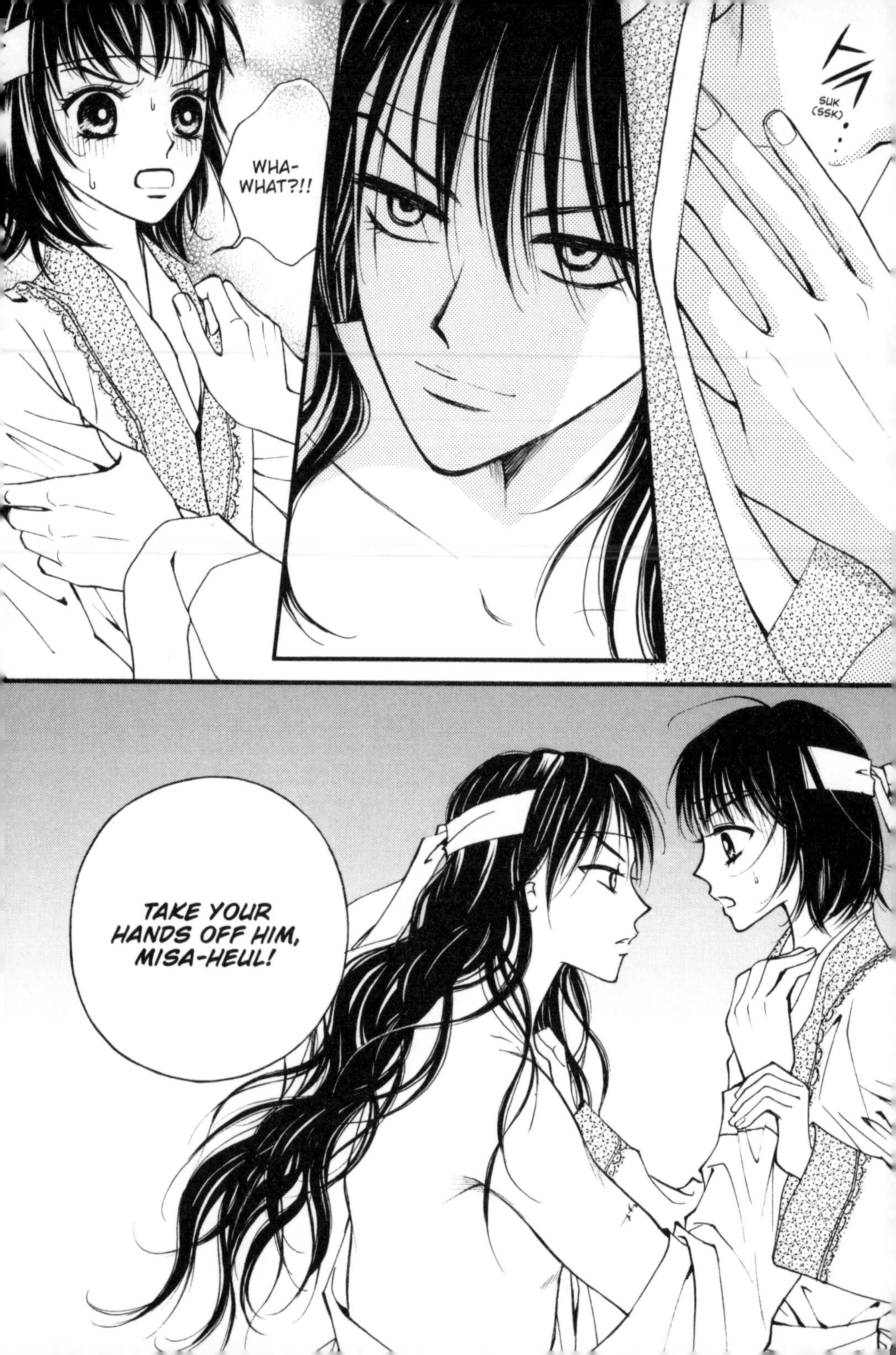
WHA-
WHAT?!!
SUK
(SSK)
TAKE YOUR
HANDS OFF HIM,
MISA-HEUL!

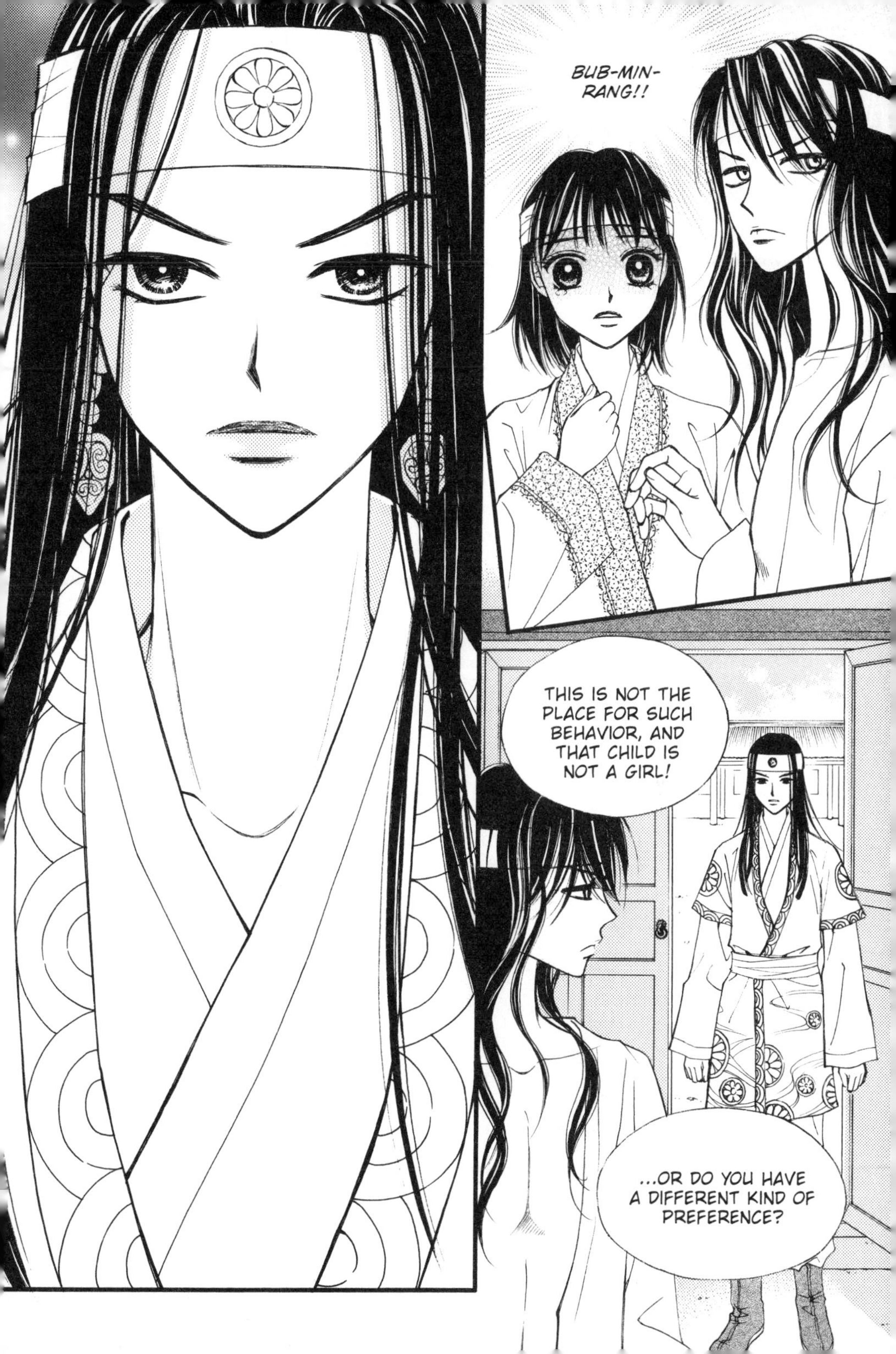
BUB-MIN-RANG!!
THIS IS NOT THE PLACE FOR SUCH BEHAVIOR, AND THAT CHILD IS NOT A GIRL!
...OR DO YOU HAVE A DIFFERENT KIND OF PREFERENCE?

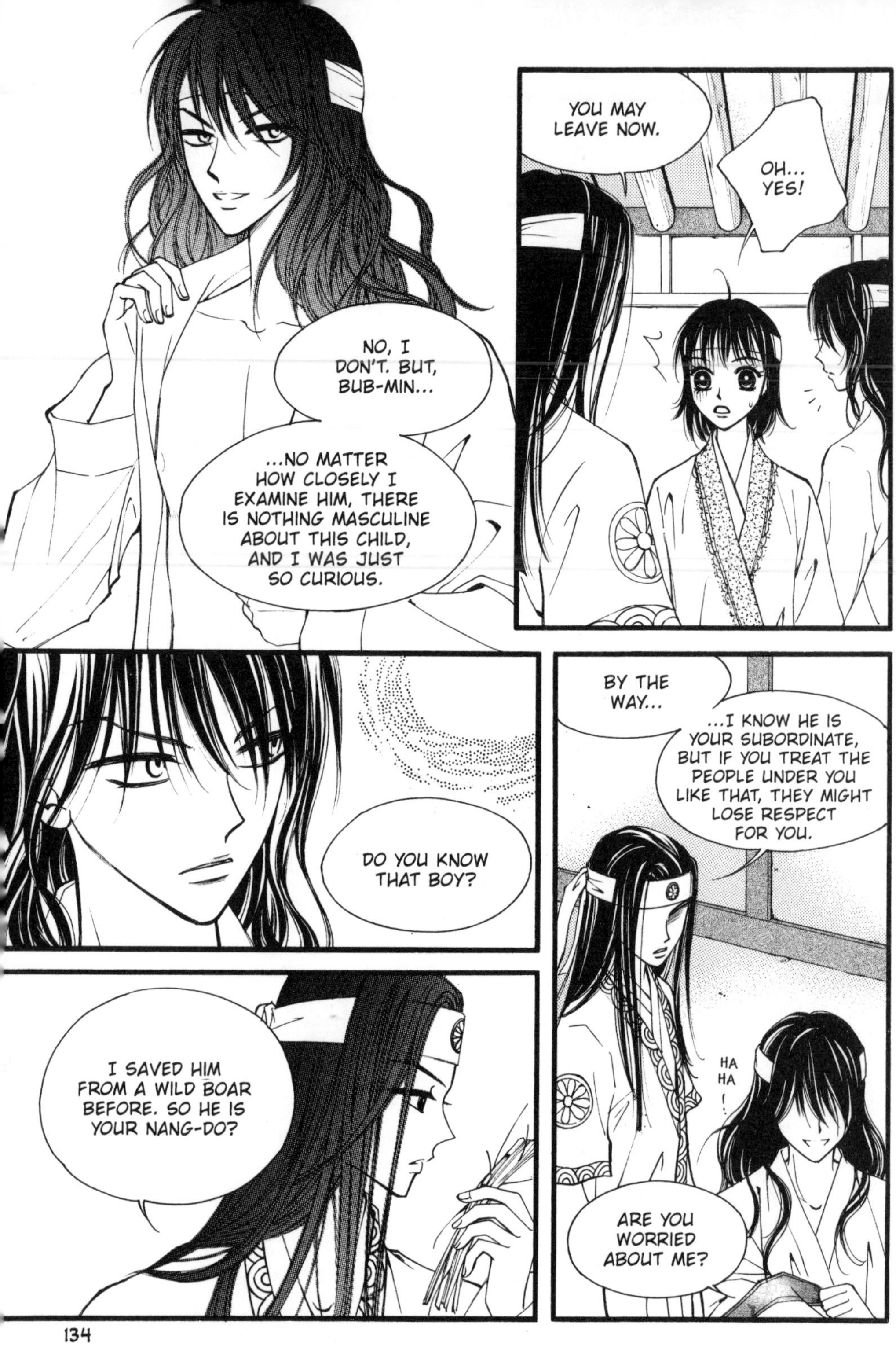
NO, I DON'T. BUT, BUB-MIN...
...NO MATTER HOW CLOSELY I EXAMINE HIM, THERE IS NOTHING MASCULINE ABOUT THIS CHILD, AND I WAS JUST SO CURIOUS.
YOU MAY LEAVE NOW.
OH... YES!
DO YOU KNOW THAT BOY?
I SAVED HIM FROM A WILD BOAR BEFORE. SO HE IS YOUR NANG-DO?
BY THE WAY...
...I KNOW HE IS YOUR SUBORDINATE, BUT IF YOU TREAT THE PEOPLE UNDER YOU LIKE THAT, THEY MIGHT LOSE RESPECT FOR YOU.
HA HA !
ARE YOU WORRIED ABOUT ME?

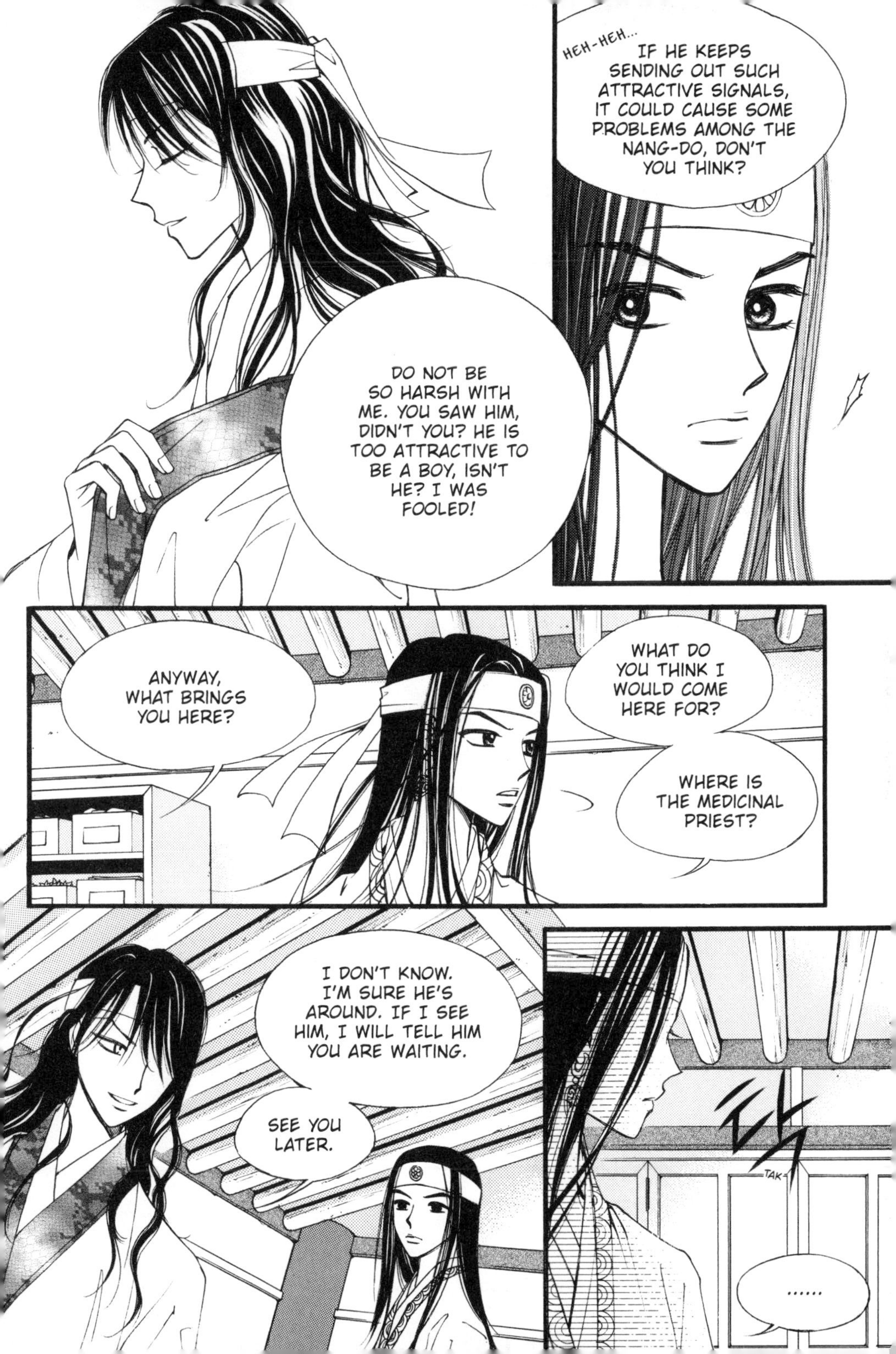
DO NOT BE SO HARSH WITH ME. YOU SAW HIM, DIDN'T YOU? HE IS TOO ATTRACTIVE TO BE A BOY, ISN'T HE? I WAS FOOLED!
HEH-HEH...
IF HE KEEPS SENDING OUT SUCH ATTRACTIVE SIGNALS, IT COULD CAUSE SOME PROBLEMS AMONG THE NANG-DO, DON'T YOU THINK?
ANYWAY, WHAT BRINGS YOU HERE?
WHAT DO YOU THINK I WOULD COME HERE FOR?
WHERE IS THE MEDICINAL PRIEST?
I DON'T KNOW. I'M SURE HE'S AROUND. IF I SEE HIM, I WILL TELL HIM YOU ARE WAITING.
SEE YOU LATER.
TAK
......

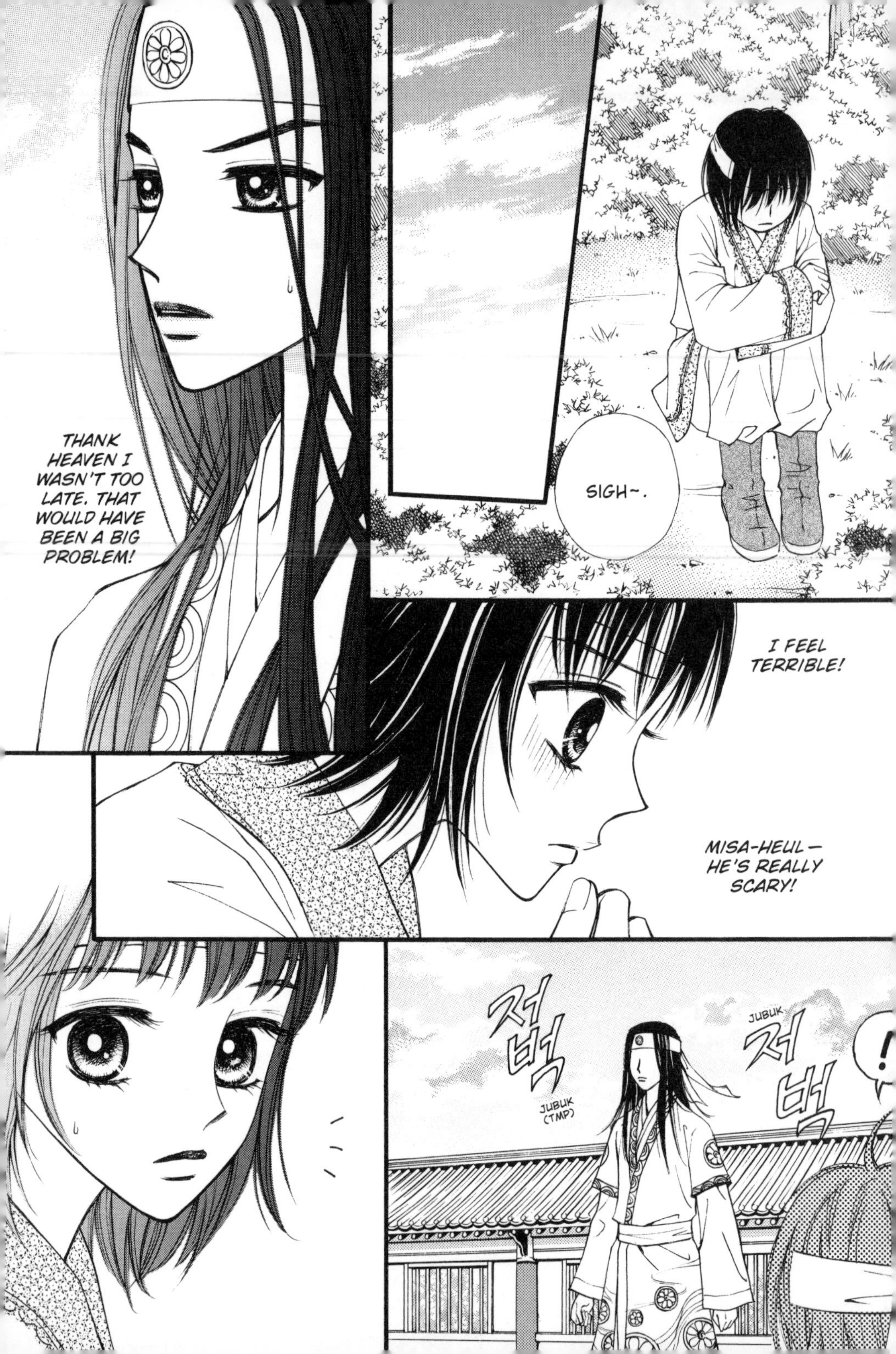
THANK HEAVEN I WASN'T TOO LATE. THAT WOULD HAVE BEEN A BIG PROBLEM!
SIGH~.
I FEEL TERRIBLE!
MISA-HEUL— HE'S REALLY SCARY!
저벅
JUBUK (TMP)
JUBUK
저벅
!

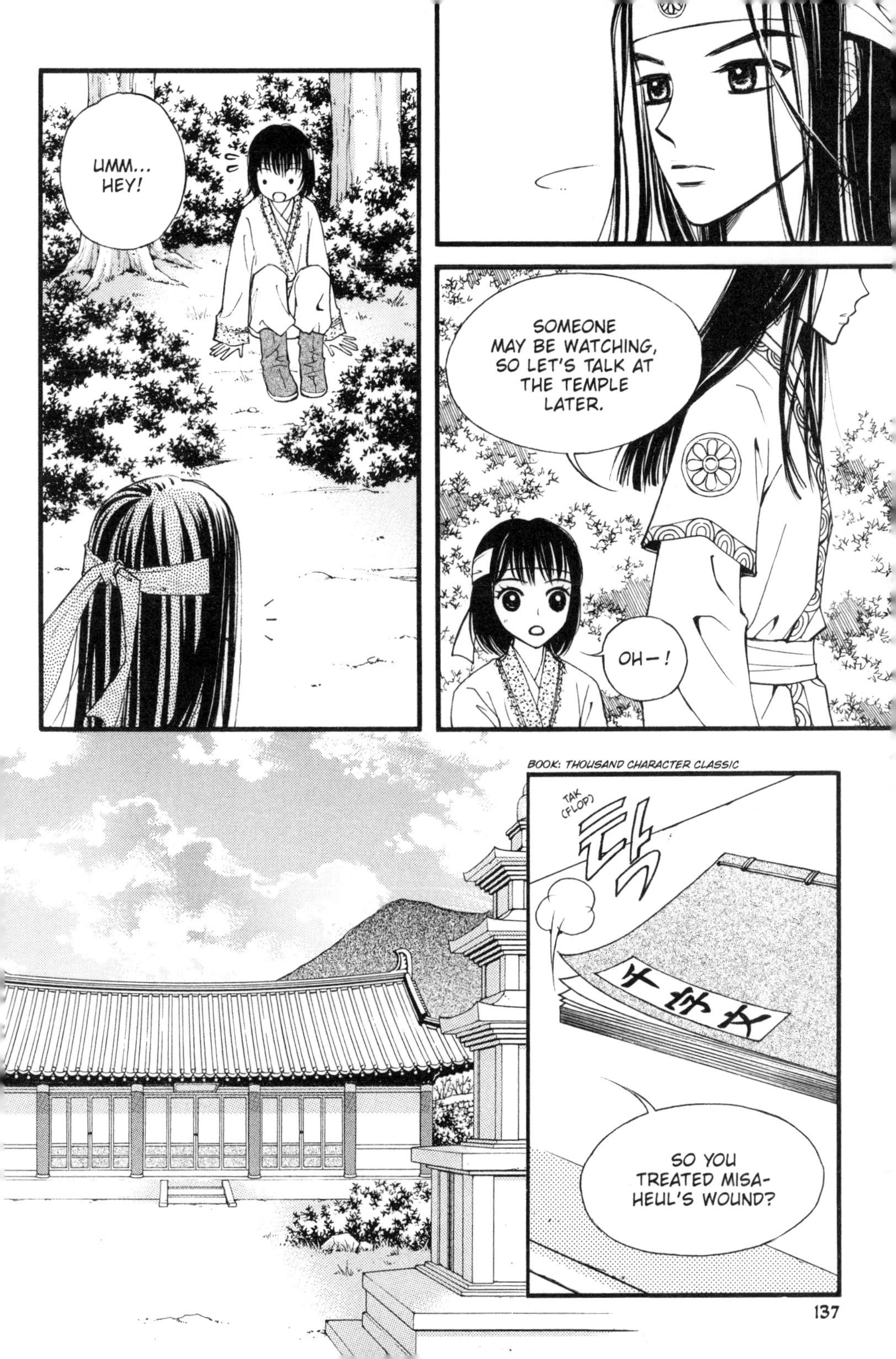
UMM... HEY!
SOMEONE MAY BE WATCHING, SO LET'S TALK AT THE TEMPLE LATER.
OH—!
BOOK: THOUSAND CHARACTER CLASSIC
TAK (FLOP)
SO YOU TREATED MISA-HEUL'S WOUND?

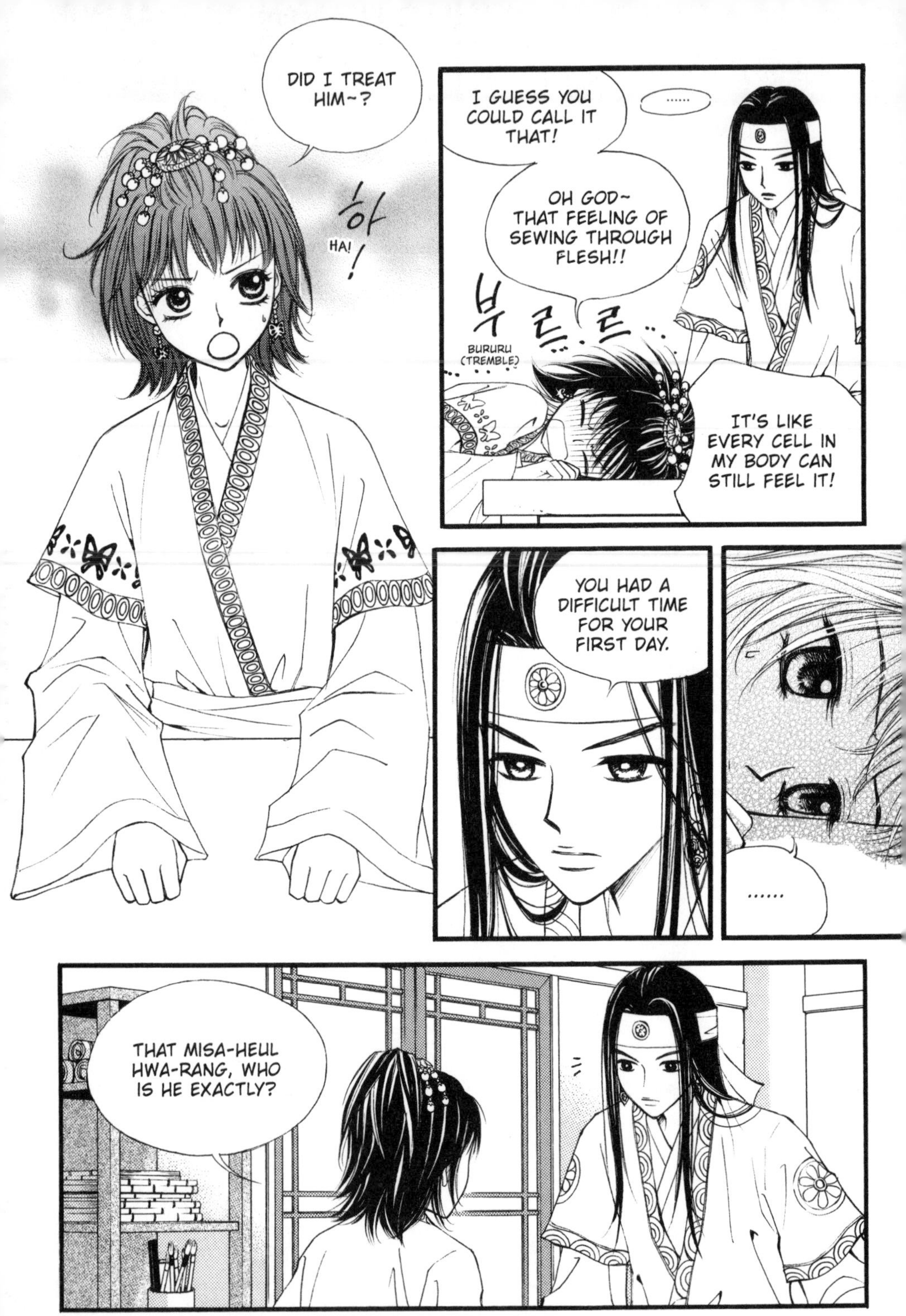
DID I TREAT HIM~?
하
HA!
I GUESS YOU COULD CALL IT THAT!
......
OH GOD~ THAT FEELING OF SEWING THROUGH FLESH!!
부르르
BURURU (TREMBLE)
IT'S LIKE EVERY CELL IN MY BODY CAN STILL FEEL IT!
YOU HAD A DIFFICULT TIME FOR YOUR FIRST DAY.
......
THAT MISA-HEUL HWA-RANG, WHO IS HE EXACTLY?

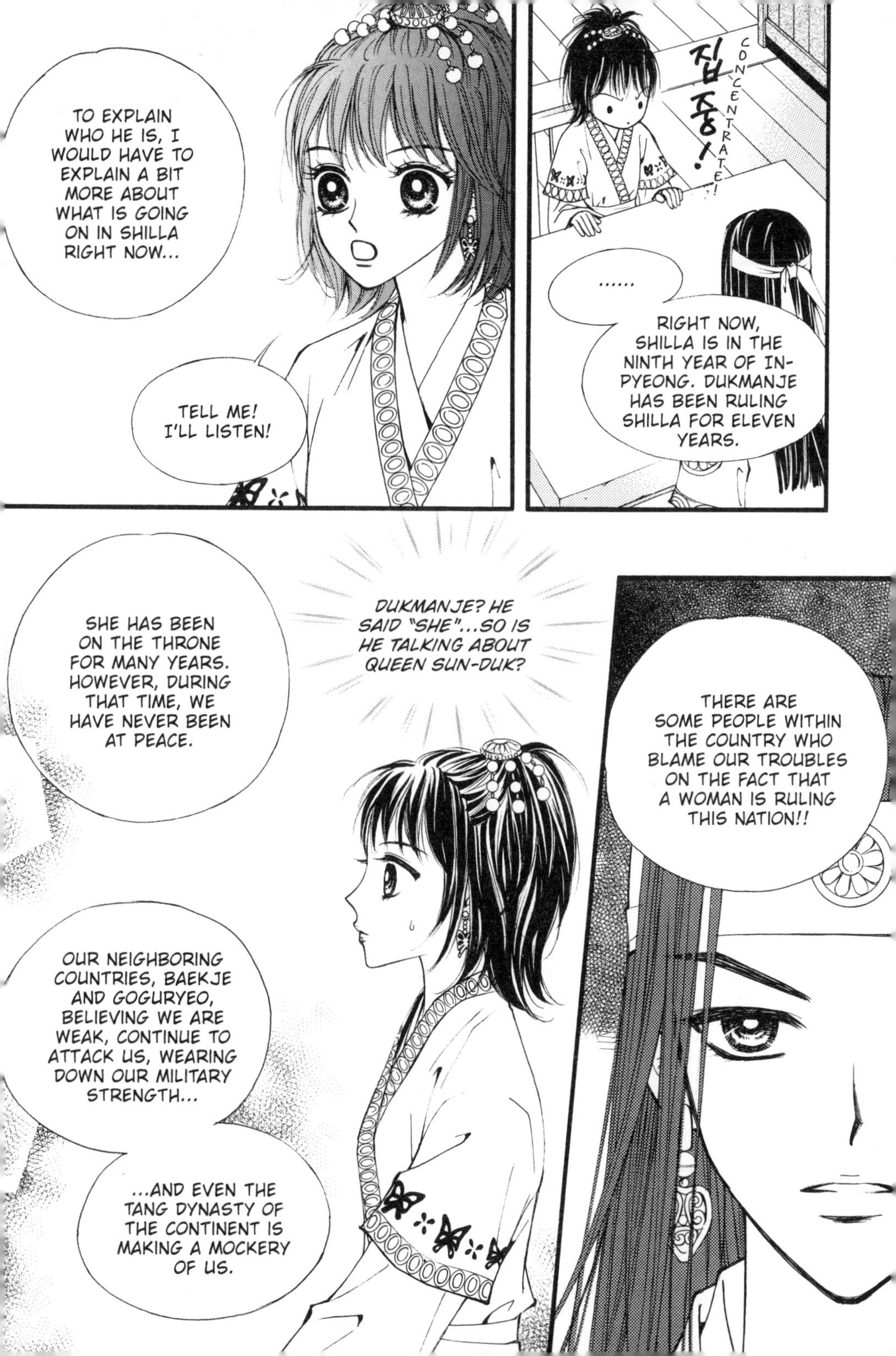
TO EXPLAIN WHO HE IS, I WOULD HAVE TO EXPLAIN A BIT MORE ABOUT WHAT IS GOING ON IN SHILLA RIGHT NOW...
TELL ME! I'LL LISTEN!
집중!
CONCENTRATE!
......
RIGHT NOW, SHILLA IS IN THE NINTH YEAR OF IN-PYEONG. DUKMANJE HAS BEEN RULING SHILLA FOR ELEVEN YEARS.
SHE HAS BEEN ON THE THRONE FOR MANY YEARS. HOWEVER, DURING THAT TIME, WE HAVE NEVER BEEN AT PEACE.
DUKMANJE? HE SAID "SHE"...SO IS HE TALKING ABOUT QUEEN SUN-DUK?
THERE ARE SOME PEOPLE WITHIN THE COUNTRY WHO BLAME OUR TROUBLES ON THE FACT THAT A WOMAN IS RULING THIS NATION!!
OUR NEIGHBORING COUNTRIES, BAEKJE AND GOGURYEO, BELIEVING WE ARE WEAK, CONTINUE TO ATTACK US, WEARING DOWN OUR MILITARY STRENGTH...
...AND EVEN THE TANG DYNASTY OF THE CONTINENT IS MAKING A MOCKERY OF US.

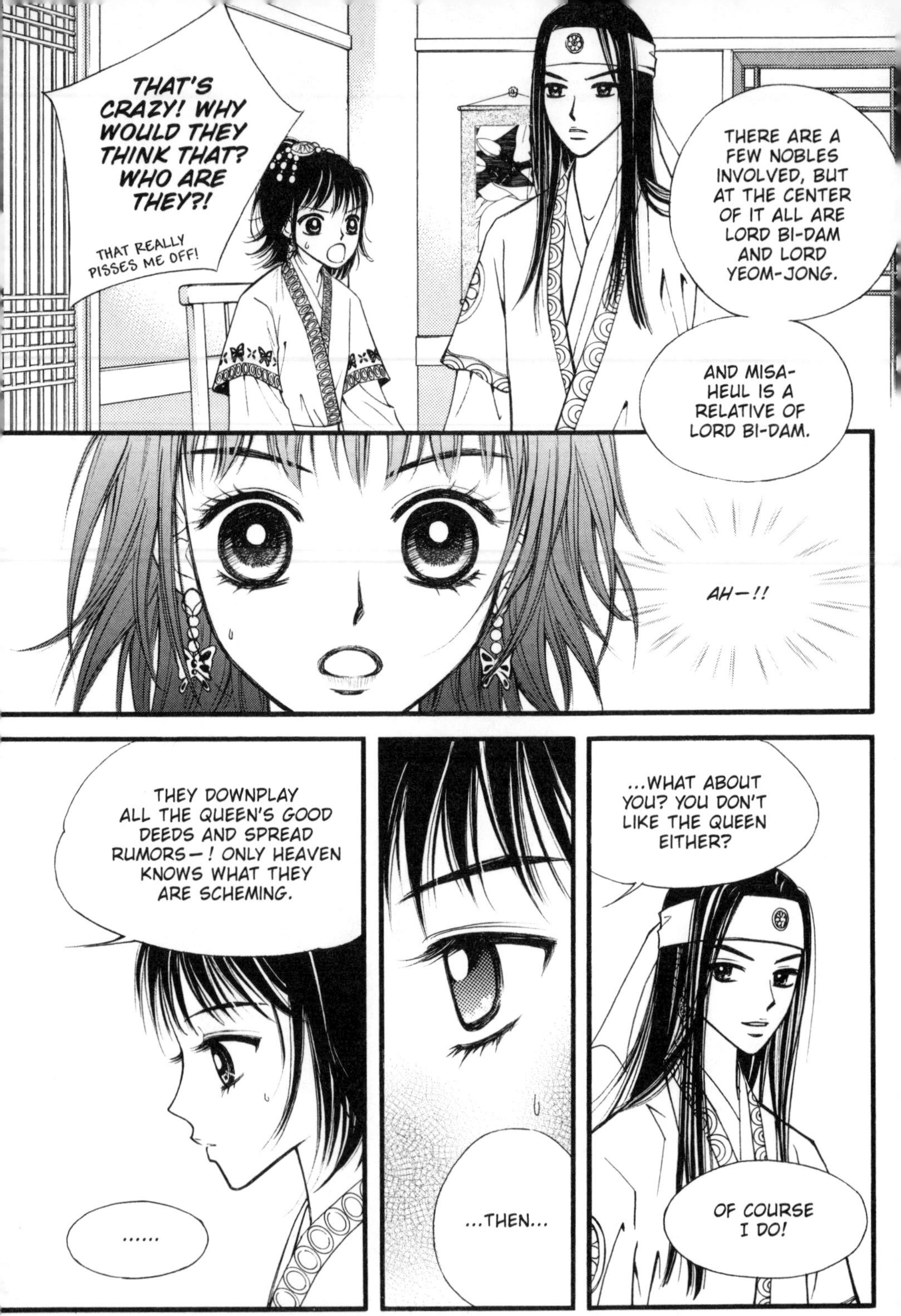

THAT'S CRAZY! WHY WOULD THEY THINK THAT? WHO ARE THEY?!
THAT REALLY PISSES ME OFF!
THERE ARE A FEW NOBLES INVOLVED, BUT AT THE CENTER OF IT ALL ARE LORD BI-DAM AND LORD YEOM-JONG.
AND MISA-HEUL IS A RELATIVE OF LORD BI-DAM.
AH—!!
THEY DOWNPLAY ALL THE QUEEN'S GOOD DEEDS AND SPREAD RUMORS—! ONLY HEAVEN KNOWS WHAT THEY ARE SCHEMING.
......
...THEN...
...WHAT ABOUT YOU? YOU DON'T LIKE THE QUEEN EITHER?
OF COURSE I DO!

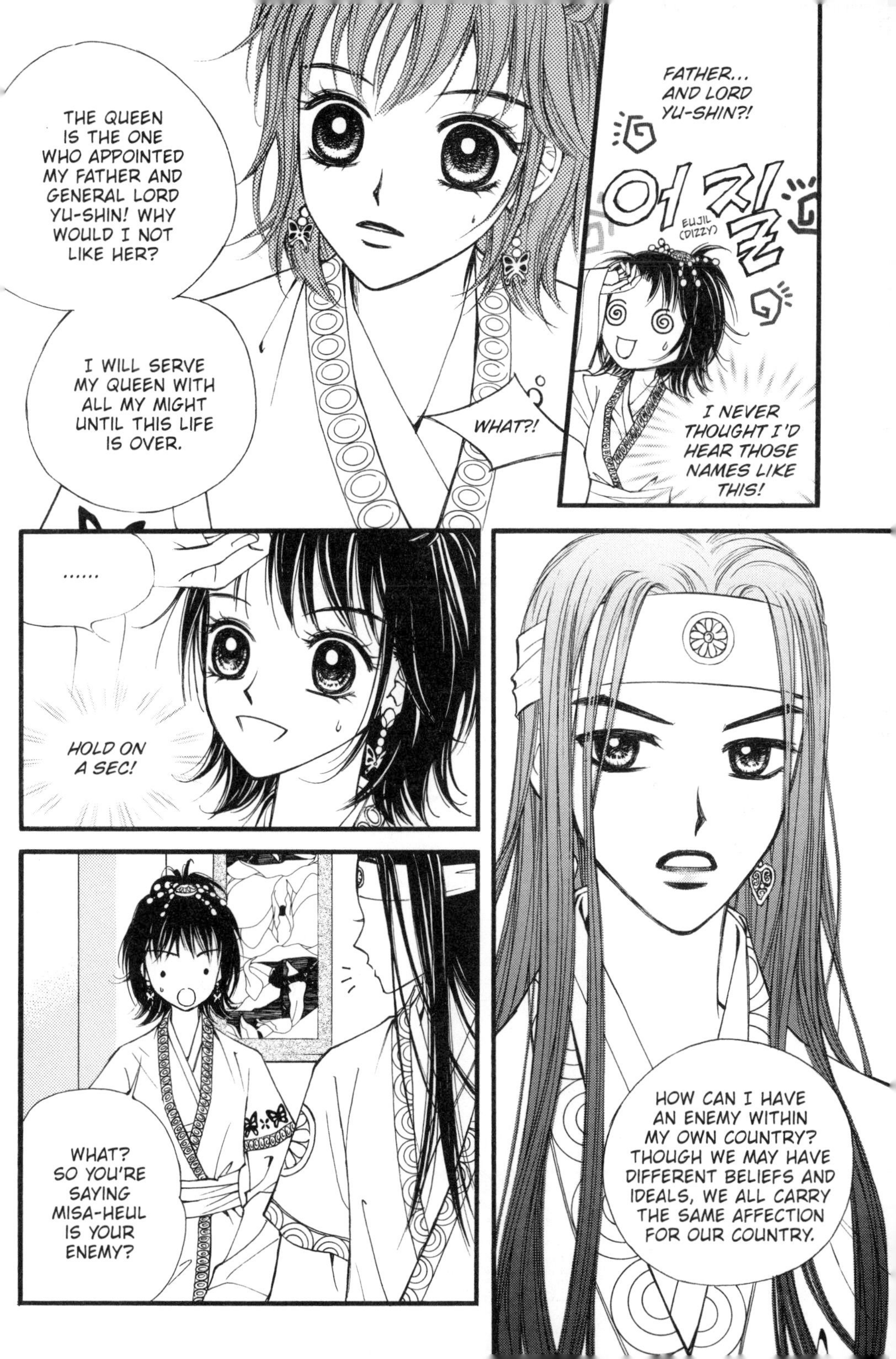
THE QUEEN IS THE ONE WHO APPOINTED MY FATHER AND GENERAL LORD YU-SHIN! WHY WOULD I NOT LIKE HER?
I WILL SERVE MY QUEEN WITH ALL MY MIGHT UNTIL THIS LIFE IS OVER.
WHAT?!
FATHER... AND LORD YU-SHIN?!
어질
EUJIL (DIZZY)
I NEVER THOUGHT I'D HEAR THOSE NAMES LIKE THIS!
......
HOLD ON A SEC!
WHAT? SO YOU'RE SAYING MISA-HEUL IS YOUR ENEMY?
HOW CAN I HAVE AN ENEMY WITHIN MY OWN COUNTRY? THOUGH WE MAY HAVE DIFFERENT BELIEFS AND IDEALS, WE ALL CARRY THE SAME AFFECTION FOR OUR COUNTRY.

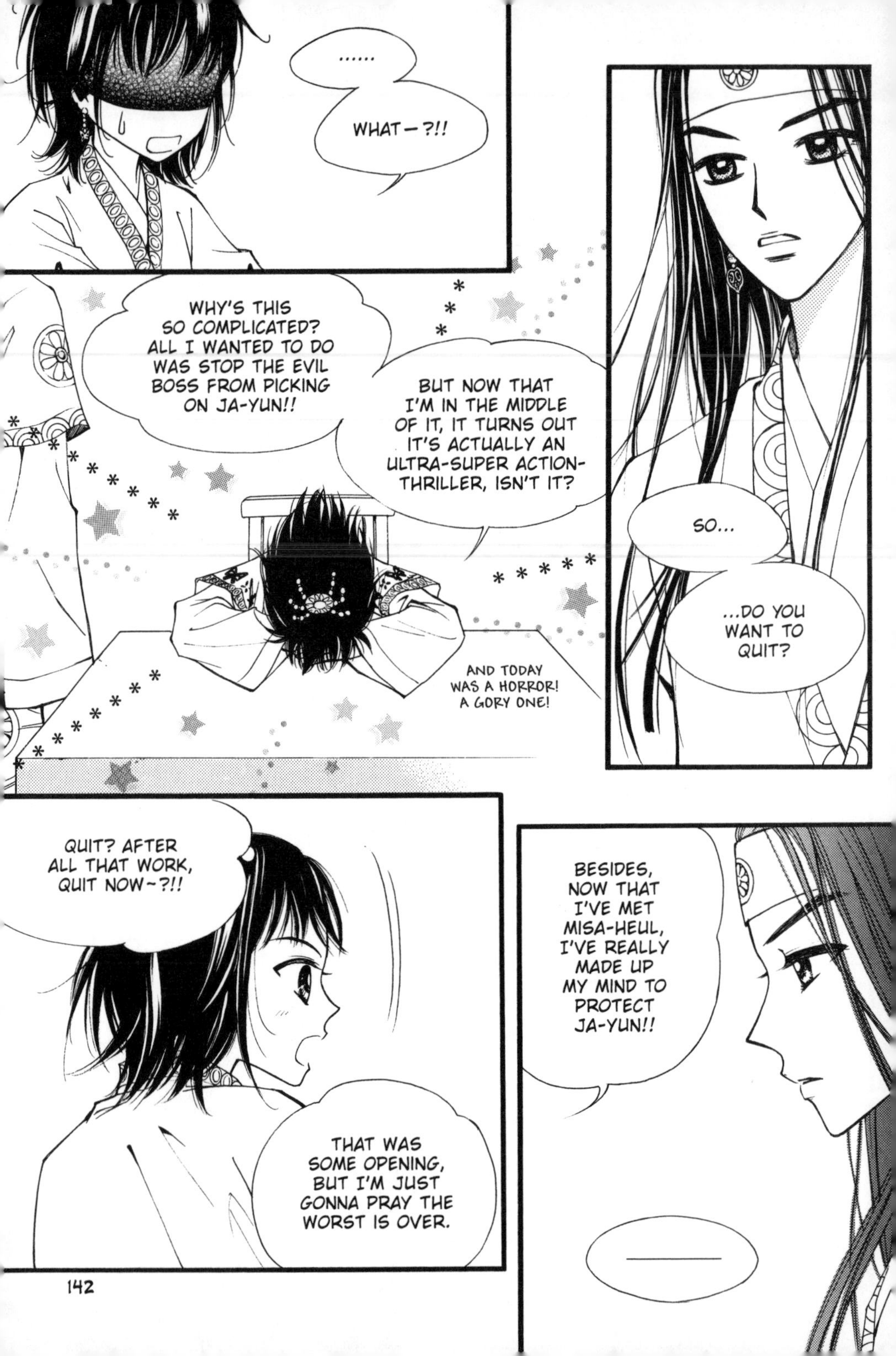
......
WHAT—?!!
WHY'S THIS SO COMPLICATED? ALL I WANTED TO DO WAS STOP THE EVIL BOSS FROM PICKING ON JA-YUN!!
BUT NOW THAT I'M IN THE MIDDLE OF IT, IT TURNS OUT IT'S ACTUALLY AN ULTRA-SUPER ACTION-THRILLER, ISN'T IT?
AND TODAY WAS A HORROR! A GORY ONE!
SO...
...DO YOU WANT TO QUIT?
QUIT? AFTER ALL THAT WORK, QUIT NOW~?!!
THAT WAS SOME OPENING, BUT I'M JUST GONNA PRAY THE WORST IS OVER.
BESIDES, NOW THAT I'VE MET MISA-HEUL, I'VE REALLY MADE UP MY MIND TO PROTECT JA-YUN!!
———

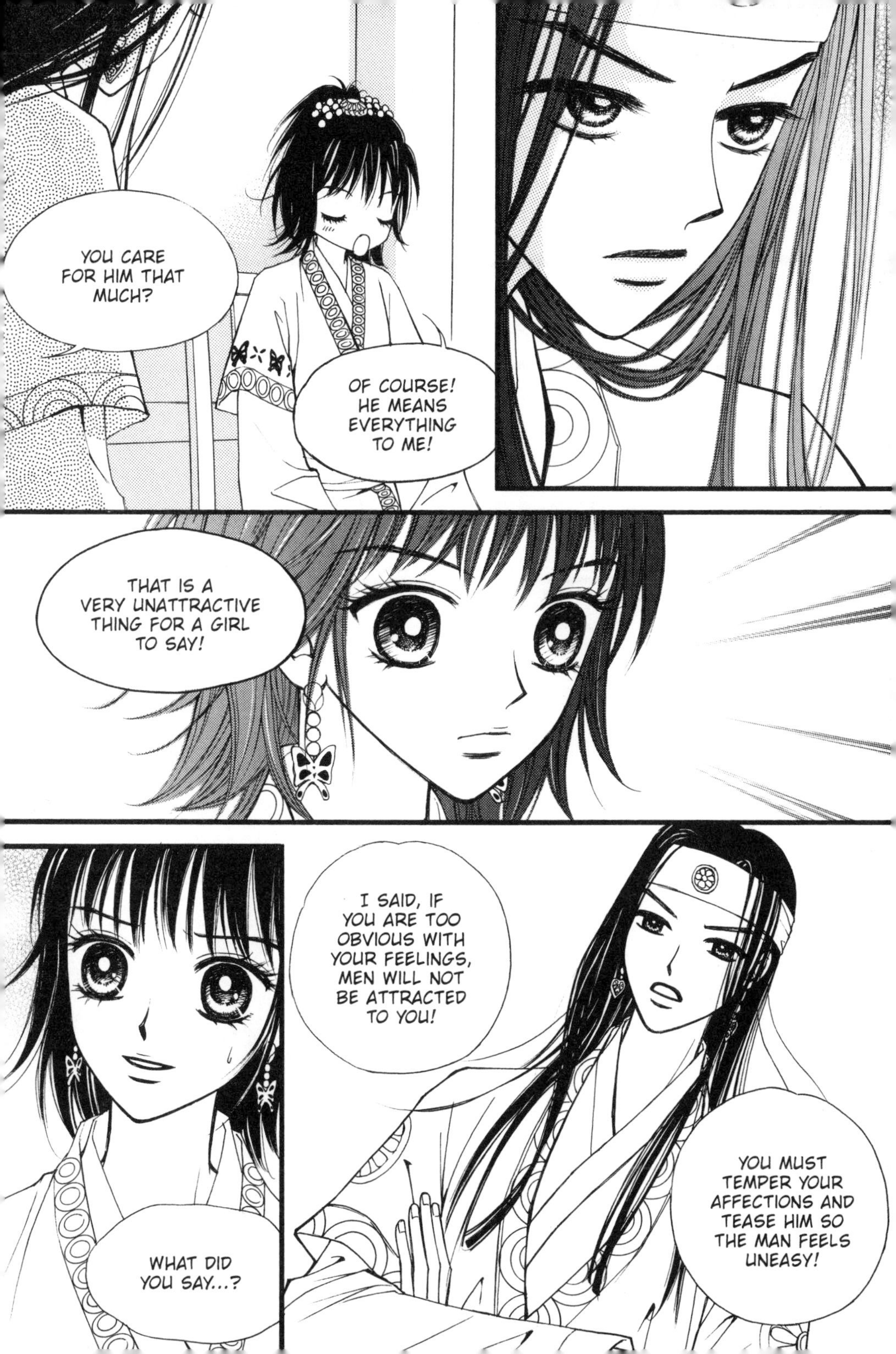
YOU CARE FOR HIM THAT MUCH?
OF COURSE! HE MEANS EVERYTHING TO ME!
THAT IS A VERY UNATTRACTIVE THING FOR A GIRL TO SAY!
WHAT DID YOU SAY...?
I SAID, IF YOU ARE TOO OBVIOUS WITH YOUR FEELINGS, MEN WILL NOT BE ATTRACTED TO YOU!
YOU MUST TEMPER YOUR AFFECTIONS AND TEASE HIM SO THE MAN FEELS UNEASY!

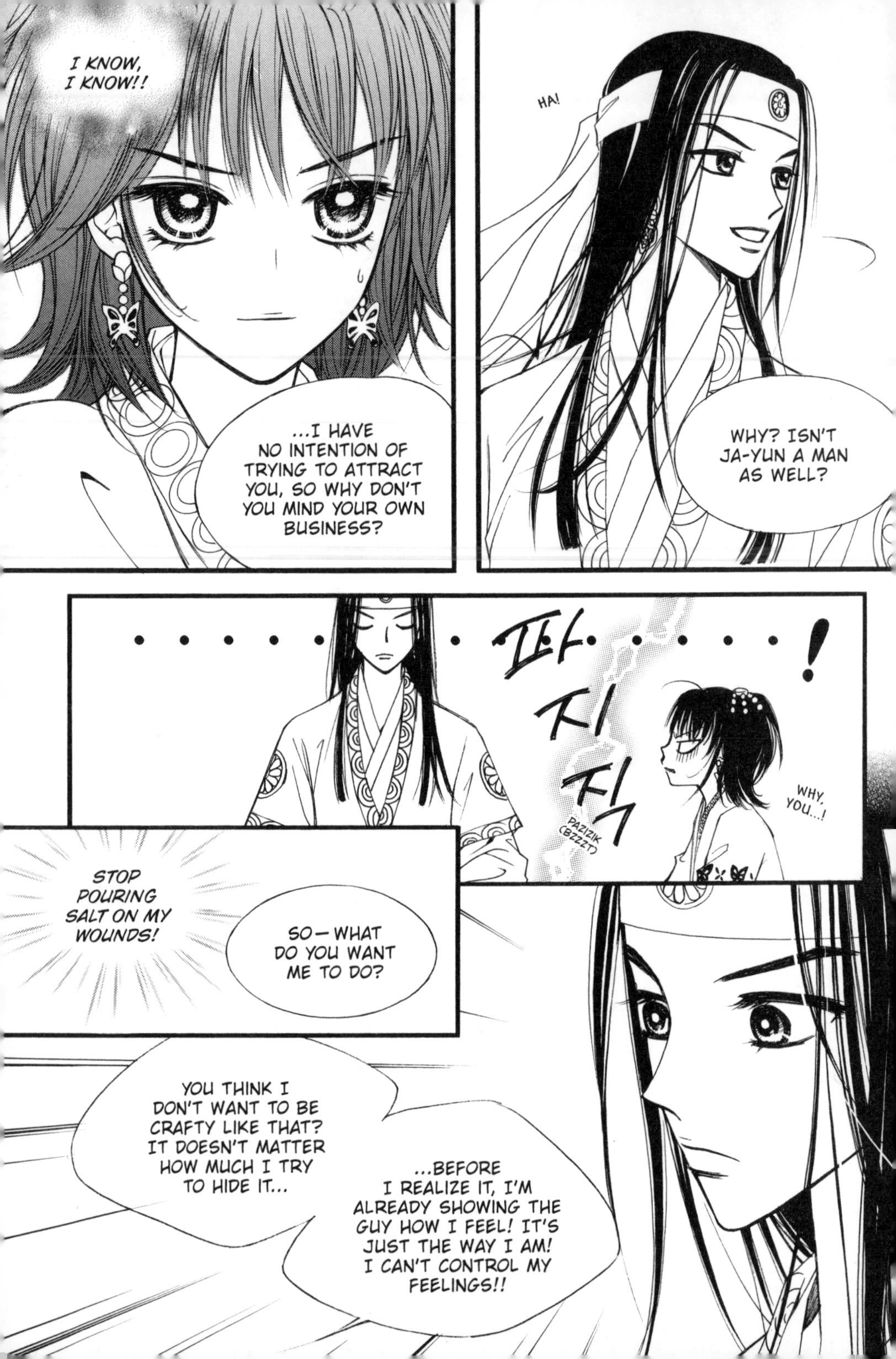
I KNOW, I KNOW!!
...I HAVE NO INTENTION OF TRYING TO ATTRACT YOU, SO WHY DON'T YOU MIND YOUR OWN BUSINESS?
HA!
WHY? ISN'T JA-YUN A MAN AS WELL?
.........!
파지직
PAZIZIK (BZZZT)
WHY, YOU...!
STOP POURING SALT ON MY WOUNDS!
SO— WHAT DO YOU WANT ME TO DO?
YOU THINK I DON'T WANT TO BE CRAFTY LIKE THAT? IT DOESN'T MATTER HOW MUCH I TRY TO HIDE IT...
...BEFORE I REALIZE IT, I'M ALREADY SHOWING THE GUY HOW I FEEL! IT'S JUST THE WAY I AM! I CAN'T CONTROL MY FEELINGS!!

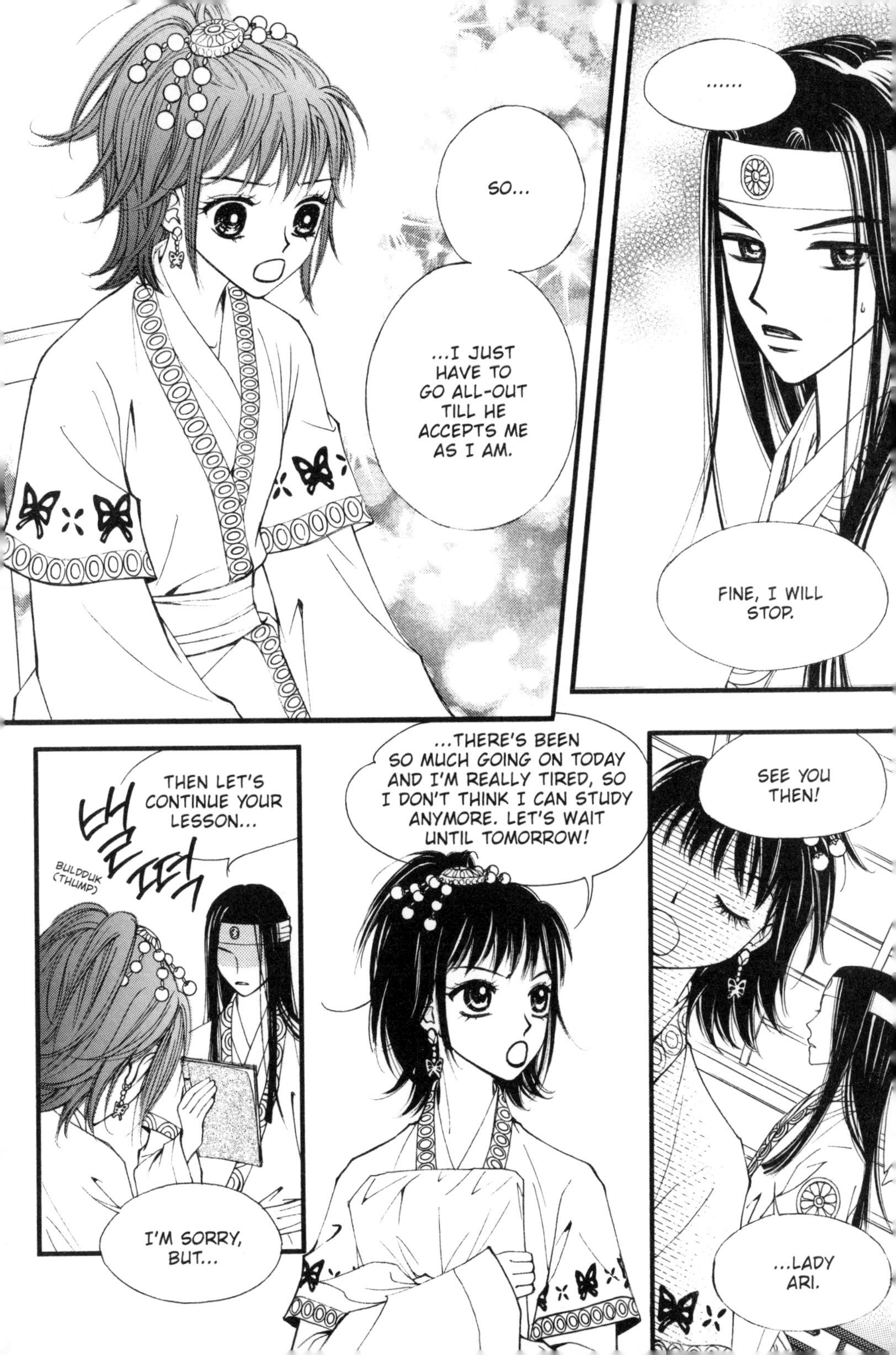
SO...
...I JUST HAVE TO GO ALL-OUT TILL HE ACCEPTS ME AS I AM.
......
FINE, I WILL STOP.
THEN LET'S CONTINUE YOUR LESSON...
벌떡
BULDDUK (THUMP)
I'M SORRY, BUT...
...THERE'S BEEN SO MUCH GOING ON TODAY AND I'M REALLY TIRED, SO I DON'T THINK I CAN STUDY ANYMORE. LET'S WAIT UNTIL TOMORROW!
SEE YOU THEN!
...LADY ARI.

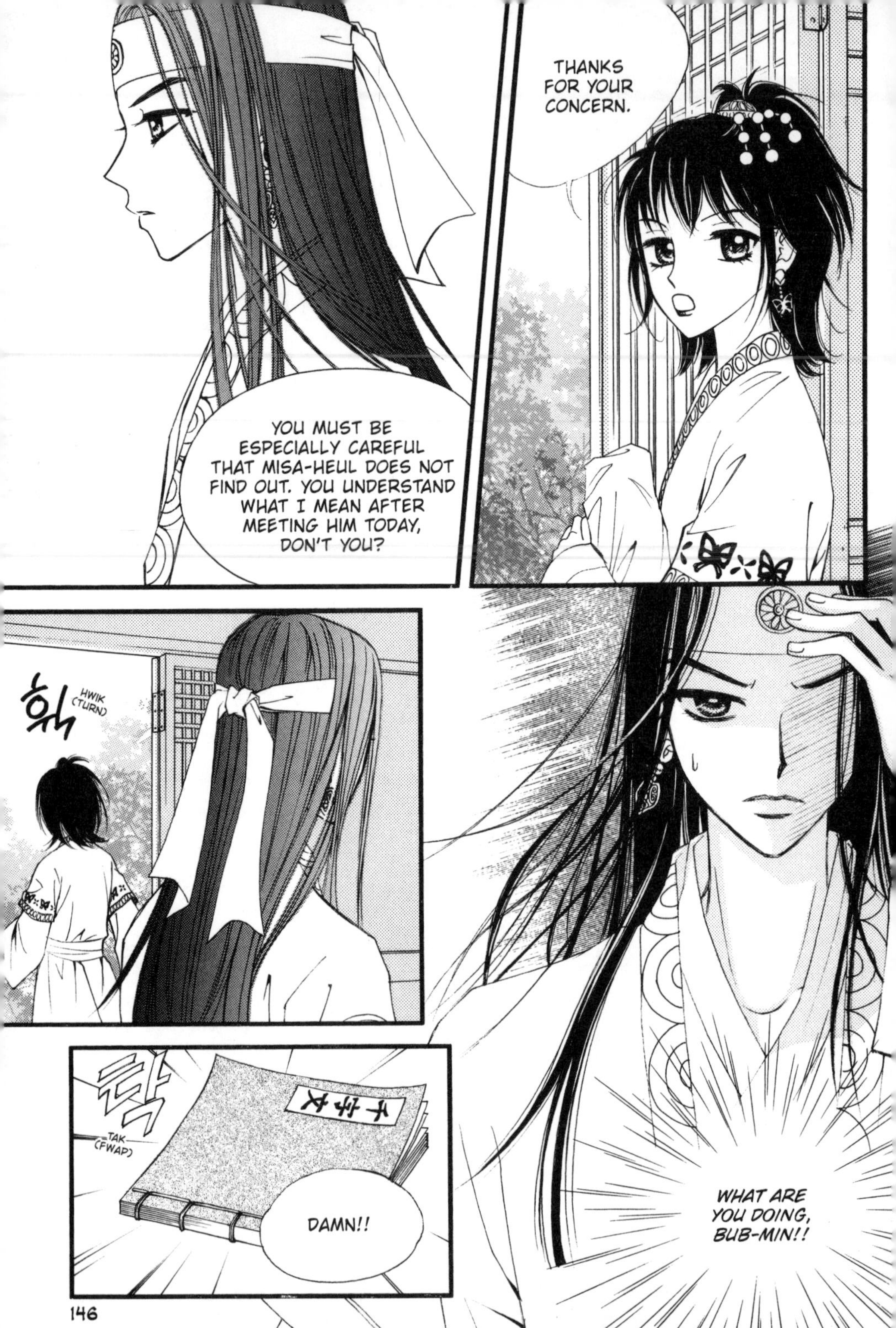
YOU MUST BE ESPECIALLY CAREFUL THAT MISA-HEUL DOES NOT FIND OUT. YOU UNDERSTAND WHAT I MEAN AFTER MEETING HIM TODAY, DON'T YOU?
THANKS FOR YOUR CONCERN.
휙
HWIK (TURN)
탁
TAK (FWAP)
DAMN!!
WHAT ARE YOU DOING, BUB-MIN!!

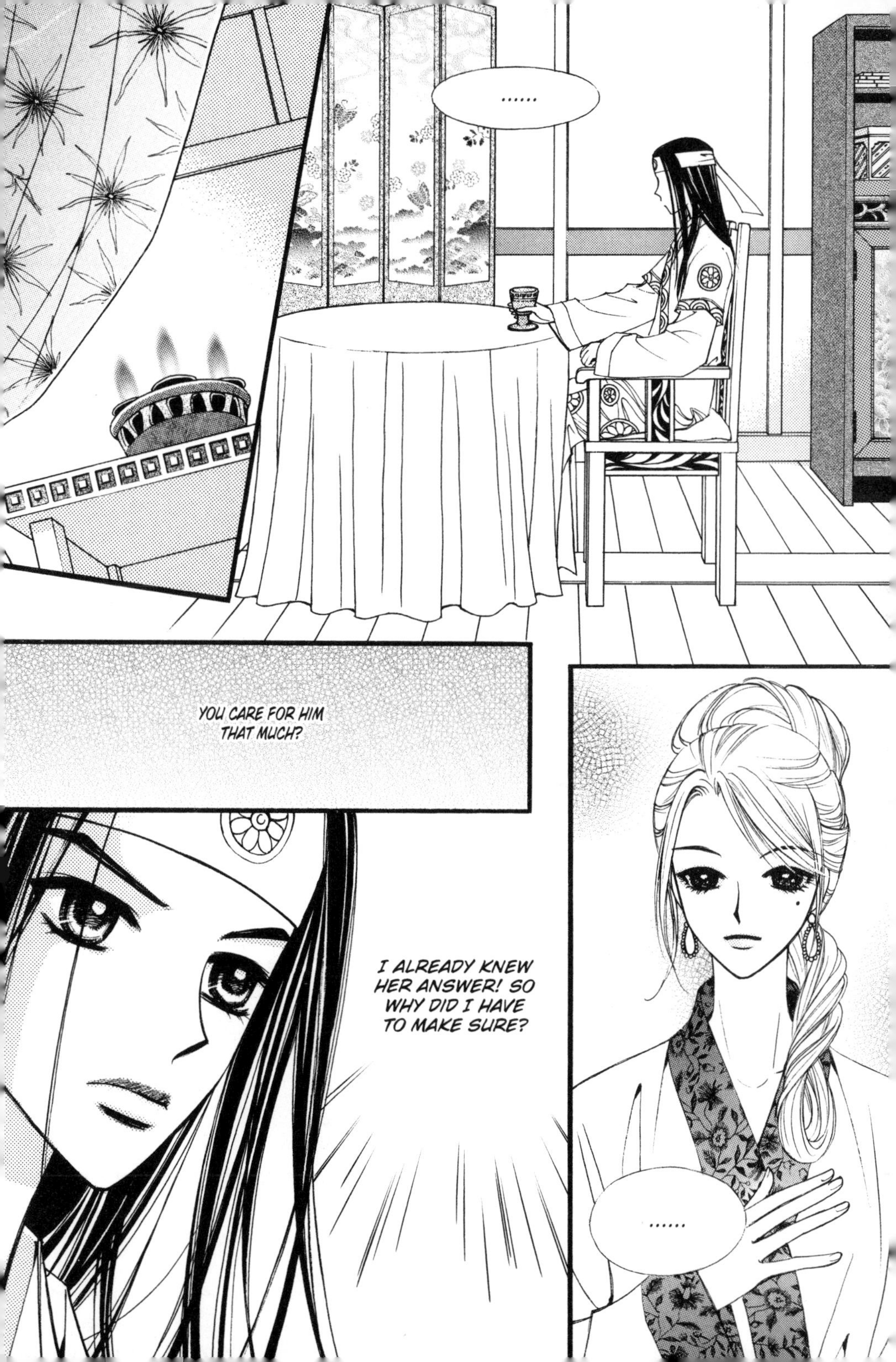
......
YOU CARE FOR HIM THAT MUCH?
I ALREADY KNEW HER ANSWER! SO WHY DID I HAVE TO MAKE SURE?
......

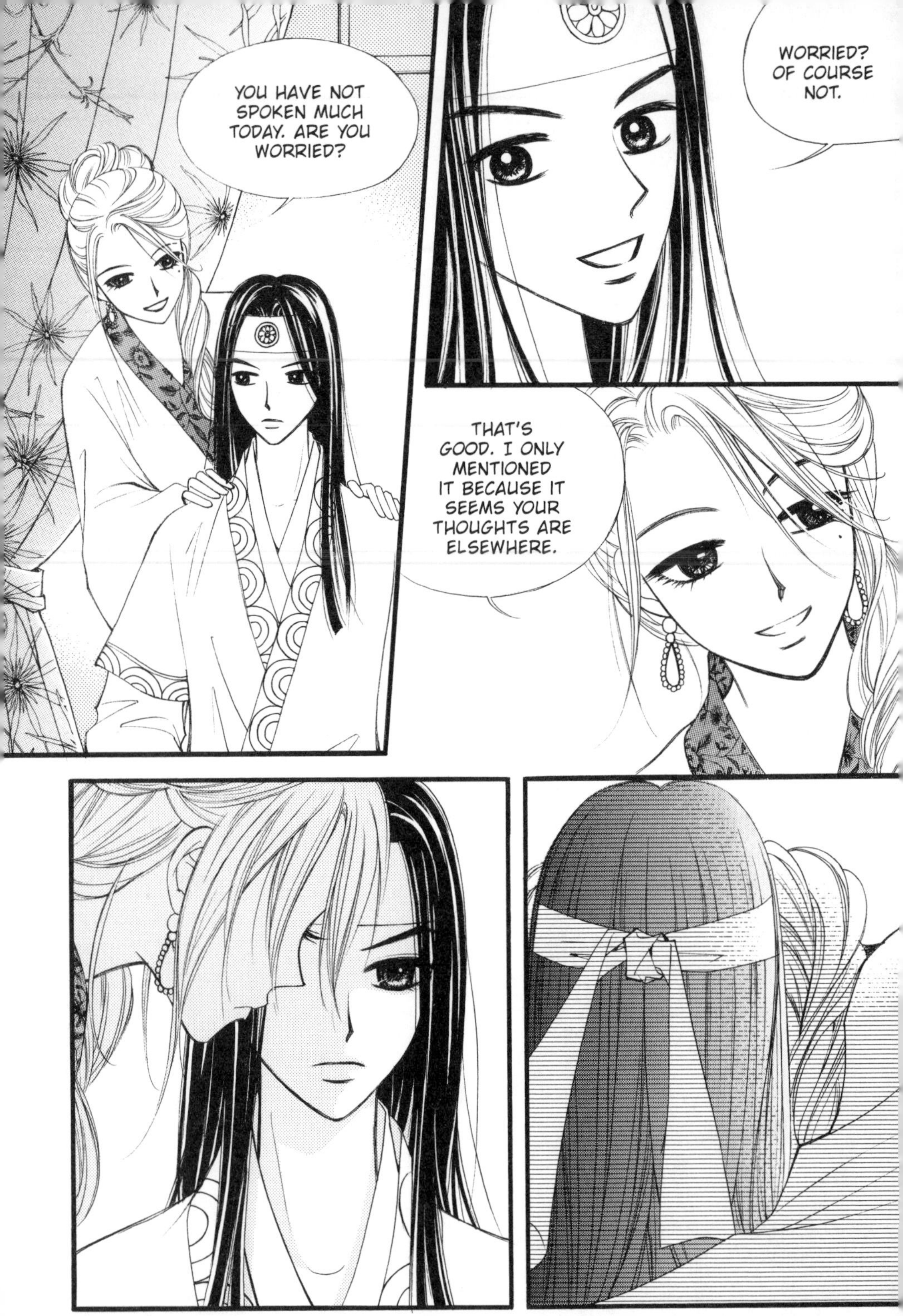
YOU HAVE NOT SPOKEN MUCH TODAY. ARE YOU WORRIED?
WORRIED? OF COURSE NOT.
THAT'S GOOD. I ONLY MENTIONED IT BECAUSE IT SEEMS YOUR THOUGHTS ARE ELSEWHERE.

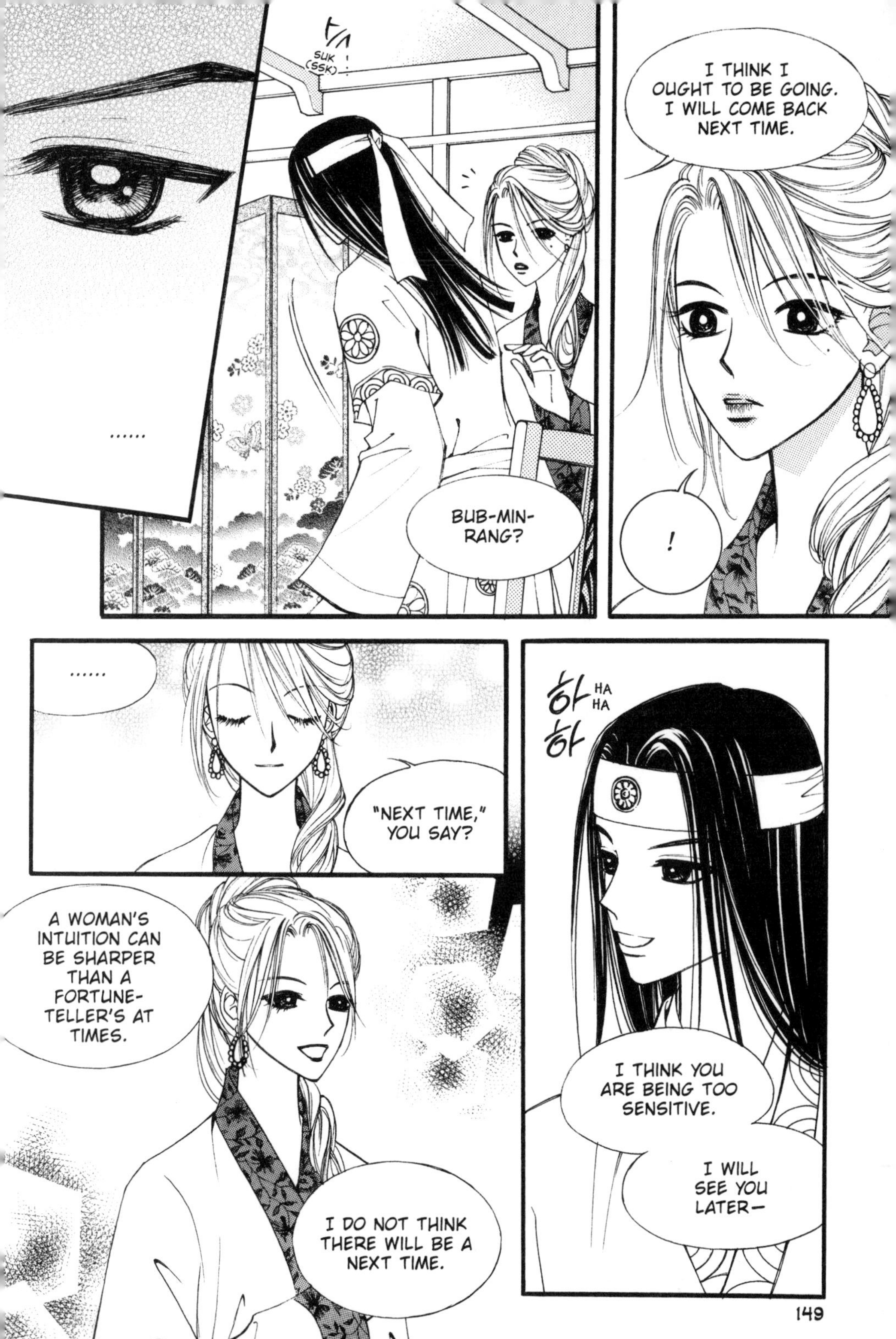
......
슥
SUK (SSK)
BUB-MIN-RANG?
I THINK I OUGHT TO BE GOING. I WILL COME BACK NEXT TIME.
!
......
"NEXT TIME," YOU SAY?
A WOMAN'S INTUITION CAN BE SHARPER THAN A FORTUNE-TELLER'S AT TIMES.
I DO NOT THINK THERE WILL BE A NEXT TIME.
하하
HA HA
I THINK YOU ARE BEING TOO SENSITIVE.
I WILL SEE YOU LATER—

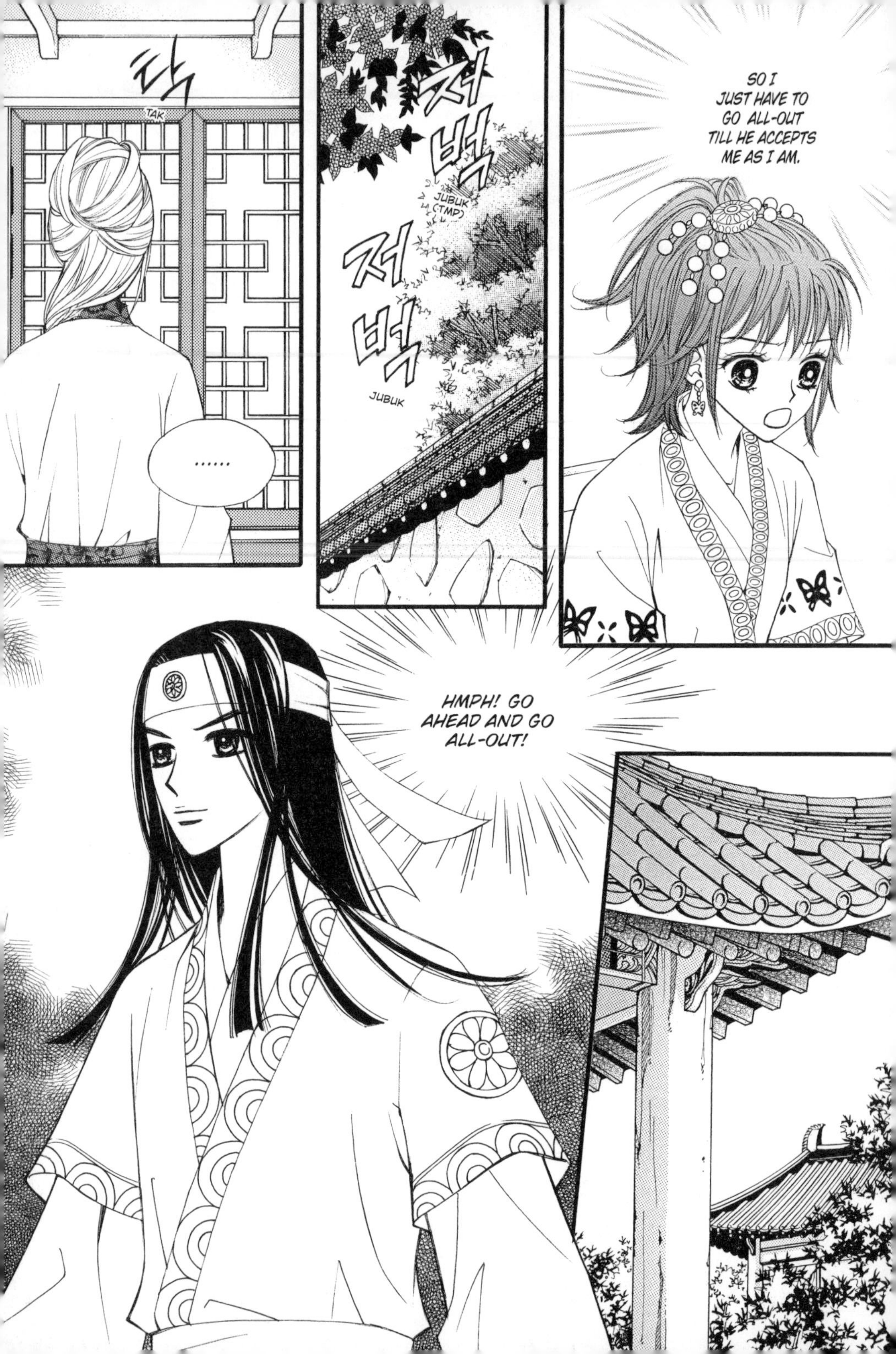
탁
TAK
......
저벅
JUBUK (TMP)
저벅
JUBUK
SO I JUST HAVE TO GO ALL-OUT TILL HE ACCEPTS ME AS I AM.
HMPH! GO AHEAD AND GO ALL-OUT!

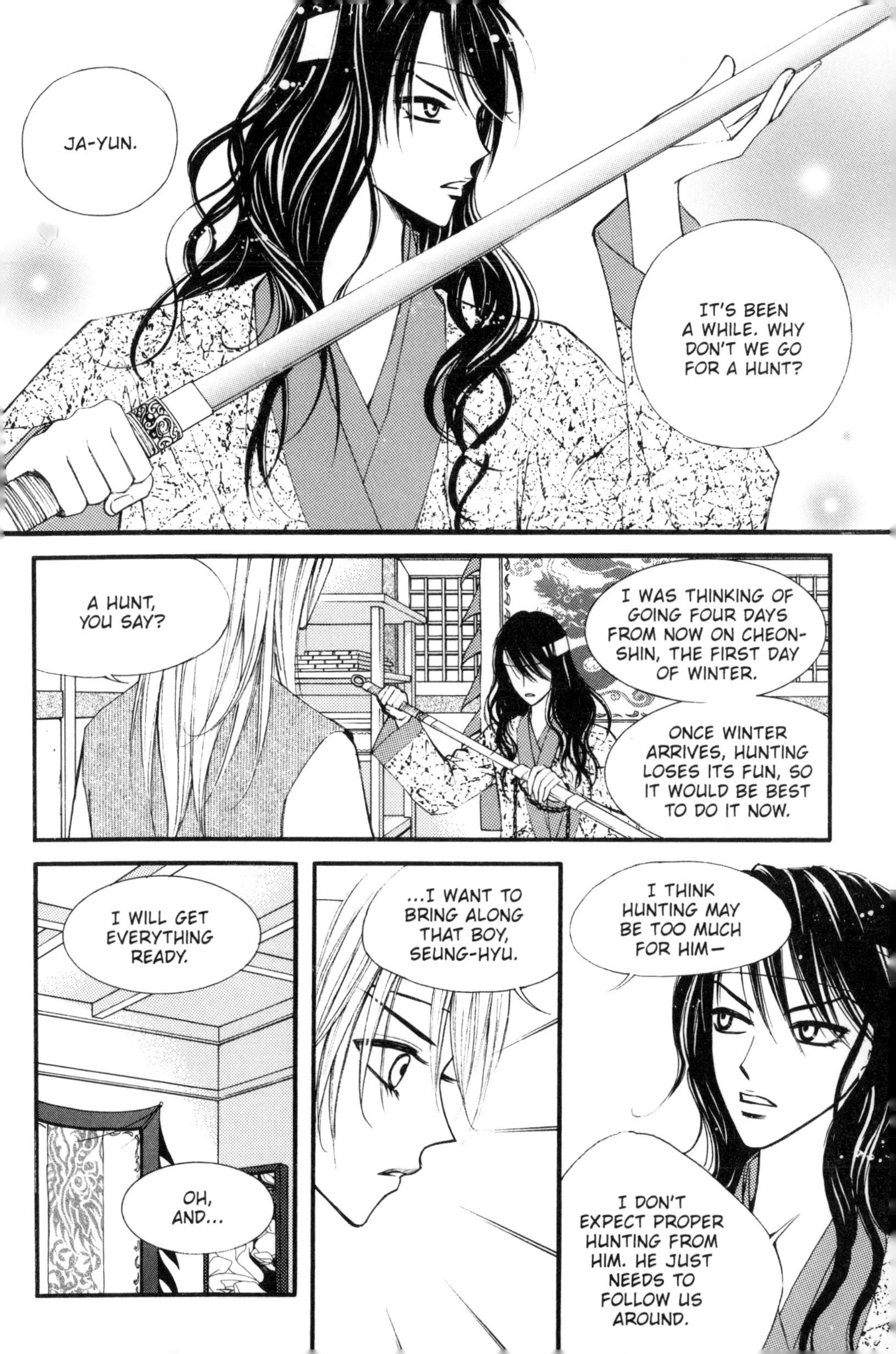
JA-YUN.
IT'S BEEN A WHILE. WHY DON'T WE GO FOR A HUNT?
A HUNT, YOU SAY?
I WAS THINKING OF GOING FOUR DAYS FROM NOW ON CHEON-SHIN, THE FIRST DAY OF WINTER.
ONCE WINTER ARRIVES, HUNTING LOSES ITS FUN, SO IT WOULD BE BEST TO DO IT NOW.
I WILL GET EVERYTHING READY.
OH, AND...
...I WANT TO BRING ALONG THAT BOY, SEUNG-HYU.
I THINK HUNTING MAY BE TOO MUCH FOR HIM—
I DON'T EXPECT PROPER HUNTING FROM HIM. HE JUST NEEDS TO FOLLOW US AROUND.

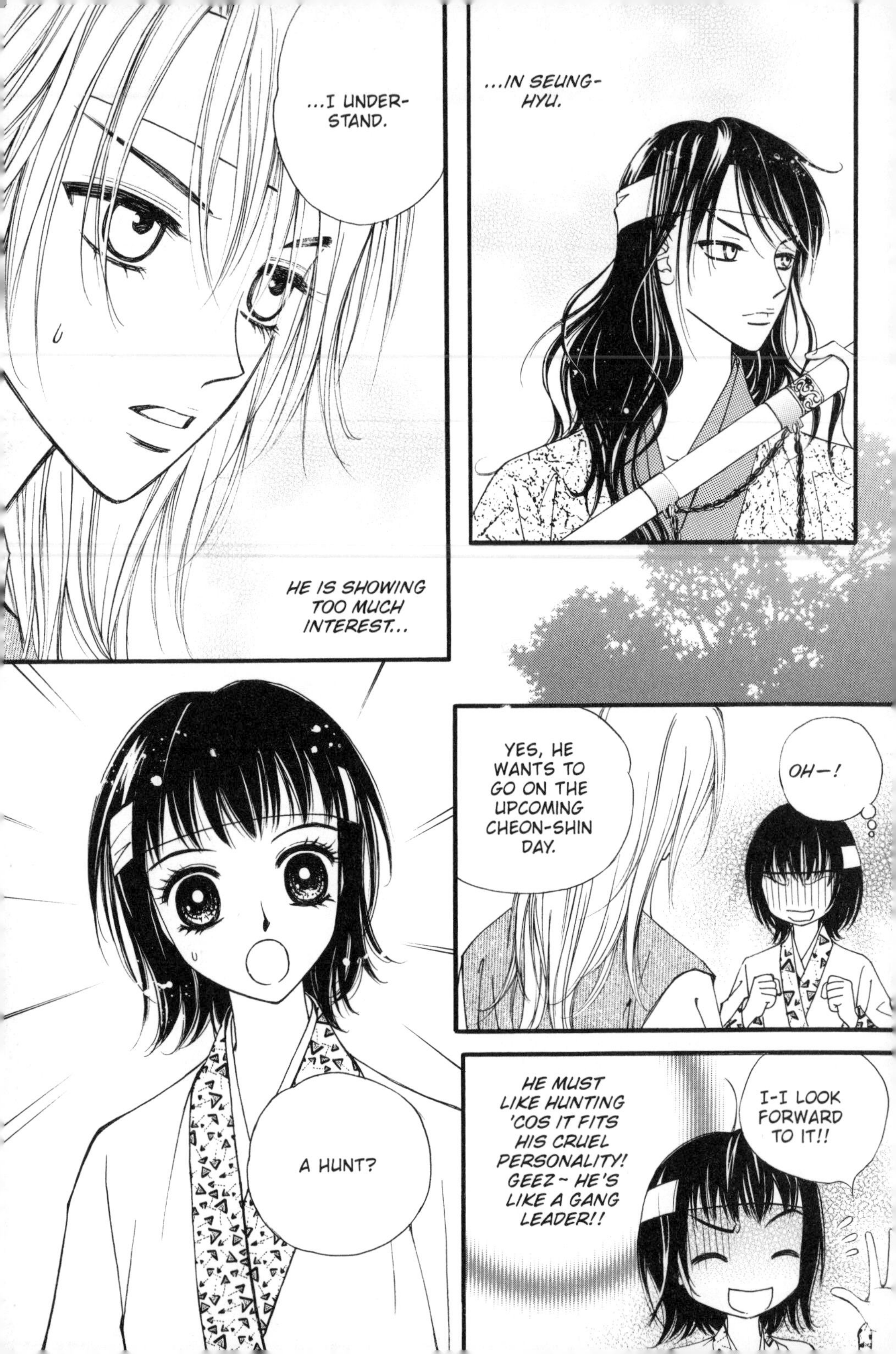

...I UNDER-STAND.
HE IS SHOWING TOO MUCH INTEREST...
...IN SEUNG-HYU.
A HUNT?
YES, HE WANTS TO GO ON THE UPCOMING CHEON-SHIN DAY.
OH—!
HE MUST LIKE HUNTING 'COS IT FITS HIS CRUEL PERSONALITY! GEEZ~ HE'S LIKE A GANG LEADER!!
I-I LOOK FORWARD TO IT!!

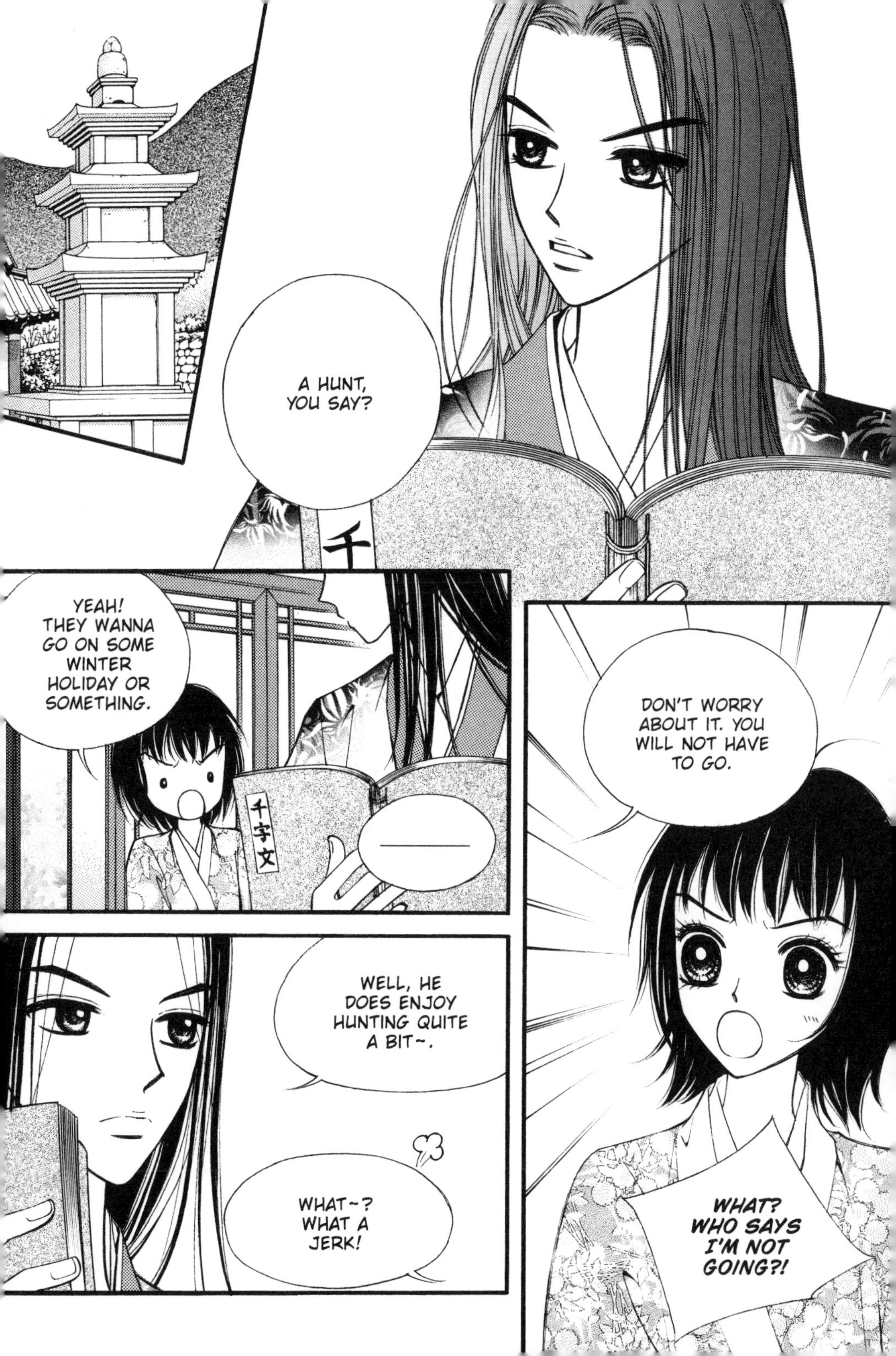
A HUNT, YOU SAY?
千
YEAH! THEY WANNA GO ON SOME WINTER HOLIDAY OR SOMETHING.
千字文
——
WELL, HE DOES ENJOY HUNTING QUITE A BIT~.
WHAT~? WHAT A JERK!
DON'T WORRY ABOUT IT. YOU WILL NOT HAVE TO GO.
WHAT? WHO SAYS I'M NOT GOING?!

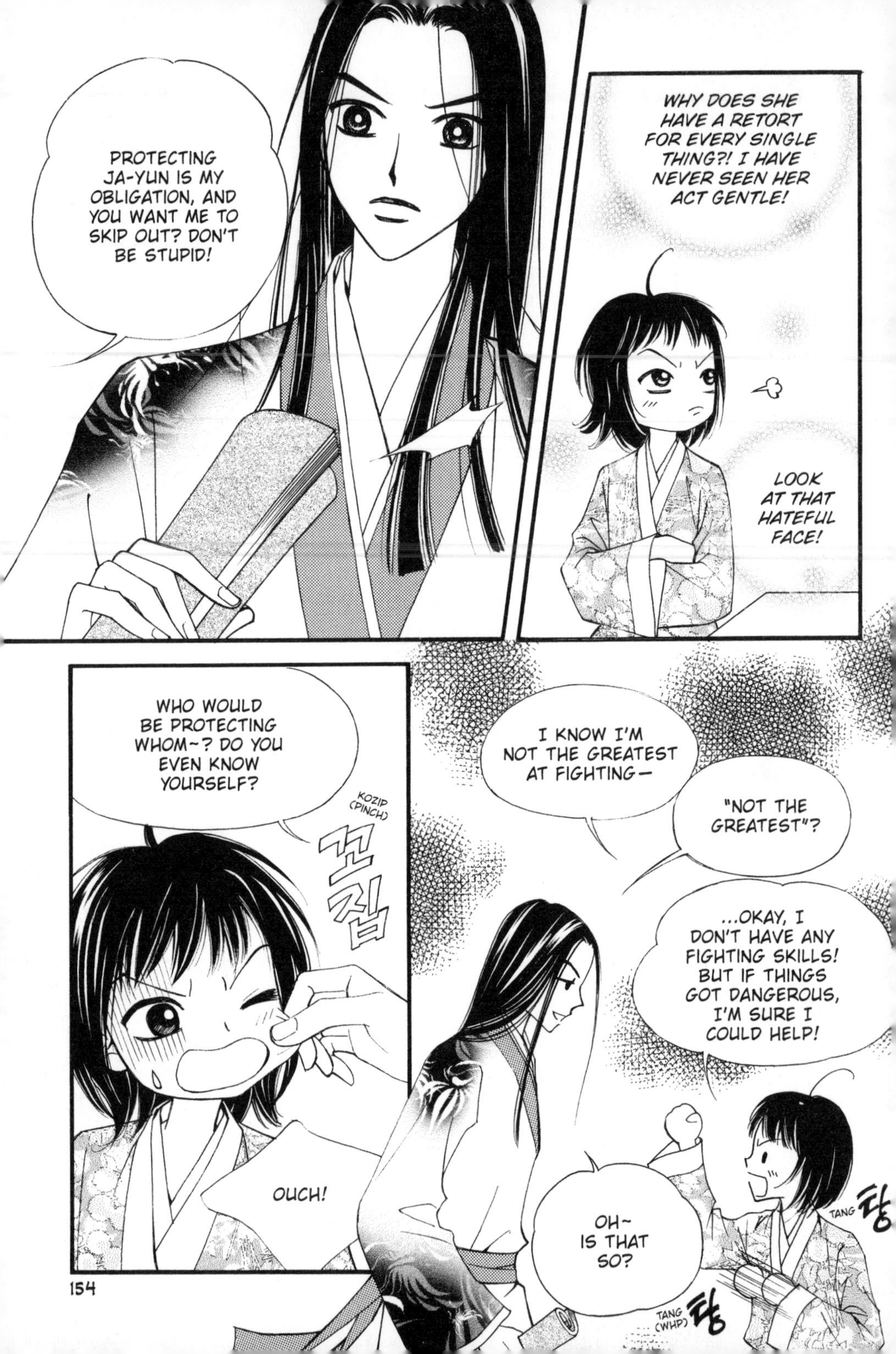
PROTECTING JA-YUN IS MY OBLIGATION, AND YOU WANT ME TO SKIP OUT? DON'T BE STUPID!
WHY DOES SHE HAVE A RETORT FOR EVERY SINGLE THING?! I HAVE NEVER SEEN HER ACT GENTLE!
LOOK AT THAT HATEFUL FACE!
WHO WOULD BE PROTECTING WHOM~? DO YOU EVEN KNOW YOURSELF?
KOZIP (PINCH)
꼬집
OUCH!
I KNOW I'M NOT THE GREATEST AT FIGHTING—
"NOT THE GREATEST"?
...OKAY, I DON'T HAVE ANY FIGHTING SKILLS! BUT IF THINGS GOT DANGEROUS, I'M SURE I COULD HELP!
OH~ IS THAT SO?
TANG
탕
TANG (WHP)
탕

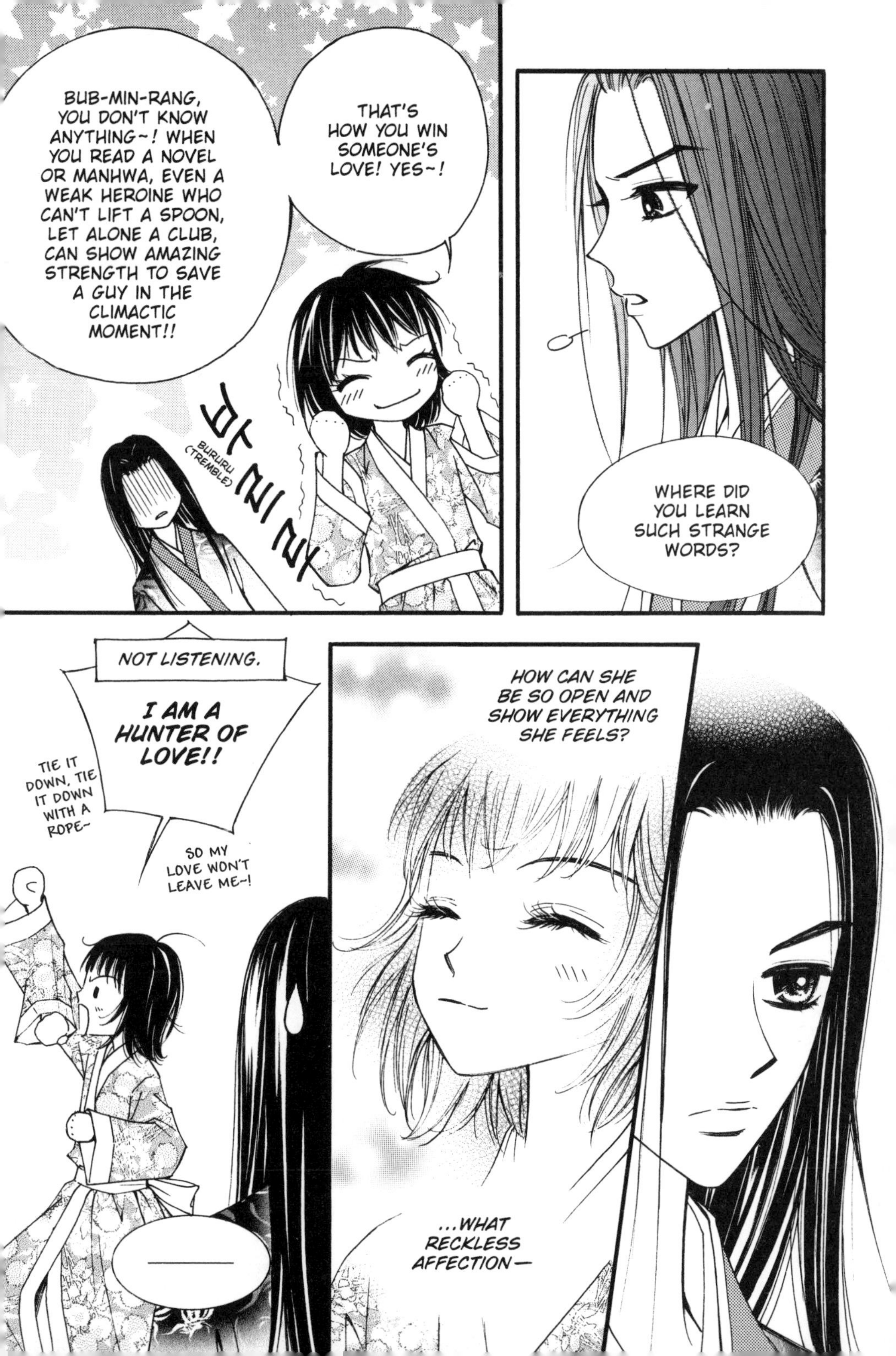

BUB-MIN-RANG, YOU DON'T KNOW ANYTHING~! WHEN YOU READ A NOVEL OR MANHWA, EVEN A WEAK HEROINE WHO CAN'T LIFT A SPOON, LET ALONE A CLUB, CAN SHOW AMAZING STRENGTH TO SAVE A GUY IN THE CLIMACTIC MOMENT!!
THAT'S HOW YOU WIN SOMEONE'S LOVE! YES~!
BURURU (TREMBLE)
WHERE DID YOU LEARN SUCH STRANGE WORDS?
NOT LISTENING.
I AM A HUNTER OF LOVE!!
TIE IT DOWN, TIE IT DOWN WITH A ROPE~
SO MY LOVE WON'T LEAVE ME~!
———
HOW CAN SHE BE SO OPEN AND SHOW EVERYTHING SHE FEELS?
...WHAT RECKLESS AFFECTION—

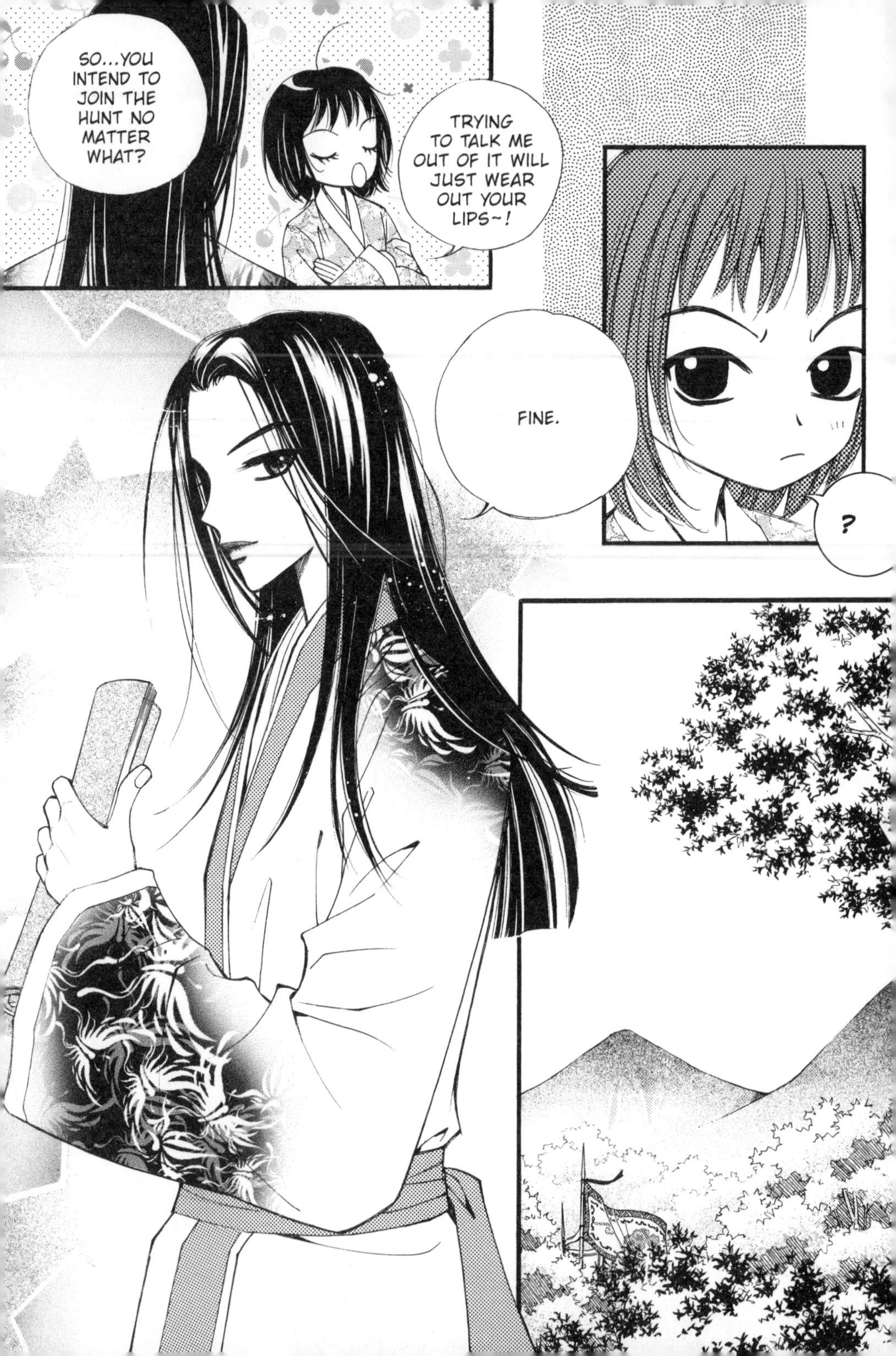
SO...YOU INTEND TO JOIN THE HUNT NO MATTER WHAT?
TRYING TO TALK ME OUT OF IT WILL JUST WEAR OUT YOUR LIPS~!
FINE.
?

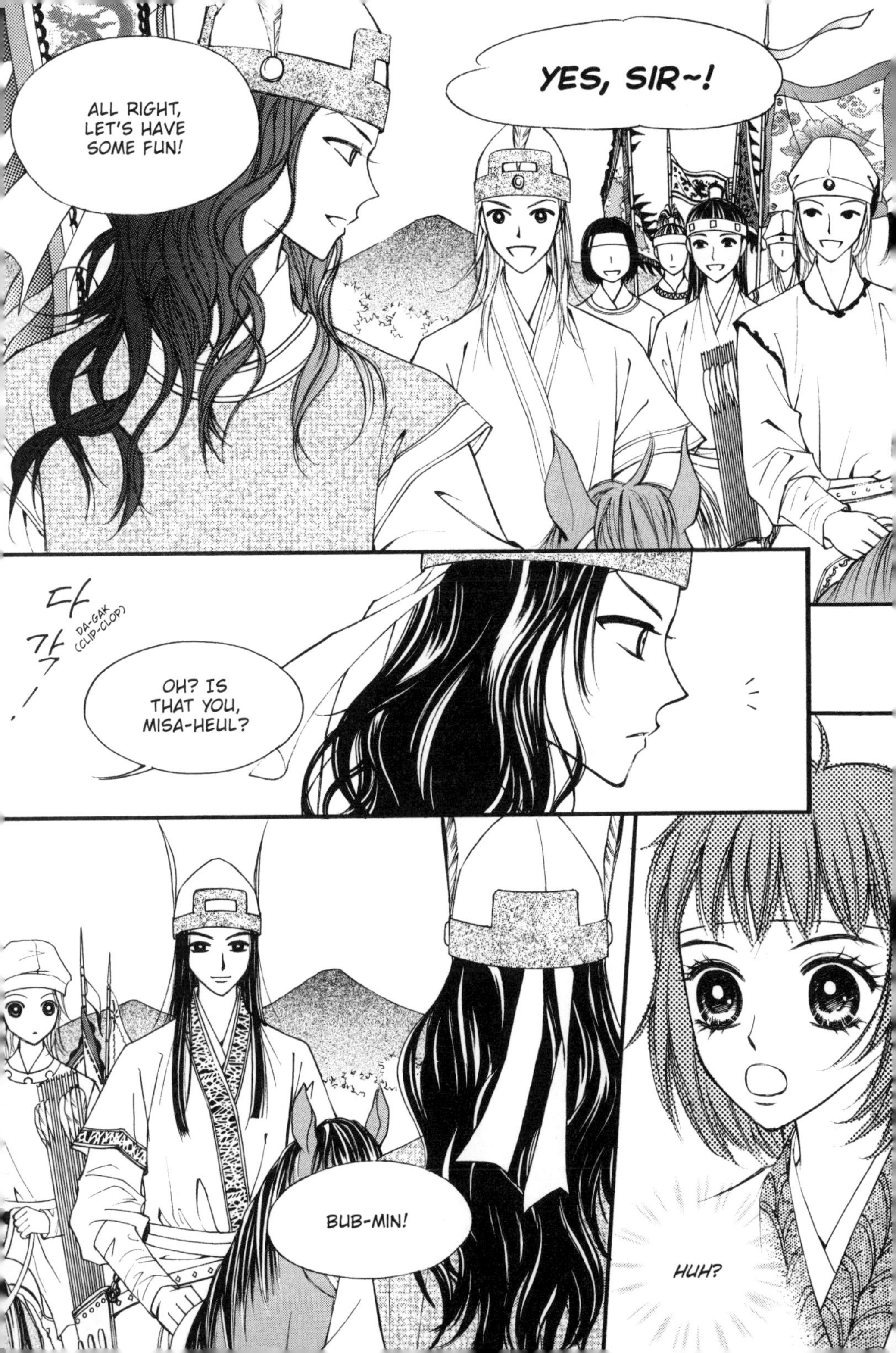
ALL RIGHT, LET'S HAVE SOME FUN!
YES, SIR~!
다각
DA-GAK (CLIP-CLOP)
OH? IS THAT YOU, MISA-HEUL?
BUB-MIN!
HUH?

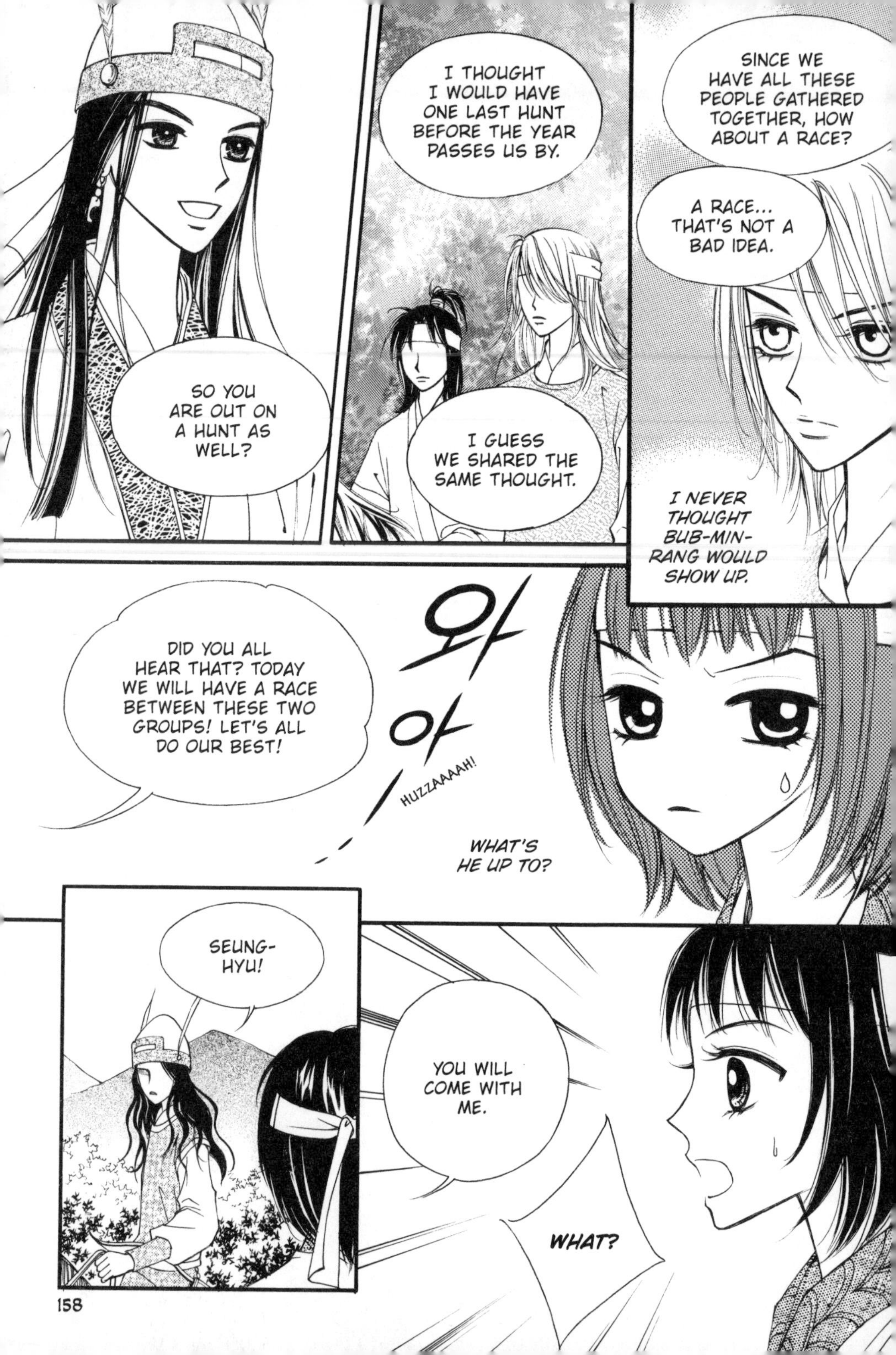

SO YOU ARE OUT ON A HUNT AS WELL?
I THOUGHT I WOULD HAVE ONE LAST HUNT BEFORE THE YEAR PASSES US BY.
I GUESS WE SHARED THE SAME THOUGHT.
SINCE WE HAVE ALL THESE PEOPLE GATHERED TOGETHER, HOW ABOUT A RACE?
A RACE... THAT'S NOT A BAD IDEA.
I NEVER THOUGHT BUB-MIN-RANG WOULD SHOW UP.
DID YOU ALL HEAR THAT? TODAY WE WILL HAVE A RACE BETWEEN THESE TWO GROUPS! LET'S ALL DO OUR BEST!
와아
HUZZAAAAH!
WHAT'S HE UP TO?
SEUNG-HYU!
YOU WILL COME WITH ME.
WHAT?

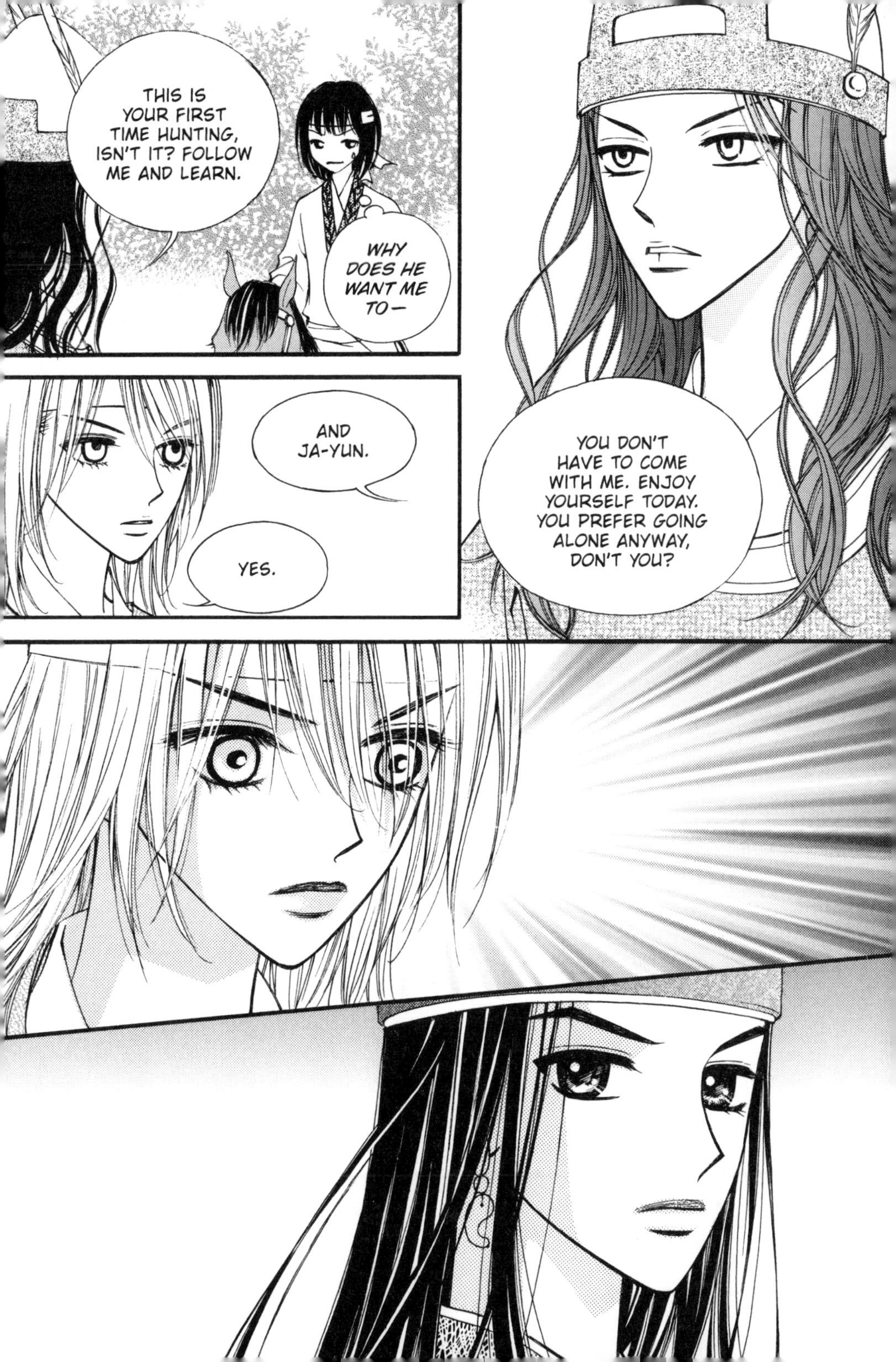
THIS IS YOUR FIRST TIME HUNTING, ISN'T IT? FOLLOW ME AND LEARN.
WHY DOES HE WANT ME TO—
YOU DON'T HAVE TO COME WITH ME. ENJOY YOURSELF TODAY. YOU PREFER GOING ALONE ANYWAY, DON'T YOU?
AND JA-YUN.
YES.

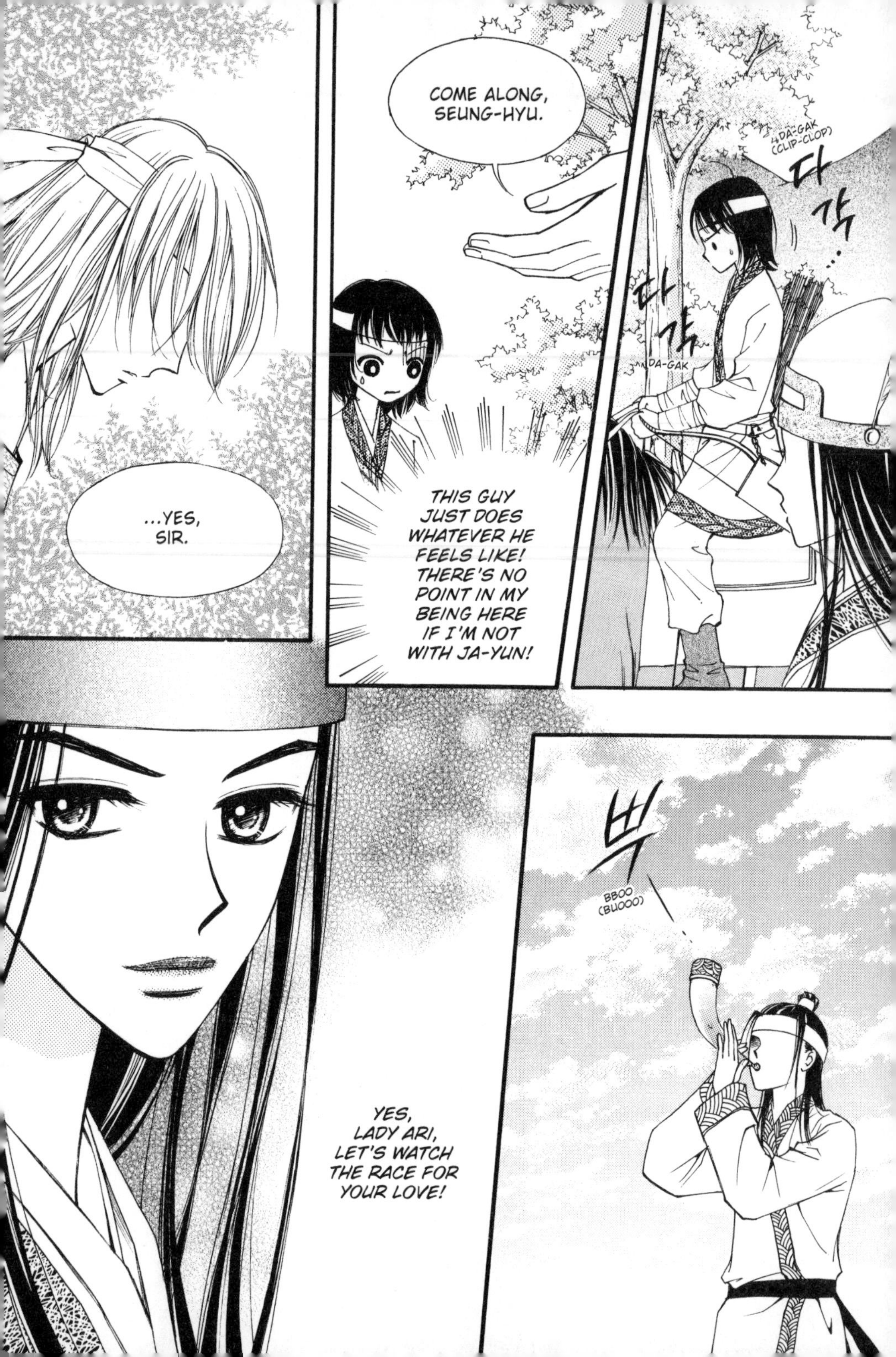
...YES, SIR.
COME ALONG, SEUNG-HYU.
THIS GUY JUST DOES WHATEVER HE FEELS LIKE! THERE'S NO POINT IN MY BEING HERE IF I'M NOT WITH JA-YUN!
다각...
DA-GAK (CLIP-CLOP)
다각
DA-GAK
YES, LADY ARI, LET'S WATCH THE RACE FOR YOUR LOVE!
뿌
BBOO (BUOOO)

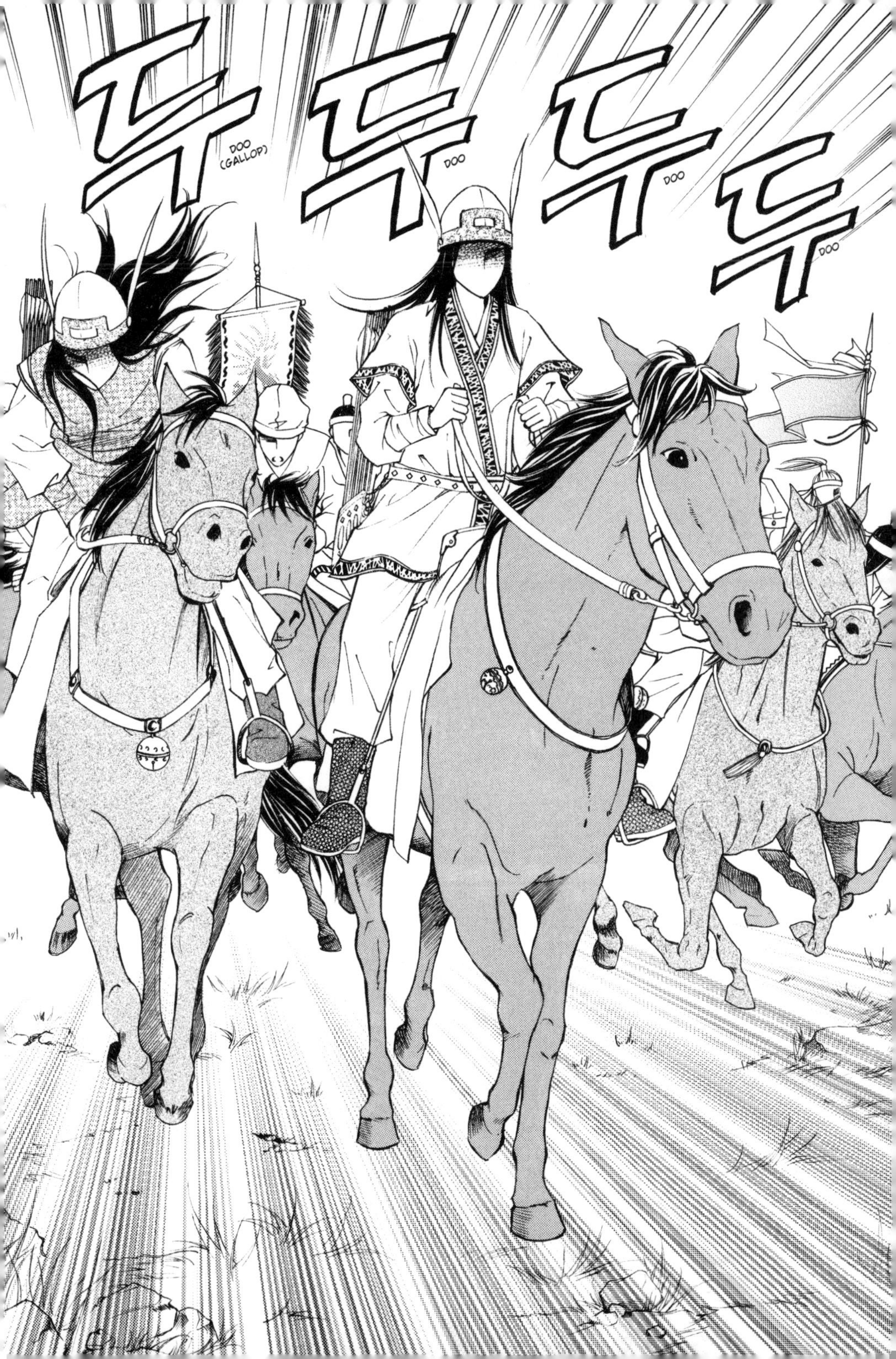
DOO (GALLOP)
DOO
DOO
DOO

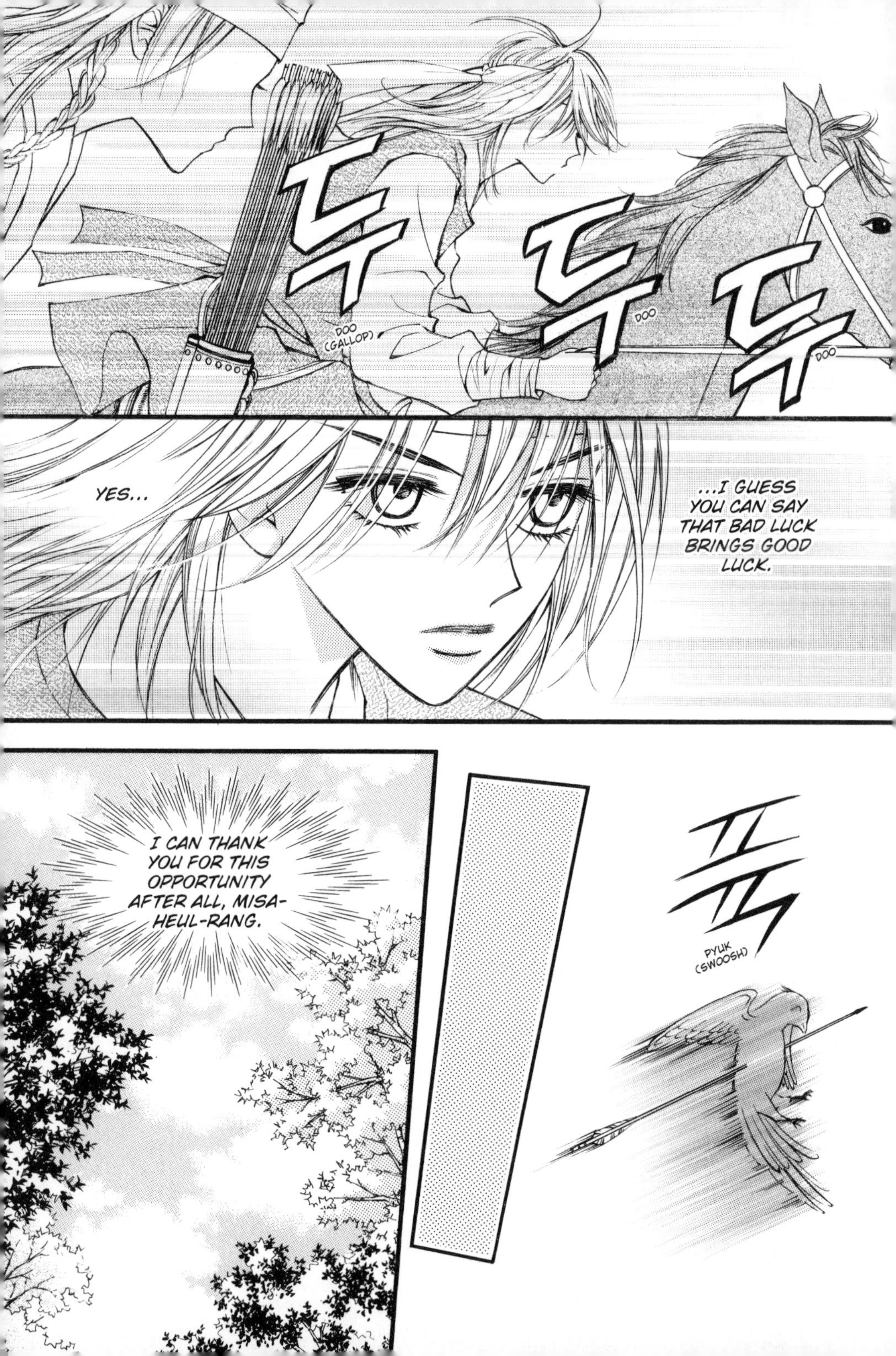

DOO (GALLOP)
DOO
DOO
YES...
...I GUESS YOU CAN SAY THAT BAD LUCK BRINGS GOOD LUCK.
I CAN THANK YOU FOR THIS OPPORTUNITY AFTER ALL, MISA-HEUL-RANG.
PYUK (SWOOSH)

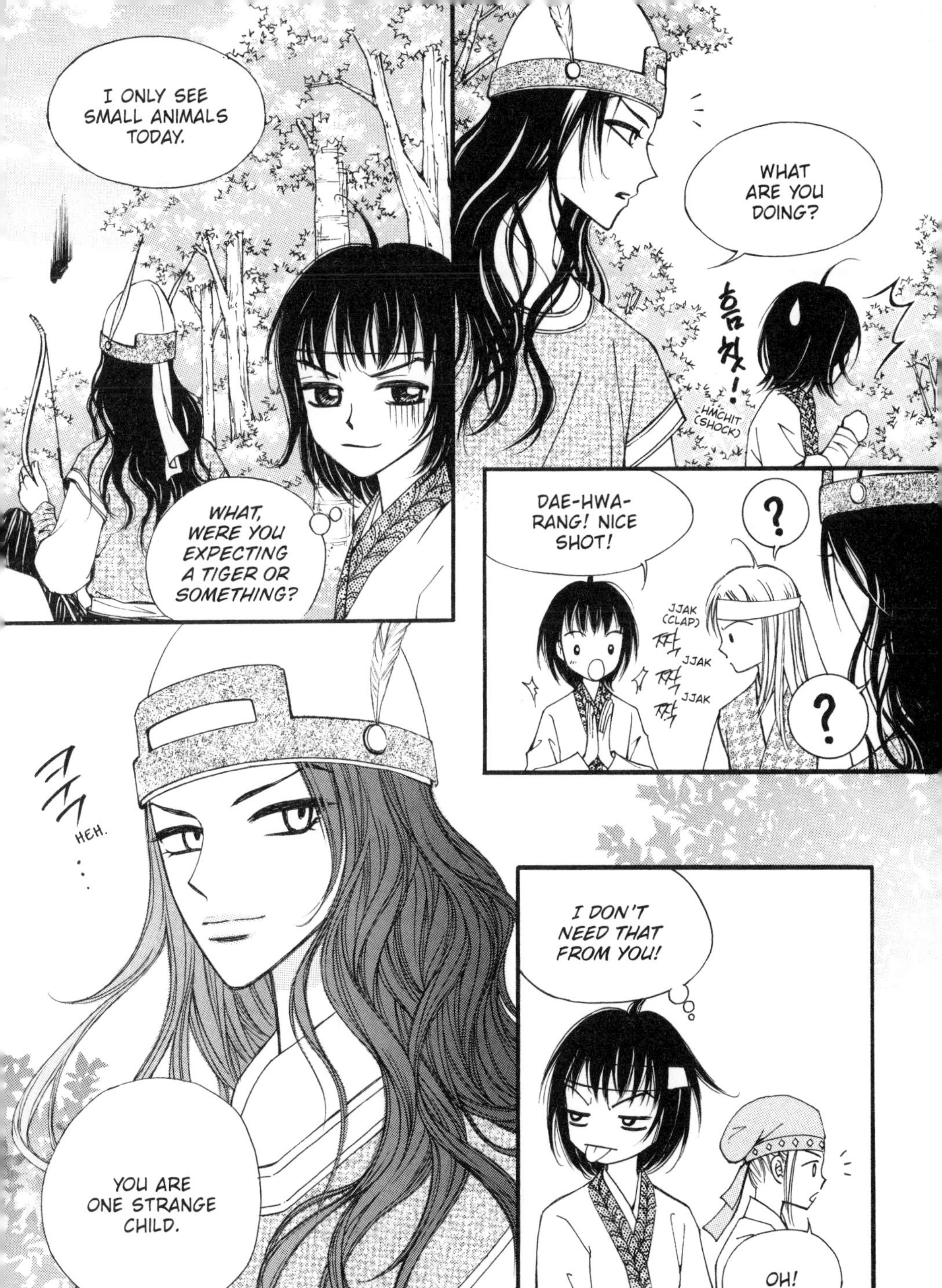

I ONLY SEE SMALL ANIMALS TODAY.
WHAT, WERE YOU EXPECTING A TIGER OR SOMETHING?
WHAT ARE YOU DOING?
흠칫!
HMCHIT (SHOCK)
DAE-HWA-RANG! NICE SHOT!
?
JJAK (CLAP)
짝
JJAK
짝
JJAK
짝
?
HEH.
...
YOU ARE ONE STRANGE CHILD.
I DON'T NEED THAT FROM YOU!
OH!

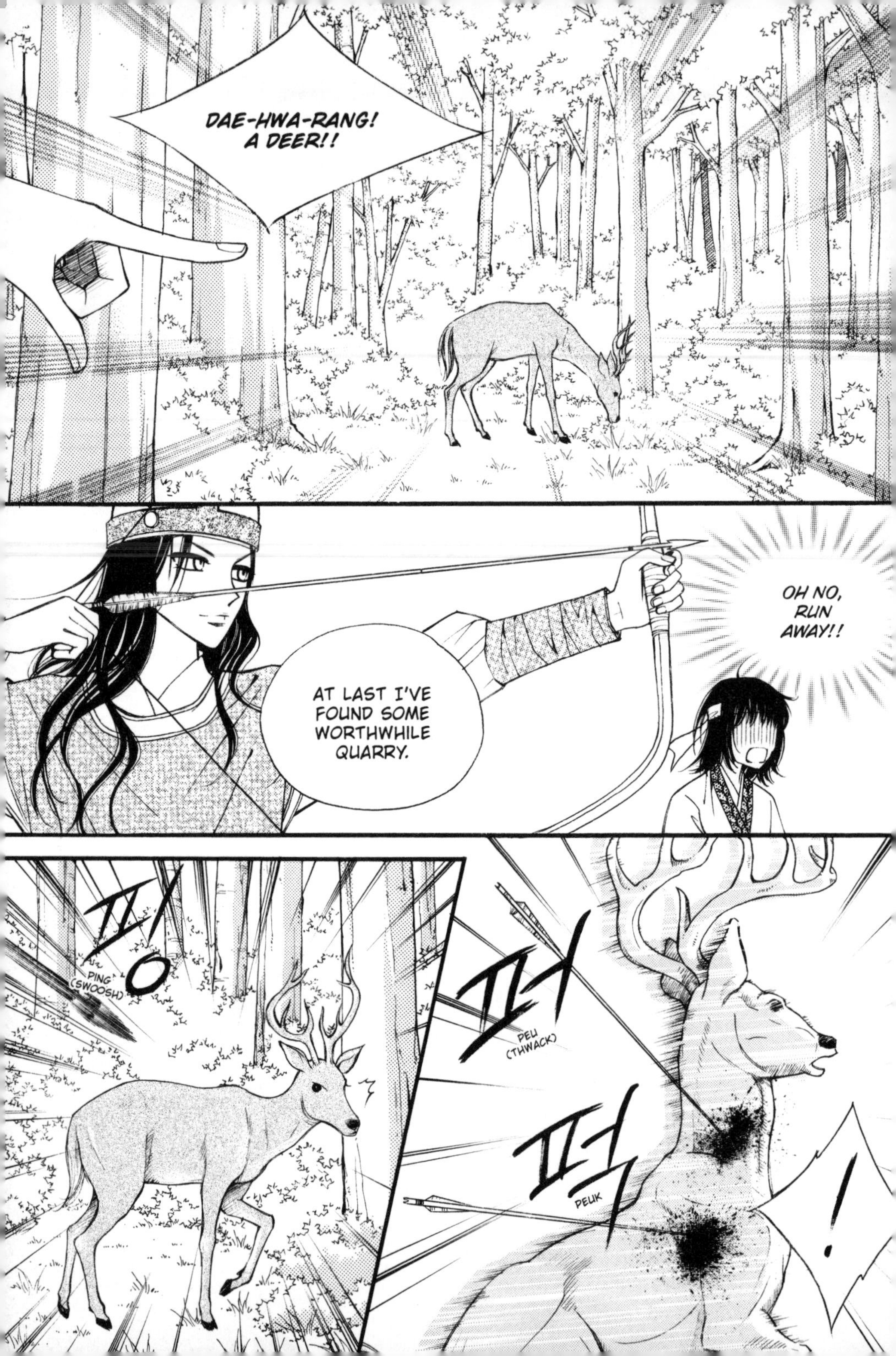
DAE-HWA-RANG! A DEER!!
AT LAST I'VE FOUND SOME WORTHWHILE QUARRY.
OH NO, RUN AWAY!!
PING (SWOOSH)
PEU (THWACK)
PEUK
!

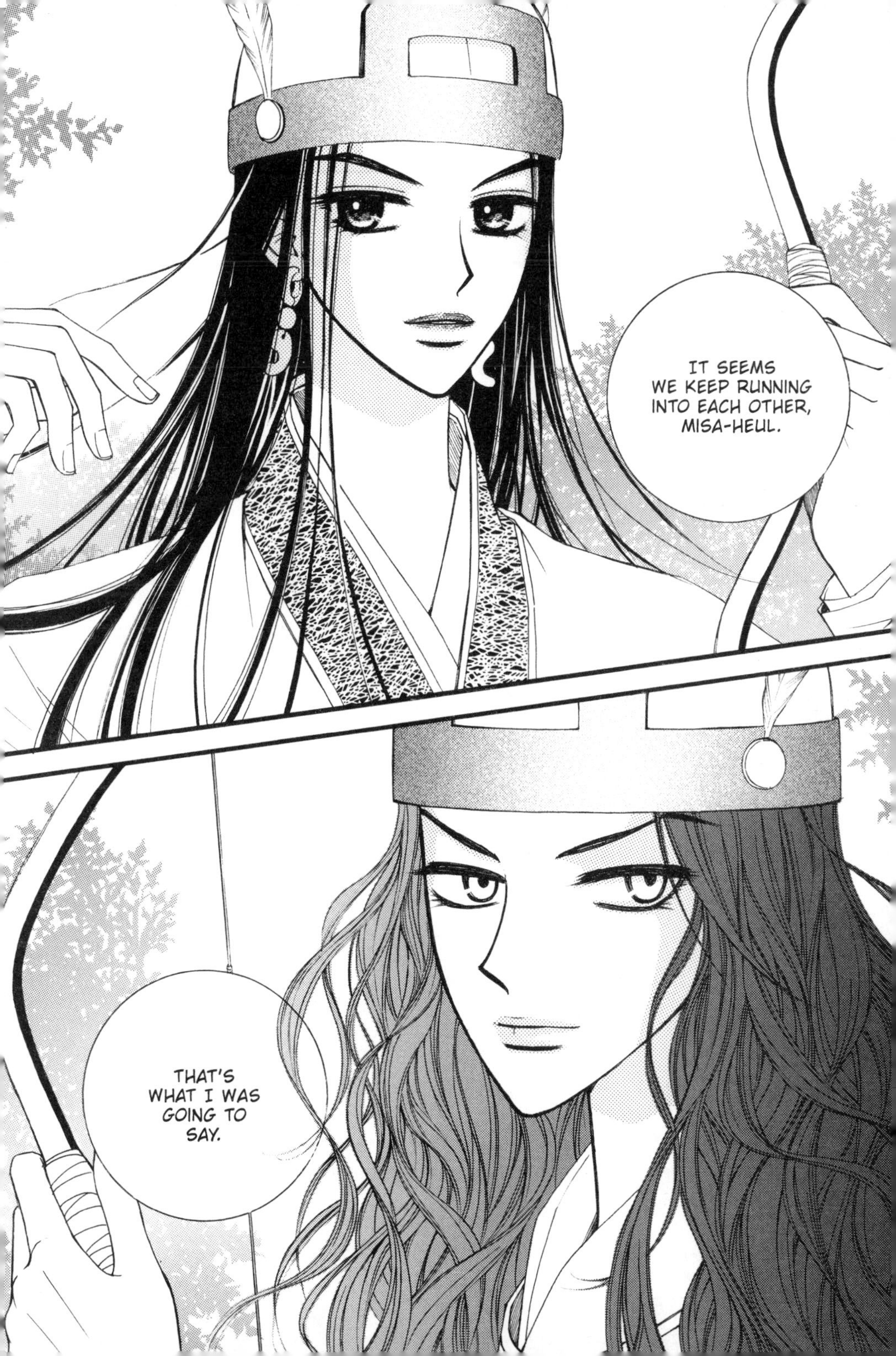
IT SEEMS WE KEEP RUNNING INTO EACH OTHER, MISA-HEUL.
THAT'S WHAT I WAS GOING TO SAY.

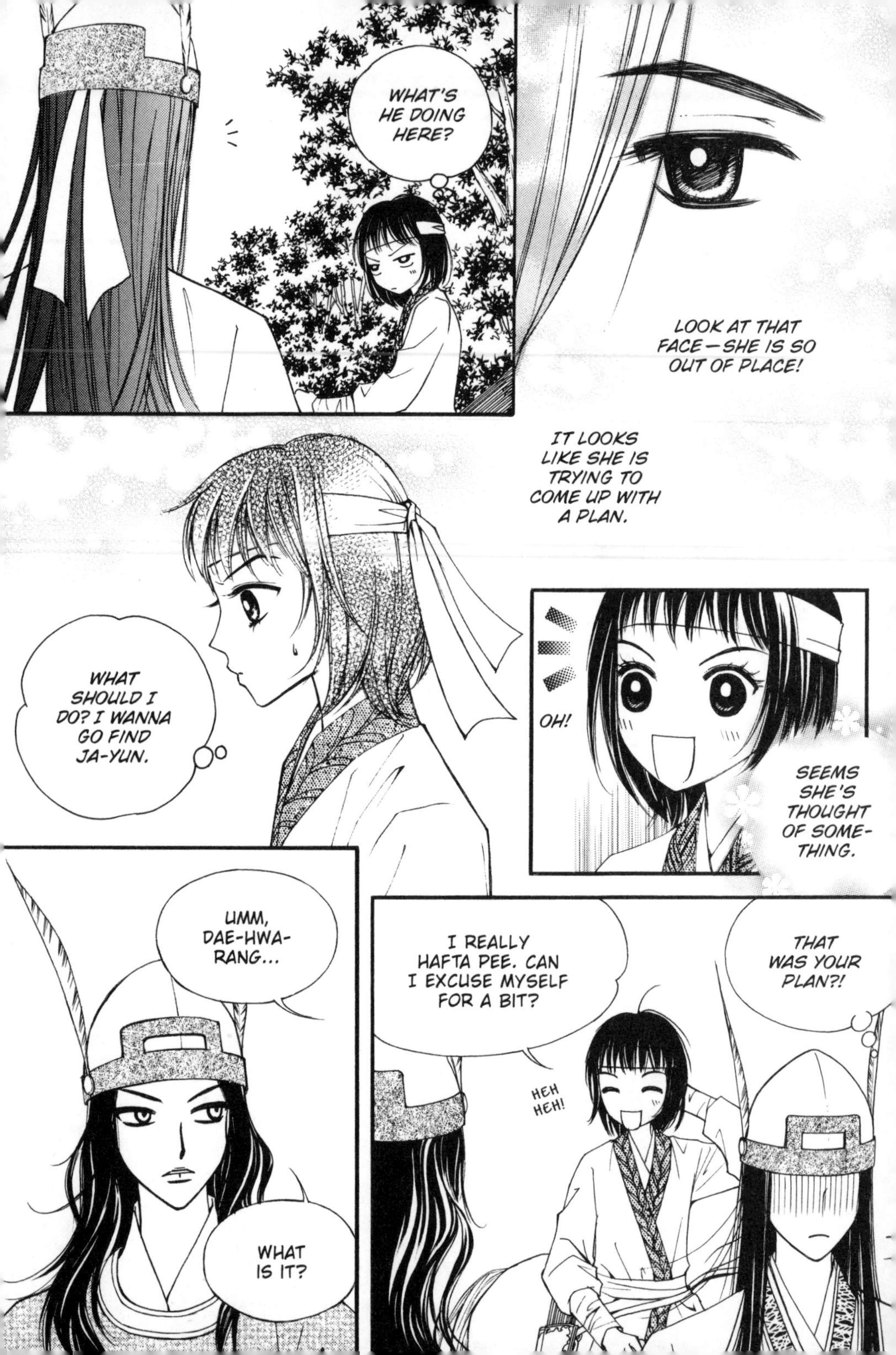
WHAT'S HE DOING HERE?
LOOK AT THAT FACE—SHE IS SO OUT OF PLACE!
IT LOOKS LIKE SHE IS TRYING TO COME UP WITH A PLAN.
WHAT SHOULD I DO? I WANNA GO FIND JA-YUN.
OH!
SEEMS SHE'S THOUGHT OF SOME-THING.
UMM, DAE-HWA-RANG...
WHAT IS IT?
I REALLY HAFTA PEE. CAN I EXCUSE MYSELF FOR A BIT?
HEH HEH!
THAT WAS YOUR PLAN?!

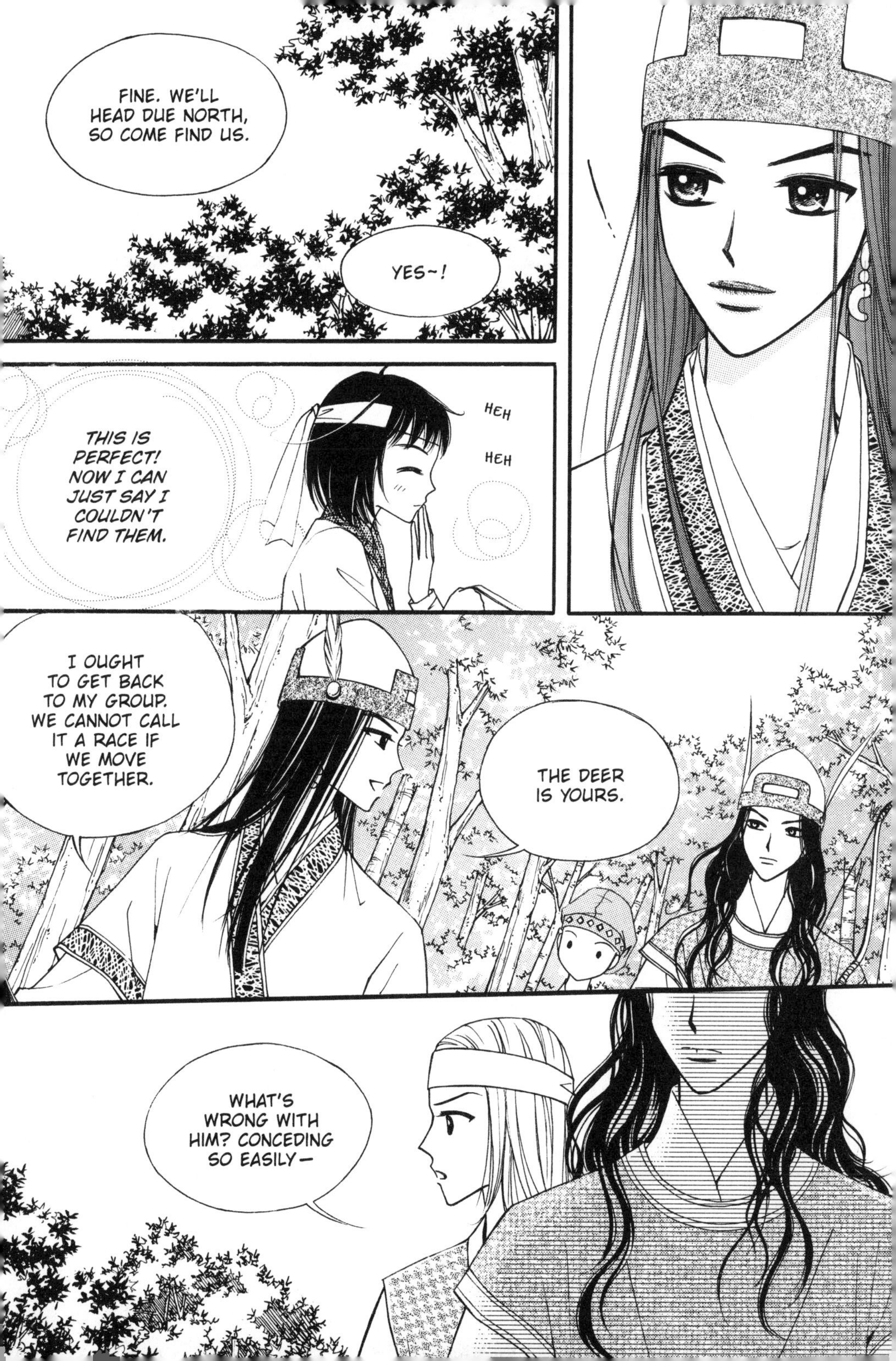
FINE. WE'LL HEAD DUE NORTH, SO COME FIND US.
YES~!
THIS IS PERFECT! NOW I CAN JUST SAY I COULDN'T FIND THEM.
HEH
HEH
I OUGHT TO GET BACK TO MY GROUP. WE CANNOT CALL IT A RACE IF WE MOVE TOGETHER.
THE DEER IS YOURS.
WHAT'S WRONG WITH HIM? CONCEDING SO EASILY—

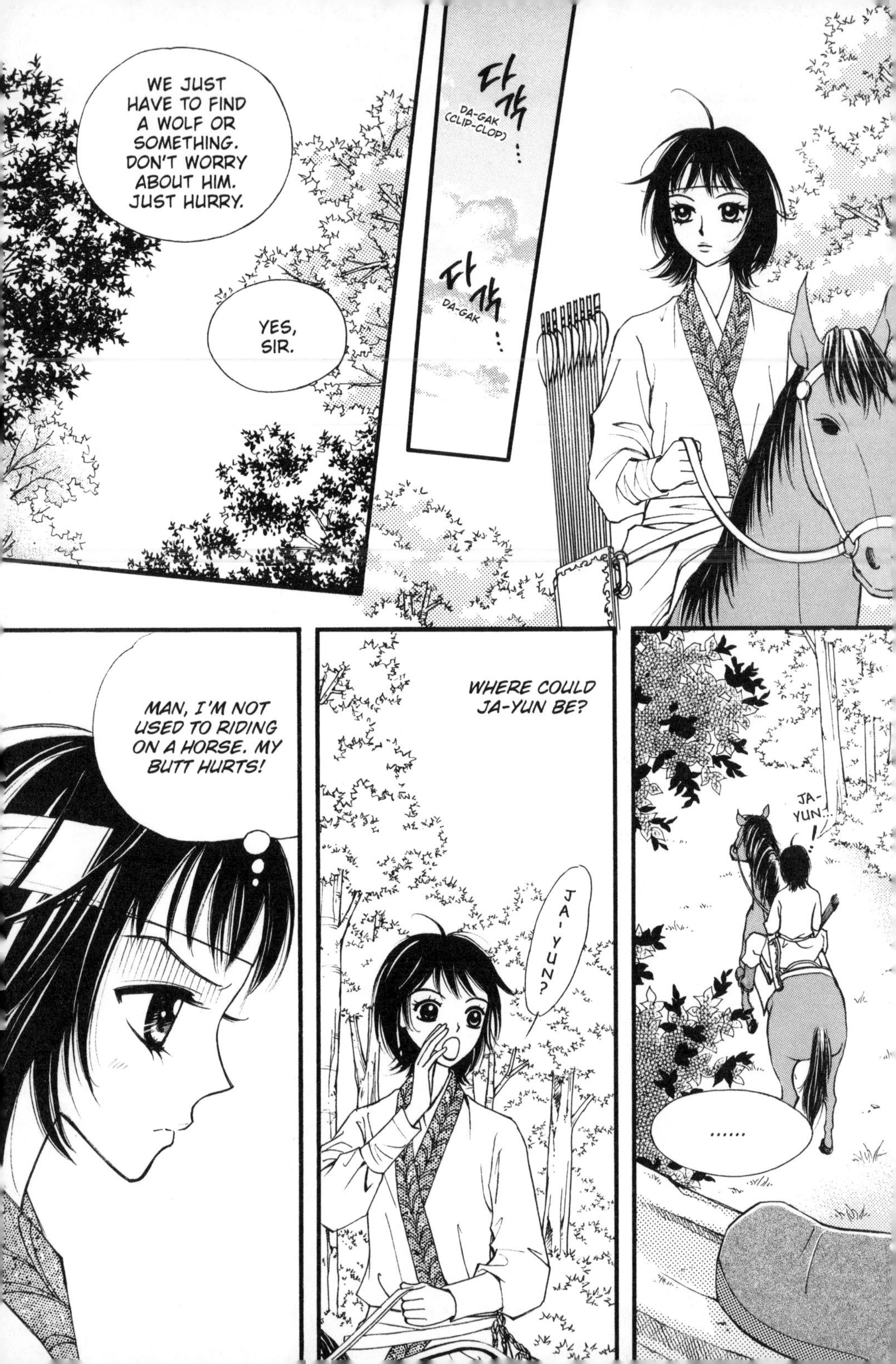
WE JUST HAVE TO FIND A WOLF OR SOMETHING. DON'T WORRY ABOUT HIM. JUST HURRY.
YES, SIR.
다각 DA-GAK (CLIP-CLOP)...
다각 DA-GAK...
MAN, I'M NOT USED TO RIDING ON A HORSE. MY BUTT HURTS!
WHERE COULD JA-YUN BE?
JA-YUN?
JA-YUN...!
......

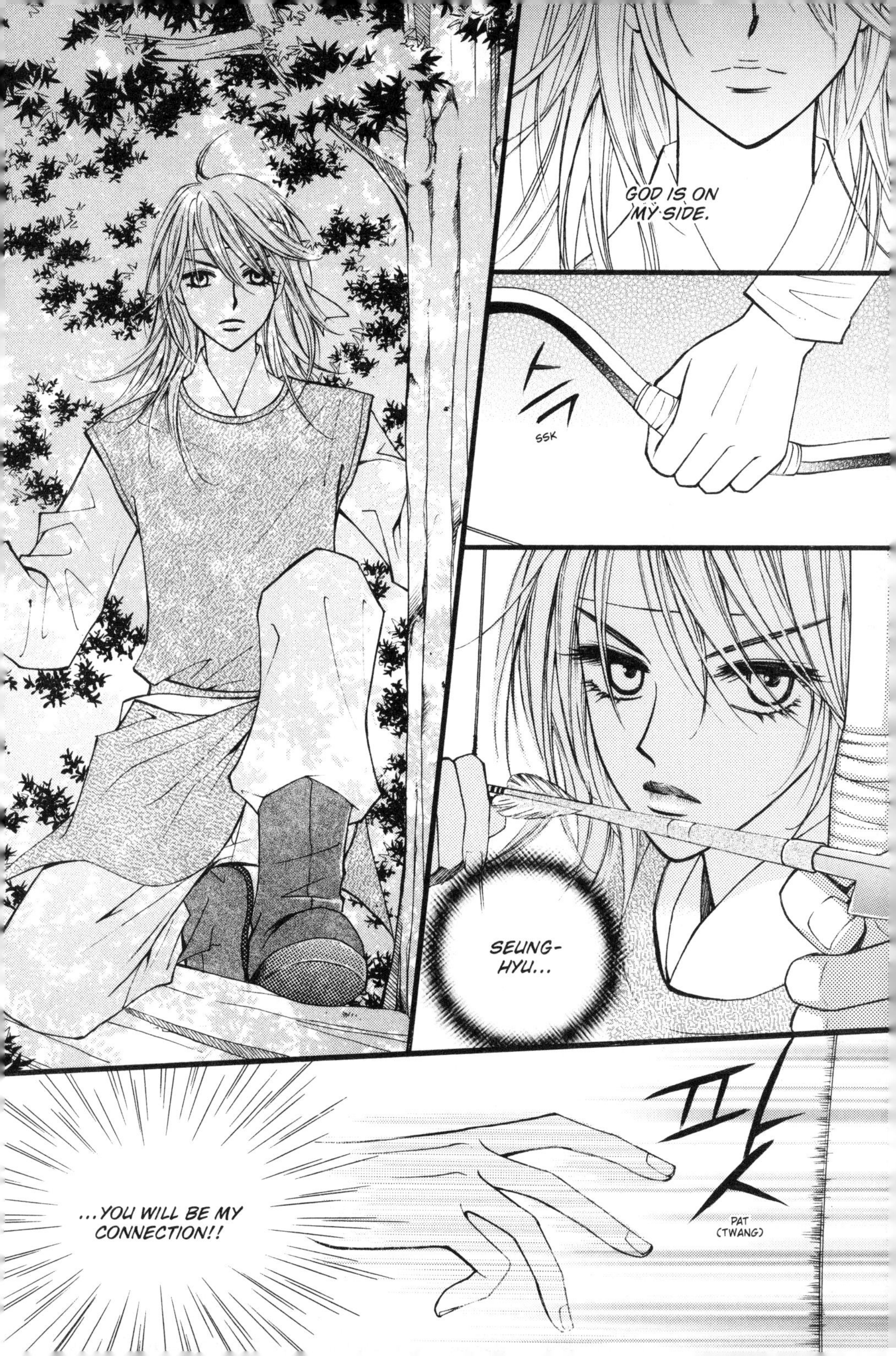
GOD IS ON MY SIDE.
SSK
SEUNG-HYU...
...YOU WILL BE MY CONNECTION!!
PAT (TWANG)

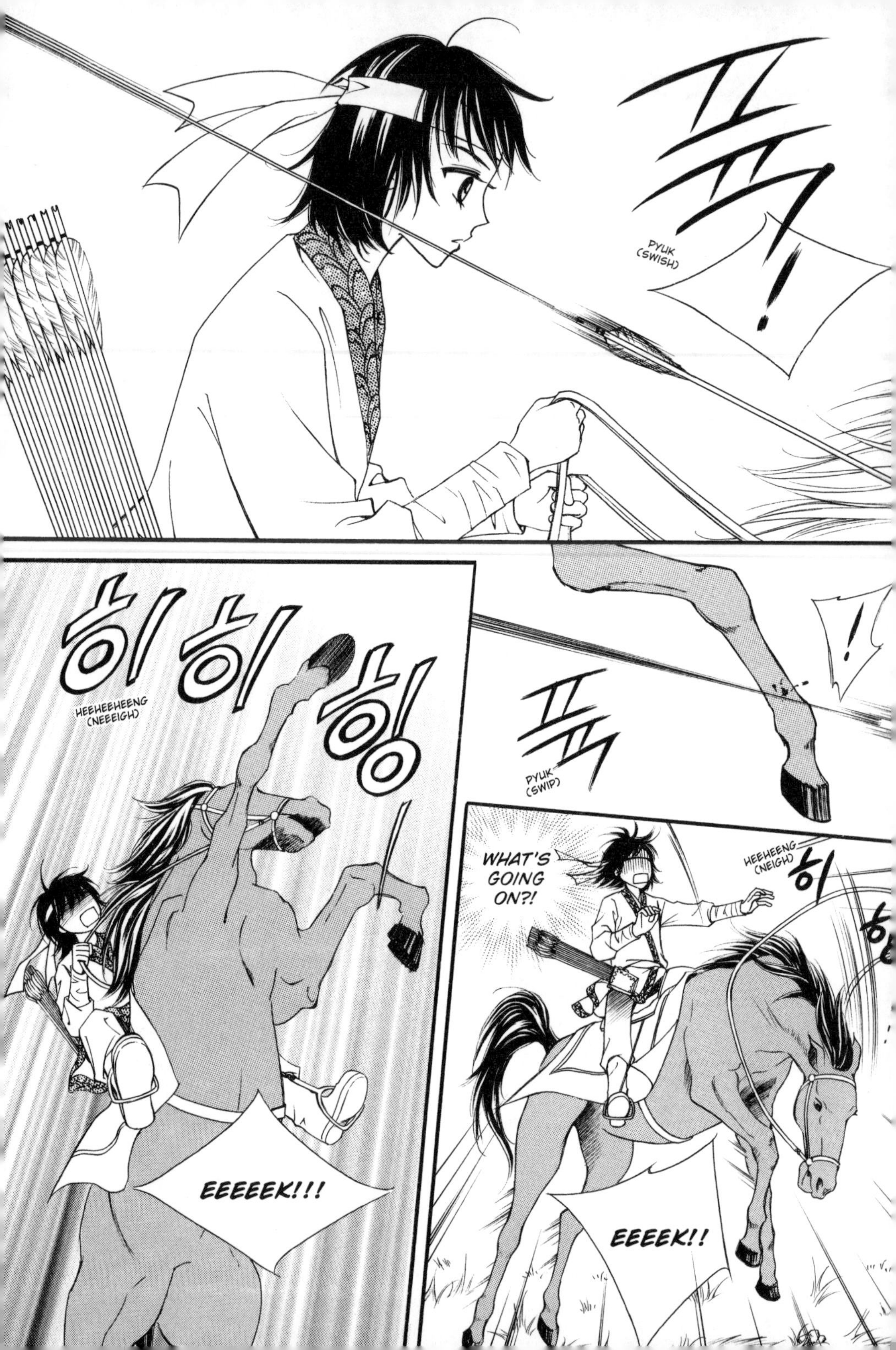

퓩!
PYUK (SWISH)
히히힝
HEEHEEHEENG (NEEEIGH)
EEEEEK!!!
!
퓩
PYUK (SWIP)
WHAT'S GOING ON?!
HEEHEENG (NEIGH)
EEEEK!!

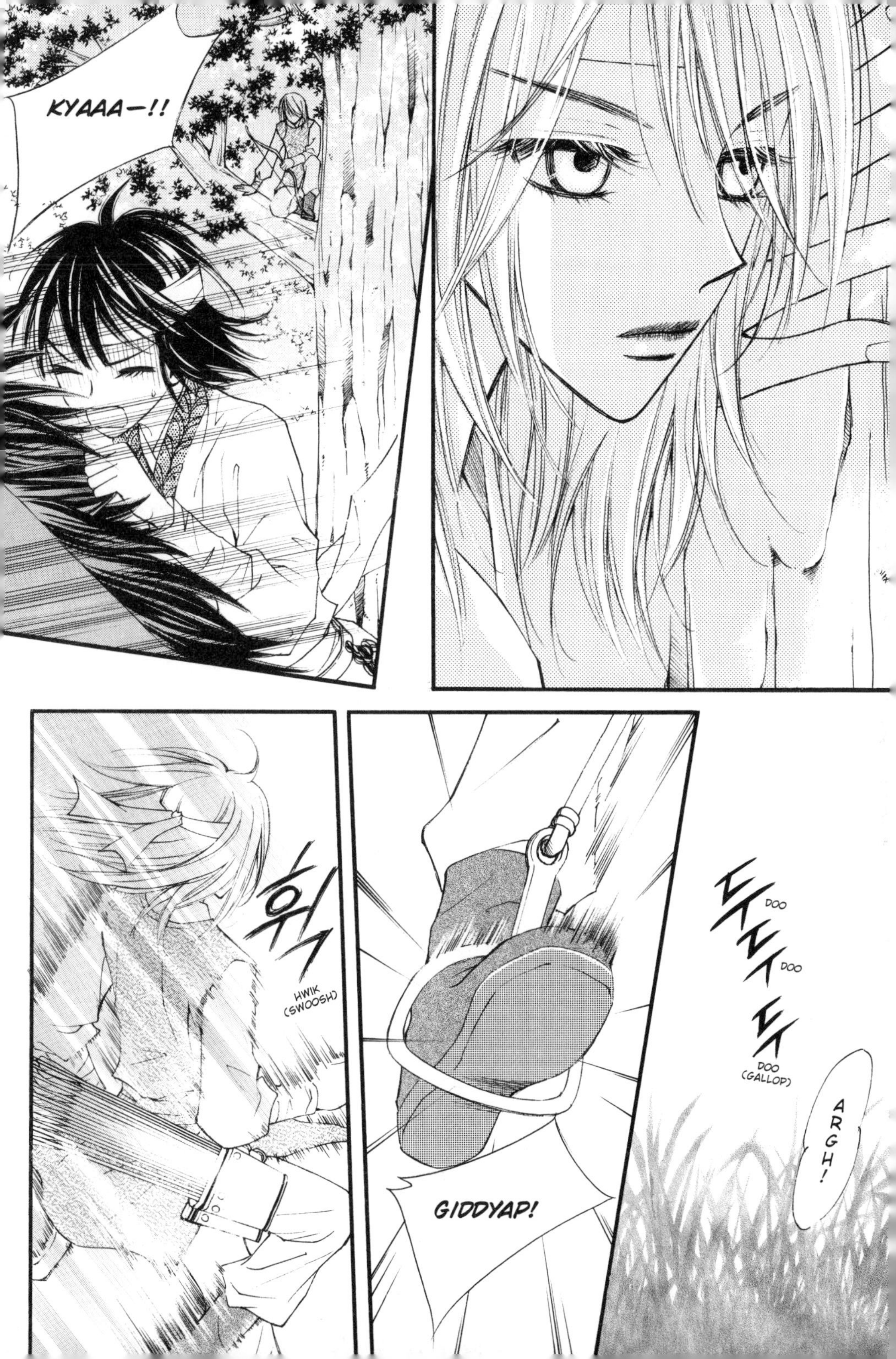
KYAAA—!!
HWIK (SWOOSH)
GIDDYAP!
DOO
DOO
DOO (GALLOP)
ARGH!

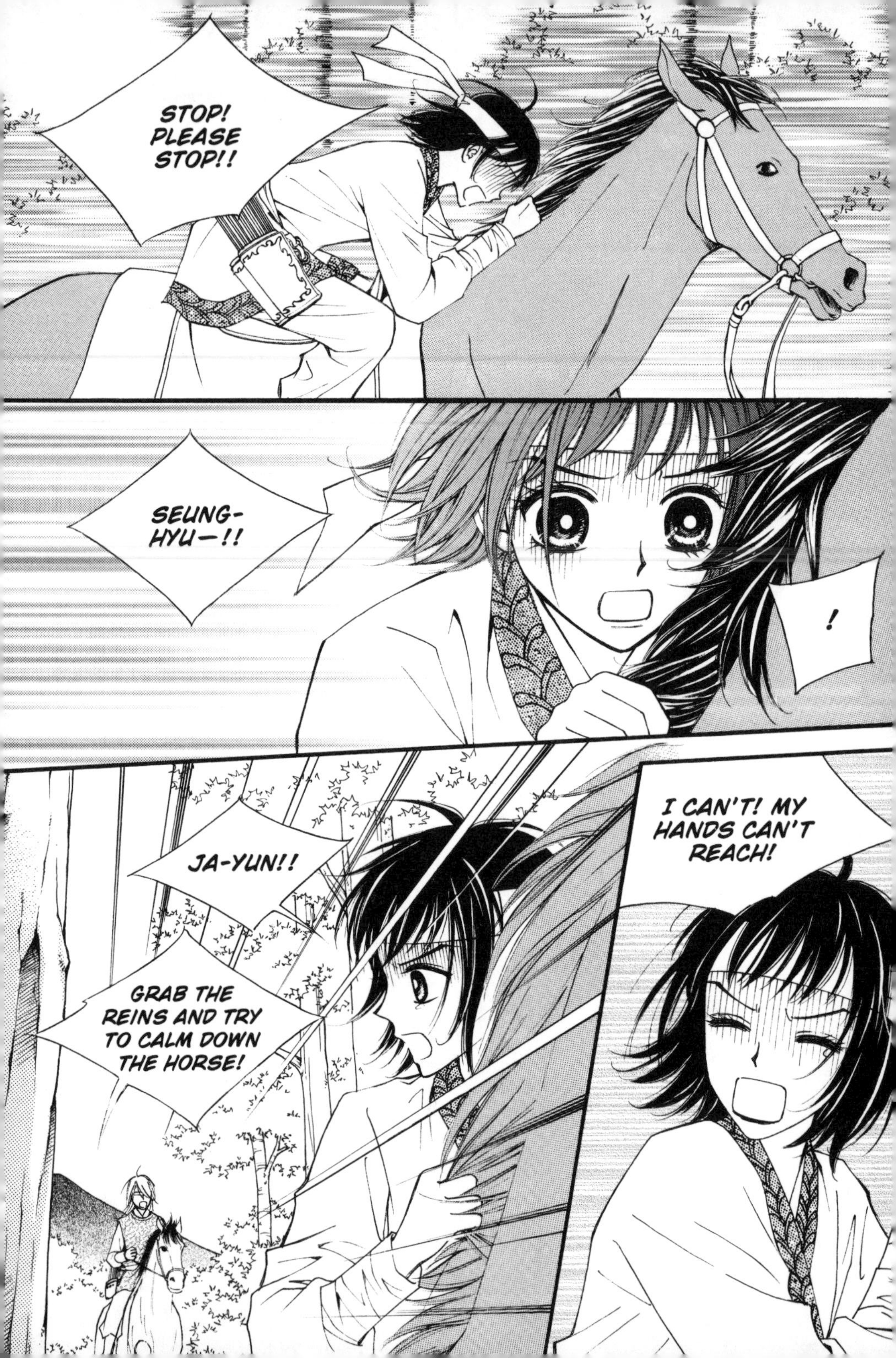
STOP! PLEASE STOP!!
SEUNG-HYU—!!
!
JA-YUN!!
GRAB THE REINS AND TRY TO CALM DOWN THE HORSE!
I CAN'T! MY HANDS CAN'T REACH!

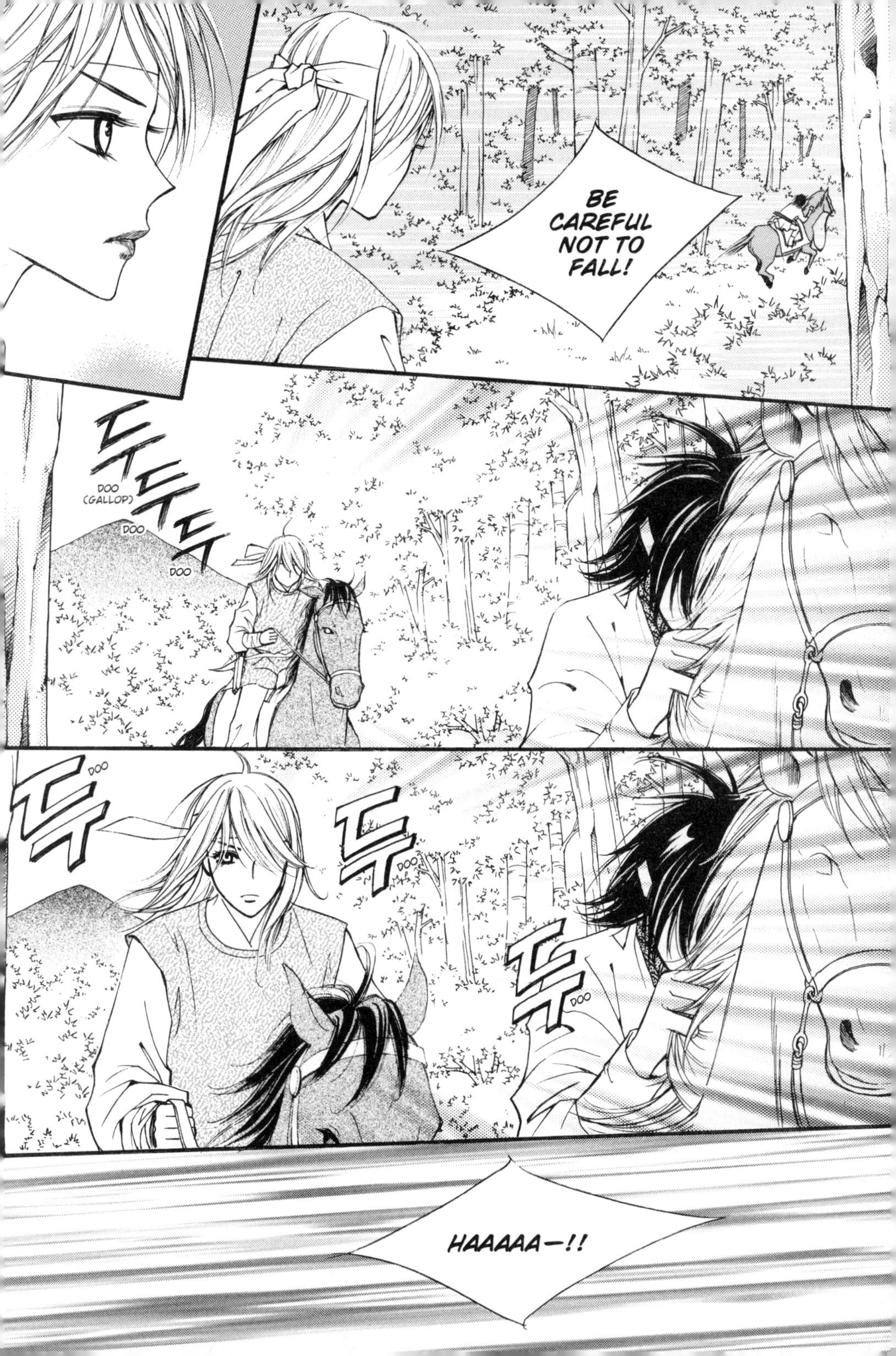
BE CAREFUL NOT TO FALL!
DOO (GALLOP)
DOO
DOO
DOO
DOO
DOO
HAAAAA—!!

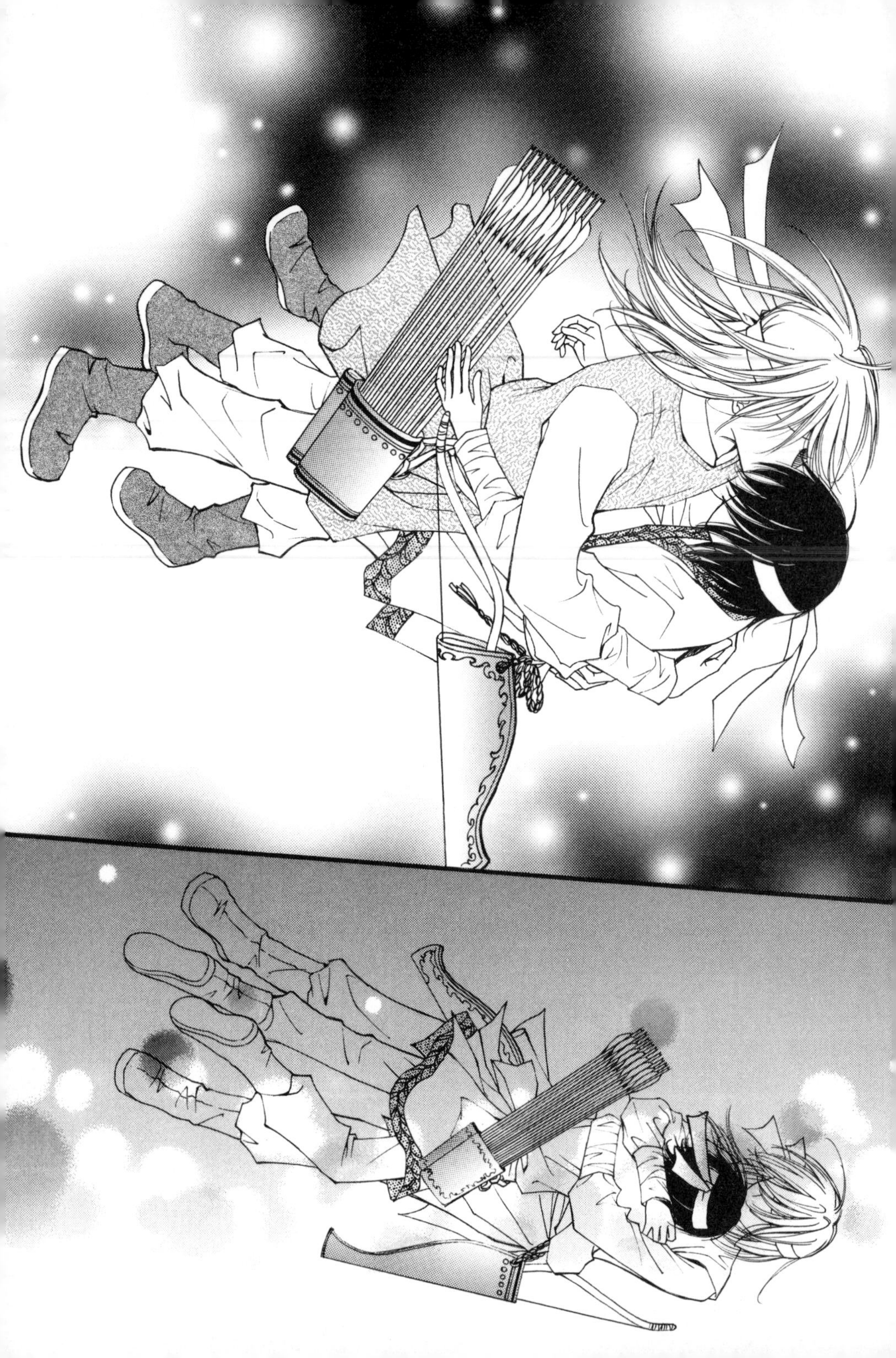

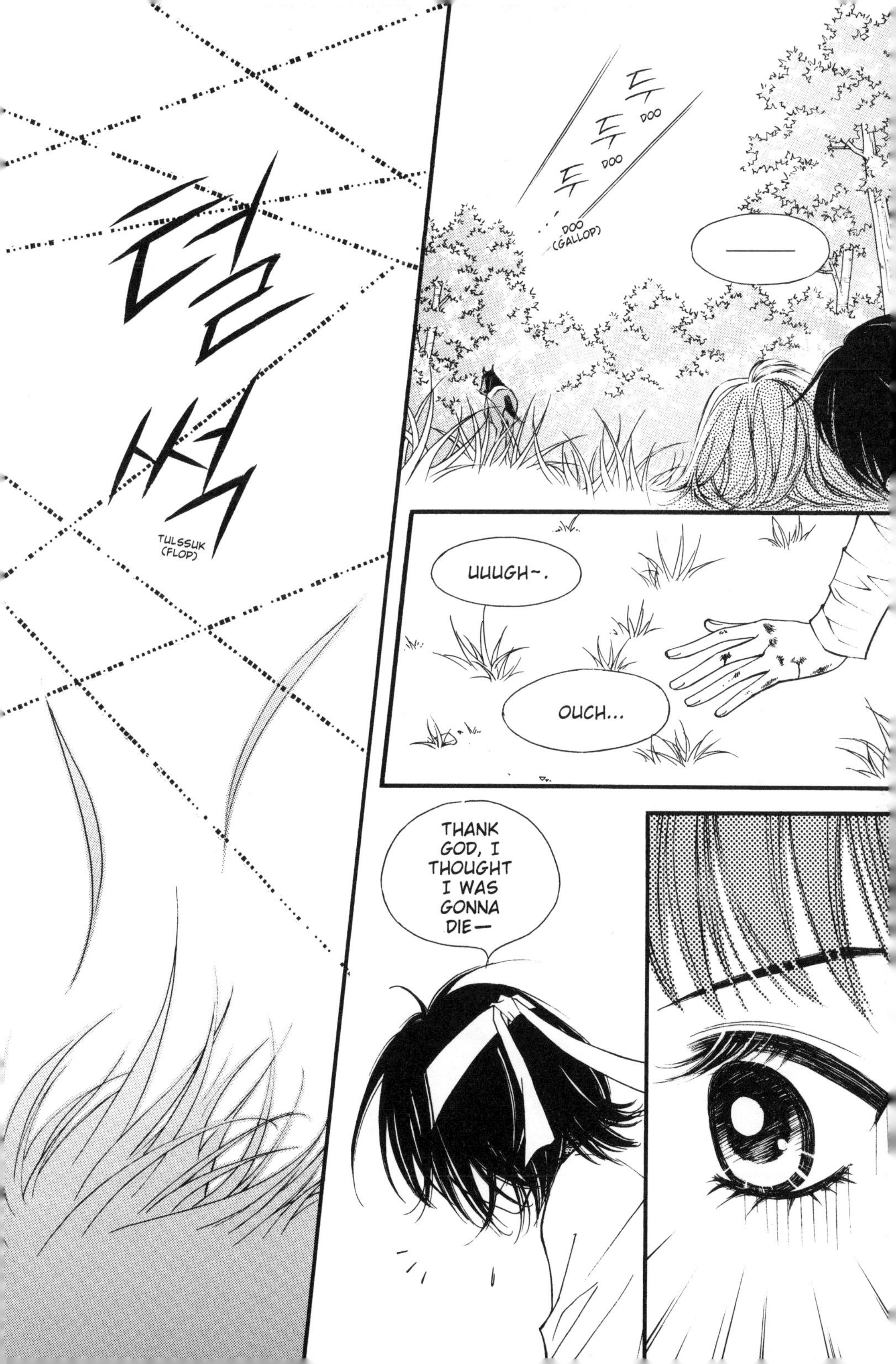
털썩
TULSSUK (FLOP)
두 두 두
DOO
DOO
DOO (GALLOP)
——
UUUGH~.
OUCH...
THANK GOD, I THOUGHT I WAS GONNA DIE—

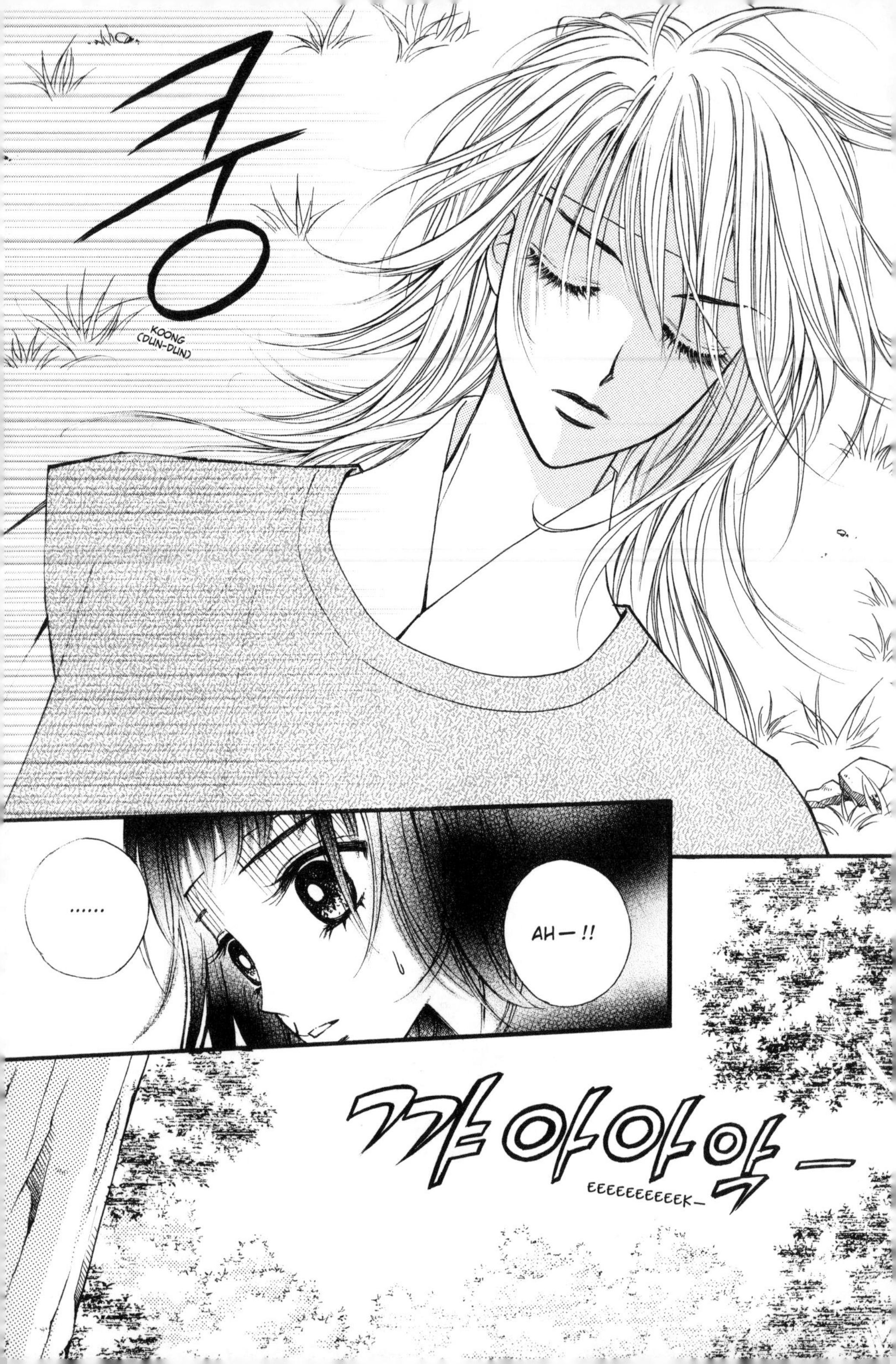
쿠웅
KOONG
(DUN-DUN)
......
AH—!!
꺄아아악—
EEEEEEEEEEK—

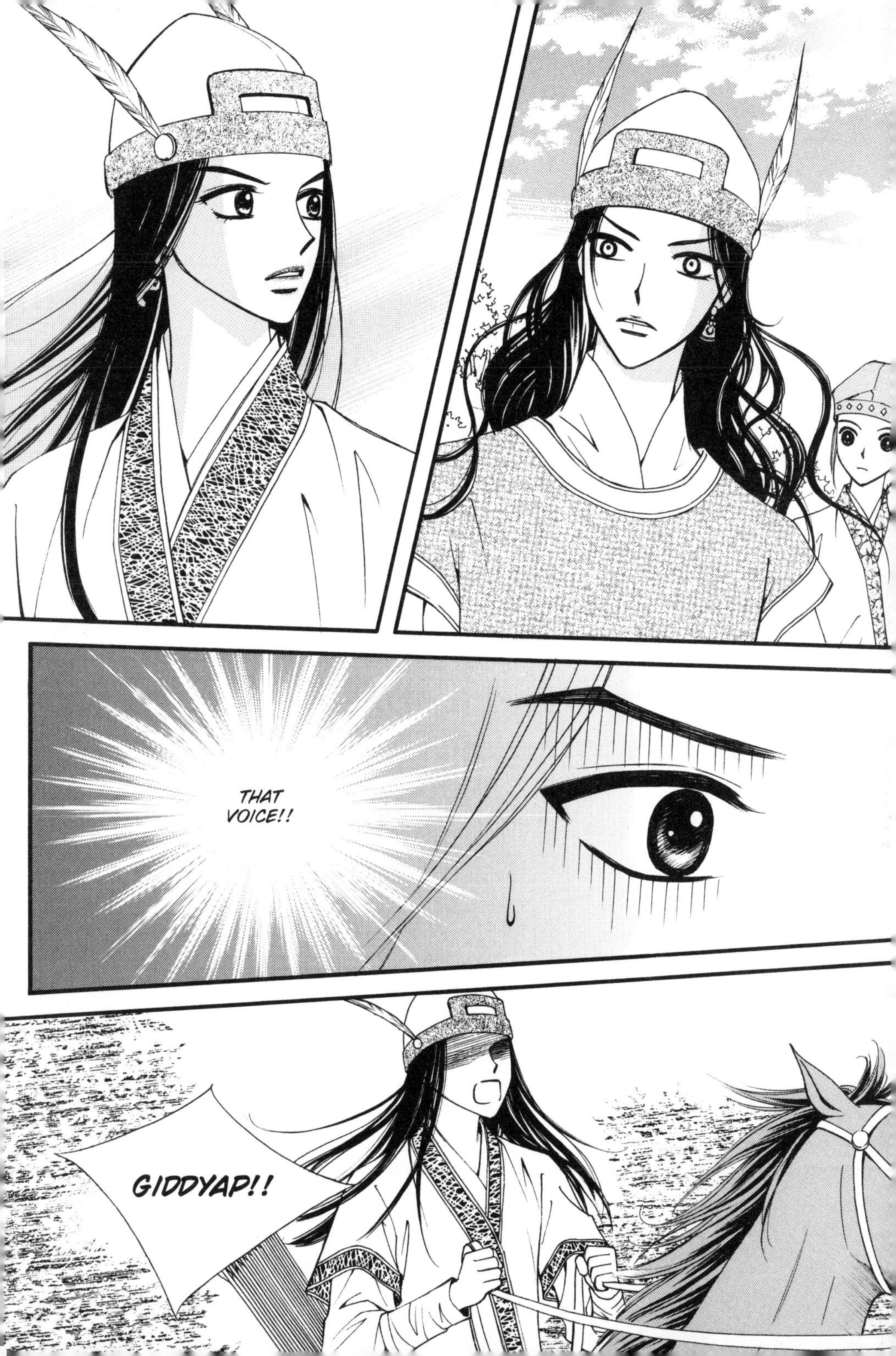
THAT VOICE!!
GIDDYAP!!

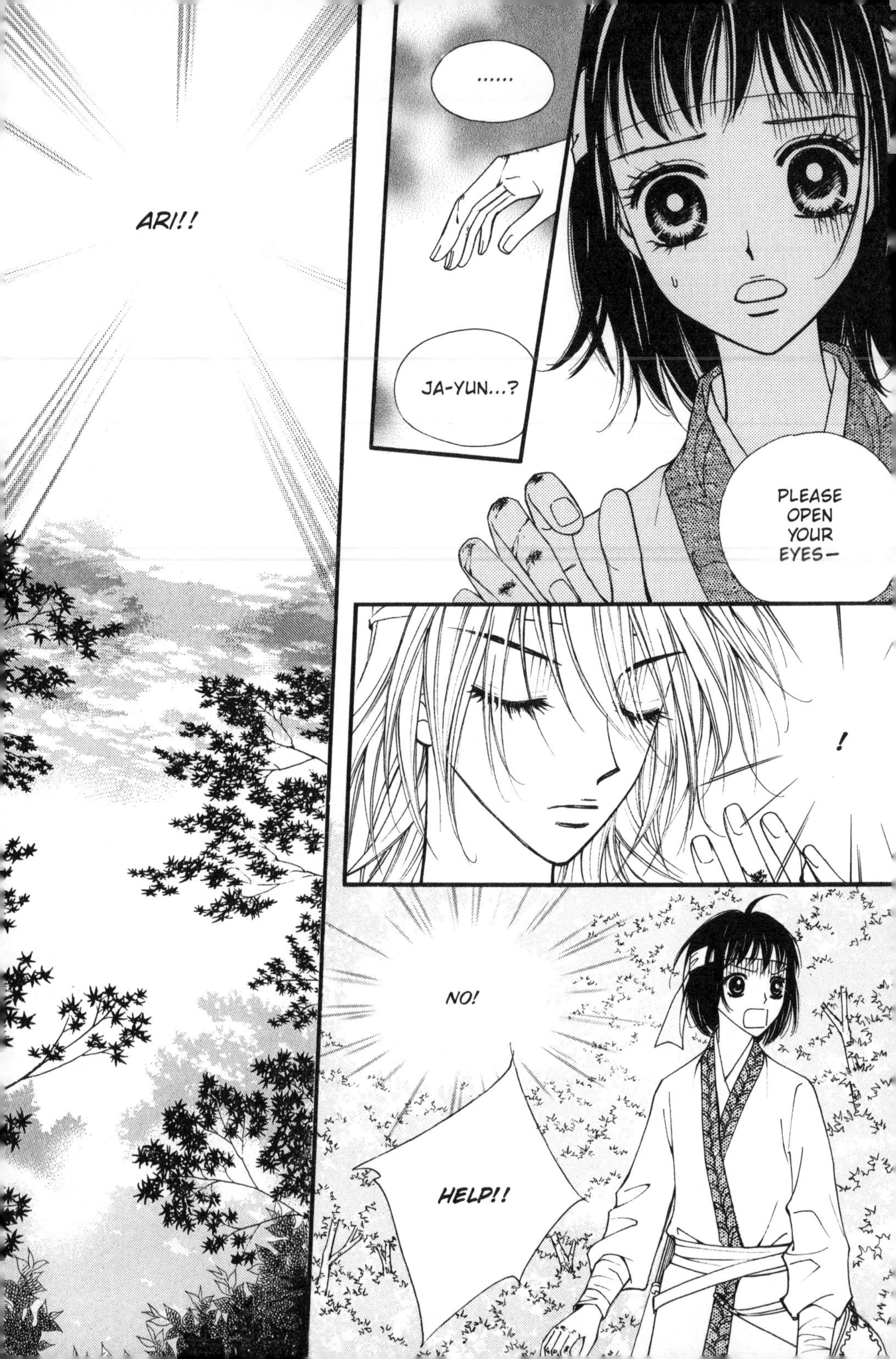

ARI!!
......
JA-YUN...?
PLEASE OPEN YOUR EYES—
!
NO!
HELP!!

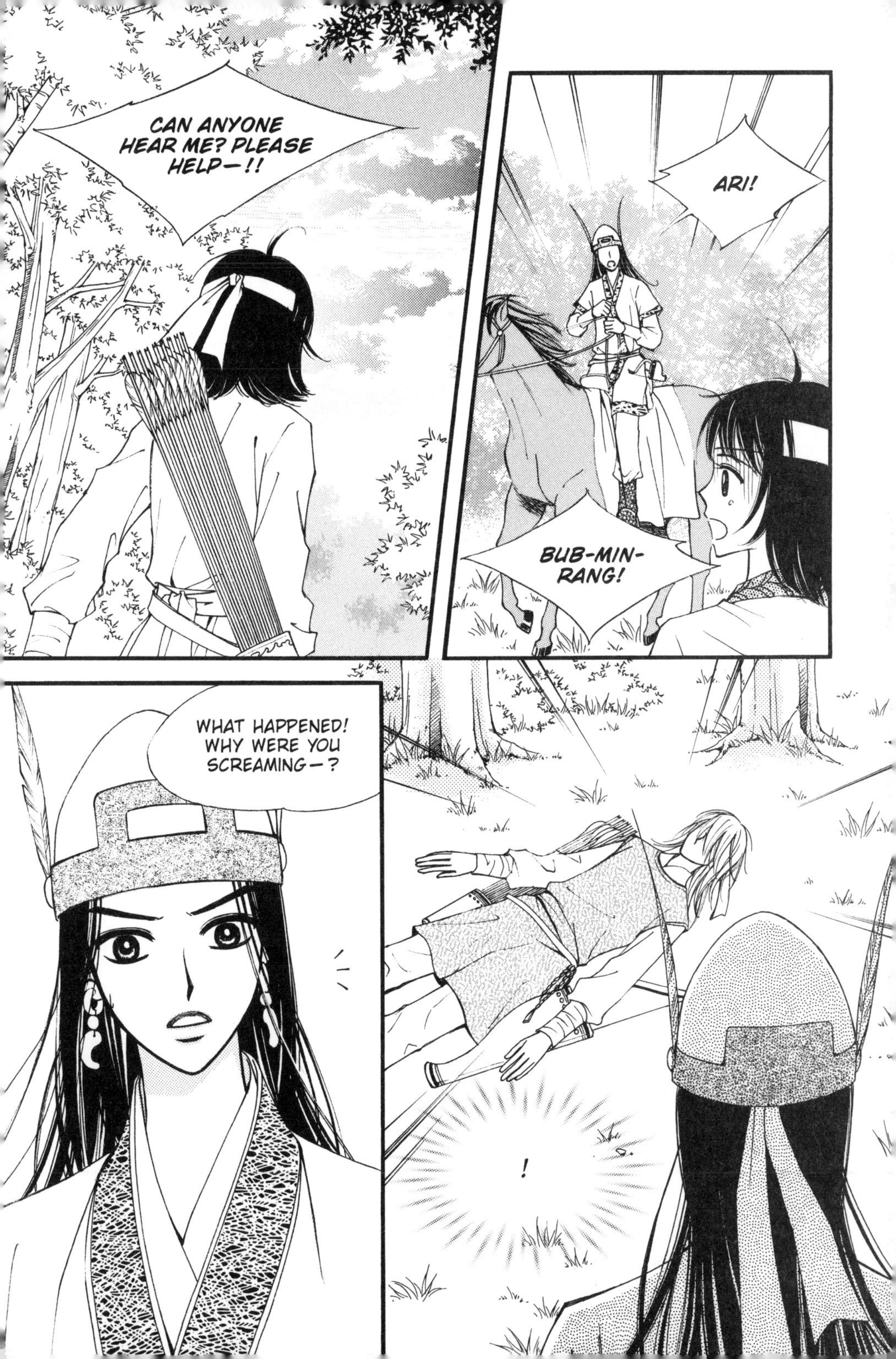
CAN ANYONE HEAR ME? PLEASE HELP—!!
ARI!
BUB-MIN-RANG!
WHAT HAPPENED! WHY WERE YOU SCREAMING—?
!

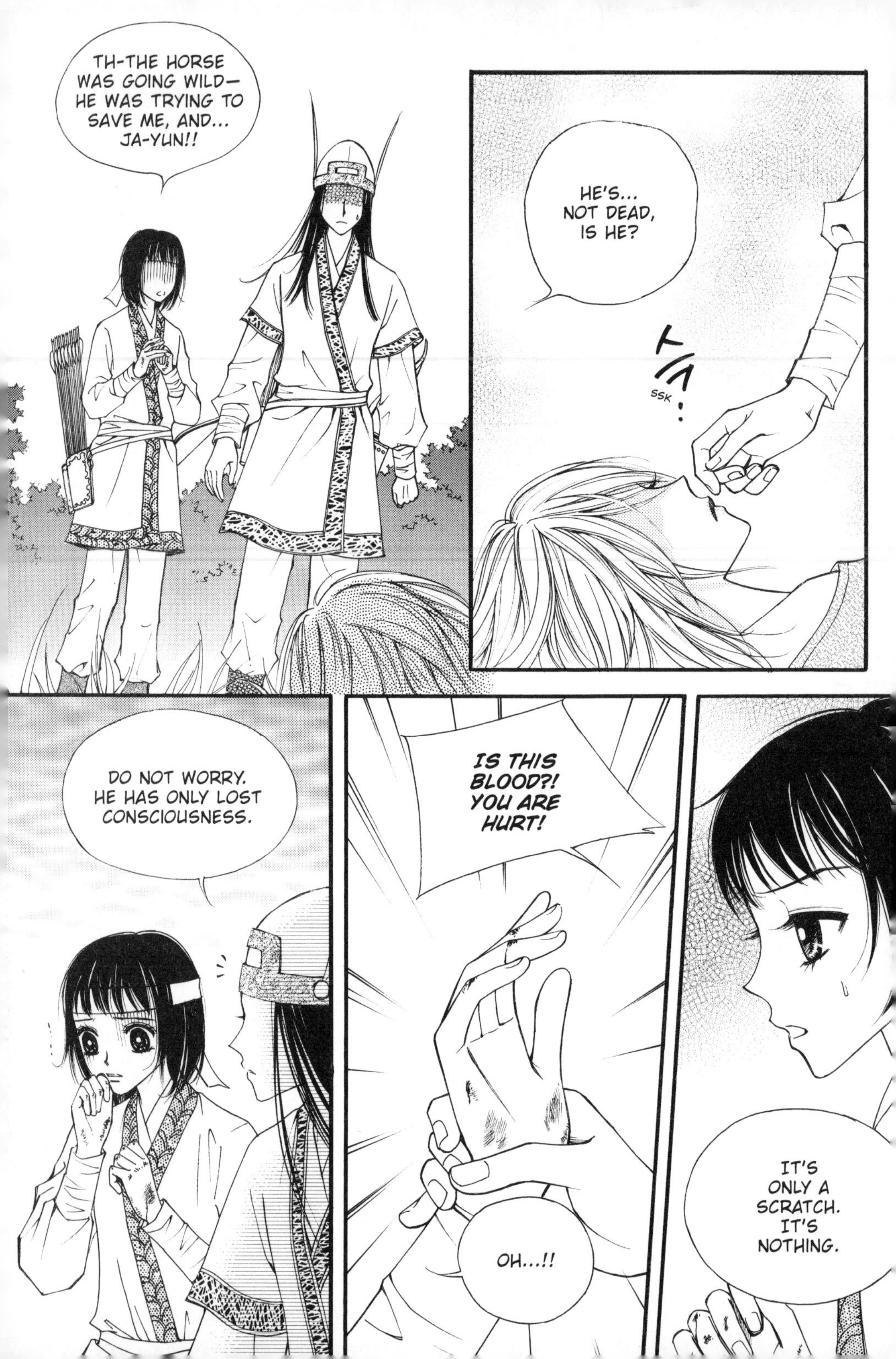
TH-THE HORSE WAS GOING WILD— HE WAS TRYING TO SAVE ME, AND... JA-YUN!!
HE'S... NOT DEAD, IS HE?
SSK
DO NOT WORRY. HE HAS ONLY LOST CONSCIOUSNESS.
IS THIS BLOOD?! YOU ARE HURT!
OH...!!
IT'S ONLY A SCRATCH. IT'S NOTHING.

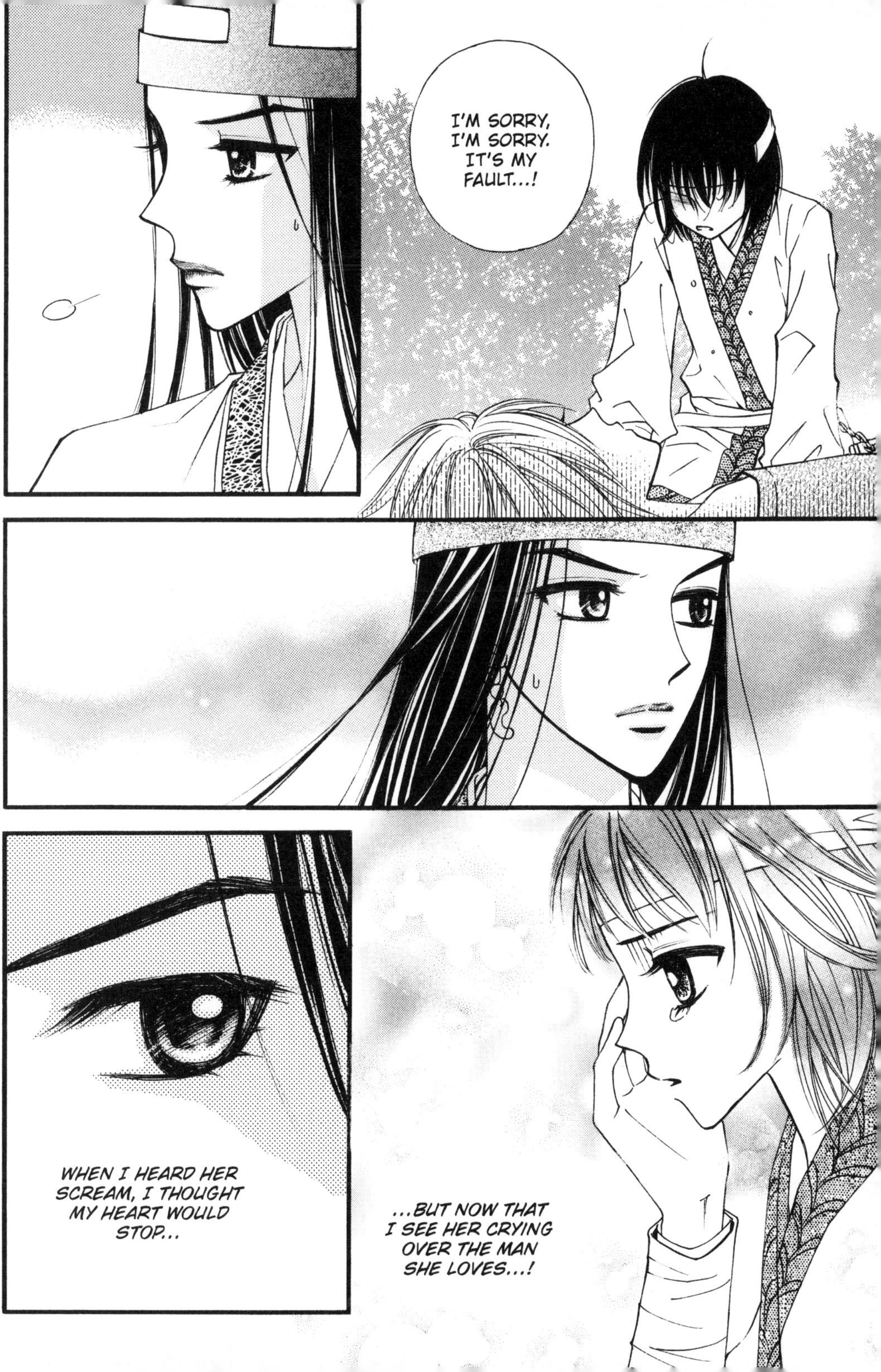
I'M SORRY, I'M SORRY. IT'S MY FAULT...!
WHEN I HEARD HER SCREAM, I THOUGHT MY HEART WOULD STOP...
...BUT NOW THAT I SEE HER CRYING OVER THE MAN SHE LOVES...!

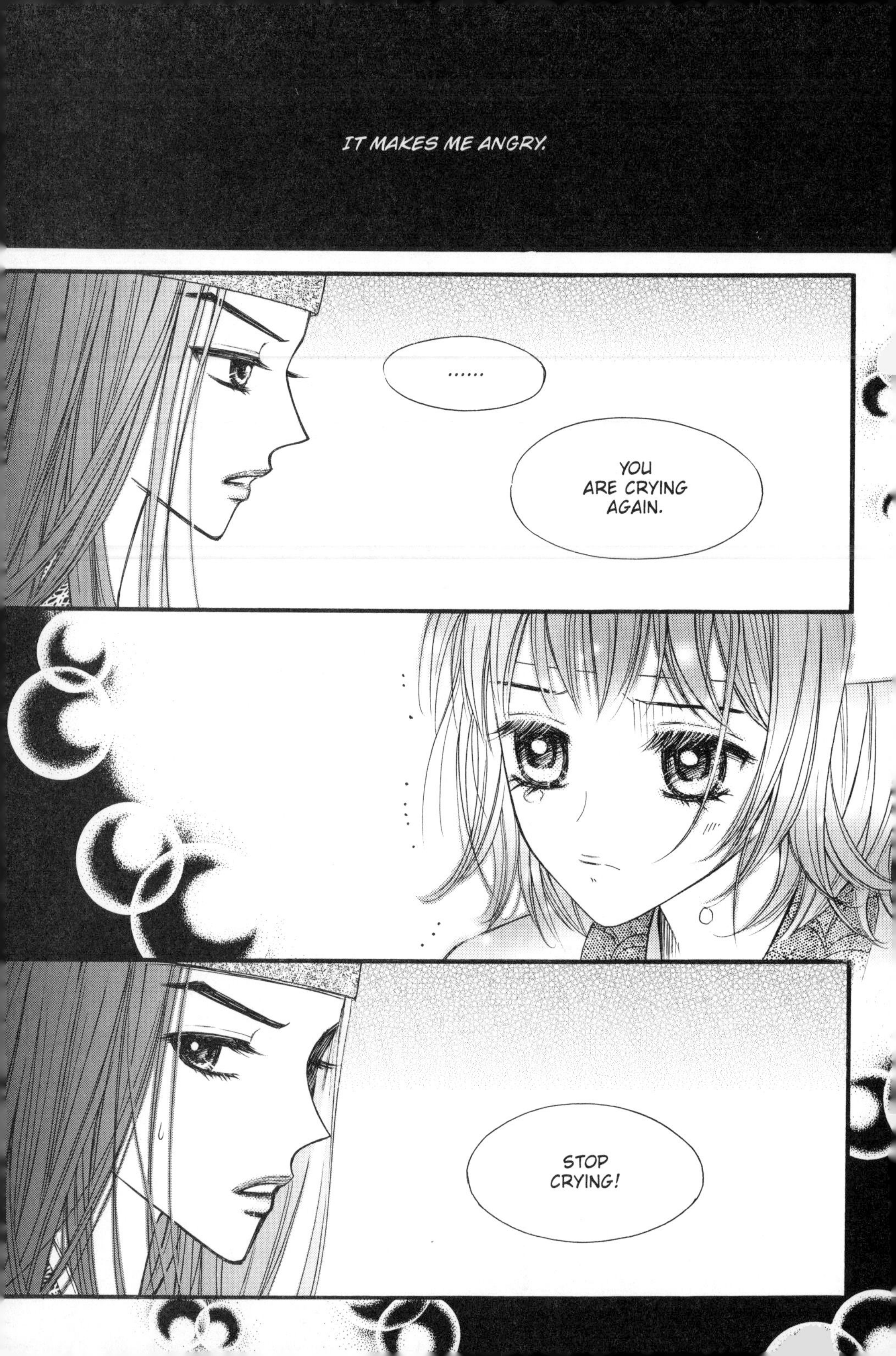
IT MAKES ME ANGRY.
......
YOU ARE CRYING AGAIN.
STOP CRYING!

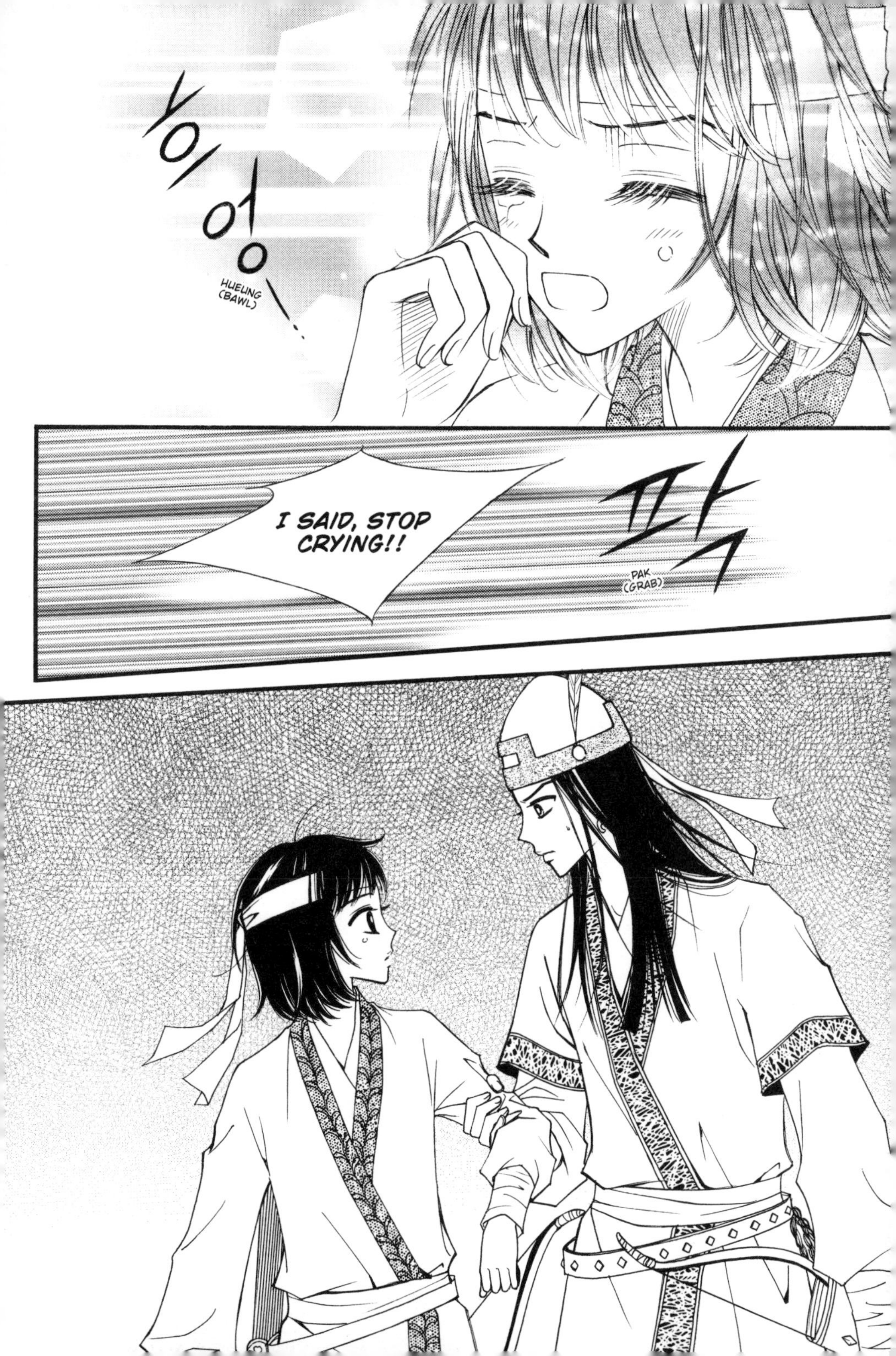
HUELING (BAWL)
I SAID, STOP CRYING!!
PAK (GRAB)

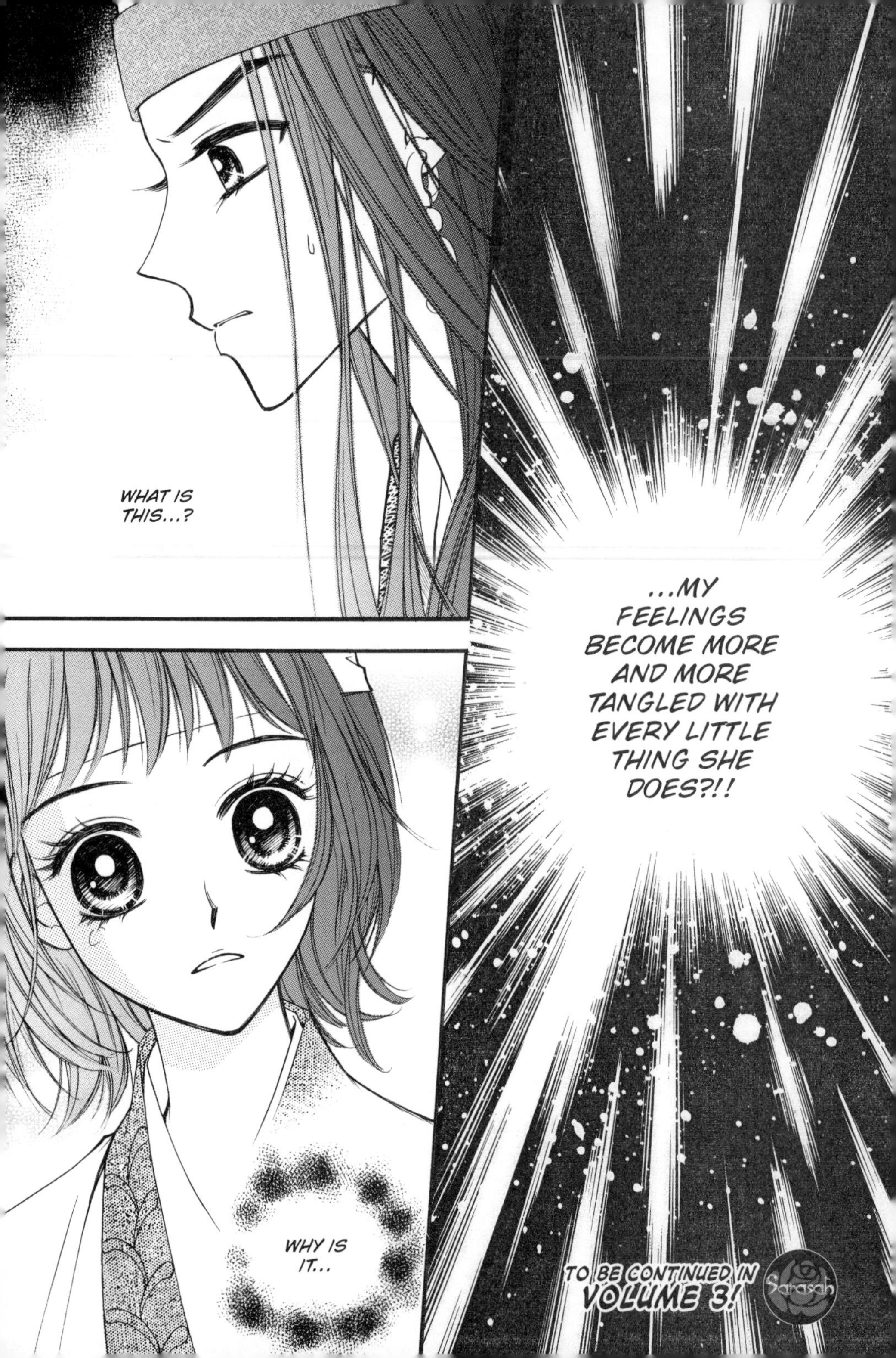
WHAT IS
THIS...?
WHY IS
IT...
...MY
FEELINGS
BECOME MORE
AND MORE
TANGLED WITH
EVERY LITTLE
THING SHE
DOES?!!
TO BE CONTINUED IN
VOLUME 3!

TRANSLATION AND HISTORICAL NOTES

GENERAL NOTES

Hwa-Rang: A leader within Hwa-Rang-Do. (-Rang is added as a suffix to one's name, i.e. Bub-Min-Rang.) Each Hwa-Rang has many Nang-Do beneath him.

Hwa-Rang-Do: An elite group of youths in Shilla. It was an educational institution as well as a social club where members, who were mostly sons and daughters of nobility, gathered for all aspects of study. This group developed into a more military organization and was most famous for its members exceptional archery skills.

Nang-Do: A term referring to a member of Hwa-Rang-Do.

Nang-Meun (or Seondo-Meun or Seon-Meun): A training place for Hwa-Rang.

Page 7
Yebu: A government division of Shilla.

Page 18
Nang-Jeok: A list of all the members of Hwa-Rang-Do.

Page 67
-nim: An honorific suffix, like "-san" or "-sama" in Japanese.

Page 104
-hyung: A suffix used by boys to address an older brother or older brother figure.

Page 107
Gakji: A ring that protects the thumb from the snap of the string during archery.
Jumtong: The bow handle.
Jeolpi (Serving): The section of the bowstring where the arrow is pulled back that is reinforced to make the bowstring last longer.
Jumpi: The grip of the bow.

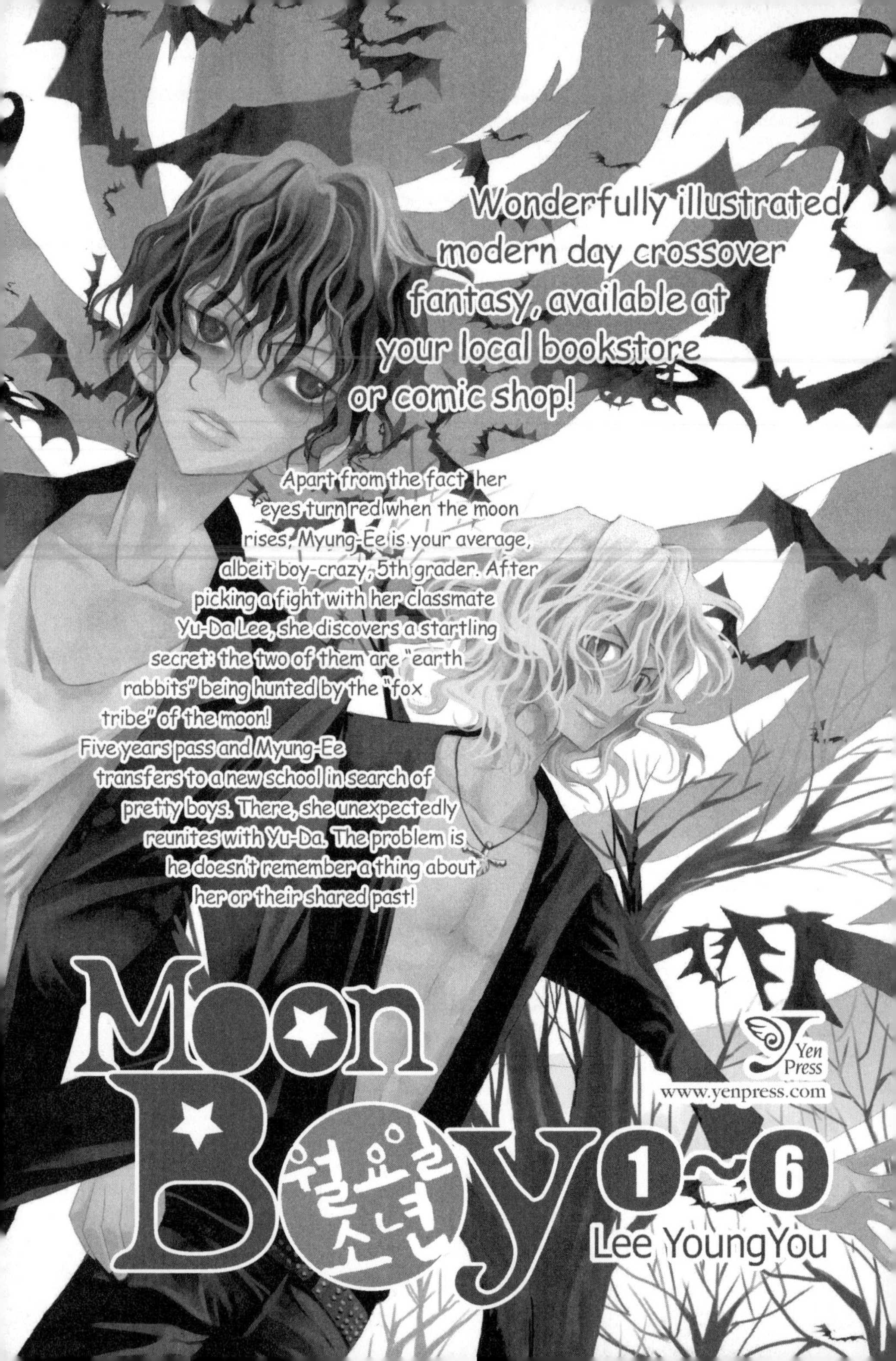

Wonderfully illustrated modern day crossover fantasy, available at your local bookstore or comic shop!
Apart from the fact her eyes turn red when the moon rises, Myung-Ee is your average, albeit boy-crazy, 5th grader. After picking a fight with her classmate Yu-Da Lee, she discovers a startling secret: the two of them are "earth rabbits" being hunted by the "fox tribe" of the moon!
Five years pass and Myung-Ee transfers to a new school in search of pretty boys. There, she unexpectedly reunites with Yu-Da. The problem is he doesn't remember a thing about her or their shared past!
Moon Boy
월요일 소년
1~6
Lee YoungYou
Yen Press
www.yenpress.com

Totally new Arabian nights, where Shahrazad is a guy!

Everyone knows the story of Shahrazad and her wonderful tales from the Arabian Nights. For one thousand and one nights, the stories that she created entertained the mad Sultan and eventually saved her life. In this version, Shahrazad is a guy who wanted to save his sister from the mad Sultan by disguising himself as a woman. When he puts his life on the line, what kind of strange and unique stories would he tell? This new twist on one of the greatest classical tales might just keep you awake for another ONE THOUSAND AND ONE NIGHTS.

Yen Press

www.yenpress.com

Available at bookstores near you!

One thousand and one nights 1~8

Han SeungHee · Jeon JinSeok

Yen
Press
www.yenpress.com

Becoming the princess... Isn't that every girl's dream?!

Monarchy rule ended long ago in Korea, but there are still other countries with kings, queens, princes and princesses. What if Korea had continued monarchism? What if all the beautiful palaces, which are now only historical relics, were actually filled with people? What if the glamorous royal family still maintained the palace customs? Welcome to a world where Korea still has the royal family living in their everyday lives! Only for this one high school girl, Chae-Kyung, is this a tragedy, since she has to marry the prince — who apparently is a total bastard!

THE ROYAL PALACE
Goong

vol.1 ~ 7

Park SoHee

The newest title from the creators of <Demon Diary> and <Angel Diary>!

Once upon a time, a selfish king summoned the monstrous Bulkirin into the real world. The monster killed half of all human beings, leaving the rest helpless as to what to do. That is, until one day when a hero appeared and defeated the Bulkirin with the legendary "Seven Blade Sword." But…what does all this have to do with 8th grader Eun-Gyo Sung?! First, she gets suspended from school for fighting. Then, she runs away from home. The last thing she needed was to be kidnapped—and whisked into the past by a mysterious stranger named No-Ah!

Legend

Available at bookstores near you!

1-6

K a r a · W o o S o o J u n g

Yen Press

www.yenpress.com

Available at bookstores near you!

CHOCOLAT
1~7

Shin JiSang · Geo

Kum-ji was a little late getting under the spell of the chart-topping band, DDL. Unable to join the DDL fan club, she almost gives up on meeting her idols, until she develops a cunning plan–to become a member of a rival fan club for the brand-new boy band Yo-I. This way she can act as Yo-I's fan club member and also be near Yo-I,

How far would you go to meet your favorite boy band?

who always seem to be in the same shows as DDL. Perfect plan...except being a fanatic is a lot more complicated than she expects. Especially when you're actually a fan of someone else. This full-blown love comedy about a fan club will make you laugh, cry, and laugh some more.

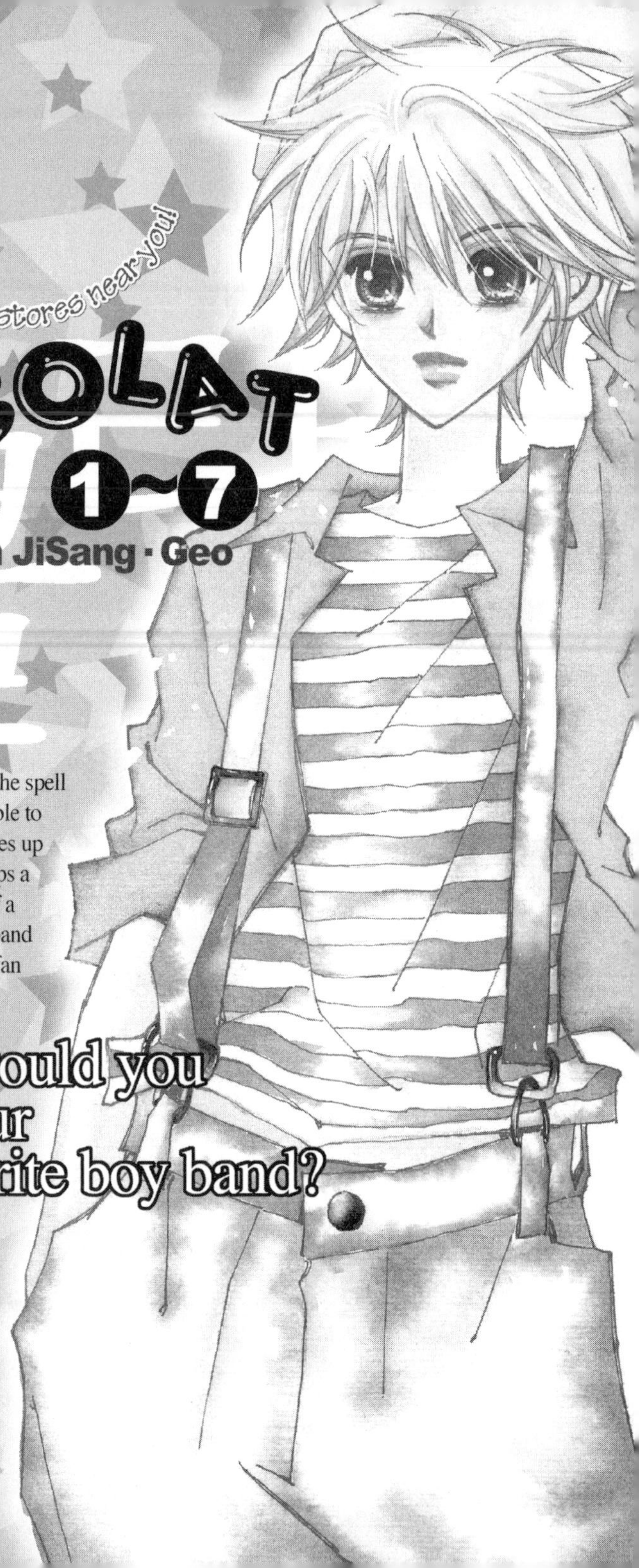

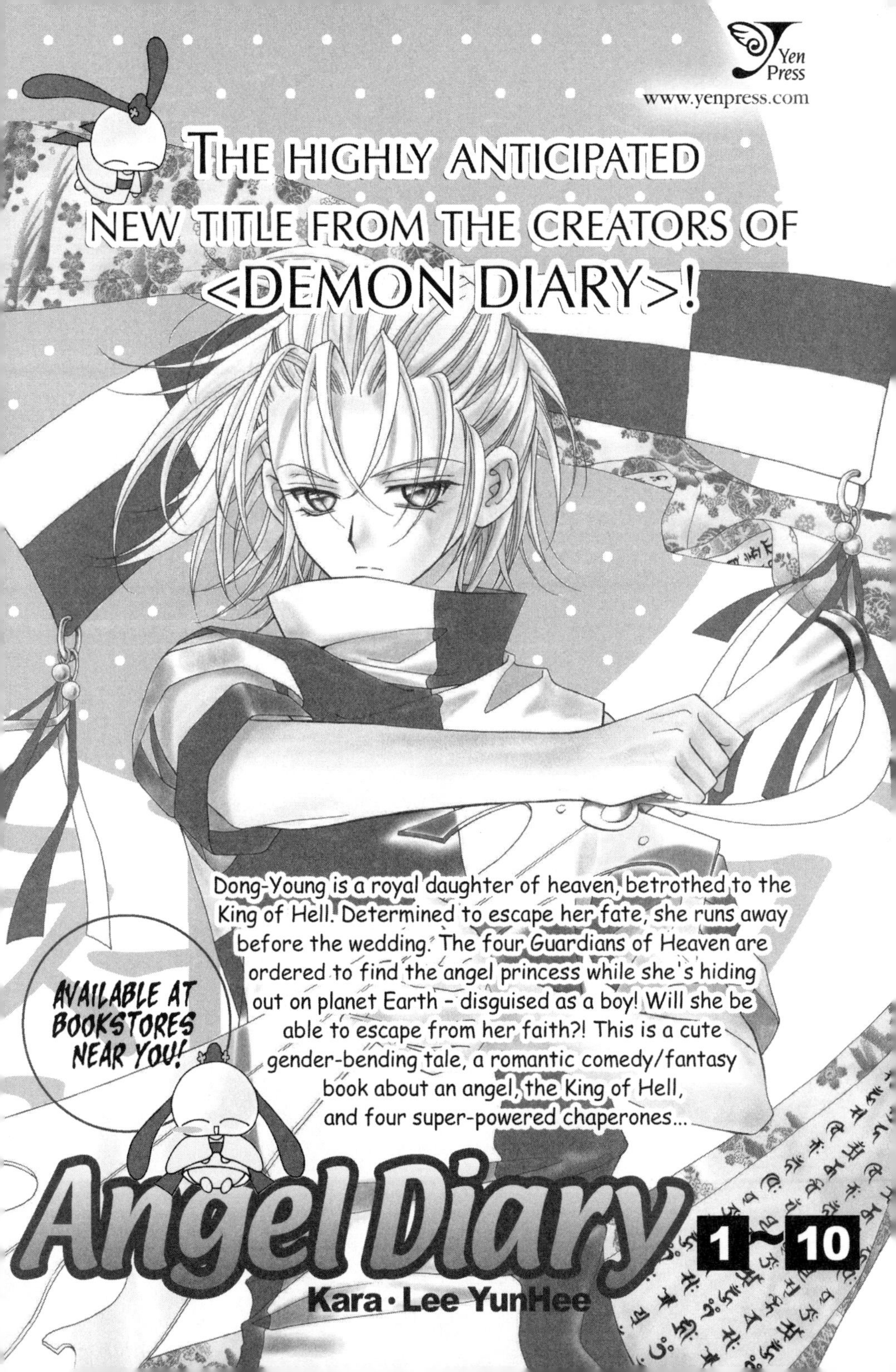
Yen Press
www.yenpress.com
THE HIGHLY ANTICIPATED NEW TITLE FROM THE CREATORS OF <DEMON DIARY>!
Dong-Young is a royal daughter of heaven, betrothed to the King of Hell. Determined to escape her fate, she runs away before the wedding. The four Guardians of Heaven are ordered to find the angel princess while she's hiding out on planet Earth - disguised as a boy! Will she be able to escape from her faith?! This is a cute gender-bending tale, a romantic comedy/fantasy book about an angel, the King of Hell, and four super-powered chaperones...
AVAILABLE AT BOOKSTORES NEAR YOU!
Angel Diary
1~10
Kara · Lee YunHee

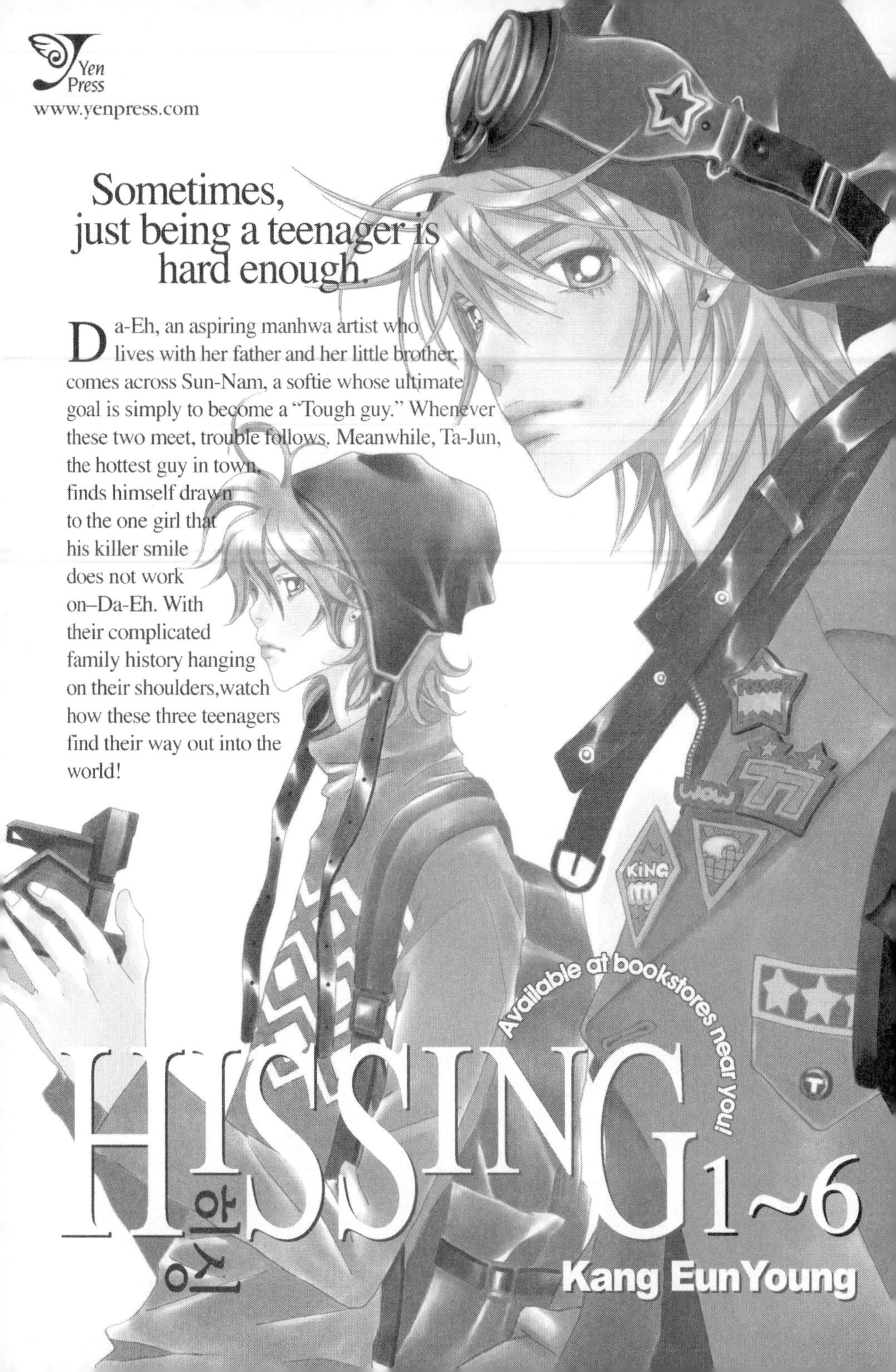
Yen Press
www.yenpress.com
Sometimes, just being a teenager is hard enough.
Da-Eh, an aspiring manhwa artist who lives with her father and her little brother, comes across Sun-Nam, a softie whose ultimate goal is simply to become a "Tough guy." Whenever these two meet, trouble follows. Meanwhile, Ta-Jun, the hottest guy in town, finds himself drawn to the one girl that his killer smile does not work on–Da-Eh. With their complicated family history hanging on their shoulders,watch how these three teenagers find their way out into the world!
Available at bookstores near You!
HISSING 1~6
Kang EunYoung

THE MOST BEAUTIFUL FACE, THE PERFECT BODY,
AND A SINCERE PERSONALITY...THAT'S WHAT HYE-MIN HWANG HAS.
NATURALLY, SHE'S THE CENTER OF EVERYONE'S ATTENTION.
EVERY BOY IN SCHOOL LOVES HER, WHILE EVERY GIRL HATES HER OUT OF JEALOUSY.
EVERY SINGLE DAY, SHE HAS TO ENDURE TORTURES AND HARDSHIPS FROM THE GIRLS.

A PRETTY FACE COMES WITH A PRICE.

THERE IS NOTHING MORE SATISFYING THAN GETTING THEM BACK.
WELL, EXCEPT FOR ONE PROBLEM... HER SECRET CRUSH, JUNG-YUN.
BECAUSE OF HIM, SHE HAS TO HIDE HER CYNICAL AND DARK SIDE
AND DAILY PUT ON AN INNOCENT FACE. THEN ONE DAY, SHE FINDS OUT
THAT HE DISLIKES HER ANYWAY!! WHAT?! THAT'S IT! NO MORE NICE GIRL!
AND THE FIRST VICTIM OF HER RAGE IS A PLAYBOY SHE JUST MET, MA-HA.

vol.1~8

Cynical Orange

Yun JiUn

SARASAH②

RYU RYANG

Translation: June Um

English Adaptation and Lettering: Abigail Blackman

Yen Press
Hachette Book Group
237 Park Avenue, New York, NY 10017

Visit our websites at www.HachetteBookGroup.com and www.YenPress.com.

Yen Press is an imprint of Hachette Book Group, Inc. The Yen Press name and logo are trademarks of Hachette Book Group, Inc.

First Yen Press Edition: November 2009

ISBN: 978-0-7595-3016-4

10 9 8 7 6 5 4 3 2 1

BVG

Printed in the United States of America